BRIGANDS KEY

Discard

BRIGANDS KEY

KEN PELHAM

FIVE STAR
A part of Gale, Cengage Learning

GALE
CENGAGE Learning·

Detroit • New York • San Francisco • New Haven, Conn • Waterville, Maine • London

GALE
CENGAGE Learning®

LIBRARY OF CONGRESS CATALOGING-IN-PUBLICATION DATA

Pelham, Ken.
   Brigands key / Ken Pelham. — 1st ed.
   p. cm.
   ISBN 978-1-4328-2578-2 (hardcover) — ISBN 1-4328-2578-X
(hardcover) 1. Archaeologists—Fiction. 2. Murder—Investigation—Fiction. 3. Florida Keys (Fla.)—Fiction. I. Title.
PS3616.E359B75 2012
813'.6—dc23   2012003843

Published in conjunction with Tekno Books and Ed Gorman.
Find us on Facebook– https://www.facebook.com/FiveStarCengage
Visit our Web site– http://www.gale.cengage.com/fivestar/
Contact Five Star™ Publishing at FiveStar@cengage.com

Printed in Mexico
2 3 4 5 6 7 16 15 14 13 12

For Laura

ACKNOWLEDGMENTS

Many thanks to those who helped, and most of all to Dr. Frank Diefenderfer for his insights into dental forensics, and to Larry Bedore for help with technical aspects of the work of medical examiners. For their advice and support, Melanie Griffey, Susan Meyer, and Diana Morrison. For his keen, unsparing editorial eye, Gordon Aalborg. For photography, Jeff Goodfellow. For website help, Mike Arlington. And, of course, for their love and support and avid readership across the years, my endless gratitude to my daughters, Amy and Jenny, and to my wife, Laura.

CHAPTER ONE

Carson Grant was happiest surrounded by ghosts. The good kind. The ancient, long-dead kind. So Tuesday morning he was ecstatic, anticipating a swim with ghosts in an ink-black cave at the bottom of the sea.

The sun had kept its end of the deal, warming the Gulf of Mexico to a slow boil through midmorning. Clouds billowed over the western horizon, white, limned in slate.

His twenty-four-footer, *Lost Expedition,* rose and settled on the waves. The name, it had frequently been pointed out, begged disaster. He didn't care. He'd endured his share of disasters and reasoned that reverse karma worked as well as any.

Grant opened the small ice chest and withdrew a highball glass, a jug of pulpy orange juice, and a bottle of Dinsmoor Scottish vodka. He scooped ice into the highball glass, poured a shot of Dinsmoor, and drenched it in orange juice. He studied the drink, grimaced, and hit it with another shot. He toasted the good weather and drank it down. The morning dive that couldn't be improved by an icy screwdriver was a myth, like Sasquatch. With less hair.

He slipped over the transom and took a seat on the dive deck, dangling his legs in the warm sea. He squeezed his mask against his face, cinched his weight belt tighter, shouldered into his BC vest and air tank, took in the mouthpiece, and slipped under the water, knowingly and deliberately committing the cardinal sin of diving alone, the province of fools and divers

9

with short life expectancies.

Hell with it. Playing by the rules had gotten him nothing but screwed. He played by his own rules now. No job, no money, just his own rules. He could do archaeology without politics just fine, and without funding with no small effort.

He'd lucked onto something big.

The water was glass, as clear as it gets in the Gulf. He peered to the bottom, thirty feet down. There, amid rock and sand and swaying grasses, lay the object of his desire. Grant upended and kicked his fins, propelling himself to the dark hole in the sea floor to search for ghosts.

A stingray, buried in the sand, shook off its cover in a small cloud and darted away as he neared.

He paused at the entrance to the cave, admiring a miracle of nature. Here he was, twenty-two miles off the Florida coast in the Gulf of Mexico. In *fresh* water.

He glanced at the surface above. *Lost Expedition*, its hull a dark spear point against a bright, watery sky, bobbed slowly with the waves. All good. The anchor line was holding. If the boat pulled free and drifted away, he would die out here. Being foolish had a definite downside, and a doctorate in archaeology wouldn't float him twenty-two miles.

Grant turned back to the cave and swam into its mouth. A current flowed from the cave and pushed at him. He pulled his regulator mouthpiece out and took a drink of the ocean, tasting it, swallowing it. Fresh water, in the salty open sea.

Despite his current unemployment and poisoned reputation, a boatload of colleagues still owed him their jobs. He'd called in one of the debts, pestering Ginnie Pavlic at Cape Canaveral. He'd given her the range of the limestone shelf, a hundred miles of it, and prodded her for satellite geothermals.

"How many?" she'd asked with her trademark sigh.

"Come now, Ginnie. All of them."

"How about last summer's images?"

"Not good enough. I need winter imagery. Cooler water. Shot on a calm day, one-foot swells, max."

"Is that all? How about a nice café latte while you wait?" It had been February at the time, water temperature in the sixties. All she had to do was slide his request to the top of the list. Shouldn't be too hard. After some wrangling over blackened grouper and cheap Riesling, Ginnie produced the images. They were worthless. Grant promised pricier wine and badgered her into refining the geothermals to hundredths of a degree. She nixed the wine but delivered the new images.

There among sheet after sheet of blue images were a dozen yellow dots scattered along the sea floor, the proof of slightly warmer water in the sea. Proof of a freshwater submarine spring.

The aquifers underlying Florida hold at seventy-one degrees, give or take, year round. A spot reading of seventy-one in a sea of sixty-degree water hinted that fresh water from the inland aquifer was spilling from the bottom of the sea. Of the springs identified, only the two within six miles of shore had been discovered and a couple more were rumored by fishing crews. This one, the largest and most enticing by far, may have gone undiscovered another hundred years if not for his innovation.

The vent boiled from the top of a ragged cliff that teemed with a kaleidoscope of sea life. He gripped the rocky edge of the vent to anchor himself. The current pushed against him steadily, suggesting that this spring was fresh all the time. Most offshore springs pumped out brackish water, the freshwater flow insufficient to keep the heavier saltwater from intruding. Some were so weak they reversed flow with the tides, the saltwater pushing the fresh back upstream, inland, underground, ruining drinking water. The problem worsened each year as people crowded in, and thirsty lawns and bad habits sucked the aquifers dry.

A shadow, large, dark, and scary, flashed to his right. Grant spun to face it, thinking shark. Big, toothy shark. He was relieved and disappointed to see a giant grouper, bigger than himself, darting from his sudden movement for a friendlier hole.

He fidgeted with his BC vest and regulator, flipped the switch on his lamp. The beam illuminated the dark interior of the cave and he pulled himself in one handhold at a time.

Claustrophobia, his old demon, revved his heartbeat up a notch. This is crazy, he thought. Not too late to choose the better part of valor.

The vent was the narrow point. Just inside, the cave broadened into a room twenty feet wide by an indeterminate length, its far side vanishing into darkness beyond his beam.

The walls and ceiling glowed with gorgeous sepia, deeply creased here and there with black. The water was liquid diamond, yet the cavern was barren, a desert undersea, in stark contrast to the teeming environment just outside the cave. Grant had expected this; the freshwater resisted the saltwater creatures outside and the constant pressure kept life from drifting or swimming in. Crawlers, like crabs, could drag themselves inside but they'd have no reason to stay in a desert with nothing to eat.

Silt carpeted the bottom. He fanned it gently, swirling away a wisp of brown, exposing the rocky bottom. Respect the silt, he reminded himself. He drifted, studying the floor, searching.

A small bump in the silt gave away the prize. He whisked it clean, uncovering an angular, serrated flake of stone.

Pay dirt. He scooped up the stone and studied it. He'd take it back to shore, research it, photograph it, go by the book, but he knew what he had. The stone was chert, a crystallized chunk of limestone, worked into a razor-edged weapon. A spear point.

He began to compose text in his head, describing, speculating, expounding. He stopped himself. Bad habit, that. Cart before the horse. He pocketed the spear point and whisked away more sand and silt. Bits and pieces of a long-ago culture began to appear. A fish hook carved from bone. A digging tool. A shell fashioned into jewelry. He left them untouched, much as he wanted to gather them all up. The spear point was enough for now. The day was young and he could set a work grid before it was over. Proper archaeology, done the right way. Despite his reputation, he knew he was among the best. He snapped a few more photos, secured the camera to his belt, and headed back to *Lost Expedition* to fetch gear for the grid.

But before he got out of the cave, something caught his attention.

The human mind works in mysterious ways. It seeks familiarity in a scary universe. It sees human faces in clouds, human manners in cats, Jesus in pizza toppings. Anything remotely human registers in the mind. Sometimes it's a trick of the light. Sometimes it really is human.

In a dark crevice of rock a shadowy shape registered in Grant's mind. He swung his lamp beam toward it. Weird rock forms were always worth a look.

The beam illuminated the pale nude body of a man.

He stared at the body, his thoughts swirling. He was twenty-two miles from shore, in an undiscovered cave at the bottom of the sea. With a dead guy. Impossible, impossible.

The guy looked fresh. Grant preferred finding bodies thousands of years old. Good and dead. Not recently dead.

He'd done his share of fetching the recent dead, much as he hated it. In a previous life, three years ago, he regularly pulled unlucky and stupid divers from wet graves in the drowned caverns that laced Florida. He did it because he was good at it and because a pesky conscience demanded he do so. But he hated it. The eyes of the victims stared into your soul, scarring it. And regularly reintroduced themselves in your dreams. When he'd gotten away from body retrieval on his last trip to Guatemala, he swore he'd never fetch another stiff.

Fresh was a relative term. He was used to locating the bodies of divers who'd perished within the last few hours. This one looked a bit more worn. The flesh had lost the pallor of the new, was puckered and drawn. Couple days old, maybe? Grant had little knowledge of these things.

He gave a gentle kick and drifted closer to the body. He felt an uncomfortable stirring in his gut and could feel his face flushing hot, even in the cool water of the spring. Don't lose it now, he thought. He knew what he had to do.

The current had wedged the body into the crevice and pinned it there. The current also wanted to push Grant right onto it. He gripped the rock, anchoring himself inches from the body. It was turned half away, the face hidden. Grant had a sudden, uneasy thought. The guy's not dead. He shook the thought away. Don't get stupid. Course he's dead. Stick to the job.

Grant realized he'd stopped breathing, and sucked deeply on his regulator, drawing a long breath. Easy does it . . .

The body was that of a white man. Average height, average build. Grant reached out and touched the body, suppressing his revulsion. The flesh was soft, yielding, but not overly so. He put his hand on the shoulder and slowly turned the body to face him. The eyes were glassy, sunken, sickly.

Eyes, the poets say, are windows to the soul. The poets are misinformed. The eyes of the dead are windows to eternity and emptiness, and when you stare into them in an underwater cave, you see your own death.

Grant felt a twitch in his gut, and another. His stomach lurched and its contents surged upward, burning his throat and mouth. He spat out his mouthpiece and vomited into the clear water, into the face of the dead man.

CHAPTER TWO

Gerald Hammond stubbed his cigarette and sprayed a blast of freshener into his mouth, wondering why he bothered. Everyone in Brigands Key knew he sneaked a smoke now and then. He'd been the only doctor in town worth a flip in twenty years and no one was going to run him out on account of smoking, so long as he had the decency to not cough smoke into their faces.

He cupped his hand in front of his mouth and blew. Not bad. He stretched his back, listening to its satisfying pops, and went to the bathroom adjoining his office and studied his reflection in the mirror. A slight paunch, only a few wrinkles, and the wispy brown hair atop his head had not given up the struggle. Yet.

Satisfied, he stepped into the exam room. A gentle rap came at the door. "The doctor is in," he called.

Jill leaned her head around the door, smiling. "Emma is here for her eleven A.M.," she said, stepping aside and swinging the door open. Emma Watterson entered, pushing a dinged-up aluminum walker.

"Emma! You look fine today," Hammond said. "Like Audrey Hepburn in *Bringing Up Baby.*"

"That was Katharine."

"*The Philadelphia Story,* then."

"You two have fun," Jill said, handing him Emma's file and closing the door behind her.

Hammond flipped through the file, although he already knew

it and her inside and out. "So, Emma, you turn seventy tomorrow. Congratulations."

"I could die tomorrow."

"You're too mean to die. You're strong as a horse."

"Horses my age get sent to the glue factory."

"Emma, be still. Let's listen in on your heart." He placed the stethoscope against her chest. "Are you ready for City Council's big tussle next week?"

"A hundred percent ready."

"You going to tell me which way you're voting?"

"I'm an aging hippie. You know my position."

"Stubborn thing."

"Carpetbaggers don't always win, Jerry."

Hammond wrapped up her physical and jotted down a quick scrip and escorted her to Jill's desk. Jill was on the phone, taking hurried notes. "Couple of these a day," he said, "and you'll be doing cartwheels."

"Will I be able to play piano?"

"Not while doing cartwheels."

As Emma stepped out, Jill punched a button on the phone, set it down, handed him the note. "Time to change hats, Jerry. Randy's got a John Doe coming in."

Hammond read the note. "Cancel my afternoon. Tell him I'll be at the Icebox in five minutes."

The Brigands Key medical examiner's lab was a Spartan affair in the back of the police department. Hammond had badgered the City Council skin-flints for years about the inadequacies of the Icebox, its lack of chill at the top of the list. Cold, he reminded them again and again, the lab must be cold. But that runs up the electric bill, they argued. Why keep a room bitter cold all year for one or two bodies a month? So instead of chilly he got lukewarm. When alerted that a body was on its way, he would rush over and crank the thermostat down. Half the time the body arrived before he did and lay on the slab festering. Unacceptable, he told the Council. Tough, they responded. They could always find another medical examiner.

Which was malarkey. They pretended they were doing him a favor, supplementing his meager practice with a meager public servant's salary. It was the other way around. He was keeping a job they'd never be able to fill.

He wasn't really even employed by them; he was an employee of the State of Florida. An associate medical examiner. Not many two-light towns had an ME of their own. Most relied on the medical examiner's district, in this case District 8, operating out of Gainesville. Brigands Key got an ME of its own purely on account of the island's remoteness.

Hammond drove the three blocks across town from his office to City Hall, feeling guilty about using an excuse for not getting the exercise, although it was legit. The sooner he could ice the Icebox, the better. Even so, his car was a steam room, bottling the Florida summer up tight. He got a rolling sweat before he completed the one-minute drive. Wonderful. One surefire recipe for ruining forensics evidence was to sweat on it like a pig.

The Brigands Key Police Department stood to one side of City Hall, suitably humbled by the elegant old brick building. Hammond pushed through the door and was welcomed by the cool breeze within. Behind an old steel desk, Tom Greenwood's face bobbed up eagerly. Something big was afoot.

"What's on the docket, Major Tom?" Hammond asked.

"Got us a body, Doc. Found out in the ocean by that dude from Gainesville. He radioed from way out and just now got to the dock. Randy's bringing the body in, be here any minute."

"Know the identity?"

Greenwood shook his head eagerly. "John Doe," he said, relishing the phrase. Law enforcement in Brigands Key usually

17

amounted to making high school kids ditch cigarettes. Discovery of an unidentified body was like Pearl Harbor.

"I'm assuming you've got my AC going in the Icebox?"

"Um, I had some leads to follow up, a bunch of them. I was fixin' to."

Hammond hurried past, giving the deputy an anguished look. "You're killing me, Tommy."

At the end of the hall, he fumbled with his keys and rattled open the ancient wood and glass door that was stenciled importantly with "Medical Examiner."

The Icebox belched a wave of warm air into his face. He flicked on the lights and twisted the thermostat. With a clunk, the old unit hummed and a breeze fanned him.

He quickly set up his workstation, swinging lamps into play, rolling out trays of tools. He could set up for two bodies at a time, three in a pinch, but the place was never meant for this kind of work and a single cadaver was the number appropriate for the scale of the room. One is the loneliest number, his mind sang off-key. And the best number when it's a stiff. Not a stiff, he reminded himself. A little sensitivity, if you please. Someone's husband, boyfriend, son, father, grandfather.

He glanced at the clock. Five minutes had passed and the room was reasonably chilled and neat. He looked over the small lab, satisfied that it was as ready as it would get, considering its limitations. All that was missing was the stiff. Damn. Did it again.

A clatter came from the hallway. A moment later the door swung in. Police Chief Randy Sanborn pushed through, nodding to Hammond.

"Welcome . . . to my laboratory," Hammond said in an asthmatic Peter Lorre voice.

"Got a customer, Jerry."

"A nonpaying customer."

"Glad you find it so funny."

Hammond swallowed his grin. Don't joke with The Chief. Not today. Not when he had that look. Sanborn was too serious, too political and way too cozy with the Council and, like himself, a repatriated lifer on Brigands Key. The island had a habit of reeling back in those that strayed.

Sanborn pulled a gurney in after him. A heavy bag lay upon it. The door swung back shut, but quickly reopened. Carson Grant looked in, hesitated.

"Come on in, Grant," Sanborn said. "Law enforcement on Brigands Key is not quite as formal as in the big city. Jerry, this is Dr. Carson Grant. He found John Doe."

"I've seen you around town," Hammond said.

"I suspect no one moves around here without drawing attention."

"That'd be right. Sit. I'd shake your hand, but despite this medieval lab, we're not total hicks. Got to follow some protocols when doing forensics."

The gurney was wheeled in and parked adjacent to the operating table. The body bag was unzipped and Hammond and Sanborn transferred John Doe onto the table. Sanborn administered a thanks-for-your-big-help glance at Grant. Grant shook his head. "Uh-uh. I fished him out of the ocean and brought him ashore. I entrusted him to your capable hands from that point."

"Yeah, I've got some questions about that," Sanborn said. "Mind if I work while you work, Jerry?"

Hammond shook his head. He punched a button on a battered tape recorder.

"Hell, Jerry, we bought you a laptop with voice recognition software. Why aren't you using that?" The police chief was edgy, and it showed.

"It never works. Give it back and get me a real lab and a

beautiful assistant if you want to spend money." Hammond glanced at his watch and announced the time and date for the recorder. "White male, age is a guess, early twenties." He stretched a tape from head to toe. "Height, five feet, ten inches. Weight, one-seventy-one, maybe altered due to immersion in water. Need to do a bit of research on that." He glanced at Grant. "You found him naked?"

"Yep."

"Where?"

"In a freshwater spring, twenty-two miles offshore."

Hammond made a small sound. "A spring? Offshore? Is that a joke?"

"Offshore marine springs are real. There are a couple dozen known on both coasts of Florida."

"How can that be?"

"Florida's only a third the size it was during the last ice age. The coastline then was miles further out, the oceans several hundred feet lower, the water locked up in glaciers. The rainfall that hits the state seeps into the limestone and sometimes flows out in springs. Some springs happen to be on what was once dry land."

"The springs are for real," Sanborn said. "But I've lived here all my life and never heard about one anywhere near here."

"That's because I just discovered it this morning."

"The fishermen hereabouts never discovered one."

Grant shrugged. "So?"

"So how'd you manage it?"

"Satellite imaging. Wave of the future and all that." Grant nodded toward the body. "Was it a drowning?"

"Too soon to tell," Hammond said. "No overt signs of trauma, no wounds. Maybe a heart attack."

"Know the guy?"

Hammond cocked his head. "Nyet, Comrades. Never seen

him before. Randy?"

"Nope. Out of town sport fisherman, most likely. Probably got drunk and fell overboard."

Grant hesitated. "I don't think so. He was wedged into a spring crevice, pinned in place by the out-flowing current. There's no way a dead body or a drunk could wash into a spring, against the current."

"I know a little about offshore springs," Sanborn said. "Some of them reverse flow with the tides."

"Not this one. Constant out-flowing water pressure."

"Could he be a diver? Could've swum into the spring and then died."

"If he did he did it in a cave thirty feet below the surface, with no gear. And no clothes."

"You didn't see any other boats?"

"I passed a few sport boats five miles out, fishing the first reef. A couple of commercial fishing boats a little past that. Nothing within fifteen miles of the spring."

"I'm going to need a fix on that spring."

Grant began to speak, stopped. "I'd rather not give it, but I'm guessing my preferences don't mean much."

"You'd be guessing right. Your hole in the ocean is a possible crime scene. Why don't you want us there?"

"You're law enforcement. You do crime scenes. I'm an archaeologist. I do archaeology scenes. The two don't mix."

"You think we'll screw up your site."

"I know you will."

Sanborn let the challenge hang in the air. His fingers drummed softly. "You've dicked around with a possible crime scene. Didn't you stop to think about that?"

"I did."

"And you dicked it anyway. I could lock you up right now."

"Arrest a good Samaritan? Doesn't seem prudent. I could

have just left the guy where I found him, don't forget. I was worried he might drift free and never be seen again."

Another silence. "What kind of archaeology is done twenty-two miles out? Sunken ships?"

"I'm looking for human habitation sites."

"Expecting to find Atlantis, are you?"

"As I said, during the ice age that area was dry land. Florida was wonderful for ice age cultures. Lots of game, not bitterly cold like the rest of the continent, not buried under a mile-high sheet of ice like the Midwest and New England. A freshwater spring was prime real estate to Paleo-Indians. You had year-round, crystal clear drinking water."

"I need to see what you found."

Grant hesitated for the slimmest of moments. "Who said I found anything?"

"I believe I did."

"I found rocks and sand."

"And a dead man. Let me ask once more. What else did you find in the Goddamn spring?"

Grant studied him for a moment. He reached into his pocket, withdrew a cloth, and unfolded it, revealing a stone spear point.

"Hey, your memory has improved. And you remembered a weapon. How about that."

"It's an artifact, not a murder weapon."

"Who said anything about murder?"

"That's where you're going with this."

Hammond glanced from Sanborn to Grant. Redirect them, he told himself. "At a glance, I'd say the body's a day or two old. More or less. Randy, that's your starting point."

"And your best guess as to cause of death?"

"You want guesses, hire a bookie. I'll open him up in a few minutes. You're welcome to watch, but no one hardly ever sticks around for that."

"I hate to break with tradition." Sanborn rose from his chair. "Get me some dentals if you can. I'll be back in a bit to lift some prints. Dr. Grant, where will you be staying?"

"On my boat."

"Wrong answer. Your boat is hereby impounded. Get yourself a room at the Morrison and don't think about leaving. At the moment, I have a few questions. And I want straight answers. Let's go chat."

Grant shook his head, a look of disbelief on his face, and headed for the door.

Hammond watched them go and turned back to his subject. He was now alone in a cramped, dismal lab with a pale John Doe, a recently deceased mystery man. The creepiness of the lab—quiet, gloomy—began to press in on him. The body stared at the ceiling, eyes like fogged glass. Found in a submarine spring.

Something was wrong with this picture. Dreadfully wrong.

He lifted John Doe's right arm, drew the hand close. He felt the palm, squeezed it, felt its cool pale flesh dent and refuse to return to form. He spread the pliable fingers, bent them forward and back. Where was the rigor mortis? A day or two old, he'd told them. Best guess. But what was whispering in his ear that he had no idea?

The spear point lay upon a towel on Randy Sanborn's desk. Sanborn hovered over it with a magnifying glass. He picked it up, held the glass close, hoping to coax some kind of clue out of it. Hoping to see evidence that it was a fake. He thumbed the blade's edge, surprised at its jagged sharpness. He occasionally flipped through a book on Indian arrowheads and spear points, holding Grant's point close to the pictures, comparing. He didn't know what he expected to find. Maybe an inscription saying "made in China."

The piece was evidence of a sort. Not necessarily an alibi for Grant, but at least a good excuse. Maybe. Undersea Indian villages? Okay, that idea was too bizarre to be a lie. Grant was an archaeologist and here was the fruit of his supposed labor. But he'd been stubborn and shifty right up until he realized Sanborn was going to invade the spring, like it or not. Then he described all manner of bone chips, hooks, and potsherds littering his magical spring. It would have been nice if Grant had brought them in, but the guy claimed he couldn't screw with "context."

Sanborn knew a couple guys he could call and check out the story. And he sure wasn't going to take Grant at his word.

His radio chirped. "Randy, Julie Denton would like a few minutes," Jackie said.

Sanborn sat up straight and sucked in his stomach just a bit, feeling like Pavlov's dog. "Send her in." He surveyed his office, did a quick straightening of the papers on his desk, squaring them up. He reached into his desk drawer and pulled out a worn paperback copy of Hemingway's *To Have and Have Not* and set it on the edge of the desk, nice and square. Julie loved Hemingway and there's no way she could miss it. He'd already finished reading it, a couple of weeks back. It was good stuff, island stuff, rumrunners and all, and reminded him a lot of Brigands Key. Julie would only care about a really literate guy and he'd been devouring books lately. If this was what it took . . .

He suddenly felt pretentious and scooped the book back into his desk drawer.

The door opened and Julie entered. "I hear you've got something," she said.

Not Hemingway, he thought sourly. "Word gets around. I barely had time to get back to my office."

"Inconvenient?"

"Julie, we always have time for our friends in the media."

"The 'media,' " Julie said with a narrow smirk. She took a seat opposite his desk without waiting to be asked, moving with feline grace, leaning forward as was her habit. She pulled a beaten Rays baseball cap off her head, letting her dark brown hair cascade waves that glowed in the afternoon light. She tucked a strand behind her ear. Sanborn swallowed.

"Randy, you've got a John Doe."

"We have an unidentified adult male. It's a bit too soon to go melodramatic."

"The highlight of the week on this rotten island was Old Lady Cole backing into Hammond's mailbox. You've got a body; that's the biggest story in five years. It's five-thirty now, but I'm not leaving and my paper isn't shutting down tonight until this story is written and printed for tomorrow morning."

"Like I said, we haven't got anything yet."

"Right. You got the word this morning and the body before noon. You've been all over town talking to people, calling people. You've got story. Even dead ends are news when it comes to dead bodies."

He drummed gently on his desk. "Okay, but be gentle with me." He related the pertinent facts in chronological, intentionally boring order. No embellishment, no speculation. It was a lesson learned the hard way in Tampa, back when he was wet behind the ears, back before he learned the hard way about big-city law enforcement. Back before he came home and begged for a spot in the Brigands Key Police Department.

Julie Denton, he had told himself a thousand times, was not the reason he returned to Brigands Key.

Julie listened closely to his report, scribbling furiously. When he finished, she glanced up. "That's it?"

"You'll be the first to know when I get more."

"We both know that's not true. I'll get the story out first but within a day you'll be getting calls from every big paper in the state. I'm not stupid. This is a big, bizarre story at any level. If I don't get the scoop now, I never will."

Sanborn shifted uneasily in his chair. "The mayor won't be too crazy about this."

"The mayor's in line for a quote. Probably composing it as we speak."

"All right. Can we talk off the record?"

Julie set her notepad and pen down. "Off the record. For the moment. I'll let you know when that changes."

"See this?" Sanborn motioned to the spear point.

"I was waiting for you to bring it up."

"This is what Grant says he was after."

"You don't believe him?"

"Let me put it this way. The odds against a lone diver finding a fresh body in a cave no one has ever seen before, almost two dozen miles out to sea, stretch credibility way beyond my limits."

"What do you know about Grant?"

"Not enough. I've got this, though. Trouble follows him. He used to be a rising star in archaeology then threw it all in the toilet with some ridiculous claims. He took a sabbatical, returned to work, and led a disastrous expedition to Guatemala. People died and no satisfactory explanation ever came forward. He shows up in Brigands Key and—surprise, surprise—we have a mysterious death."

"Mysterious? I heard it was a drowning."

Sanborn said nothing, and realized that his fingers were still drumming. He willed them to stop.

Julie picked up her notepad. "Now we're getting somewhere. On the record. Let's start from the top."

Julie glanced at the clock in the printing room. Two A.M. Wednesday already? She rubbed her eyes, more to clear them than to keep awake. The clean smell of newsprint and ink were coffee enough, and she was not stopping until the morning edition was stacked and ready to roll.

She didn't have much. Randy was evasive, true to his nature. Hammond, even more so. But they'd told her more than they'd realized.

She'd pushed at Randy to let her see the body. She could run a photo, help them identify John Doe. No dice, he said, claiming some obscure rule or other. That would be a last resort; she knew what buttons to push if it came to that.

The press hummed and clattered, and the sheets slipped through with satisfying rapid-fire clicks.

She glanced at the headlines of yesterday's edition. Fishing report. Weather report. The never-ending squabbles between the City Council and Gulf Breeze Properties, the hotshots down in Tampa pushing the Bay View project. The Council making veiled threats about Mayor Johnson's pension. Small-town politics. Small-town crap.

She exhaled slowly, and skimmed her writing. Satisfactory at best. It was hard to get excited about crap, and her prose reflected it.

Now she had something she could sink her teeth into. She was going to give it her best and not get scooped by the biggies. The crap stories could wait. The fishing report was essentially the same every day and no one gave a flip about the mayor's pension except the mayor.

The first copies of the morning edition rolled off. Julie picked one up, smelled it, felt it. It was hitting the street in three hours. She tossed the paper back onto the stack. Hitting the streets, indeed. There were four hundred homes on Brigands Key. How many streets could there be? She should count them some day. When she had a spare three minutes.

She returned to her computer and uploaded the story to her online edition. After the papers were delivered, she'd fire off an electronic copy to Associated Press. She'd have a byline that would be circulated to newsrooms all over the state, maybe all over the country.

Some editor somewhere would have to notice.

CHAPTER THREE

In her dreams, Kyoko Nakamura is lost in a pueblo, in the dark . . .

She walks through low dim rooms. Dirt floors, rough walls. Following the sound of crying, searching. The sick and the dead all about. No sound but the crying of an infant.

The crying, growing louder. High and pained. Closer now.

Ducking through a low door into a dark and windowless room. The darkness dissipating, the dead, close air luminous, glowing with swarming microscopic life.

In the center of the room in a bundle of rags, the crying baby.

She approaches. Rats scurry and crouch with yellow glowing eyes in the shadows.

The baby turns to her, its cry intensifying. It is smeared with its own wet filth.

A Navajo boy. She reaches out, touches him. He recoils, shrieks, clutches her hand, and dies. And his grip upon her only tightens . . .

Kyoko awoke with a start, gasping, her heart thudding. She turned to the red glowing numbers on the clock. Four A.M. She got up, trembling, stumbled toward the bathroom, and turned on the shower. She would not get back to sleep and she knew it.

Kyoko slid her security card through the slot and the door hissed open. First in the office. She took a small victory in beating the Atlanta rush hour.

Small victories. The only kind she scored anymore.

29

The aroma of freshly brewed Arabica coffee filled the room and she thanked herself for setting the timer the night before. She poured half a cup and finished it off with another half of heavy whipping cream. And three sugars. Then another, to drive the night fog away. And to get ready for Paul Greer.

She settled into her desk chair and switched on the computer. She warmed up with a quick online sudoku before toggling the screen to CNN for a look at the headlines. If a relevant story reached cable before she knew of it, she wasn't doing her job. The Centers for Disease Control paid her to be the first to find trouble.

She scrolled her screen away from CNN and ran a quick scan of online medical journals, finding reports of a half-dozen cases the CDC had been tracking for a couple of months. There was a food poisoning outbreak in Oregon related to a shipment of bad chicken from Virginia. With emphasis on deadlines and time management, Americans were becoming coolly efficient at shipping illness. When it absolutely, positively, has to be there overnight—cut a corner or two. Who'll notice?

She nervously opened the report from the New Mexico field office. The hantavirus in Taos Pueblo had all but disappeared. Finally. It had taken down a few careers with it, almost including her own.

She opened the screen menu labeled RURAL OUTLETS/ MISC UNUSUAL DEATHS. A group of stories appeared, all from small-town newspapers and police blotters. Off-the-radar sources, where hot zones first showed up, before anyone had a fix on what was going on. A combine accident in Idaho, a strangling in upstate New York, an unsolved death in the Arizona desert. That one was clear as glass, the symptoms obvious, a case of strychnine poisoning. Why couldn't they figure it out? Small-town criminal investigation left a lot to be desired and it wasn't helped by any brilliance of medical examiners in the backwaters. She made a note to call the Phoenix office.

Zipping through stories, she paused over one proclaiming "Nude Body Recovered Offshore." Can't go wrong with nude bodies, she thought. "Police Baffled." Drownings were hardly baffling. She read the byline. Julie Denton, *Brigands Key Gazette*. Some little town in Florida. She read further.

"The body of a white male, approximate age early twenties, was found yesterday twenty-two miles offshore in the Gulf of Mexico. The body was found by researcher Dr. Carson Grant under thirty feet of water in a submerged freshwater spring . . ."

She read on. No sign of foul play, no boat, nothing. Kyoko sat back, thinking. She again read the story. The police chief was being coy but hinting at murder.

How did this Grant guy manage to find a body like that?

Brigands Key. She typed in a quick search and pulled it up. Small barrier island. That figured. Island dwellers had a gift for weirdness. It huddled a hundred and twenty miles north of Tampa, sixty west of Gainesville, and fifty south of nowhere.

There would be no point in bringing it forward to the higher-ups' attention just yet. No hint of disease. Waste of time, taxpayers' money, blah blah blah. Yet the acquisition of an impossible body was setting off an internal alarm. The one she'd ignored—to her sorrow—in Taos.

An hour later, Paul Greer finally buzzed her, summoned her to his office. "Close the door, please, Kyoko," he said when she entered.

Uh oh, she thought.

Greer was a severe little man with a round head and pointed features. Birdlike. She waited while he took a phone call as soon as she took a seat. He laughed and joked and turned his back to her. Had to be terribly important, that call.

He at last hung up and turned to her. "Any news, Doctor?"

Good morning to you too, she thought. "The usual. Oregon's

31

on top of things. Mendoza is giving them an earful."

"Good man, Mendoza. The best diagnostician I've worked with."

Kyoko felt the invisible dagger. She was the ranking diagnostician and had taught Mendoza the ropes. Let it go, she thought. "Heard anything about the research opening?"

Greer had a damn-the-bad-luck look on his face.

"You didn't even recommend me, did you?"

"That's not why we're meeting, Kyoko. Things have gotten . . . complicated. Where are we on Taos?"

"The follow-ups are clean. Most of the families have moved to neighboring towns, still waiting for the all-clear. They're more than a little angry. The second and third units are fanning out from the pueblo, checking every nook and cranny that could hide hantavirus. Chicken coops, barns, tool sheds. We've exterminated hundreds of rats and mice. Not a single rodent still lives in the stricken towns."

"A whole month without another case."

"Our luck is holding, sir."

"Luck? That's not a strategy, is it? Don't *ever* use that word outside this office. The Secretary just left yesterday evening, you know."

"So I'm told."

"She made it clear that President Rawlings will not abide another Taos. The New Mexico delegation is raising hell in Congress and laying the blame at the President's feet."

"Does Tom Rawlings understand viruses? We're at their mercy. Does he understand biology at all?"

"That isn't the issue. The virus left the pueblo after the initial two deaths and next thing we know, we've got seventeen dead in three towns. You didn't give us a clear picture at ground zero, Doctor."

"I told you exactly what was going on."

"Two days too late. The virus had migrated by then."

"I followed the protocols to a tee, Paul. You know, the ones you wrote."

"You were the ranking physician on site. The Secretary sees that. She wants a head. Whose doesn't matter, as long as it's someone from Special Pathogens. I didn't give her one. Not yet."

"Not yet?"

"She's not going to let this pass."

Kyoko studied him. A dead electricity filled the space between them. "What's this meeting about, Paul?"

"I'm placing you on notice. For your own good. Another screw-up like Taos, and even I can't save you. In the meantime, your work must be impeccable. Flawless. For now, I just want you out of the office and out of my sight—and the Secretary's sight. I've got damage control to do. I want you to take some time off."

Kyoko began to speak, thought better of it. Time off? What the hell for?

A smile flickered across Greer's face.

"Time off," Kyoko finally managed. "Fine. I could use a vacation. Tomorrow soon enough?"

"Don't be hasty. Next Tuesday will suffice. It's budget time and I need the numbers for your section before you go." He paused. "The Secretary arrives next Wednesday for another little pow-wow."

"Fine. Vacation. I think I'll go to Florida."

Greer brightened with an effort. "Ah, a little fun and sun. Anyplace in particular? I peg you as a South Beach type."

Kyoko felt her fingers digging into her armrest. "No. A little place called Brigands Key."

Charley Fawcett eased the door of his mobile home shut, trying to slip out unnoticed. The screen door slipped from his grasp and slapped against the doorjamb. His mother swung the door wide a split-second after he'd vaulted down the concrete steps to the dead lawn. "You be home real quick, soon as work's over, back in this house. Your daddy doesn't need to be chasing after you tonight. He's real tired of that."

No, just real drunk, Charley thought. At eighteen, he was old enough to know that much. "Bye, Mama. Soon as Roscoe calls it a day, I'll be home."

The sun hung low in a pale yellow sky but the morning was hot. Roscoe would be at the boat ready to go, pissed about something. Time was wasting. Time was money.

Charley hopped on his bike, a rattle-trap fat-tire affair, and pedaled down the lane of the trailer park and onto Thursby Street, then onto Main. Brigands Key was a rotten little berg but at least he could negotiate the whole frigging town in twenty minutes on a bicycle.

He coasted past Brigands Key High and through downtown, past City Hall and the post office, past the police department. The office of the *Brigands Key Gazette* was still lit. Julie Denton was locking up, a haggard but contented look on her face.

Charley zipped across Main and coasted down the slight slope of Dock Street and skidded to a stop in the gravel at the foot of the dock, sluicing up a satisfying cloud of limestone dust that subsequently settled on him and clung to his sweat-damp skin. He coughed up dust and chained his bike to a stop sign.

Roscoe Nobles looked up from the deck of the trawler *Electric Ladyland*. "Fawcett, you're five minutes late. You think this is a charity outfit?"

"Sorry, Mr. Nobles. Won't happen again."

"You say that every day. Shit, boy, you finished high school in May. It's August now. I been paying you good money three months and you still treat this like some kind of high school

34

circle jerk. It ain't. This is my livelihood. Unhitch the cleats and get on the damn boat."

"Sorry, Mr. Nobles," Charley repeated, this time making eye contact. "I'm a punk, no doubt about it."

Roscoe eyed him, deciding whether or not he was being mocked. Satisfied that he was, he stepped behind the wheel in the small cabin and switched on the key. The engine sputtered and belched blue smoke and rumbled to life. Roscoe spun the wheel and throttled gently up and pulled away from the dock. "Fish are probably all gone by now."

"We going after grouper today?"

"Grouper, reds, whatever gets stuck in the net. Think I'm stupid, college boy?"

"No sir."

The harbor of Brigands Key nestled on the inland waterway side of the island, away from the rougher waters of the Gulf. Roscoe steered out into the channel, careful not to draw wake and the ire of other captains, and followed the channel markers out and around the northern end of the island, passing through the shadow of Hammond Lighthouse. Clearing the point, Roscoe opened his traditional bottle of whiskey, poured a couple fingers into a thermos of coffee.

"Some kinda shit yesterday, huh, Charley?" Roscoe wasn't a total asshole once he got a little booze in him and would quickly drop the name-calling and address Charley by name. That made some sense; anyone that named a boat after a Hendrix album couldn't be all bad.

"What shit is that, Roscoe?" Charley asked, feeling comfortable enough to use first names.

"That U of F guy found a body out in the ocean. It's in the paper." He tossed the *Gazette* to Charley.

"I heard of it." Charley skimmed over the story.

"I ain't buying it."

35

"Why not?"

"Grant . . . he ain't a local."

Charley rolled his eyes. Of all places, Brigands Key had no right to arrogance, yet it was a defining trait. "So?"

"So he's up to something. You really believe he's looking for Indian mounds under the sea? That's a good 'un."

"He's an archaeologist. What do you expect him to be after?"

"Come on, Charley, grow up. You ain't in high school no more. A man's after two things: money and pussy. Having the first gets you the second. Indian mounds, my ass. Grant's up to something."

"I don't think anyone mentioned Indian mounds."

Roscoe grinned conspiratorially. "Bet no one mentioned treasure, either."

Oh boy, Charley thought. Here we go. Roscoe's ultimate fantasy. "You think he's on a treasure hunt?"

"There's dozens of shipwrecks within an hour's boat trip of Brigands Key. Most of them ain't been identified yet, and I guarantee you there's a bunch more ain't been found. Grant's hiding something. Didn't you notice the paper didn't say where the body came from?"

"So the newspaper and the police are in on it, too?"

"Grant won't tell them the location."

The island and mainland receded in the distance. Salty wind blew through Charley's hair and the open sea filled his senses. At moments like this, he loved going out each morning with Roscoe. Although he'd lived his whole life on an island, he rarely got to go out on the water until he got this job. His sporadically employed father never owned a boat, and his mother wouldn't set foot on one.

"Chief Sanborn knows the spot," Charley said at last.

Roscoe shot him a glance. "How do you know?"

Charley tried a confident shrug. "This is big stuff for Brigands

Key. When the paper didn't reveal the location, I got curious."

"Yeah?"

"I hacked Sanborn's computer this morning before work. That's why I was late."

"Holy damn, Charley! You're odd, but you got your moments."

Roscoe was a miser with compliments, and Charley blushed. "Piece of cake," he said. "Sanborn's not real big on computer security because nothing ever happens around here and because he knows nobody on the island is worth a damn with the digital age."

"He underestimated one of us."

Charley grinned.

"So. You going to tell me or not?"

"I don't know, Boss. I kind of feel like it's a threat to the case and to Dr. Grant's work."

Roscoe groaned. "Look. If Grant ain't told Sanborn, he's hiding something, and it ain't arrowheads and baskets. If he has, Sanborn's going to blunder all over the place and screw up his little project anyway."

"I don't know."

"You ain't the pushover I thought. Tell you what, Charley. You got something good and I'll throw in fifty bucks on top of your wages."

Charley hesitated. "Cash? Today?"

"Don't get greedy, son. I'll add it to your paycheck."

"Good enough. Sanborn wrote a report and saved it as a .pdf file on his computer. It was ridiculously easy to open. His password is 'Theodore'."

"That's his damn cat's name!"

"Guys like that think that's some kind of unbreakable code. Anyway, the Chief's computers are networked with City Hall's. Get into one of them, you get into them all."

"Yeah, but what's he got?"

"An Indian spear point is all he produced. Says there's more. Teeth, hooks, stuff like that. What you'd expect."

"I say he got that junk from some other site and is using it as a cover. Where's his treasure, boy?"

"It rounds to twenty-nine degrees, thirteen minutes north, by eighty-three, twenty-eight west."

"Not enough. I need GPS coordinates. Grant's probably not the guessing kind."

Charley hesitated and pulled a slip of paper from his pocket and handed it to him. "I figured you'd want it. Grant's precise; he logged the position out to fourteen decimal places."

Roscoe read the paper, rummaged through his console, found a paper clip, and attached the note to a dirty notepad hanging from the console.

Charley laughed. "You know, Roscoe, you really should get yourself a laptop. Get with the times."

Roscoe shook his head. "I got a computer. I use it to look at dirty pictures and steal songs. I keep the important stuff the old-fashioned way."

"How come?"

" 'Cause of guys like you. You broke into the police computer and had your way, and that's the most sensitive shit in town. You hackers, you can steal my stuff from the other side of the world. No sir. My way is safer. There's folks here in town would like nothing better than a look at my files."

"Any moron could break into your house and steal your stuff."

"Not my stuff. All my important stuff is in code. And I use dozens of codes. Somebody cracks one of them, and it'll only be good for a little bit of my stuff. Computer hackers are smart but lazy sons of bitches. They can't do it electronically, they don't want to bother. Nobody else on the island is smart enough to figure this out." Roscoe studied him for a long moment, a peculiar, appraising look in his eyes. "You'd be the only guy on the island I figure is smart enough for code-breaking."

Charley squirmed, pretended to look out to sea.

"Relax, kid," Roscoe said. "I don't bite. Listen close; when Old Roscoe kicks the bucket, you keep looking for them lost trails, you hear?"

"Yeah sure, Roscoe."

"And get your education. What did you say you were going to study in college?"

"Physics, I guess."

"Well, ain't you the egghead? That's fine, but read your Shakespeare."

Charley nodded.

"Read your Shakespeare, kid. I mean it."

"Shakespeare. Got it."

Roscoe swiveled the screen on his GPS finder out of the sun and wiped it with a fist. He looked at the paper on which he'd scrawled Charley's coordinates and looked up at the southwestern horizon. He swung *Electric Ladyland* west so sharply Charley, leaning against the starboard gunwale, nearly toppled overboard.

"As luck'd have it," Roscoe said, "the reds are biting over yonder."

Forty minutes later, Roscoe throttled down and the boat slowed to a crawl, rocking gently over its own following wake, its powerful outboards grumbling. Charley glanced eastward. Although he could just see the tiny spire of the lighthouse, a pinpoint over the water, they were no longer within sight of land and he felt a vague dread, his mind whispering that the whole world was ocean and that a half-inch-thick wooden hull was all that separated him from a wet, lonely death.

Roscoe peered at the horizon. Charley shaded his eyes and squinted into the distance in the same direction. He could make out a small white speck. Roscoe rummaged through a plastic crate, found his old Bushnell binoculars, and trained them on the speck. "It figures," he said. "Randy Sanborn's already parked over the professor's mystery hole. Got his dive flag raised. Son of a bitch."

"You gonna ease over and take a look, Roscoe?"

Roscoe didn't answer for a moment, seeming to weigh things in his mind. "Nah," he finally said. He picked up a small, bright orange book off the console and thumbed through it, pausing over a couple of pages, reading silently. He replaced the book, pushed the throttle forward, and swung about to port. "Let's go get some mullet from the channel while the gettin's good."

"I thought we were going to catch reds and grouper instead."

"You got a lot to learn, college boy."

Sanborn knew himself to be just a half-assed diver, having logged too few dives to consider himself anything but. Given the woeful, systemic lack of staff he contended with, it was smart to become a jack of all trades. Hence, his diver status. Made perfect sense for a coastal town the size of Brigands Key, though until now he'd never had a single need to call upon that ability. It always looked good on his bio and now it was coming in handy.

As luck and cheap government would have it, Sanborn was diving without a fellow officer. The department had only himself trained as a diver. Greenwood was topside, minding the boat, thinking about lunch. There was no one left to buddy with and he didn't want to bring along just anyone to wreck his investigation by screwing with evidence and hunting arrowheads.

So he'd asked Julie Denton to join him. She jumped at the chance. Serendipity happens. She was the only available, trustworthy dive buddy in town and he had a legitimate reason for asking her to join him on this dive. He could kick himself for not having thought of this years ago.

The spring was exactly where Grant had said, pinpointed by GPS to within five feet. Technology. No end to it. It'd behoove folks to not throw out the old techniques just yet, though. One honker of a solar storm could knock out every satellite orbiting the planet and GPS would be nonexistent once again, stranding travelers and deleting bank accounts everywhere.

Sanborn drifted close to the mouth of the spring, a diamond of clear water. Chalk one up for Grant; the outsider had discovered a miracle of nature right under the noses of Brigands Key lifers and know-it-alls.

Julie held back. Sanborn motioned her forward and she eased alongside. She caught him staring and her eyes iced over. He tried to smile, realizing he must look ridiculous. Smiles through facemask, mouthpiece, and octopus hoses come out like grimaces.

Julie had agreed to not touch anything and to not enter the cave. Just keep hold of his safety line and fish him out if need be. She had no equipment for underwater shots but he'd located the clunky, twenty-year-old underwater camera the City purchased long ago, squirreled away in a closet of never-used equipment. Julie would have to compose from her own notes and memories.

Sanborn flipped the switch on his lamp. Nothing. He jiggled it and the beam lit the water. He swept the beam about in the cave. Clear and spooky. He hesitated and pulled himself in against the current.

The cave was broad and deep and foreign, and its walls shivered as he swept them with the beam. Nothing struck him as peculiar, but then he didn't know what he'd expected. He saw no sign of ancient human habitation. No wigwams, no spears, no canoes. Just rocks and sand.

He negotiated the left side of the cave, feeling the knobby

gray wall with his hand. A sudden dread crept into him and he glanced nervously back toward his exit, to make sure he always had it in sight.

Grant had said the body was wedged into a niche, trapped in place by the flow of the current. Sanborn shone the light about, searching. There were three sizable niches in the wall. He pulled himself toward the nearest and studied it. A band of sand, dazzlingly white, blanketed the bottom like snow. He reached out his hand, recalling Grant's certainty that the local bumpkins would screw up his important research. Don't want to disappoint the good professor. He stirred the sand, scattering the flakes into a cloud.

He uncovered a tooth, a molar.

Resisting the urge to snatch it up, he unhooked the camera from his belt and swung it forward. He aimed and clicked, the flash illuminating the dim cave like daylight. There's your Goddamn context, he thought. He set the camera aside and tucked the tooth into a small plastic bag.

Continuing around the room, Sanborn gently fanned the bottom, clearing away the snowflakes. He found a large, flat bone, picked it up, turned it, felt its thickness and weight. Way too big for a human. Looked like a hip bone. He was no zoologist, but hell, he watched Animal Planet. Big things, mastodons and bison and camels, used to roam Florida, way back when. This had to be something like that.

Intrigued, he again brushed the cave bottom, clearing away two inches of sand, and uncovered a seven-inch tooth that curved and tapered like a scimitar to a fine, wicked point. Sabertooth. Ice Age Florida was a scary place. He could see why this appealed to geeks like Grant. He was a kid all over again. He tucked the dagger of a tooth in a separate bag. Another five minutes netted a broken spear point and half a dozen more teeth, both human and animal.

Another object caught his eye. There was nothing prehistoric or exotic about it. He picked up the heavy black—totally modern—nightstick and ran his fingers along it, feeling the nicks and dents and scratches that whispered a history of brute force.

He swept the room with light once more and let the current carry him out through the mouth of the cave. He motioned Julie to the surface and followed her. Tommy helped them onto the deck of the boat and they shrugged out of their dive gear. Sanborn spread his finds, except for the nightstick, out on the deck.

Tommy crowded in. "What you got, whale bones?"

"Nope. Some kind of extinct animals, I imagine. Got some Indian stuff, too. Teeth, another spear point. Part of Grant's story checks out."

"Unless he planted this stuff to back up his story."

Julie reached for the human teeth. "May I—?"

Sanborn shrugged. "I reckon they're all Indian teeth. John Doe has all his intact, not missing any. So go ahead. I'll turn these over to Grant after I make him sweat a while."

Julie picked up the teeth and turned them over, then replaced all but one, an incisor. "You may not want to give this one back just yet."

"Why not?"

"It has a filling."

CHAPTER FOUR

The intercom buzzed. Gerald Hammond jumped and slapped down his scalpel. "What now, Jackie?" Biggest autopsy ever in Brigands Key and interruptions were the rule of the day. No one understood "No Interruptions." He should just drag the corpse back to his office where he had complete control. Here at City Hall Annex he was just another public employee.

"Randy's back off the water," Jackie said cheerfully. "He's hauling in Dr. Grant."

"Terrific," Hammond said.

He had canceled his patients for the remainder of the day and toiled in blissful silence, having locked the door and unhooked the phone, pestered only by Jackie's frequent inquiries. The hours had passed and his unease had grown.

The door clattered open and Sanborn entered. Grant followed, scowling, no doubt snatched away from his favorite soaps.

Sanborn dragged a stool close and motioned Grant to do the same. Grant ignored him, ran a hand through his dark hair, and leaned against a stacked cabinet and plunged his hands deep into his pockets, his scowl deepening. Great.

Sanborn spoke first. "I hear you've got a cause of death and it isn't drowning."

Hammond nodded toward Grant. "Who invited James Dean?"

"I suggested he come along."

"Am I a suspect?" Grant asked.

"Everyone's a suspect. Except me."

"You going to tell me how bad you ruined my site?"

"It's not your site anymore."

"We'll see."

Hammond shifted uneasily. "This is why I didn't want him here," he said. "Now then. Mr. Doe here was murdered."

"You said there wasn't a mark on him."

"There isn't, almost." He leaned close to the body. "I've done a standard Y-incision of the torso. Good specimen, really. This guy was in great shape. Take a good look. Can you spot any injuries, any trauma? Apart from my having splayed and gutted him like a fish."

Sanborn crowded in, studying the cadaver, glowering. "Just give me your damned report."

"Follow me." Hammond went to a corner sink, washed up, and took a seat at a garage-sale desk and began typing on a computer keyboard. He swiveled the monitor toward them. On screen, John Doe lay intact and unopened, naked to the world. In the corner of the screen, a counter ticked off the time of filming.

He dragged the mouse and the images advanced in time, then settled on an image and zoomed in on the man's chest until the camera was practically on top of it. "Right there," he said, pointing with the cursor to a spot a couple of inches right and below the left nipple. "See that?"

"What?"

"Christ, you're blind. Right there." The cursor drew a circle the size of a dime. Within the circle, a tiny, almost invisible, mark lay. "Puncture wound, right through the heart. The diameter is less than a millimeter. This guy was stabbed with an implement like a long needle or ice pick. Very lethal, very hidden."

Sanborn studied the image. "And the internal damage?"

"Whoever did it jiggled the point inside the victim to ratchet up the trauma."

"Anything else?"

"The trachea is crushed."

Sanborn straightened and held his arms out, slowly crooking one, drawing the other inward toward himself in a stabbing motion, working through movements. "The killer seizes John Doe from behind, clamps his left arm around the victim's neck, cutting off oxygen. The victim panics. The killer finishes him off with a stab into the heart." He whistled softly. "The whole thing is over in seconds. Professional work."

"You're a savant, Randy."

Sanborn took a small plastic bag out of his pocket, set it on the desktop, and opened it. He withdrew five human teeth and lined them up. From another bag he withdrew the nightstick and set it beside the teeth. "What kind of grill has John Doe got?"

Hammond opened the dead man's mouth. "Pretty healthy one, I'd say. A couple small cavities, no crowns, caps, bridges. Not missing any, teeth are all intact."

"Got his dental molds and x-rays yet?"

"Course I do. You sign for it and I'll overnight them to the FBI to see if anything comes up. Fingerprints, too."

"Send a tissue sample for DNA typing while you're at it." Sanborn turned to Grant. "Tell me about Indian teeth."

"Paleo-Indians had hard, worn teeth. No daily intake of sugar to rot them. They would wear down through tough chewing on grains and nuts."

"These are all paleo teeth?"

"If you thought so, you wouldn't be asking." Grant studied the teeth for a moment and picked up an incisor and turned it over in his palm. He handed it to Hammond. "This one's recent. It has a filling."

Hammond examined the tooth. Sure enough, it bore a sizable filling in the back. The root had been sheared off. "John Doe's not missing an incisor. This tooth belonged to someone else."

"The murderer was in the spring with John Doe and got his tooth knocked out," Sanborn said. He handed the nightstick to Hammond. "With this, I'll wager. You need some real force to break a tooth loose underwater. John Doe didn't go easily." He looked at Grant.

"For Christ's sake," Grant said. He opened his mouth wide.

Sanborn peered into Grant's mouth, pushing his head to one side and back again. He released him and stepped away. "Not missing any. Could stand a little flossing, though."

"Maybe I had an accomplice," Grant said.

"Maybe." Sanborn turned again to Hammond. "You fixed the time of death?"

Hammond looked nervously away. "This isn't Hollywood. Evaluating time of death isn't an exact science."

"Let's have it."

"John Doe appears to have been dead less than a day when he arrived here. Less than half a day."

Sanborn leaned in. "Okay. Tell me why."

"Lack of discoloration. The skin should have started changing color between twelve and twenty-four hours. This one looked good."

Sanborn studied the body. "Looks a little blue to me."

"He does now. A day later, he's supposed to be blue."

"He looked pretty unnatural yesterday too."

"That was discoloration due to gravity. The blood settling in the lowest areas. I'm talking now about discoloration due to decomposition."

Sanborn looked at Grant. "You claimed you found the body around ten yesterday morning."

"That's when I *did* find it."

"And you arrived there at nine."

"I spent an hour getting my gear ready, starting notes, mainlining hard drugs."

"So John Doe was murdered and left in the open sea in an undiscovered spring either that morning or night, hours before you discovered the spring. Those are some pretty incredible odds, Dr. Grant."

"Good to see you come to grips with it."

"Any ideas?"

"It's a damned strange world."

"Jerry, what else you got?"

Hammond's mouth felt dry. "John Doe died between a couple weeks ago and a couple of months ago."

"You just said he's been dead less than a day!"

"I said he appeared to have been dead less than a day." Hammond went back to the corpse and selected a forceps and gently probed the intestines. "This isn't pretty. Leave now if you're squeamish." He pulled open the flap of skin that covered the intestines, exposing a gray, collapsed mass. "See how the tissue has broken down? This is the result of enzyme action and consistent with nine days."

"No smell and no exterior degradation," Grant murmured.

Hammond glanced at him. "Correct. Why isn't he breaking down outside the body cavity? In decomposition, there are four general stages. You have fresh, or autolysis; you have bloated, or putrefaction; you have decay, or putrefaction with carnivores; and you have the dry, or diagenesis."

"I know all this, Jerry," Sanborn said, his face clouding.

"Decomposition is a gang-bang," Hammond said. "Enzymes, bacteria, insects, carnivores—they all demand a piece of the action. Enzymic decomposition is what we call autolysis. Your digestive tract is chock full of enzymes like hydrochloric acid.

Strong stuff, right? While you're alive, your gastrointestinal tract produces mucus that keeps your guts from dissolving. When you kick the bucket the natural protections cease but the enzymes don't. They start to break down gastrointestinal tissues. You get a perforated stomach and intestines, even some of the esophagus. The enzymes seep into the lung cavity and the abdomen, continuing the digestion. The lungs break down rapidly in the enzymes and you get a bubbly, bloody fluid. That's pulmonary autolysis. In advanced cases, the fluid is a brownish-green. Stinks to high heaven.

"Now if this guy were a drowning victim, pulmonary autolysis would be even faster, because drowning sparks convulsive vomiting, which draws gastric enzymes into the lungs." Hammond eased the chest cavity apart. "Look closely. Tell me about the lungs."

Sanborn swallowed audibly as he leaned in. "They're gone," he said after a moment.

"Completely. Not removed, but dissolved by autolytic process. They turned to fluid and leaked out through the nose and mouth. That would indicate that the body has been dead for a week or two.

"Brain tissue also undergoes autolytic breakdown, just not as fast. Much slower." He motioned to the John Doe's head, the top of which was covered with a white cloth. He removed the cloth, noting with some satisfaction the sick look on Sanborn's face. "I've removed the front of the skull. The brain is gone. All that's left is a disgusting sludge. But that would have taken weeks in the brain. See, Randy? Fresh outside. Unfresh inside. The chronology of decomposition is all wrong. It simply makes no sense."

Sanborn shook his head. "That can't be right. There are a bunch of qualifiers with the rate of decomposition."

"True. Exposure to oxygen affects the rate. Tissue immersed

in water takes twice as long to decompose as tissue exposed to air. Still not enough to explain the discrepancy."

Grant looked up. "Oxygen? This was not seawater he was in. It was fresh spring water. Springs have lower oxygen levels than other water bodies."

"That would add a little time to the rate. Not a lot. What else you got about springs?"

"They're chilly and pure. Not much in the way of microbes."

"Okay, we add a few days extra. I'm concerned about something else. Anthropophagy."

"Flesh-eating," Sanborn said. "See, I paid attention in class."

"Wonders never cease. This guy should have been scavenged. Crabs should have lined up at the buffet table. Fish would nibble. Sharks would gobble up whole chunks of him."

"There weren't any fish or crabs in the spring and the body was a good forty feet in from the vent," Grant said. "Saltwater marine life doesn't have much liking for freshwater. And the current is strong. It would take quite an effort and will for sea life to work upstream into the cave."

"Was the body floating?"

Grant shifted. "He was wedged into a niche. Pinned there by the current."

"Floating freely or resting on the floor?"

"Resting on the floor."

"Bodies sink when they're new and float when they putrefy. The gases produced by bacteria render them buoyant. There's a primary flotation between twenty-four and seventy-two hours of death. Once the initial gases are dispelled, the body sinks until it bloats and rises again. John Doe here isn't bloated. Not even a little. He doesn't stink. There's no breakdown of the lips or eyelids, which should go quickly.

"Here's my quandary. If this gentleman has been dead long enough for enzymes to completely dissolve lungs, stomach, intestines, and brain, he should also be in an advanced state of bacterial putrefaction."

Sanborn leaned back, his eyes fixed on John Doe. "So why isn't he?"

"Now comes the good part." Hammond opened a refrigerator and withdrew a small tray of microscope slides. He switched on the light of the binocular microscope and placed a slide under the scope, looked into the eyepieces, twisted the focus knob, and stepped back. "This slide is muscle tissue from the lower abdomen. Be my guest."

Sanborn peered into the microscope. After a moment, he said, "I don't see anything."

"Exactly. The tissue should be crawling with bacteria. Instead, they're absent."

"All the slides are like this?"

Hammond nodded. "The body, gentlemen, is completely sterile."

Sanborn was quiet for a moment, studying the cadaver.

Hammond made a nervous, clipped laugh. "Starting to sink in, isn't it? Time of death is unknowable. This guy's free of bacteria, like he was pickled in alcohol or formaldehyde. Like Lenin. Only he wasn't. Preservative chemicals are absent." Hammond shook his head. "I'll put it all in my report because I have to, and I'll pray that no one outside Brigands Key ever gets wind of this. Why? Because I'll be a laughing-stock, an incompetent sawbones out in the sticks who doesn't know his ass from a hole in the ground." Hammond leaned forward and his voice dropped. "Because what I'm telling you is, simply put, impossible."

ON the EDGE, with Charley Eff
  Greetings, Blog-People!
  The Old Man takes one look this morning. "The hell are you

going?" he bellows. The Old Man has a limited but effective vocabulary.

"Work," says I.

"That drunk ever going to pay you?" At this point, Mom pops in and pops right back out. She's a superhero when the Old Man hits the bottle before breakfast. Her super power is her ability to disappear into thin air. Which is not a lot of use to me.

"I get paid in a week or so," I lied. I got paid yesterday and cashed it and stuffed it in my underwear drawer.

"I want to see the check before you cash it."

"But, Father, Roscoe pays in cash," I lied. "Minimum wage." (That much was true.) "Keeps his books lean and clean." Such bullshit. No way am I letting the Old Man see my check. "Forty hours a week," I lied. It's more like fifty. The Old Man would drink up every penny I make. I can't scrape enough nickels together to get me into college, but maybe I'll get enough to buy that beat-up old Chrysler the mayor's trying to unload. Then I'm gone for good.

When I was twelve, I had a paper route for the Brigands Key birdcage liner. I made twenty bucks that first week. The Old Man drank eighteen of it then beat the hell out of me. I quit the route that day. The Old Man found out and beat me again.

I gotta get off this freaking island.

Roscoe's okay. A moron, but okay.

The Old Man is a little guy. A shrimp, really. By the time I was fourteen, I was bigger than him. He stopped hitting when he had to swing up at me. Coward! He wanted to, 'cause I was bigger AND smarter than him. He felt cheated when he lost the edge in size.

Anyway . . .

Big News in Hooterville sur la Mer! Dead guy was found

out in the ocean. No one knows who he was or how he got there. There's this professor dude in town who found the body. Professor Dude seems normal, but living here you grow a skewed idea of normalcy. Inbred bunch of island 'necks. They're already whispering about Professor Dude. Poor guy doesn't know what kind of snake pit he stumbled into. More later . . .

Peace Out,
Charley Eff

Grant rolled over on the marble slab that the motel staff claimed was a mattress and looked at the glowing red numbers of the alarm clock. Two A.M. Thursday already. Wednesday was wasted and it was looking like that would be the norm. He sat up, kicked off the bed covers, stretched.

He pulled on a pair of shorts and a tee-shirt and slipped out of the room, barefoot. Probably stupid to go out barefoot but what the hell. He thought best in strange towns on late-night walks in bare feet.

He headed down the quiet street and reached the dock and followed it to its end. He looked over his boat, toying with the idea of boarding, but decided against antagonizing Sanborn further. He took a seat, dangling his feet over the water, and stared at the dazzling stars overhead. The thunderclouds had blown away, leaving a clear black sky, best appreciated in towns on the edge of a sea. A midsummer night's dream. He spotted the constellation Perseus and leaned back to watch.

John Doe haunted him.

He'd seen his share of the drowned, having pulled a number of them from underground rivers across Florida. John Doe was different somehow.

A meteor streaked across the blackness, a white thread stretching and disappearing in less than a second. Summer's annual Perseid shower was in its waning days but patience should reward him with more meteors every few minutes.

Soft waves lapped against the piers below, and a cool salty breeze drifted in off the Gulf, calming him. Weariness settled in. His eyelids drooped and his head nodded.

There was a flash of blue light in the darkness.

He snapped back to wakefulness and looked about. Must be a patrol car prowling, flashing lights at drunks like himself.

Nothing. The streets were as deserted as before.

He looked up at the sky. A pale blue glow hung there, fading, fading. Gone.

He blinked, rubbed his eyes. Was it really there? He wasn't sure what he'd seen, or dreamed. The sky was black and starlit once more. The stardust of the Perseids continued to rain.

He'd heard of the fabled "flash of green" over the water. He didn't believe in it. Old sea-dog stories were mostly nonsense. Mostly. He'd never heard of a flash of blue.

He got to his feet and headed back toward his room.

CHAPTER FIVE

Charley sat on the gunwale of *Electric Ladyland,* balancing himself, trying to imagine a suitably manly pose in case a girl from school happened by. He glanced at his watch. Roscoe was fifteen minutes late. That had to be a record. Roscoe's super power was punctuality. Everybody needed a super power, although nearly all were worthless in the scheme of things.

Sixteen minutes. The fish weren't going to wait, as Roscoe pointed out every morning. Funny thing, though. The fish always waited and Roscoe always caught them.

Roscoe late. It just didn't happen. Charley wished he had a cell phone. All the kids had one. Maybe he'd blow his next paycheck on one, a good one with video and cool apps. But that would decimate his college fund.

Charley heard that college students had an unwritten pact with professors: If the instructor was fifteen minutes late, class was canceled, absences excused. It sounded like bullshit, it was so alien to life in Brigands Key.

Roscoe was now seventeen minutes late, but Charley didn't move. The last thing Roscoe would want to hear was that the college boy had blown off an honest day's work because some tweedy eggheads let kids skip class without repercussion.

The last of the Brigands Key fishing fleet, Frank Salazar's *Mustang Sally,* heaved off and moved out into the channel, the throaty rumble of the engines shaking the water's surface, blue smoke coughing from the exhaust. Frank waved. "Roscoe sleeping one off, Charley?"

Mustang Sally rounded the tip of the island, throttled up, and rolled out to the open sea. *Electric Ladyland* was the last commercial boat moored. Another first.

Twenty minutes. Roscoe wasn't coming. Drunk, like Salazar said.

Roscoe could drink anyone under the table (another super power), but his code required abstinence during the work week.

Charley walked to the foot of the dock and looked down the street in both directions. Maybe Roscoe was at Merrill's Bait and Tackle, picking up something or other. Roscoe hated Merrill, but Merrill's was the only game in town. Charley crossed the street and entered. Merrill scowled and stopped what he was doing and watched like a hawk. Anyone under fifty was out to steal from him. Charley asked, "Mr. Merrill, has Mr. Nobles been in this morning?"

Merrill swept the air with his hand. "You see him here?"

"I thought maybe he popped in. He likes your store. He steals shiners when you're taking a crap." Charley slammed the door on his way out.

He unlocked his bike and pedaled down Main to the south side of town, slowly, then faster and faster. Something was wrong with Roscoe. Probably the flu. Nah. Roscoe never got sick and if he did he'd be fine with the idea of getting everyone else sick, so long as he didn't miss a day of work.

Roscoe's house on Lee Street was a weathered, peeling Victorian, one of the oldest in town. It had been built by the Nobles clan in 1878. The family had prospered, and prospered even more during Prohibition until Roscoe's great-grandfather was paid a visit by the FBI and went to prison and the family fell into ruin and lost the house. Roscoe fulfilled a twenty-year-old promise to his father and purchased the Victorian. Roscoe was the last of the line and lived alone in his bachelor's paradise.

Roscoe the bachelor. Charley wondered about that. Roscoe talked as nasty as one could about his conquests of the opposite sex, yet Charley had never seen him with a woman. A few business associates, all men, came by periodically. And Roscoe's weekends were typified by jaunts down to Tampa, to see "family." Whatever. In Brigands Key, that kind of thing didn't exist. Charley didn't pry and Roscoe didn't talk, and Charley was glad he wasn't the only misfit in town.

Charley leaned his bike against the front steps and climbed to the broad, shady porch. The morning paper lay unopened. Roscoe's Chevy pickup sat in the gravel driveway.

Charley banged on the ancient, sagging door, making it rattle. "Roscoe, you here?" He tried the knob. Locked. He peered through the dirty front window but could see little, except that the room was hideous.

Charley circled the house, calling Roscoe's name. Still no answer. He returned to the front porch.

No big deal. Simple explanation. Roscoe had a little business that needed attention in Ybor City and someone gave him a ride. Happened all the time. A guy needs a little release now and then. That's what everyone claimed.

Roscoe was fine. He'd be back tomorrow.

Charley had a hard time convincing himself as he pedaled away.

Susan Walsh finished reading the *Brigands Key Gazette* online edition for the third time, closed her laptop, and squared it neatly on her desk. No big deal, she told herself. People die every day.

She cradled a cup of steaming coffee with both hands and turned to the vast window of Bay Tower. The afternoon sun was peaking through after a sudden storm. The sunset would be spectacular over Tampa Bay this evening.

"People die every day," she said quietly. Tampa was rife with homicides, disappearances, unexplained deaths, and no one cared. Why get worked up over one death up in Brigands Key?

She read the story once more.

There was just one death. Probably a drowned, drunken fisherman. But in the sticks things like this riled people up. She didn't need that, not now, not with the project at a critical point. Passions were running high over Bay View. She had City Council in her pocket but the good citizens were ready to string them all up.

This could mushroom. Rumors would fly, accusations would be leveled, all because of timing. In five days the Council would vote and Bay View would be a done deal. The good news: Pierce hadn't mentioned it and didn't know about it. And what the boss didn't know didn't hurt him.

She wanted to kick herself. Playing close to the vest was her talent and was supposed to be a good thing, but it hadn't served her well lately. Yet instincts had gotten her this far in life without disaster. Without big ones, anyway.

Susan turned back to her laptop and typed in a few commands, assigning an out-of-office reply to all incoming emails. She picked up the phone. "Beth, mark me out for the next couple of days. I'm driving up to Brigands Key first thing tomorrow morning. I'll be there until the vote next Wednesday. The skids need a bit of greasing."

Julie Denton stared at the computer monitor, scrolling through headlines on MSN. Nothing going on in the world that affected her little paradise, she thought, switching off the website. She leaned back wondering where that sentiment had come from. It's all news, regardless of scale, regardless of location. She was a news junkie and the news had run her life.

Everything was connected in some way. The price of grouper

in Brigands Key, somehow, someway, affected the outcome of elections in Thailand, and vice versa.

So why was she disaffected by the events of the world this morning? Wednesday's edition of the *Gazette* had been the biggest in years. She'd gotten phone calls from the *Tampa Tribune* and the *Miami Herald*. Today's paper had some follow-up, a little background. John Doe had bumped the fishing forecast and that tropical depression down by Cuba right off the front page. Yet the bigger picture was out there, tantalizing and elusive. She should be out pounding the pavement, drawing out the story. Grant, Hammond, and Sanborn knew more than they were telling.

Yet here she sat, a malaise gripping her. She'd felt it from the moment she'd awoken at five. Maybe she was entering middle age. That would stink.

She closed the Internet and started a new document file. She'd found out a little about Grant's checkered past and could use it to fill out page two. She began typing and stopped after one paragraph as sudden queasiness took hold. It passed, and she read back what she'd just written.

Her prose style, when she was at the top of her game, was sharp, crisp, and insightful. Like Hemingway's. Maybe not that good. But Hemingway whacked and whittled and crafted a line thirty or forty times if need be. She didn't have that kind of time. And what she'd just written was far from her best.

Her stomach twitched, butterflies, and she felt a flush come into her face. She touched her brow and felt the sweat there.

Wonderful, just wonderful, she thought. Story of the year and she was getting a flu. Unacceptable. What would Hemingway do? Drink a fifth of whiskey and get back to work.

Her stomach twitched again, gurgling. She rushed to the bathroom and rummaged through the medicine cabinet and found a bottle of Pepto. She checked the expiration date. Close enough. She opened the bottle.

Before she could get a glass of water filled and the medicine into her mouth, her guts lurched. She dropped to her knees over the toilet and the contents of her stomach blew up and out of her throat, the smell and taste burning her throat. Tears squeezed from her eyes. She heaved again and again until there was nothing left, and then she heaved some more.

At last, the violent expulsions ceased. She rinsed her mouth out, splashed cold water on her face, and went to the old leather sofa in the lobby and lay down, trembling. Digging for the truth would have to wait another couple of hours.

CHAPTER SIX

Friday morning and for the second straight day, Charley sat on the dock waiting for Roscoe, this time with no belief that he actually would show. After a half-hour he gave up and cycled past Roscoe's house. The newspaper hadn't been picked up.

He worked up his nerve and pedaled to the police department. Inside, a really old lady in her forties smiled like a cartoon when he entered. He stammered about filing a missing persons report and she showed him in to Chief Sanborn's office.

"Mister Sanborn," he said, "I'm Charley Fawcett."

"I know who you are, Charley."

Charley blushed, surprised anybody knew him. Of course, cops didn't really count. That was the one bunch you didn't want to be popular with, his old man liked to say. He chased the thought from his mind and described his worries about Roscoe to Sanborn.

"Charley, how long have you known Roscoe?" Sanborn asked.

"I've seen him around my whole life."

"Not what I mean. How well do you *know* him?"

Charley hesitated. "Real well, for a few weeks. Long as I've been working on his boat."

"You know Roscoe has two lives? One that's all about fishing and working, and another that doesn't include or concern Brigands Key?"

"I kind of figured that out."

"Then you know Roscoe disappears for days at a time. I

expect that's what he's done right now."

"It's not like him to ditch work without a word. He's the hardest-working man I've ever met."

Sanborn considered this for a moment. "Tell you what. I'll check around a bit. You too, but be discreet. Word gets out about Roscoe's second life and his first life here on the island comes to an end. You understand what I'm saying?"

Charley nodded. "How'd you know about Roscoe?"

"I know a lot of things Brigands Key would rather not think about."

Charley searched the Chief's face for lies.

Sanborn seemed to read his mind. "Don't worry, son," he said. "He'll turn up."

"I've got to go."

"You see him, you let me know, okay?"

Charley gave a wary nod and left.

He pedaled again past Roscoe's house. He emptied the mailbox and hid the mail on the front porch behind a greasy box of boat motor parts, glancing first at some of the letters. One was a flier from some bar called Holiday Nights in Ybor City. A couple of dudes in top hats and tuxes grinned knowingly in the letterhead. Charley glanced about and tore the letter open. There was a big week-long bash going on at Holiday Nights, apparently.

Somehow, Charley couldn't picture Roscoe Nobles—scruffy, uncouth, tactless Roscoe—in top hat and tux. But you never know.

The Holiday Nights event was already in progress and winding down. If Roscoe was there, the letter did him no good. If he was not there, it also did him no good. Charley stuffed the letter and envelope into his pocket and sped away on his bike.

He turned down Main and headed into town. No point rushing home to hear his father's drunken tirades. He'd get that soon enough. He could hang out in the library, see if he could disable the anti-porn filters. Just for kicks.

Gerald Hammond arrived at his office earlier than usual. Despite John Doe and all, he still had a business to run and paperwork and patients still to deal with. Mystery was good for the soul but didn't pay the bills.

He parked in his favorite spot, in the shade of the ancient live oak that sheltered his little building and its small, crushed-shell parking lot. Jill had not yet arrived. She was always early, setting things up for his schedule. As he unlocked the front door, a weathered Lincoln Town Car pulled in. Emma Watterson. Unscheduled, of course.

He offered a look of concern as she climbed out of the car. Emma, the hypochondriac's hypochondriac. Reliable, if nothing else. Odd, though; she didn't have her walker. "Emma, you shouldn't be driving. And your appointment's not until next Thursday." He pushed the office door open and stepped aside, holding it for her.

"Jerry . . ."

Emma staggered forward, her face ashen, and fell. He caught her and eased her in through the doorway. Her nails dug into his arms. She looked into his eyes, trembling, and he saw in her face something he'd not seen before, after all her varied and imagined maladies. He saw pain and fear.

"Emma, what—?"

Clinging to him, she leaned to one side and her body trembled and she vomited onto the floor, the yellow bile splashing onto his leg. She slumped and sagged. Hammond wrapped his arms around her and guided her into the exam room and lay her on the table. She shuddered violently.

He took her pulse. Rapid-fire, but weak. Her face was ghostly pale.

Where the hell was Jill?

Emma vomited again, very little this time. She turned to him, her eyes pleading. Her head tipped to one side and her eyes turned glassy and rolled up under her eyelids.

Her struggles ceased and she settled back with a sound like a sigh.

Hammond, one hand still upon Emma to keep her from slipping onto the floor, reached for the wall phone with the other, cradled it between ear and shoulder, and punched in Jill's number.

The phone rang five times before Jill's husband, Marty, answered.

"Marty, tell Jill I need her here right now."

"Doc, she's sick in bed. I was about to call."

"Emma's here." Hammond lowered his voice. "She's in seriously bad shape. I need Jill right now."

"Let me put it another way. Hell no. Jill's not coming in. She's shaking something awful, vomiting her guts out."

Hammond got a sinking feeling. "Okay, keep an eye on her, Marty. Get her plenty of water to drink. Aspirin if she gets a fever. She gets any worse, you bring her in. Not as an employee, as a patient." He hung up the phone.

"Looks like it's just us, Emma," he said. He strapped the blood-pressure cuff around her arm and pumped it tight.

Out in the lobby, the little bell hanging on the front door jangled brightly, announcing an arrival. "Anyone here?"

Hammond recognized the voice. "Be with you in a second, Burt. I'm a little short-staffed right now. Did you have an appointment?"

"Naw, Doc. But you got to help me. I'm real sick."

Hammond had a sudden stab of fear in his gut. He wasn't a big believer in coincidences.

Don't get ahead of the moment, he told himself. Three sick

persons do not an epidemic make. It's just a little summer flu.

Four terrible, wet hours later, Emma was dead and Burt James was slipping in and out of consciousness.

Randy Sanborn hesitated outside the mayor's door, listening to the muted voices beyond. This was a rush meeting, called only a half-hour ago. He was ten minutes early but they'd started without him, no doubt by design. Politicians liked to get their stories straight before conflicting agendas were allowed.

Fine. If that was the game, he could play it, too. He decided against knocking, hoping to catch an unguarded word or two. He swung open the door and stepped quickly in. The conversation stopped as if someone had thrown a switch.

The mayor cast quick, knowing glances to his other guests, then collected himself. "Ah, Randy, thanks for coming on such short notice."

"Apparently I'm late, Ralph." Sanborn glanced about at the small group. Mayor Ralph J. Johnson, all three-hundred pounds of him, leaned back in his brown leather wing chair behind his vast oak desk, in his trademark short-sleeve white shirt and too-short tie, a semi-smile plastered on his face. Clay Abbott, the city manager, hovered at Johnson's elbow in one of the cheap guest's chairs that made guests feel not quite comfortable nor welcome. Abbott nodded slightly to Sanborn.

Sanborn was surprised and a little pleased to see Artie Blount. The feud between Mayor Johnson and Blount was a constant source of amusement, so Blount's presence meant that something big or sneaky was afoot.

The last member of the group was a slender blond woman smartly dressed in corporate gray and white. Not a local, not by a long shot. Her smile was practiced.

"Randy," Johnson said, "You know Susan Walsh, of course, with Gulf Breeze Properties, out of Tampa."

Of course he knew her. Everyone knew her.

Walsh offered her porcelain hand. Sanborn took it and felt her give a gentle squeeze. Alarm bells sounded in his mind. He released her hand quickly and took a seat.

The door swung open and Hammond entered, breathing heavily.

"Ah, Jerry," Johnson said happily. "Good of you to come. I'll have 'em locate another chair."

"Don't bother. I've got a problem at my office, as you know. I can give you ten minutes and then I'm out of here."

"We best be efficient then," Johnson said. "Randy, Jerry, we've got a busy little town all of a sudden."

Sanborn nodded. Let them deal the first hand.

"First, John Doe," Johnson continued. "Now this little flu outbreak."

"You diagnosed influenza?" Hammond asked. "I surely didn't."

"You called it a flu this morning."

"I said it might be a flu. As cases arrive, I'm not seeing enough symptoms of flu."

"Semantics. An outbreak of something."

"Of something."

"How many have you got?"

"I've got three patients in my office right now, waiting on me to get back. I've sent four home already this morning. My nurse is home, sick in bed. And Emma . . ."

"So sad to hear about Emma, Doc," Blount said.

"Well, she was seventy years old," Johnson said. "And chronically sick."

"Her many illnesses were imaginary and inflated," Hammond said. "This one was real. What's more, Burt James passed away a half-hour ago. Same symptoms."

Johnson leaned suddenly forward. "Burt died?"

The question hung, answered by silence.

"Mayor," Abbott said, "we had two city employees, Myriam and Bobby, call in sick today. I suspect a number of people are sick that Doc doesn't know about."

"I have no doubt," Hammond said. "When people are sick, the doctor only sees the tip of the iceberg. Whatever it is, it's deadly."

"This illness, is it related to John Doe?"

Hammond shook his head. "John Doe was murdered."

The mayor grunted. "Well, that's something."

Sanborn cleared his throat. "That doesn't mean they're unrelated. It just means cause of death is not the same."

"Have you figured out who he is, Randy?"

"There are no missing persons that fit his description. No sport or commercial fishermen in the area reported missing."

"He's not a local," Blount said. "That's huge."

"For once we agree, Mr. Blount," Walsh said.

"I wouldn't go that far, Susan."

Sanborn looked directly at the mayor. "Why is she here?"

"Calm down, Randy. Susan's firm has a big stake in our community."

"Lots of businesses have a big stake in our community. Why does hers get the inside track?"

"My question exactly," Blount said.

"Randy, you're stepping over the line," the mayor said. "Don't forget your place."

"Don't start, Ralph."

Susan Walsh leaned forward, smiling brilliantly. "Mayor, Chief Sanborn is right, Gulf Breeze is just one concerned party here. We're Brigands Key's biggest fans and our interest is of course financial. No secret in that. We stand to make a lot of money here, but the big winners will be your community. Our community. We've committed our talent and fortune to Bay View and Brigands Key, and naturally we want the community to prosper before we break ground."

"*If* you break ground," Blount said. "That's not decided yet."

"True, we're here at the discretion of the good citizens of Brigands Key. If we're told to hit the road, so be it. But we'll do our best to convince you of our value."

"What a load of crap. The Council votes on Wednesday on Bay View, and what do you know? Emma's death leaves you sitting pretty. What fortuitous, well-timed luck."

"Be careful what you suggest, Mr. Blount."

"You're selling but I'm not buying and neither is the majority of the town. And you know what? I hear we're missing another councilmember. Another 'no' vote."

Johnson's eyes widened.

"He's right, Mayor," Sanborn said. "Roscoe Nobles has up and disappeared."

"Where?"

"Disappeared means we don't know. His boat-hand, Charley Fawcett, said Roscoe hasn't shown up for work for two days."

"Goddamn it, why wasn't I told? Find him! This is the biggest vote on the island in the last quarter-century. I want everyone there."

"I'm sure he'll turn up."

"If he doesn't," Clay said, "we still have a quorum. And the Council, by charter, is required to vote if there's a quorum."

Susan smiled, too brightly. "We're confident that we're already there, Clay. If Mr. Nobles doesn't show, it's three to one in our favor. If he shows, it's still three to two in favor."

Johnson looked down at some papers on his desk.

"Right, Mayor?" Susan asked.

"We'll listen to the arguments and then we'll vote, Susan. That's always been my position."

There was a brief, freighted silence.

"Of course, Ralph," Susan murmured.

Hammond tapped his watch. "You get five more minutes of my time. Sure you want to use it on issues that don't concern me?"

"What are we up against?" Sanborn asked.

"Not sure. Signs point to a virus, not a bacterium. Seems highly contagious. To cover the bases, I've given antibiotics to the patients just in case it is a bacterial infection."

"Well, just stick a sample under the microscope and see if it's a virus or a bacterium," Abbott said.

"Not that simple, Clay. A virus is ten-thousandth the size of a bacterium, way too small to see with a tabletop microscope. You'll need a scanning electron microscope."

"Don't you have one?"

Hammond rolled his eyes. "Appropriate me two hundred grand and I'll buy a half-decent used one today."

"Then how do doctors diagnose a virus?"

"Day to day, by the look of things. Certainty requires tests."

"Do the tests, then."

"I'm working on it. I've overnighted cultures to Garrett Labs in Tampa. Results will take several days on one test, two weeks on another."

"What symptoms are you seeing?"

"Diarrhea, muscular pain, joint pain, severe vomiting, dehydration, nausea, disorientation . . . and two deaths. The severity varies from patient to patient. Symptomatically, it looks like viral gastroenteritis. Noroviruses are prime suspects in gastroenteritis and sudden epidemics."

"Whoa, whoa. 'Epidemic' is a scary word. Let's not get ahead of ourselves."

"Let's not kid ourselves, either."

"Could it be environmental? Food poisoning, contaminated drinking water, gas leak?"

"I can't rule them out. Hell, scallops are in season and everybody on the island is gobbling them down. Oysters are easily contaminated with norovirus, so maybe scallops are, too."

Susan leaned forward, touched Johnson's arm. "Mayor, you need specialists. Now. But they can get expensive in a hurry. With your okay, I'll have Gulf Breeze hire the best and foot the bill. We'll have them here tomorrow."

"You can get them here on a weekend?"

"We'll make it worth their while."

"Mm, proactive," Abbott said.

Johnson beamed with buzzword happiness. "I like it."

"Nothing like putting the fox in charge of the henhouse," Blount murmured.

"Artie, you got an objection?" the mayor snapped.

Susan touched the mayor's arm. "Gulf Breeze will place the firms directly under the city's supervision." She looked directly at Blount. "But if you insist, Artie, the city can pay for the whole thing."

Blount began to speak, then leaned back, saying nothing.

"I like it," Johnson repeated with finality. "Especially the part where someone else pays. Hire the firms."

ON the EDGE, with Charley Eff

So I go to work this morning like a good little proletarian. Roscoe's not there again. That's two days. Yippee, right? No, Roscoe's always there. But not now. Dude up and ran off, no word, no nothing. The hell am I supposed to do? Can't take the boat out for him . . . I'd sink it before I cleared the channel. I checked Roscoe's house five times to see if he's around. Nope. When I get back home this morning, the Old Man is waiting. Crap, he's going to lay into me for quitting a good-paying job, which I didn't, but the Old Man has his mind made up that I'm worthless. And what does he do? Nothing. Looks at me, growls, goes back to bed. Not feeling good. Man, I catch a break.

A hangover can be a true friend.

I see Tyler Fulton today. Captain America. Football hero. Tyler got his redneck kicks knocking my books out of my hands at school the last three years. Funny thing, he was my best friend in elementary school, before he turned Jocko Homo. Son of a bitch sees me on my bike today and beans me with a rock. His buddies think that's the height of hilarity.

Roscoe's full of shit but I'm worried about him. Weird thing today . . . a package arrives in the mail. No return address. Postmarked Wednesday. I tear it open and inside is this used book, "The Big Little Book of Codes." It's all about codes and code-breaking. For beginners. I knew right away it had to be from Roscoe and that gave me a little spark of hope. But then I realized that was the last time I saw Roscoe. A little parting gift, I guess.

I hate this place.

Peace Out,

Charley Eff

Carson Grant opened his eyes and rubbed them. The late afternoon light slanted through the window. He glanced at his watch. Christ, it couldn't be that late. He sat up in bed, felt his stomach lurch, and saw a million specks of blackness swim in his eyes, swarming the edges of vision.

Archaeologists brought home more than data and artifacts from their jaunts into the remote muddy corners of the world. They brought home parasites and bacteria and viruses. Vivax malaria had been Grant's cross to bear for fourteen years now, his bouts with it coming and going. There was no cure, only treatment.

His personal remedy was vodka and orange juice. He poured himself a particularly mean screwdriver and knocked it back.

He reached to the window, his guts protesting, and yanked the blinds shut. He sank back into bed and dragged the covers over his face, dreading the coming of the inevitable violent chills of malaria.

CHAPTER SEVEN

Early Saturday, Charley pedaled past Morrison Motel and slowed to a stop. Professor Dude was staying at the Morrison.

Grant hadn't been in town but a couple of days when he turned up with a mystery corpse. Roscoe hadn't trusted Grant's motives, not one bit. Now Roscoe was missing.

Charley pulled his bike under a towering magnolia and waited. He had nothing to do and he could do that here as well as anyplace else.

An hour later, Grant emerged, squinting against the bright morning light. He looked worn out and rotten, his face sporting a rough stubble, his eyes dark, his face pale. He hesitated in the doorway, rubbing his chin, and headed to a dinged-up brown Ford truck.

Charley followed Grant the short distance to downtown. The guy could have walked it in ten minutes and he didn't strike Charley as the lazy type. Must be sick with the flu that was going around. Grant hadn't been out and about much in the last day or so.

Grant parked outside Chapman's Drugs and went in. Charley brought his bike up and leaned it against the outside wall without locking it. He slipped inside, feeling like a secret agent, which was a little more grown-up than a superhero.

He sauntered among the aisles, pausing at the magazine rack and picking out a random publication. A muscle mag. Oily bodybuilders with square little heads were knotted into piles of muscles. Charley quickly replaced the magazine and picked up a racing mag. Stupid redneck writing, but at least there were girls in bikinis on every page.

Grant browsed the aisle of over-the-counter drugs and selected a couple of bottles of pills. He took them to the cashier and plopped down some cash. Mr. Chapman rang him up and glanced over Charley's way. "Hey, Charley, you gonna buy that or just smudge all the pages up?"

Cover blown. Charley pretended not to hear.

He followed Professor Dude out, hanging back a dozen yards, wondering what he was doing, playing cop. No other choice, he told himself. The Mayberry cops were rubes, only with Barney Fife in charge instead of Andy. They couldn't catch a cold with a plague going around.

Plague?

The bug everybody was catching was not unusual. Was it? Maybe his subconscious was speaking to him. Did Roscoe catch something and die?

Professor Dude was nowhere in sight. Charley glanced north and south along Main. Grant must've slipped into someplace next door. To the right was the post office, to the left was Carla's. It being Saturday, the post office was closed, but Carla's was open for breakfast, the smell of pancakes and bacon drifting on the breeze. That would be where he went.

He hurried toward the restaurant.

As he cleared the corner of the drugstore, an arm reached out and collared him from behind and pulled him into the alley and pinned him against the wall.

"Okay, son," Grant said, releasing him. "I'm the suspicious stranger in town and one yelp from you will land me in real hot water, so I'll not lay another hand on you. Why are you following me?"

"I'm not."

"You were watching my room for an hour before I came out. You've got to be the world's worst spy."

"I was just looking for something at the drugstore. For my dad's cold."

"You're a worse liar than you are a spy." Grant shook his head. "I'm going back to my room to throw up some more. Don't follow me." He turned and started away.

"You're sick, too? You haven't been out much. Bet you didn't know half the town is sick."

"People get sick."

"And some die. Maybe you brought a plague to Brigands Key."

Grant turned and looked at him, incredulity in his eyes. "That what you think? I'm some kind of Typhoid Mary, spreading filth and pestilence wherever I go?"

"Not what I think. Others do."

"This is entertaining but I'm going."

"Did you kill that guy? For the treasure?"

Again Grant turned. "Treasure? I'm an archaeologist. It's my fate to be impoverished."

"My boss thinks you killed him."

"Who's your boss?"

Charley hesitated.

"Spit it out, kid."

"Roscoe."

"Look, I'm not from your little hamlet. Give me the whole name."

"Roscoe Nobles. I work on his fishing boat."

"Should I talk to Mr. Nobles about slander?"

"If you could find him. He's been missing three days. Maybe you killed him, too."

"Ah, so that's why you're skulking about. Listen. I don't know you or your boss. Why would I kill him?"

"For the treasure."

"Paleo-Indian artifacts are a treasure, an intellectual one. You wouldn't get rich selling them." Grant paused. "You're serious, aren't you?"

"A stranger shows up in town, a dead guy shows up, Roscoe goes missing, everyone gets sick. I guarantee you the mayor and Chief Sanborn are talking about it."

"What's your name, kid?"

"Charley Fawcett."

"Charley, I'm Carson Grant."

"Yeah, I know. Ex-Professor Grant. Discredited and disowned archeologist. Doing independent research now."

Grant laughed. "Kid, you're a piece of work. You've been checking up."

"Piece of cake in the information age."

"Computer geek, huh? Beneath salty man of the sea exterior. I'd never have guessed."

Charley's eyes narrowed suspiciously. "No need for sarcasm, sir."

"What, the geek thing? Sorry."

"No, not that."

"What then?"

"No one's called me a man before."

"Aren't you a man, Charley?"

Charley studied him. "I got to get home now."

Grant stepped aside. Charley edged past him back onto the sidewalk on Main.

"Charley, keep me posted, okay? About your boss."

Charley quickened his pace.

Other eyes watched Grant and Charley from the bakery across the street. The watcher scribbled a few notes on a PalmPilot and noted the time and date.

Grant and the kid were probably the smartest two people in town. That was obvious. Therefore they were about the only two that could screw everything up. They weren't yet at that point, but you never underestimate smart, resourceful people. Grant struck him that way. The kid, too, but why was a mystery. The kid was a snot-nosed know-it-all, the kind you beat up and stuff into a locker for kicks. This kid had a depth to him, though.

"One croissant to go," Myles the baker said, pronouncing it "kroy sant."

The watcher snapped shut the PalmPilot, took the croissant, and slipped out of the bakery. Then strolled down the block and opened the bakery bag. Smelled okay, but that was an illusion. The watcher unwrapped the croissant and took a bite.

Cardboard, stuffed with sawdust. Yummy.

Disgusted, the watcher tossed the pastry into a trash can. Inedible, like most food here. It would be nice to be done with Hicksville once and for all.

Randy Sanborn rapped sharply on the medical examiner's door.

"It's open," came the response.

City Hall was quiet as a tomb but Hammond was there, working on a Saturday. John Doe had a lot of people working long hours. Sanborn let himself in and eased the door shut. Hammond sat at the corner desk, peering at a transparent plastic bag. He waved Sanborn over. "You washed up, I hope."

"Yep." Sanborn dragged a chair close and took a seat. "Any progress on John Doe?"

Hammond picked up the plastic bag and waved it. In it was a tooth. "Got some interesting things to report."

"A dental match?"

"Nope. Florida Department of Law Enforcement search comes up negative, no matches."

"FBI?"

"No luck there either. Trying to match dental records is a crapshoot anyway. John Doe or his murderer would have to be a convicted felon for them to have a record of either."

"What then?"

"I had a hunch about this guy so I drove down to Tampa to meet with Aaron Calder. He's the top dental forensics expert in the whole country, a real historian of dentistry."

"And?"

Hammond placed the tooth on a black felt pad and swung a magnifier over it. "Remember, the tooth was broken out violently. Look closely at the filling."

"Looks like a regular tooth to me," Sanborn said.

"Ah, but it's a front tooth, an upper incisor. Appearance is important. You don't want an ugly amalgam in the front for the world to see. This cavity was filled with a silicate cement, designed to mimic the natural tooth. Very common practice."

"So that proves nothing."

"Calder x-rayed the tooth. Take a look." Hammond opened a manila folder and withdrew two x-ray mylars. "The one on the left is of a patient of Calder's. The patient had a silicate cement filling put in a month ago and he talked her into a follow-up x-ray. See how clean the bond between tooth and filling is? Now look at this x-ray of John Doe's murderer's tooth."

"It's got a line or smudge between the tooth and filling."

"Exactly. Good workmanship, though, for its time. They've just gotten better at it."

"What are you getting at? Dental work a few years old?"

"Seventy years old."

Sanborn set the tooth aside. "Jerry, I don't have time for jokes. On Wednesday you said the guy had been dead a day. Then you said it was a few weeks, tops."

"I've been telling you all along there was something screwy with the time of death. The enzymic decomposition, the body's sterility . . . it's all wrong. This tooth amplifies it a hundred times."

"Maybe the killer's dentist was a hack."

"Calder also ran some mass spectrometry and an old-fashioned touch test." Hammond opened a small case to reveal ten teeth. "Calder gave me these on loan. These are anterior teeth from around North America, South America, and Europe. Go ahead, pick each one up, feel the silicate cement on each."

Sanborn did so.

"Now feel the mystery tooth."

"It feels different," Sanborn said.

"It was hand-molded in place. That hasn't been done in decades. Here's the good part: Calder's tests identified the material as a porcelain enamel from the thirties."

"He made a mistake. Or the killer got his dental work in a third world shit-hole somewhere. Maybe he's Eastern European, maybe he got it in an Eastern bloc backwater before the Soviet Union collapsed. Albania, Bulgaria, Ukraine . . . those places are fifty years behind the times, maybe a hundred years behind in the countryside."

Hammond shook his head. "Damn it, Randy. This stuff hasn't even been manufactured in seventy years."

"That's impossible."

"I've got a pet theory. The body was frozen for decades, thawed, and placed in Grant's little spring within the past week. The long freeze sterilized the body; placement in a fairly germ-free environment protected it even further, and so internal enzymes worked before bacteria could gain a foothold."

Sanborn slapped the desktop. "That's a damned sleuth puzzle-book solution! What are the chances of the body being placed in a spring just days before the spring is even discovered?"

"Slim to none. But there's no other explanation."

"Wrong. This filling material is produced somewhere in this

world that your dental historian doesn't know about, and that's a good thing. If the places these bad boys are produced are that rare, once we find them we'll have a clue to Mr. Doe's killer."

"You going to help with this search? I kind of have my hands full, being a godlike healer of the sick and all."

"I'll make some calls. Someone knows where this stuff is made."

ON the EDGE, with Charley Eff

Spooky weirdness in Hooterville! There's this strange sickness going around. People getting sick left and right. Walking around, listless, dull . . . no wait, that's every day. But this time there seems to be a good excuse.

My Old Man lays in his skivvies in bed all day, groaning, getting up to piss and puke. Won't go out. Won't hit me. Small blessings.

Roscoe's still missing. I can feel it in my bones: he's dead.

Professor Dude collared me. I'm such a pussy. Guy's like forty years old, but he manhandled me like a baby. Don't get me wrong. He's not a perv (I don't think). I tail him and get nabbed. He should have beaten the shit out of me. I would have, but like I said, I'm such a puss. Professor lets me go instead. He's not so bad. Next to me, he's the smartest guy in town by a wide margin. But that's not saying much.

We got a murder victim and now we got three people dead of flu. Storms are brewing. One way out on the ocean, one here on the island.

Later, Charley Eff

Charley logged off his blog and stretched in his creaky desk chair, its broken spring protesting and sagging under his weight. It was early still; lunchtime. He grabbed the half-eaten bag of corn chips and stuffed a handful into his mouth. A bit stale, but tasty. He wiped the rim of his Mountain Dew and washed the chips down.

He browsed the Internet a little longer, pulling up some old comic book web pages. *Iron Man. Silver Surfer.* Good stuff. And his favorite, *Vampirella.*

God, what a loser I am, he thought.

He closed *Vampirella* and tried to get interested in the news on CNN. Failing that, he drummed idly for a minute.

He had to do something. Roscoe was missing. Something bad was afoot.

He opened the Brigands Key municipal homepage. It came up slowly. What a shock. The site was a mealy-mouthed pile of tripe when it finally did. Mayor's Welcome. Brigands Key Happenings. Things to Do in Brigands Key. Now that was a short list.

Fluff and nonsense. Nary a mention of John Doe or rampaging illness. See no evil, speak no evil, post no evil on municipal website.

He scrolled down the menu list of departments and came to the police department. Not much info, just staff names, office location, and bragging about a new patrol car.

That sparked an idea. Charley found Mayor Johnson's email address and tried it. He could send messages to it, of course, but there was no archive of emails.

He knew a bit about Florida law, the one they called sunshine law. All government documents, including electronic ones, were public record. He doubted that bit of enlightenment had seeped into Brigands Key and he was sure the mayor would not willingly let his emails see the sunshine.

Charley settled back and assaulted the mayor's email archives. They were secured and blocked, as expected. No problem. The mayor wasn't smart enough and the city wasn't sophisticated enough to keep a good hacker down. In a shade under an hour, the mayor's archived messages suddenly opened and stretched out in a long list.

Charley selected the most recent. Something about ordering a new desk set. Garbage. Charley opened the next couple of messages. More garbage. The fifth was a message from Chief Sanborn:

Mayor, I know you're anxious but we're having difficulty identifying the unknown person. Time of death is problematic. Hammond has good data and more questions, as do I. We'll get back with you as soon as possible. Thanks for your patience.

Charley reread the message. It was innocuous, but Sanborn had inserted a giveaway. Time of death is problematic. Government-speak. Sanborn was reporting without really saying anything. The mayor was technically "informed."

Charley spent the next hour reading dozens of the mayor's emails, his faith in government eroding by the minute. The guy was a boob. How'd he manage to get elected in the first place, let alone reelected six times?

Historians complained that the digital age was making their jobs impossible. Men and women of influence no longer put their thoughts on paper, to be collected and preserved by historians, shining a light on the times. Electronic messages were ephemeral, vanishing at a keystroke, leaving nothing for history. Made sense, but Charley wondered if maybe the world wouldn't be a better place if no one was forced to wade through the doodlings of morons. Whatever, Johnson's correspondence would not be missed by historians. Hell, probably no one read it even now.

Charley selected what seemed to be the most important messages and deleted them, grinning. He'd done his good deed for the day.

He scrolled the list of city employees and found Dr. Gerald

Hammond. He hesitated; Doc was everyone's pal and his stuff actually should remain private.

But Charley was already in deep. He opened Hammond's email account.

The account was not as stuffed with messages as Johnson's but then Hammond was a city employee only in the loosest sense. What caught Charley's eye was the number passed between Hammond and Sanborn over the past two days. There were dozens.

Charley selected the most recent and opened it.

Hammond: *Thought any more about what I told you?*

Sanborn: *There's a better explanation somewhere.*

Hammond: *There's not.*

Sanborn: *Find me something I can work with, Jerry. I'll bet my life John Doe or his murderer was from rural Eastern Europe.*

Hammond: *You can look, but I'm telling you, John Doe has been dead sixty, seventy years.*

Sanborn: *I'm taking this conversation offline.*

Charley quickly found and opened Sanborn's email archive. That whole back and forth with Hammond had been deleted. Sanborn was nervous about the exchange. Silly man. Anything could be resurrected by the right hacker.

Charley read the remaining emails and printed them. He took a drink of Mountain Dew, his mind racing with possibilities. He opened the *Vampirella* web page again and studied the graphics. Holy shit, he thought.

He turned again to his computer and opened his blog and began typing furiously.

ON the EDGE, with Charley Eff
  Curiouser and Curiouser.
  People get sick. People die. Dead strangers turn up. Happens every day, right?
  Not in Hooterville.

Place was always a little weird, populated by inbred island folk and all. But this is off-the-charts.

Barney Fife and Doc Holliday are keeping stuff from the hicks, even from the mayor (okay, can't fault 'em there).

You, Dear Readers, have been getting off on my postcards from the edge. All six of you. (Ha ha.) I told you about John Doe. I told you about the Great Plague of Brigands Key. Thought I knew a thing or two.

I didn't know shit.

John Doe is dead but fresh. Way dead. Way fresh. How dead? A few days, tops? Nope. A week? Nope. Month? Keep going. John Doe is like decades old. Doc swears to it.

People are sick. Looking like crap, pale skin, sunken eyes. People dying. Virus is the official word.

Bullshit.

I've seen this before. But that was just TV, just movies.

What did that Euro director call it? Nosferatu. Undead. Max Schreck was scary as hell, but this is for real.

Maybe it's time to pack up and get outta Dodge. The smart remaining few in Salem's Lot *got out.*

There is no God. Nevertheless, I'm hanging a cross on my door tonight. Meanwhile, I gotta check on the Old Man. He's sick. Drunk, I figured. That was back when I didn't know.

Now I want to see his neck.

> *Yours, Dusk 'til Dawn,*
> *Charley Eff*

CHAPTER EIGHT

Sunday morning, Grant lingered in a hot shower, hoping the steamy water would cure him. For a moment he thought it had. It hadn't. His stomach knotted painfully, then eased. His nausea passed. He glanced at his bed and contemplated crawling back into it. No, get going, he told himself. Get some food in you.

He dressed and headed out the door.

Carla's, the little café, had grown on him. Food was good, especially breakfast. The waitress motioned him to a table nearest the town chatterers. He walked straight past it and settled into the booth in the far corner. The quiet corner.

He ordered scrambled eggs and pancakes and stared at his food when it arrived. It had lost its appeal. He stabbed the pancakes and took a tiny bite. His stomach lurched and he pushed the plate aside. He asked for a glass of orange juice with lots of ice. The waitress brought it and he took the flask of Dinsmoor vodka from his pocket and measured in two shots. The waitress frowned and left, saying nothing. He stirred the screwdriver and drank it down and closed his eyes.

"Join you?"

Artie Blount, the realtor, was standing over him, smiling amiably.

Grant nodded. "I'm not great company this morning."

"Under the weather?" Blount took a seat.

"I feel like crap. Thought I had a return date with malaria, but the symptoms are all off. It's something else."

85

"There's a bug going around. Half the town's got it and indeed, I've got a touch myself." He waved an arm about the restaurant at the empty tables. "It's usually packed in here for breakfast. In Brigands Key, you're not late for work or church if you're eating breakfast at Carla's." Blount stretched casually, making himself at home.

The waitress approached, beaming. "Why Artie, you come here to sweep me off my feet?"

"I can only hope, Maria. How about my usual this morning?"

"Two eggs over easy, two sausages, two pieces of toast. It's already on the grill." Maria tapped him on the head with her pencil. "Stay out of trouble."

Blount watched Maria walk away, smiling. "Got to love it here, Professor. How you liking paradise so far?"

"Paradise is relative. I've seen a couple you can keep."

"We like our version. Most of us, anyhow."

"Some don't?"

"Some think it can get better. Of course it can, but how we get there is a touchy subject."

"I gather you're at odds with the mayor on the doings of Susan Walsh's company. That's what I've been reading in the local paper, anyway."

"That's putting it mildly. Johnson, he's an okay guy. Sometimes the bluster obscures that. Like a bunch of small-town governments, ours is habitually a few nickels above bankruptcy. Expenses keep going up but our tax base stagnates. Hell, I know what a pickle the City is in. I'm a civic-minded guy. I perform several services for the City, gratis. The dock? I pay for trash pickup. The lighthouse? I do routine maintenance on it, even on those pitiful lights. The Coast Guard is supposed to maintain the light but they're at the mercy of a shrinking budget themselves. They don't get out here to check on the light but once a year, in April. The Historical Society makes clucking noises but they don't step up with money to maintain the lighthouse. So I do.

"These are our budget realities. Johnson struggles with it every day. He sees Bay View as the answer. He may have a fiscal point, but I see it as a quality of life thing."

"Why? You're in real estate. Big land rush like they're talking about will make you a rich man."

"That's not what life's all about, is it?"

"I've never figured out what life's about. Clue me."

"Doc, it wasn't so long ago I'd have been Bay View's biggest cheerleader. Real estate values are going to skyrocket and I could make a bundle. But you know what? I took in a little sightseeing down the coast a couple years back. Wall-to-wall condos and hotels. The coast is gone, man. When I got home, I had an epiphany. This is it, old Florida's last stand. You've seen this town. Have you seen the thunderclouds pile up over the Gulf after the sun slips below the horizon? A sky that's cobalt, crimson, pink, orange like fire? Takes your breath away. But have you watched it from a skiff, knocking back shots of bourbon, grilling mullet and snapper and shrimp right on the boat on an old camp stove, fish you caught that day, so much fish that the getting of them makes your muscles ache, the dripping juices filling your senses? That, my friend, is living. And that will be lost if Bay View goes in.

"I'm a cautious man, Dr. Grant. I'm not impulsive. Things have to add up before I act. On that day, things added up. I swore then and there I wouldn't let us lose what we have."

"You sound pretty sure of yourself."

"They say they'll protect the mangroves on the south end of the island and the grass flats everywhere else. I beg to differ. Sure, by law they can't bulldoze those wild places. But what they can and will do is flood the south end with high-end homes and a golf course. Bob and Betty High-End will look with envy upon the lush carpet of grass the Joneses have just committed. They'll do theirs even better. Pump the water, pump the fertilizer. That shit's got to go somewhere. Where it'll go is into the mangrove and grass flats. In a few years, we'll change our name to Silty Key. The nurseries for fish will collapse and we'll all be eating frozen fish sticks."

"Why exactly did you join me for breakfast, Mr. Blount?"

"You see how the town is dividing, right? It's not haves versus have-nots. Hell, we're all have-nots here. It's the have-nots versus want-mores. Public opinion is solidly against Bay View, but the Council is going with it anyway. Brigands Key is about to lose its soul."

"What makes you think I can save Brigands Key's soul?"

"I've heard how the town fathers talk about you. You're what every small town loves and hates, the outsider with brains. Everyone's watching you. If you come out against, it may just sway one or two votes back our way."

"Bay View owns most of what they need already. They'll build it now or they'll build it later."

"Wrong. If there's enough pressure, the Council and Mayor Johnson will stall the project. I'm talking years. After a while, Gulf Breeze will get tired of carrying the debt to fund this monstrosity. They've got other projects; they can't afford to tie up money and pay interest to keep a project afloat that may sink anyway. They'll take their ball and go home."

"Although some might argue, I'm a scientist, Mr. Blount. You may not know my history. Shit has hit the fan more than once and stuck to me. I have a nasty feeling it may stick to me again with this unidentified dead guy I found. You'll forgive me if I sit this one out."

Blount cocked his head sideward and tapped a finger nervously on the table. "All right, Doc. But think about what

I've said. You think fence-sitting suits you, but I'm a good judge of character. This is one of those moments a man picks a path. I have a gut feeling you'll pick the right path." Blount reached for the check. "I've enjoyed our chat. I'll get this."

Grant pushed his hand away. "Uh-uh. One thing I've learned, when someone wants something from you that you don't want to give, always buy your own meal."

Susan Walsh closed her email and snapped the laptop shut. It was getting late, twilight gathering outside her fabulous Morrison Motel accommodations.

Pierce's emails had taken on a different tone. The company was about to screw her.

Enormous fortunes were going to be made off this island and Gulf Breeze would let nothing stop that. They might endure setbacks but they'd win out in the end. They always did. But this whole thing had turned rotten in a hurry.

Small-town quirkiness, my ass, she thought. For such a tiny place, Brigands Key sure wallowed in its share of stupidity. The mayor and his staff, all empty suits. The realtor, Blount, typical small-town gadfly and shit-stirrer. Sanborn, too much time on his hands. Hammond, a chip on his shoulder, unable to make it in the big city. Denton, the newspaper publisher, smelling something big.

This place was the bastard child of Peyton Place and Green Acres.

Corporate wanted results, and soon. Susan had lain awake last night, trying to cobble together something resembling progress. Yet all she could see was a fractious little town cracking up as the big issue of their lives, the Bay View project, loomed over them. Blount was banging his drum, claiming that the John Doe murder had something to do with her project. Now he was tying the illnesses to the development projects in nearby towns. Toxins in the water, that kind of thing, and although he hadn't produced one iota of evidence, he'd managed to get others nodding in agreement. They, of course, didn't give a hoot about the environment; they just didn't want outsiders horning in on their island paradise.

Susan had put on a smiley face for the good of both the townsfolk and her evil bosses back in Tampa. Things were going well, in spite of it all, she reported. She didn't need to make everyone here happy; she just needed to make three of five councilmembers happy. And she had that. Three of five. Majority rule.

Now a councilmember was dead, another missing, both against her. She wouldn't mourn their loss. Things happen, right? That harmless old tree-hugger, Emma Watterson, hadn't inspired the opposition. And Roscoe Nobles had gone on some gay holiday. Or had he? His disappearance was of concern to the company.

Great concern.

Three-zip, a unanimous vote. But her hand was weakening. Johnson was backing out on her. If he changed his vote and Roscoe showed, there would be a tie vote. And a tie vote was a disapproval.

She felt suddenly alone. She opened her laptop again, switched on the Internet, clicked open her favorite blog. On the Edge, a pimply, adolescent rant posted by one Charley Eff. The thing was laughably anonymous, and transparent as glass. Charley Eff was Charley Fawcett, the kid that worked for Roscoe. Charley suffered a persecution complex and a heap of teen angst. That was common enough, even out here in the sticks. Being a misfit sucked everywhere.

Since Roscoe's disappearance, the blog was bound to muddy the waters, once it got to be common knowledge. And that was only a matter of time, probably days or even hours. She'd found the blog two months ago, searching the Internet for local history she could arm herself with. She'd entered the phrase "Hammond Lighthouse." Charley's blog frequently mentioned the lighthouse. Wrote some rubbish about living under the watchful eye of Hammond Lighthouse. Thought he was being poetic.

Charley's boss was AWOL and the kid was talking about vampires, for crying out loud.

She opened her email account and began typing.

Charley waited until his mother lumbered off with a load of dirty clothes to the laundry room by the trailer park office. She'd be back in a few minutes but seconds were all he needed. His dad was in bed, moaning and feeling sorry for himself. Charley swiped a beer from the fridge and cloistered himself in front of his computer.

A slew of emails were waiting. He deleted the Nigerian Prince money, easy women, and penis enlargement ads and looked at the remainder. There was one subject line that caught his eye.

Easy Does It.

He didn't recognize the email signature, but how can you ignore a tag like that? He opened the email.

You have been spreading rumors in cyberspace about your lovely seaside hamlet. That may not be the wisest of pastimes. Listen to me, Charley. Stop scaring people. Nobles is missing and you know more than you're telling.

That was all.

Charley read and reread the message, feeling his blood boil. It had been sent not more than a half-hour ago. He looked at the email signature. BrigandsKey54321. What a crappy sig. He typed a one-character response, a single question mark, and hit send. The delivery failed. No such address was recognized. He typed in a search for the address. Nothing.

The email account had been created for a one-time usage and then wiped away. The perp must have figured that equaled blissful Internet anonymity. The perp was mistaken.

"Okay, Charley, summon all your powers of geekdom." He spent the next hour searching and hacking. At last he found the infamous BrigandsKey54321.

It was that woman, the land developer everyone was talking about. Susan Walsh.

Why was she zeroing in on him? It didn't make any sense.

Or did it? The high-powered only paid attention to the low-powered when they were after something. So what did he have? A drunken dad and a scared mom. A home in a trailer park.

He had his blog and the attention of a handful of cyberspace losers. Very bankable, that. Maybe it was what he had to say. Plague. Vampires. Walsh was selling land and dreams, which is difficult when your product has gone into the toilet. The land was tainted and the dream becoming a nightmare.

Charley was a beacon of truth. She would not be a big fan. Beacons of truth were bad for business.

He had—maybe—a job on a fishing boat. He had a missing boss.

Could she have a bone to pick with Roscoe? Worse, did she have something to do with his disappearance? It didn't seem likely. She was this cosmopolitan superwoman. Roscoe was this anti-stereotypical, coarse, scruffy gay fisherman. Yet he was on the City Council and could vote on her livelihood.

But Roscoe had also been onto something big, if you believed him.

She knew something Charley didn't.

★ ★ ★ ★ ★

Susan Walsh squirmed on the stiff double bed in her room. The ancient air conditioner roared in the darkness, blowing a gale across her. She lay in the dark, spinning about under the covers, trying to find a comfortable position.

There was none. The bed was a slab and the room smelled of disinfectant trying to mask mildew and other unknowable, unpleasant odors.

These were, by all accounts, the only accommodations in town. That would change. She made a mental note to push for a decent hotel in the development plans.

Of the dozens of trips she'd made to the island over the last three years, this was the first time she'd spent the night. If she had any say, it would be the last. This was purgatory.

Outside her window, the pink neon of the motel sign flashed. Morrison Motel. Vacancy. Air Conditioning.

God, she'd never get a decent night's sleep here.

Where had Nobles gone?

She checked the clock. It was after one. Brigands Key had shut down hours ago, everything but that blinking pink sign.

Small-town life. Postcard stuff. Mom and apple pie. Quaint as could be. She could deal with this. The move to Tampa from Chicago was bad enough, but she'd managed. What was one more slip down the cultural ladder?

She sat up and fumbled about the nightstand for a cigarette. At least in the sticks the Nazi notion of nonsmoking rooms had not yet taken root. She lit the cigarette and inhaled deeply, the glowing red tip comforting her. The digital display on the alarm clock clicked and counted off minutes.

At last she crushed out the cigarette and kicked the covers off. She pulled on jeans and a tee-shirt, found her keys, and slipped out.

Her car was parked next to the archaeologist's. His room was at the end of the building and he'd become a bit of a mystery celeb here. She wondered about him. Grant was cute in a tweedy, professorial way, with an appealing roughness just underneath. Not much earning potential. Still, he was educated and maybe worth talking to. She'd make an effort to bump into him soon.

Except that she'd heard he was sick.

The talk of a plague was a bit unsettling. Certainly something was happening, but the locals were seizing on anything as gossip fodder.

Susan switched on the Mercedes and pulled out onto Main and cruised slowly through town. Quiet as a tomb.

She put the windows down and let the breeze, fragrant with the sea, blow through her hair. That was something she could like about this place. You were never more than a stone's throw from the water.

The town fell away and she reached the north end of the island, nearly deserted, the old lighthouse towering above, its small lights blinking red and green.

She turned the car about and headed south, rolling again down Main before turning onto Lee Street, the lane of grand old Victorians of the nineteenth century. The houses lacked the cute flourishes urban renewal hipsters slapped on. The Lee Street Ladies were true to their original days, if you overlooked the satellite dishes.

The Ladies gave way to a row of vacant lots, recently bought and dozed of their fifties block homes by Gulf Breeze. Standing at the end of the vacant lots and before the empty sixty acres just beyond was the weathered Victorian of Roscoe Nobles. Susan slowed to a stop.

The timing of Roscoe's disappearance couldn't have been better or worse. Gulf Breeze had put in an offer to him, upped it, upped it again. Good money, more than his rattrap was worth. The guy hadn't budged and the company put pressure on Susan to make the deal happen.

She admired the old pile of sticks. The house was dark but its elegance came through even at night. It was the real deal and had withstood a half-dozen hurricanes in its century of existence. A shame it had to go.

A flicker of light from within the darkened house caught her eye. She stopped the car and leaned closer to the window.

There was nothing but blackness in the windows.

Put it in gear and move on, she told herself. Nothing to see here. Several minutes passed, with no return performance, no flicker.

Behind her, out over the Gulf, a slow thunderstorm drifted across the water, towering blackness, miles out to sea. Distant lightning sparked silently. That's all it was, a reflection of faraway lightning on the black windows of Roscoe's house. Smoke of a distant fire.

She sighed with relief and shifted the car back into drive.

She hesitated.

Roscoe was still missing. If he stayed missing, it was only a matter of time before Sanborn came here and started rooting around in the old house.

That would most certainly be bad for business. And career-ending for her.

Certain correspondence between Roscoe and Gulf Breeze would be found and brought to light, correspondence that might not shine a favorable light upon the company and some of its more high-pressured tactics. So far, Roscoe had never brought that correspondence up, as it implicated him as well, but Susan had no doubt that he'd kept copies as insurance.

A light rain, a wet edge of the faraway storm, began to fall. Light enough for cover, not hard enough to discourage her.

"This is nuts," she murmured, and pulled the car down the

block to park under a magnolia. She killed the engine and lights and sat in the dark, tapping on the wheel.

She had a sinking feeling. Pierce had gone off on her when she broke the news about Roscoe's sudden absence, as if it were her fault. He'd reminded her of certain delicate information Roscoe might still possess. Pierce would be the one to land on his feet, not her. He'd stack the deck against her.

She studied the house. Roscoe hadn't been seen in a couple of days and the place was clearly empty. She could slip along the side hedge and easily reach the porch unseen. Ten minutes. She could allot herself that much. Get inside, find his papers, grab them all if need be. Just get rid of any Goddamned incriminating slips of paper. Then she'd be back to her car, again in the impenetrable shadows of the hedge. She could pull it off. Ten minutes.

She rested her hand on the door latch, took a breath, and slipped out into the rain, easing the door shut. She glanced about and moved into the shadows off the street and hurried along the hedge toward the house.

She ducked in beside the porch, mercifully sheltered under the eaves, and dry. She listened. Hearing nothing, she crept up the steps and onto the porch. A floorboard creaked ever so gently underfoot and she froze, her heart quickening.

The rain fell harder, drumming on the tin roof, drowning out the sounds of the world. It was unlikely—impossible, really— that anyone would hear or see her in the rainfall. Her confidence grew and she eased close to a window and peered in.

Blackness inside. Her confidence grew.

She moved to the next window. Nothing. In the third window, she again found only darkness, but the quality of the darkness stayed her. Something about it was different.

It shifted ever so slightly.

She caught her breath. Light and dark are simply that. Light and dark. One was the absence of the other. A matter of degree. Darkness only shifts in response to light.

Someone was inside.

The dark shifted again, and Susan realized that a dim light was coming down the stairs inside. It flickered and went out. The interior was plunged into blackness.

She moved back a few inches from the glass, suddenly aware that although the interior may be invisible to her, she might not be invisible from it. As she leaned away, lightning flashed in the distance behind her, illuminating the porch for a half-second in ghost light. Her breath had condensed into a tiny cloud on the window pane. She fought the urge to reach out and wipe it away.

The rain beat down, harder now. The darkness inside was complete. She began to doubt her own eyes. Lightning flashes, the shimmering reflections of the rain, the claustrophobic quality of the island night, all had tricked her senses. She was a city girl. City nights were simply darker versions of the day. Not like this.

There really was nothing—no one—in the house. She exhaled deeply.

The Fawcett kid had been spouting his nonsense about Brigands Key. Charley's last blog had taken a paranoid turn, something about the mysterious sickness sweeping Brigands Key, about the ageless unidentified corpse from the sea. About the undead walking around.

A shiver went through her. Get a grip, girl, she forced herself to think. There was no stupidity like that of the gullible, and there was no such thing as vampires.

Yet the night had a feeling of its own here. Spooks be damned; it was stupid to be prowling around like Nancy Drew. She backed away from the window, careful not to step on the floorboard that had creaked before. She should go.

But she couldn't. She couldn't leave those damning letters unaccounted for. They were the loose ends that would send her to jail.

Behind her, the floor creaked.

She wheeled about as lightning lit the night. An arm's length away, a dark silhouette stood, wet and dripping. Her heart leaped and fear engulfed her. She screamed. A powerful hand clamped against her mouth and shoved her against the wall. Her attacker pressed hard against her, pinning her.

"Should have stayed in tonight, Susan," a voice whispered.

Lightning flashed and flickered. Something thin and metallic and malevolent glinted in the instant of light, something drawn. It suddenly struck deep inside her. Searing white pain beneath her ribs blinded her thoughts, threatening her consciousness.

She lashed out blindly. The point that had buried into her was torn free, then struck her again.

The pain bit deep inside. She could feel the needle-like blade working, exploring, damaging.

Darkness fell like a shroud across her eyes, her mind shutting down to fight the pain. She slumped, vaguely aware of the blade still twisting and turning deep inside her.

The world dimmed and fell apart.

CHAPTER NINE

Kyoko Nakamura left Atlanta the night Susan Walsh died. She sped south on I-75, not stopping until Valdosta. A restless night's sleep, a quick, greasy breakfast, and back on the road by eight A.M.

She'd planned on leaving Tuesday as Greer had instructed, when the only urgency had been his artificial timetable. She scrapped that idea and packed her things and left on Sunday night, a hell of an odd time to start a vacation.

Plans can change in a hurry.

Her departure was sudden and precipitous. Reviewing the news leaking out of Brigands Key, reading that kid's blog, a sense of dread had come over her.

She thought about Taos, and the seven people that had died before CDC reacted. By then the contagion was out of control.

Taos would not happen again. Three confirmed dead in Florida. That was enough for her. She'd called Greer that night, interrupted his dinner with his wife, and informed him that she was headed south to investigate, officially or unofficially.

Unofficially, was Greer's angry response. And on her own dime and her own time. Three deaths, all among the elderly? That was weak and somewhat alarmist. So she had hurriedly packed and left by nine P.M, swinging first by the office to gather equipment. Without authorization, of course.

The eye of the news had yet to zero in on the island, but something was seriously wrong on the Florida coast.

Two hours from the island, she tried to call the town's mayor. He was out. An hour later, he was still out. No, she couldn't have the mayor's cell number. She called the local medical examiner, a Dr. Hammond. No answer. She left him a message. It was the third message she'd left him over the last two days and she didn't expect a response to this one either.

She would simply have to drop in unannounced.

With good luck and good weather, she'd be in Brigands Key by noon. Good weather. The radio eagerly reported that Tropical Storm Celeste would likely reach hurricane status by the afternoon, drifting west into the Gulf of Mexico, heading for Brownsville, maybe even Galveston. At most, Brigands Key would get choppy surf.

She crossed her fingers. Vacations on barrier islands during hurricane season were an iffy proposition at best.

Kyoko drove slowly through town a couple of times, drinking in the sights, enjoying the smallness. A complete pass through, one end to the other, took all of five minutes. Compare that to Atlanta—well, you couldn't. You couldn't even guess where Atlanta began and ended.

This was easy. She could get used to this.

The island didn't match her notion of a Florida island. No coconut palms, no condos, no broad, sandy beaches. She'd be leaving her bathing suit in her bags. But it wasn't a bad look. Mammoth live oaks and magnolias spread muscular, moss-draped limbs, shading the island from the blistering sun far better than palms would. Instead of beaches, there were marsh grasses swaying with the breeze, in water that shifted in color from green to cobalt with each passing cloud, and tangles of mangrove, dark and thick and mysterious.

The waterfront was lined with paint-peeling fishing boats and trawlers. Nets hung in the sun, wet and drying, men and boys going about their work, scrubbing, scraping, mending. The smell of fish throughout.

Brigands Key was not a resort island. It was a working town of broad shoulders and weathered tans, a fishing town, its pace slow and purposeful.

She parked at Brigands Key City Hall and got out. Hot, sticky air struck her and she instantly felt flushed. She slammed the car door and hurried inside. The slow pace, so quaint a minute ago, found urgency with the heat. Atlanta suddenly didn't seem so bad.

Inside, cool air greeted her, thank heavens. She wondered if she'd held her breath from the car to the building.

The receptionist, Kay (her nameplate read), greeted her with a look more surprised than gracious. "Help you, ma'am?"

"I'm Dr. Kyoko Nakamura, Centers for Disease Control, Atlanta." She handed a card to the woman. "Homeland Security," she added, feeling it might add a little gravity. "I'm a few minutes early. Mayor Johnson is expecting me."

"Homeland Security? We don't get many terrorists here in Brigands Key, miss."

Miss. Small-towners were certainly presumptuous. "Doctor," she replied. "The mayor, please?"

Kay pointed to the clock. "You're more than a few minutes early. The mayor's at lunch."

"When will he be back?"

"Maybe an hour. Maybe not."

Kyoko sighed, exasperated. "Will you please tell me where I might find him?"

"I tell you where to bother him on his lunch hour, he'll have my hide."

"Thank you so much for all your valuable help. I'll find him myself." Kyoko turned and left, aware that Kay had snatched up a cell phone and was dialing furiously.

101

She went out to the street and looked up one side and down the other. The downtown was a few blocks at most and wouldn't have more than three or four places to eat. The first was directly across from City Hall. She marched out into traffic, jaywalking defiantly, raising a hand to ward off oncoming cars.

Carla's Café was a down-home kind of place, and Carla had evidently been talked into making that a cute theme, and had cluttered the otherwise unassuming restaurant with country kitsch, no doubt fabricated in the countryside surrounding Beijing. The kitsch was overdone and on sale and collecting dust. But the place smelled good, like just-right meatloaf and cornbread. And it was blessedly cool inside.

The place was obviously popular with the locals and each of the twenty-odd tables was occupied. All heads turned and looked at her on cue. Guess they didn't see a lot of Asians in Brigands Key.

Kyoko surveyed the diners and headed for a large table in the back, occupied by four men. The largest of them was closing his cell phone, watching her with a look-what-we-got-here smile. She recognized him from the City's website. It was slathered over with pictures of the mayor, talking to townsfolk, kissing babies, breaking ground, being mayorly.

"Mayor Johnson," she said. "So good to meet you."

"Dr. Nakamura, I presume," the mayor replied, chuckling. "Kay tells me you're CDC."

"That's right."

"And Homeland Security."

Kyoko said nothing.

"That's a good line and it worked on Kay. CDC is under Health and Human Services, not Homeland Security."

Kyoko said nothing.

"Don't think we're all hicks, Doctor. It won't fly."

"My apologies, Mayor. May we start over?"

"Maybe." Johnson motioned to his companions. "Proper introductions. This is our city manager, Clay Abbott; Chief Randy Sanborn; and Dr. Hammond, our medical examiner. A colleague, eh?"

"Pleased to meet each of you. Dr. Hammond, I assume you've shared my concerns with everyone here?"

Hammond nodded.

"Body language tells me you're unhappy."

Before Hammond could respond, Johnson interrupted, his voice hushed. "Dr. Nakamura, this is not the best time and place to discuss sensitive issues."

"It is absolutely the time; you have a crisis on your hands. But if you want to find a more private place, please feel free."

Johnson picked up the check, glanced at it, and dropped fifty dollars on the table. "Follow me," he said. "I'd like you to meet my mistress."

Vivian Schuster, making her late-morning rounds, rapped on the door of Room 14 at Morrison Motel. There was no answer and she unlocked and pushed the door open.

A groan emanated from the bed in the dark room. The college guy, Grant, wasn't even out of bed yet. "What is it?" he grumbled.

She glanced at her watch disapprovingly. It was almost noon! Lazy city-slickers. "Cleanup, sir. I got to change the bed and tidy up."

"Come back tomorrow."

"Mister, you said that yesterday."

"I meant it yesterday and I mean it today. Come back tomorrow."

Vivian commented with an audible *hmmph*. "I'll just leave some clean towels, then."

"You do that." Grant stirred and turned to face her.

Vivian ignored him and replaced the towels in the bathroom. There was a faint odor of vomit in the small room.

Despite Dr. Grant's rudeness, Vivian felt compelled to wipe down the bathroom quickly. "Lovely, guv'nor," she said, affecting a Cockney accent. She imagined it sounded like the real thing and it amused her to slip into a different foreign accent in each room. She should have gone to Hollywood, become an actress. She might still.

She let herself out and continued down the motel landing, pushing her cleaning cart that overflowed with brooms, mops, and towels. The next room was vacant and the one next to that she changed and cleaned, giggling and remarking aloud, even though she was alone inside, in her favorite voice, the French Maid.

The next room belonged to the Tampa girl, Susan Whats-Her-Name. Susan hadn't been overly friendly. Downright sullen, in fact. When she wasn't barking orders about.

Vivian knocked. "Iss maid," she said in a gruff Boris-and-Natasha cartoon accent. "Iss time for clean."

There was no answer. She rapped again, a bit louder. "Maid service." Still no answer. She unlocked the door and pushed it gently inward. The room was dark, still, due to the army-grade curtains on the windows. "Iss Moose and Squirrel?" she inquired.

She flipped on the light switch and pulled the cart through the door behind her, humming the "Rocky and Bullwinkle" theme.

She reached to strip the bed and froze. Susan was still in it. "Mees? Iss time for clean."

The woman didn't stir. Vivian began to feel sheepish and tried to back quietly away. Let the dead tired sleep in. After all, it was their nickel.

She paused in the doorway, switched the lights off, and

negotiated the cart back out onto the sidewalk. She began to ease the door shut.

In the street behind her, some punk kid blew his car horn at her, making her jump. Small-town friendliness, you bet. She'd lived in Brigands Key her whole life, but these kids didn't care if you recognized them or not. The horn blasted, loud enough to wake the dead.

Susan What's-Her-Name hadn't stirred, not one inch.

Enough to wake the dead.

Vivian leaned back in. "Miss? You okay?"

No answer. Vivian jiggled the cart, hoping for a response. Even an angry one.

She stepped inside. "Miss Susan?" She crept to the bed. The woman lay on her side, facing the far wall. Vivian reached out slowly, her hand trembling, and hesitated. There was something going around the island, people getting sick. Dying, even. A couple of her friends had decided to up and leave, go on an extended vacation, not sure where, maybe Disney World. Away from Brigands Key, any way, anywhere.

If there was something going around, it wasn't too smart to be rousting them that'd got sick. She couldn't help herself. She shook the woman.

The woman was cold and didn't respond.

Motel maid wasn't such a bad job, but job loyalty had its limits. Vivian burst out of the room, hurried down the landing, and pounded on College Guy's door.

Ellie June was the mayor's boat, a muscular thirty-one-foot cabin cruiser, outfitted for serious offshore fishing. It wasn't the biggest boat in Brigands Key Marina—some of the commercial fishing boats dwarfed it—but it was easily the most beautiful and the most expensive. Small-town politics must pay well, Kyoko thought. She wondered if it was a Guy Thing, the dominant male displaying his plumage.

The mayor lumbered aboard first, carrying his great bulk with surprising nimbleness, and held his hand out for Kyoko. She took it and he helped her aboard, the very picture of Southern chivalry. Maybe he had a good side after all. Abbott began to step onto the gunwale, but Johnson motioned him to stop. "Not you," Johnson said curtly. "Cast us off, then go run the government for a while." Abbott skulked away unhappily and began undoing the mooring lines. Sanborn and Hammond climbed aboard, sharing a smirk. Kyoko settled into a plush seat. Johnson pressed a CD into the stereo and Bach drifted from speakers all around. He pressed the starter button. With a puff of white smoke and a sudden prismatic sheen of gasoline on the water's surface, the mammoth twin engines of *Ellie June* grumbled to life. The big boat eased away from its mooring and out into the channel. The mayor guided the boat slowly through the channel. "You get the nickel tour for free, Dr. Nakamura," he said. "Now we can talk in private and honestly say that we didn't meet behind closed doors. Jerry, I believe you had a bone you were about to pick back at Carla's."

"That I do." Hammond looked at Kyoko. "We've got a handle on things here, Doctor. You pulled rank. Why, I don't know."

"No one's pulled rank yet. This is still your show, but there's a real cause for alarm and this isn't the time to get provincial. That's why CDC's involved."

"Granted, we've got an outbreak of something, but still only three deaths."

"I count four."

"No, the John Doe that came in was a murder victim. No signs of disease at all."

"How many cases of illness have been reported?"

"Thirty-one. Still only three deaths, and all three victims were elderly and in failing health."

"Thirty-one that have come to you. I've made a few calls. I called the high school. Today was the first day of classes, yet they had a twenty-two percent absence rate this morning. I even called City Hall, Mayor. Care to guess how many called in sick this morning?"

"I figure you're about to tell me."

"Eleven out of a staff of twenty-eight. Bet that's the highest absenteeism you've ever had."

Johnson's eyes had a fleeting defensiveness. "We're keeping an eye on them. We look after our own down here, Doctor."

Kyoko looked at him evenly, feeling a tinge of anger. "I'm sure you do," she said. "Nevertheless, I need to review all your cases, Dr. Hammond. I'll need the files in thirty minutes."

"Hold it right there. There's such a thing as confidentiality."

"When national security is in question, confidentiality has limits. Very definite limits." She couldn't believe the words actually came from her mouth. She'd make quite a good Nazi.

"Help me out here, Randy," Hammond said.

Sanborn leaned close. "Jerry, give her the damned files. Dr. Nakamura, you've done your homework and you know how to bullshit. You came in like gangbusters and put us on the defensive. Good for you. We won't be called obstructionists during an emergency. You've got exactly twenty-four hours to read Jerry's case files. Then you'll return them to him, not a minute late. If you don't, we can play games, too. The *Tampa Tribune* would love an opinion on the usurpation of state's rights by the federal government with your name all over it. I'm sure your bosses in Atlanta would love reading that. Now I suggest we start over and play nice. Happy, sunny faces. The model of governmental cooperation. What do you say?"

Kyoko studied him. "Dr. Hammond will have his files back in eighteen hours, Chief. And I'll expect you to keep me in the loop on your investigation into John Doe."

A smile ghosted across Sanborn's face. "Are you also FBI? Because I doubt CDC throws much weight around in criminal investigations."

Kyoko nodded carefully. He was right; she had no real claim of authority. "In the spirit of cooperation, I humbly request to be kept up on any developments." She decided, what the hell, might as well push her luck. "But please be aware; the FBI can be brought in at a moment's notice. One phone call will do it."

His eyes let her know he wasn't buying it. But all he said was, "I'll see what I can do."

Ellie June rounded the north end of the island and left the smooth water of the inland side for the choppy Gulf. A lighthouse came into view above the windswept, stunted trees. The lighthouse tower was concrete and cylindrical, painted a gorgeous orange-red that glowed in the late morning sun. Topping it, the actual light room was black steel and glass, a dark eye watching over the island.

"Hammond Lighthouse," Johnson said.

Kyoko looked inquisitively at Gerald Hammond.

Hammond cast a possessive glance at the lighthouse. "My great-great-grandfather built it. He was the best and settled here when he finished construction. The lighthouse has been here since 1868, through good years and bad, and six hurricanes. A hundred and sixty-eight feet tall. Visible at sea for over twenty miles. Best damn lighthouse in the Southeast."

"It's beautiful."

Hammond's scowl evaporated. "Still operational, too. On automatic timer. The original Fresnel lens is a real work of art. It's still up there, still intact, but no longer in use. We run a couple of blinking lights now. City can't afford to stick a codger in there to do nothing but draw a check. It's our landmark, and it pretty much shaped the history of Brigands Key. Know how we got our name? Way back when, about 1850, our growth

108

industry was ship salvage. The waters offshore are shallow for a ways out and ships were always running aground. Local entrepreneurs figured grounded vessels were fair game and would race to them and plunder what they could. A few souls got quite wealthy and it was a lot more fun than fishing. Of course, the merchant marine and their insurers disapproved. They labeled the salvagers 'robbers and brigands' and pressured the government to shut them down. It continued unabated until 1866, when the first lighthouse, a wood tower some thirty feet tall, was built on this same spot. It was only visible for a few miles out to sea but was loved by mariners, including most of the local fishermen. And hated by the salvage industry. It lasted a year until it mysteriously burned to the ground one night. It was replaced by this tower and they added two armed sentries. The salvage guys couldn't burn it down and didn't like getting shot at, so business quickly died off."

"You're a marvelous historian, Dr. Hammond."

Hammond blushed.

Kyoko turned to Johnson. "Mayor, I haven't gotten settled in yet. Would you advise me on the best accommodations in town?"

"The best and the worst. They're the same. There's only one motel, the Morrison."

Sanborn's police radio squawked statically. He picked it up, pressed the button. "Sanborn."

"Randy, this is Tommy. Better get back right away. We got another death."

"Roger." He nodded to the mayor, who began to swing the boat about. "Got a name and place?"

"Susan Walsh, Morrison Motel."

Sanborn shot a glance at Hammond. "Christ," he mumbled, raising the radio. "We'll be there in ten minutes." He set the radio down. "Well, Dr. Nakamura. Your motel is now a player in this drama."

CHAPTER TEN

The medical examiner's office left a lot to be desired. Kyoko reminded herself she wasn't in Atlanta anymore. CDC was state-of-the-art. Brigands Key was state-of-the-boondocks. She shouldn't expect CDC kinds of gear, CDC kinds of budgets, out in the provinces. But this place underwhelmed even her least expectations. Hard to believe it was an official institution.

She divided her time between quietly watching Hammond perform the autopsy and reading and rereading the case files he'd turned over. With each page, a sense of dread grew in her. Something exceedingly strange was going on here. Hammond's notes and speculations were thorough but they just couldn't be right.

He went through his paces. She watched each movement, each turn of hand, waiting for flaws to expose themselves. She hadn't spotted a single one.

Maybe Hammond was better than his facilities. Maybe. She wasn't going to concede that just yet.

Hours crept by. At last, Hammond concluded his work on the subject.

The subject. Kyoko caught herself.

Susan Walsh lay there, naked, opened, wet. Not a subject. A woman that had been.

Hammond walked past her and punched an intercom button. "Tommy, send Chief Sanborn over, can you?"

"He's been waiting for your call."

Hammond took a seat, leaned back. "Well, Dr. Nakamura," he said. "I've got results. Afraid they're not what you wanted."

A tinge of heat rose in her face. "I'm not looking for specific results, Doctor. Just honest results."

Hammond bit his lower lip. Kyoko thought she detected a tiny smirk. "Perhaps I misunderstood your mission. Let's just wait for Sanborn, shall we?" He laced his fingers behind his head and put his feet up on his desk and stared defiantly at her.

Not at all sanitary, the little prick.

A short rap came at the door and Sanborn entered. "Dr. Nakamura," he said with a small, indifferent nod. "Jerry, what you got for me?"

Hammond rose from his chair, his smirk blossoming into a tight-lipped smile.

"Results are preliminary, of course, but Susan Walsh exhibits some symptoms our other recent deaths and illnesses have shown."

Kyoko leaned forward, nodding. "She contracted the same illness? It confirms a virulent contagion."

"My, my. CDC sure closes cases in a hurry."

Kyoko fixed her eyes upon him. "Don't play games, Doctor."

"Games? Uh-uh. You've got an agenda. Quick score in the boonies, back to Atlanta for the kudos. I'm here to keep you from getting egg on your face."

Kyoko waited, her irritation growing. "I'm here to assist, as you well know."

"Right. You've been perched on my shoulder all day like a vulture, watching my every move."

"That's my job. CDC takes contagion very seriously. I'm sorry that you—"

"The deceased, Susan Patrice Walsh," Hammond interrupted, turning his back to Kyoko. "Caucasian, female, age 45, found this morning in her motel room in bed. In a pool of vomit. Bile

111

present in the victim's mouth. No sign of alcohol or drug use. No bruising, lacerations, or other obvious signs of physical abuse."

"All suggesting contagion."

"She was made to look like she'd died of the Brigands Key Plague. But I saw Susan Walsh just the night before. She was out having dinner. We chatted a bit. As I've been prone to do lately, I studied her for any signs of illness. There were none. Yet hours later, she turns up dead. Our other victims have shown obvious symptoms in a long, slow buildup before death. They did not get sick and die within a few hours."

"Poisoning?" Sanborn asked.

"She wasn't poisoned and she wasn't sick."

"But the vomit . . . you said she had bile in her mouth."

"It's not hers."

"Beg your pardon?"

"I examined her mouth. She indeed had vomit in her mouth. Quite a bit. But I also examined her throat. Not a trace of vomit there, not even microscopically."

"That makes no sense!"

"I think I see," Sanborn said. "She was stripped, placed in bed. Her murderer induced his or her own vomiting, then placed Susan in such a position as to make it appear that she died in her own vomit. The killer even smeared some in her mouth to make it obvious."

"Exactly."

Kyoko shook her head. "Why would someone do that?"

"To buy time. To throw us off. The killer knows we have a growing body count and hoped this one violent murder might get lost in the shuffle of all the other deaths."

"Then what killed her?"

"My guess, an ice pick."

Sanborn leaned forward. "Not your everyday murder weapon."

Hammond nodded. "Walsh was stabbed right here." Hammond motioned them closer and pointed to Walsh's exposed right breast. He moved the breast aside.

"I don't see anything," Kyoko said.

"That was the idea." He handed her a magnifying glass.

She took the magnifier and leaned in. A tiny mark, barely visible, was hidden in the crease of flesh below the breast.

"The external wound is practically invisible," Hammond said, "suggesting a finely pointed instrument. Like an ice pick. Internally, the damage is far greater. The killer punctured her, twice, then worked the needle around inside her before withdrawing it. It's not a random act of violence. It's stealthy and deliberate."

"I'm a disease expert," Kyoko said. "I'd have missed this."

"I've seen it once before." He glanced at Sanborn.

She looked from Hammond to Sanborn. "The John Doe?"

"Yep. John Doe was killed the same way."

"A serial killer?"

"No," Sanborn said. "A copycat."

She stared at him, confused. "But if the murders are almost identical . . ."

"Yeah. Almost. John Doe was stabbed from behind into his left breast, cleanly into the heart. Death was mercifully swift. Very professional. Susan's murderer also stabbed from behind, but took a couple of tries to do it, in the right breast. No heart puncture there. Lethal, sure, but not nearly as sure as the first. The first was the work of a pro. This was the work of an amateur." Sanborn rubbed his chin. "Got the time of death, Jerry?"

"Somewhere between 10 P.M. and 4 A.M."

"I like it. For once, you're not giving me a range of hours to years." Sanborn was silent for a moment. "Grant's room is two doors down from Walsh's in the same motel. Funny how such distinctive murders keep turning up so close to him. I wonder if he happened to be out and about late last night."

Currents of air high above the earth dipped and shifted. Hot dry air massed over Texas and drifted east. The summer sun beat down on a listless Gulf of Mexico after a warm winter, heating it to seldom seen extremes, a warm bath. The swirling low pressure that was Hurricane Celeste rounded the western tip of Cuba and turned northwest, gunning for Galveston. Weather satellites picked up the jog immediately and within minutes, huddling close to their computers, the citizens of a hundred communities encircling the Gulf of Mexico knew of it. The Internet is a wonderful thing.

The warm waters of the gulf embraced the storm. The pressure dropped. The wind grew. The sea grew.

Grant came out of a restless sleep, heaved out of it by the pounding in his head. He kicked off his covers and lay in the chilly, dark motel room. His guts twitched and calmed and the pounding grew.

The pounding wasn't in his head. It was on the door.

"Professor! Hey, Dr. Grant, get up!"

It was that kid.

Grant sat upright, rubbed his temples, and headed for the door. The afternoon light burst in uninvited, followed by the kid, also uninvited. "Charley. What a surprise."

"Professor, you look like shit."

"Thanks so much. What do you want?"

"You got the flu?"

"I've got something."

"Everybody's getting it. My Old Man. My neighbors. Everybody."

"It'll pass. It's a twenty-four-hour bug or something."

"Wow, you have been out of touch. There's talk of three dead already from it."

"Three?"

"Maybe more. There's this woman down from CDC in Atlanta. Tell me it's nothing. Go ahead. CDC doesn't bother with little stuff. Something big is going down."

Grant thought for a moment. "Seen your boss yet?"

"No, sir. He's still missing. See, the powers-that-be are trying to keep the plague small in tale if not in truth. It's the Black Death, man. The princes and priests tried to manage the truth about that too but they couldn't. The mayor's not counting either Roscoe or John Doe or Susan Walsh in the plague deaths. So we really got six dead."

Surprise lit Grant's face. "They're not counting Susan Walsh?"

"Not as a plague death. Hammond's computer notes say it's murder."

Grant shook his head sadly. "That's weird. They grilled me for two hours this morning about her but I had nothing to do with it. No mention of murder. Charley, something on this island is out of control. Mayor Johnson—I hope he's not a friend of yours—would lose his ass if it wasn't stuck to him. But Hammond and Sanborn are sharp. And Sanborn wants to get me in the worst way."

"No kidding. You know what the best thing about being a geek is? Small-town computer networks have no defense against guys like me. I've been helping myself to confidential emails. Guess what? There's a lot of talk about you. Not happy talk.

You're a very suspicious dude, you know. Hope you got an alibi."

"Thanks for the pep talk, Charley."

Randy Sanborn finished his afternoon beat and settled into the overstuffed swivel chair at his desk to polish off a boatload of paperwork he'd gotten behind on. With so much going on, the fun stuff had slipped. Time sheets, payroll, budgets. He glanced at the clock. Ten after five, but this stuff would keep him here another three hours. He slumped deeper into the chair and began scanning the paper on the top of his growing in-box pile.

Don Flowers came shuffling through the office. He gave Sanborn a tired smile and rooted through a file cabinet.

Blessed distractions.

"Don," Sanborn said.

Flowers looked up. He'd also just gotten off patrol, a foot walk. Pushing retirement, white-haired, paunchy, with a deeply pitted red nose. An old-school workhorse. Absolutely would not give up his beat.

"You got a little too much sun today. You okay?"

"Sure. A little tired."

Flowers was beet red. "Big Fella, why don't you get home already?" said Randy.

"My shift goes to seven, Boss."

"Forget shifts. It's after five and it's still ninety-seven outside. Go home and have a beer with Mrs. Flowers. I need you fresh tomorrow."

"I am a little tired," Flowers allowed.

"Go. You'll just start flapping your gums and I'll never get anything done. Go."

"Maybe I will. Thanks, Boss."

Flowers shuffled out and quiet entered the room. Sanborn glanced at the clock again and resumed reading, a list of maintenance needs for the squad cars. He picked up a pencil and checked off a couple items.

"Screw it," he said. He dropped the paper in the in-box and grabbed his keys.

He drove down US 19, cutting over to the Suncoast Parkway and following it into Tampa. The long drive was a welcome stretch of miles and solitude, at least until he hit some murderous north-side traffic as dusk gathered. Timing was good anyhow. Where he was going, you couldn't be too early if you wanted to find anyone willing to talk.

He worked his way over to Dale Mabry Drive, slowed to admire the topless bars, and switched onto JFK and found the neighborhood he sought, on the edge of downtown, in the shadow of the Moorish minarets of the University of Tampa. A hooker waved without enthusiasm and he waved back.

After a few minutes, he spotted the pink and blue neon sign of The Holiday House Bar. The place Charley had mentioned. He parked, took off his uniform shirt, pulled on a Hawaiian shirt, and went inside.

The place was dim and cool and jungly. Heavy wood and tropical plants abounded. Bob Marley was singing over the speakers, not too loudly. "Jammin." Patrons mingled about, the joint about half full. Teens to retirees. All men.

Sanborn took a seat at the bar and signaled the bartender. "Carl," his nametag proclaimed.

"What can I get for you, Sailor?"

"Rum and coke and some information would be nice."

"Rum and coke I can do. I thought you looked out of place here. Hawaiian shirt indeed. You a cop?"

"Not in Tampa."

"Where then?"

No point in lying. "Brigands Key."

Carl's eyes widened. He eased a few inches away. "What's

117

going on up there? People are talking about a plague."

Now it was Sanborn's turn to be surprised. When you're smack dab in the middle of something, you don't have perspective. Especially when you're from Brigands Key and accustomed to being invisible. He hadn't realized anyone outside the county had become aware of the sicknesses. "We have an unfortunate situation, that's for damned sure. That's why I'm here. In a roundabout way. Name's Randy Sanborn. I'm no doctor, so take this for what it's worth: something is rotten, but there's no plague. I'm police chief in Brigands Key. I'm off duty and I have zero jurisdiction here. So any help will be much appreciated."

"I'll try and be of assistance, Constable Sanborn of Brigands Key Hamlet."

Constable Sanborn. Never heard that before. Ever. "I'm looking for a guy, Carl."

"Aren't we all."

"He was a patron here. Roscoe Nobles. Heard of him?"

"Roscoe? Of course. He comes here all the time. Is he in trouble?"

"Is he here now?"

"Is he in trouble?"

"My whole town's in trouble. Roscoe is not suspected of any crime if that's what you want to know. He may be the key to figuring out what's going on and he's gone missing."

"He's not here."

"Does he come here a lot?"

"At least twice a month. Stays at the Starlight Motel down the block usually."

"If he were in Tampa, would you know it?"

"Absolutely. Roscoe would have come in by now. This is the place where everybody knows your name."

"When was he last here?"

"It's been, oh, three weeks. Do you think . . . ?"

"Plague? I don't know. Brigands Key is too small to hide in. When someone goes missing, it's usually because he had too much to drink and fell overboard. But Roscoe's boat is docked, pretty as can be."

"Maybe the vampire got him."

"Don't start that shit."

"Sorry. Don't mean to make light of it. Roscoe's a gem. Does a wonderful rendition of Robert Goulet."

"Who the hell does Robert Goulet?"

"You'd be surprised."

"Did . . . does Roscoe talk much about us?"

"A little. He's lonely there, Constable. As you might imagine. Had a few troubles with the townsfolk?"

"About this? No one really knows about his secret life there."

"A few do. He had trouble with a couple of people. Your mayor, he complained a lot about him."

Sanborn hoped his poker face was good. "The mayor?"

"Mayor Toad was after Roscoe to sell out to Gulf Breeze. Can you imagine, that gorgeous old Victorian getting torn down for condos? It's a crime."

"You've seen it?"

"I stayed in it one weekend. Roscoe's very sly."

"I guess he is. Know anything more about the mayor?"

"Roscoe is, of course, one of your local politicos. He was getting pushed to sell by both the mayor and that developer, and pushed by some realtor to not sell. He was stuck in the middle."

"He was adamant about not selling."

"He wasn't always. That developer offered him some big money. He was going to at one point, you know."

"Assume that I don't."

"Fine, Constable. Roscoe was a dreamer, but his dreams weren't panning out. His little treasure hunts were draining him

119

financially and emotionally. He began to believe what his father had always called him. A failure."

"And that changed, right?"

"Suddenly and dramatically. I'd like to think he couldn't bear the thought of watching the Victorian fall, but Roscoe's not the sentimental type. Something gave him a big change of heart."

"Know what it was?"

Carl shook his head. "Roscoe was a different person than what you knew back on your island. He was open, flippant, gregarious. But he could keep a secret better than the CIA. Big code buff, you know."

"Anything else?"

"Roscoe was getting extremely nervous over the last year or so about something. Wouldn't say what, but he thought someone was after him, and not about selling his house. We figured, yeah right, good old Roscoe the Paranoid."

Sanborn downed the remains of his drink. He took a business card out of his shirt pocket and tapped it on the bar. "Carl, listen. It's urgent that I find Roscoe. Ask around. If you see or hear from him, call me right away, any time day or night."

"I'd normally tell a nosy cop to piss off, but something tells me to trust you."

"Time is short, Carl. I've got at least two murders, a lethal illness, a missing person to solve. And that's just on the surface."

"It goes deeper?"

"Deeper than anything we can imagine."

CHAPTER ELEVEN

Grant flipped through his notebooks, pausing over a paragraph here and there. It really was damned good work. Well researched and well documented. Unimpeachable. He'd learned the hard way to go beyond the accepted norm of thoroughness. Damned if he'd slip up on that again.

It was now Tuesday morning. Exactly one week after he'd discovered the spring and it finally had a name, even if it hadn't yet been memorialized in any official way. *He* had named it. Others might try to come along and trump the name, maybe even give it some sawdust name like SS-42. Astronomers did that a lot, damning fantastic celestial objects with numerical designations. They claimed it was necessary because there were too many stars to give worthy names to. All the good names, like Aldebaran and Sirius, were taken. What rubbish. Seven billion humans on the planet, and every one had a name, not a number. How hard could it be? Astronomers had just gotten lazy.

So the spring was now and forever "Grant's Eye."

He toyed with the idea of a return dive to the spring, but that idea stank. Sanborn had barred him from his own archaeological site, not that he could give a shit about Sanborn. But the seas were picking up out on the Gulf. The mere thought of going out on a tossing boat made his stomach churn. He reached for the bottle of Pepto Bismol on his nightstand and took a swig. He returned his attention to the notebook.

A page of notes and sketches caught his attention. It was a description of the piece of wood he'd found. The truncheon. He'd heard nothing more about it from Sanborn or Hammond. Maybe that was by design.

A knock came at the door. What now? Sanborn was probably here to drag him in for more questioning.

He cracked the door and peeked out. A young woman with jet-black hair looked in. Quite a looker.

"Dr. Grant?"

"Dr. Nakamura."

"You know me?"

"This isn't Atlanta, Doctor. You're the only person of Asian descent on Brigands Key. What can I do for you?"

"You could let me in."

Grant hesitated, stepped aside. Nakamura glanced at the motel bed, the packed bags. "Going somewhere?"

"If the Gestapo sees fit."

"I'm not in law enforcement, Dr. Grant. But I'd recommend you sit tight."

"Your recommendation is duly noted. And I choose to ignore it. I'm checking out in five minutes."

"We'll see about that."

"Again I ask: what can I do for you?"

"You found John Doe. I'd like to interview you about it."

"Him. You have five minutes."

"You won't be leaving, Dr. Grant, until I say so. If you like, I can get Sanborn over here to explain it to you."

"I'll be off the island before you fetch him."

"I can also have the FBI pick you up and bring you back. A phone call is all it would take. Would you prefer that?"

"You're not FBI. You're CDC. Surgeons with badges."

"CDC has some sweeping powers these days. Maybe you haven't been following the news."

Grant shook his head, resigned. He sat on the foot of the bed and motioned her to one of the worn chairs. "Interview away, Doc. Let me warn you, though. You're in Brigands Key because of a contagion. And I'm sick."

"That's what I hear."

"And you're not afraid?"

"Neither Hammond nor I think it's a contagion."

"No? What then?"

"We're working on it. Nevertheless, if you feel like coughing, let me know." Nakamura reached into her shoulder bag, produced a recorder, and switched it on. "Now then: tell me all about your discovery of John Doe. Start with why you're out in the middle of the ocean in the first place. Leave out nothing."

"As you wish." Grant began with his background and his research and how it led to discovery of Grant's Eye, right up through his delivery of the body to Sanborn. He finished, leaned back, and watched her guardedly.

"Sounds like you broke a half-dozen Florida statutes and more than a few federal laws in your handling of the crime scene," she said.

"Recite them for me."

Kyoko hesitated.

"That's what I thought. You're not good at playing Dragon Lady, are you? You would have preferred I left the body in a hole in the ocean for Barney Fife to collect?"

Her smile looked genuine for once. "Maybe not."

"I've told you everything I know, Doctor."

"I don't think so. Let's start over, and start by calling me Kyoko. You've told me everything you think is relevant. You've been here a couple of weeks, right? Tell me what you know about Brigands Key. What's normal, what's not for this place."

"There's a Brigands Key normal that may not fit the outside

world. It's an island town. Very close-knit, very insular. Very secretive."

"Why secretive?"

"Islanders everywhere have a way about them. Stuff comes in, stuff goes out, but mind your own business. Through lean times, like the Great Depression, island towns keep on clicking. They've always been dropping-off points for everything the rest of us want. When we come barging in, buying up property, they get a little defensive. Guys that hate each others' guts will circle the wagons together."

"That's happening here?"

"You bet. The carpetbaggers are moving in, buying it up. The townsfolk are resentful, but there's a rift that's gotten acid. Some are ready to cash in. Others are clinging to the past. There's not much middle ground."

"Back to John Doe. There's something Hammond and Sanborn are keeping off the record."

"Like John Doe's age?"

"What about his age?"

"What's your guess?"

"Twenty?"

"Maybe when he died."

"And—?"

"The guy's seventy if he's a day. But what do I know about the recently deceased? I'm an archaeologist. Talk to Hammond."

Kyoko nodded ever so slightly. If she was surprised, she wasn't letting on. She seemed to be assimilating this new knowledge, fitting it with ideas of her own. Grant wondered if he'd underestimated her.

"What do you know about Roscoe Nobles?" she suddenly asked.

"Not much." Grant reached for his shoes and pulled them

on. "But I'll introduce you to someone who does."

Charley sat on the end of the public fishing pier, his feet dangling over the edge, jigging gently on his fishing rod, tickling the water with a lure. Nothing biting, as usual. Fishing was for crap around the pier and only out-of-towners and local kids with nothing better to do ever fished from it. But he had nothing better to do. No school. No job. No home life. No friends. Nothing.

A shadow appeared over him. "Charley, I thought I'd find you here." He looked up. The Professor stood over him. And that lady from CDC.

"Hey, Doc. Feel like fishing?"

"I don't feel like anything but puking."

"Maybe that'll chum up some fish for me."

"This is Dr. Kyoko Nakamura."

"From Atlanta. Got it."

"You know of me?"

"Everybody does."

"So it seems. Tell me about Roscoe."

"He's dead, I reckon."

"You were the last to see him?"

"Maybe. Everybody in town's looking at me funny, anyhow."

"Were you close?"

Charley snorted. "He wasn't close with anybody. Not around here, anyway. I liked him, though."

"Roscoe got into something, didn't he?"

Charley cocked his head. "Roscoe was your basic island entrepreneur. He got into lots of things."

"Don't play games, Charley Eff. I've read your blogs. I know what's on your mind. Roscoe's mixed up with John Doe, isn't he?"

Charley looked at her, surprised. CDC Woman was pretty

sharp. "You figured that out?"

"Yes."

Charley nodded slowly. "He thought the Professor had found something big in the ocean."

"What?"

"Pirate treasure. It's what all us hicks are after, isn't it?"

"And he went after it?"

"That's my guess. Next thing you know, he's disappeared. I looked everywhere. He dropped off the face of the earth and that's not like him."

"Charley, I need your help."

"For what?"

"I'm an outsider. So is Dr. Grant. Our reach is limited in Brigands Key. I need you to do some digging, some asking around. Something peculiar is going on. And it's related to real estate."

"Good guess," Grant said. "History is all about real estate."

"You know this town, Charley. You know the battle lines over Bay View. Get me something that's not obvious."

Charley's foot tapped nervously on the sea wall. Dr. Nakamura was sharp as a tack. Between her and Dr. Grant, the cumulative IQ of Brigands Key had tripled. This was a treat, being around super-smart people for a change. And they wanted his help. He felt a thickness in his throat, the odd feeling he got when being flattered, which was almost never.

"Will you keep me in the loop?" he asked.

"You bet."

"I'm the best researcher this rotten place has yet produced. I can come up with something."

Three hours later, Kyoko sat across from Hammond, watching him closely. Hammond was reading a bound report, his face drawn and pale, shadows underscoring his eyes. The report trembled slightly in his hands. He got through the last page, riffled them, squared them up, and placed them on his desk. "We're getting nowhere," he said glumly.

The tests were all coming back. She'd expressed samples to CDC for viral analysis and the electron microscope scans found nothing. "Process of elimination," she said. "The only way to crack this nut."

"But the nut's not cracking."

"Are we in agreement? It's not a virus?"

Hammond shook his head. "Can't say for sure. It just doesn't look like one."

"Well, what virus do you think it *could* be?"

"Malaria. West Nile. I don't know, something we don't see much in Florida."

Kyoko stabbed a finger at him. "Jerry, it's not malaria. It's not West Nile. You have the results in front of you."

"What then? Venom?"

She pursed her lips, thinking. "There are a million venoms in the world. Each attacks a victim differently. I've got CDC running a venom database. So far, no matches. Besides, none of the victims have reported any stings or bites that may have envenomated them."

"Venom can be artificially introduced."

"That's a stretch."

"It's all I've got."

"We can all but rule out food poisoning and natural toxins. The lab test found nothing in the scallops and oysters. Nothing in the shrimp. They tested every type of fish caught. Nothing. They tested milk, eggs, ice cream, butter. They tested all the meat at the grocery store. Nothing. Clean as a whistle."

"Check the whistle. They're vessels for spit, you know."

Kyoko tried smiling, with little success. "They didn't find anything in the drinking water. From the vomiting and diarrhea

127

and deaths, I had convinced myself *Vibrio cholerae* was going to show up in the water. Nothing. Spotless, in fact. The drinking water here is cleaner than Miami's and Tampa's."

"Then we're looking at two things. Either there's a virus we're missing or there's a poison at work."

Kyoko nodded. "Look at page six. Symptoms are viral, but we can't find a virus. Vomiting, bloody diarrhea, burning abdominal pain, swift death. If we're talking poison, what it says is arsenic."

"Hmm. No. You saw the tissue tests. If this were arsenic, it'd show up in body fat."

"Another poison, then." She tapped her pencil lightly on the table. "Jerry, this sickness is shifting out of our realm. Outside of bacterial contaminants, accidental spills of poisons or environmental contaminations usually do their dirty work over extended periods of time. Weeks, months, years. Powerful poisons rarely leak into the world and kill by accident. We're on the right track, and the track is pointing to a large-scale, acute poisoning. Not by accident. Someone is poisoning Brigands Key deliberately."

CHAPTER TWELVE

Tommy Greenwood glanced at his watch. Three-thirty in the P.M. Randy usually wrapped up his housekeeping tasks, the mail, the paperwork, the political phone calls by noon and would be out making the rounds by now. Yet the boss was still in his office, behind closed doors.

Sanborn's door rattled and he stuck his head out. "Tell you what. Here's ten bucks. Go grab you and me some coffee and biscuits from Carla's."

"You okay, Boss?"

"Yeah. I'll be here a while. Take a break and get us something."

In ten minutes Greenwood returned, balancing two foam cups of coffee on one hand, pinned in place under his chin, with a bag of hot buttered biscuits in the other. He twisted the doorknob and backed in. "Get 'em while they're hot."

He set the coffees down and opened the bag and inhaled the warm aroma of the biscuits. "Boss? You coming?"

He went to Randy's office, rapped lightly on the battered wooden door and pushed it open.

Randy was nowhere in sight.

"More for me," Greenwood mumbled. He slumped into his chair and reached for a biscuit.

Sanborn parked his Jeep at his house, slipped inside, and changed into blue jeans, baseball cap, aviator shades, and a work shirt. His cat, Theodore, watched imperially and made a half-hearted effort of rubbing against his leg before wandering off. Sanborn slipped out the back door and down the narrow alley onto the side street and down the road.

A half-hour's brisk walk brought him to Lee Street and Roscoe Nobles's place. Without slowing, resisting the urge to glance about, he turned up the walk and stepped onto the front porch. Act like you own the place, he told himself. Roscoe was missing and wasn't showing up. His folks passed away fifteen years ago and he had no extended family elsewhere. The only place he ever went was Tampa to hang out in bars with other guys, and they hadn't seen him. Sanborn knocked, waited, knocked again, waited again. He sniffed the air, half expecting to catch a whiff of death. The air was thick and hot and muggy, but clean. If anything had died in this heat, even this morning, even a lizard, you'd smell it. There were no large corpses to be found. The stench would knock you over from a hundred feet.

He dug in his shirt pocket and withdrew a pair of latex gloves, put them on, tested the doorknob. He withdrew a thin steel wire and wriggled it into the lock. The lock clicked and the door swung slightly ajar.

A turning point, he told himself. You go in, you break the law. You become the cop you swore you wouldn't.

Yet people were dying. There was no time to play by the book. He slipped inside and eased the door shut behind him.

The place was not exactly Spartan. The entry was a traditional Victorian hallway, wood floors, a couple of rugs, a coatrack in the corner by a gorgeous antique washstand topped by a vase of dead roses. A copy of *Southern Living* lay next to it. Across the hallway stood a half-dozen fishing rods and a couple of tackle boxes and the grimiest pair of boots that ever existed. Sanborn wasn't quite sure what he expected, but this wasn't it. Nobles continued to defy easy classification.

Sanborn opened a drawer of the washstand and peeked in. Rule Book Sanborn, he thought. Go ahead, stick your hands in, root about. You've already crossed a threshold that's habit-forming and career-ending. No search warrant. He didn't even inquire about getting one. Judge Ron Bettia was on the circuit this week and he'd throw Sanborn out on his ear. You what? You want a warrant to search this guy's house because he's gone a couple days? And he's never even gotten a traffic ticket? And he's suspected of nothing?

No chance of a warrant. Something terrible stalked Brigands Key. Bodies were piling up. And some way, somehow, Roscoe Nobles was the key.

Screw process.

He rummaged through the drawers of the washstand, then moved down the hallway.

All the rooms were open. Nothing seemed out-of-place, at least not in a sinister way. Out-of-place in a bachelor way.

Sanborn checked the bedrooms, or at least what were designed as bedrooms. One was more or less a junk room, stuffed with moldy, broken-down antique furniture, boxes of dishes, stacks of fishing and sports magazines, tools piled in a corner. The next room was completely empty. Nothing but a coat of dust. Without footprints.

The master bedroom lay on the right. It looked lived in. The bed wasn't made, dirty dishes covered the nightstand. Sanborn crossed the room, the pine floorboards creaking with his steps. Sanborn picked a coffee mug from the stack of dishes, sniffed it, set it down again. A cockroach scurried away.

He opened the closet and rustled the clothes hanging there. He stooped, checked the flooring, not exactly sure why. A hunch. Finding nothing, he pulled the bed apart, came up empty.

One bedroom left.

It was set up as an office. A pigsty office. Coffee-stained papers covered a scratched oak desk and books were stacked on the floor all about. Maps of Florida, the county, the Big Bend, were pinned haphazardly on the walls.

A computer monitor and keyboard occupied the center of the desk. Only the peripherals. The computer itself was missing. He sifted through the desk drawers, searching for file discs, removable drives, memory sticks.

Nothing. He rummaged through the litter of papers. Bills, canceled checks, junk mail. Ledgers for the fishing boat, receipts, schedules. The tide tables, a list of fishing spots, and notes about the competition.

A footlocker in a corner below the wall map caught his attention. He tried it, found it unlocked. Inside were a collection of books and notebooks. He picked up a pair. *Florida Shipwrecks. Pirates of Old Florida.* He set them aside and fished out more titles and lurid covers. *Gaspar's Treasure. Lost Treasures of Florida. Tales of the Spanish Main.*

A patina of dust covered the edges and corners of the room, but was nonexistent about the desk and in front of the footlocker. Typical bachelor pad, periodically swept at best. He slid the footlocker out a bit. Sure enough, it left a shadow in the dust. Hadn't been moved in a long time, although the lid was free of dust. Obviously got opened a lot, just not moved.

A couple of feet away a rectangle of clean floor lay etched in the dust.

Sanborn lifted the footlocker and set it upon the clean rectangle. It was smaller than the rectangle.

There had been a second footlocker and it was missing.

His radio crackled. "Randy?" It was Jackie. Something in her voice scared him.

"This is Sanborn."

"Randy, we need you back right away."

"Be right there. I'm ten minutes from the office."

"Not the office, Randy. At Doc Hammond's. Now."

Sanborn lugged the heavy footlocker out to the porch and set it behind the porch swing, covering it with a potted plant. He got his cell phone out and dialed.

"Hello?"

"Charley, this is Chief Sanborn. I've got a little job for you." And he told the kid where to find the footlocker.

The waiting room was full, the first time Sanborn could ever remember seeing that. And no receptionist. Seven people sat about, ashen-faced, unspeaking. Nicole Porter, high-school prom queen two years ago, sat in a corner, terror in her eyes. The door clattered as Sanborn let it shut behind him.

Hammond, his face drawn and creased, appeared from behind the far door. He motioned Sanborn inside.

Officer Don Flowers lay on the examining room table. He turned slowly and looked glassy-eyed at Sanborn, without recognition. He was in a hospital gown, its front soiled by vomit. The white light of the overhead fluorescents bathed the room, giving all color a razor's-edge brilliance. Sanborn prayed it was the light that was making Flowers look so deathly pale.

"Don—" Sanborn began.

Flowers doubled over in a spasm, clutching his stomach. His bladder released and urine soaked his gown. His hand went slowly to his head, the fingers brushing through his thin gray hair. The hand suddenly clenched and tore a fistful of hair out by the roots, his nails digging into his scalp.

"Don!"

Flowers's other hand shot toward his scalp. Sanborn seized the hand and pinned it against his body. Flowers struggled weakly, silently, and relaxed with a slow rasping escape of air.

He opened his palm, stared at the blood under his nails, shuddered, and lay still.

CHAPTER THIRTEEN

ON the EDGE, with Charley Eff

Funny Things: A couple cars came to town today and spilled their contents onto the mean streets of Hooterville Sur La Mer. Pasty Goths, down from Milwaukee, dressed head to toe in black.

They're my age. They're not from here. I'm drawn to them. A moth to flame. A fly to shit.

I want to be them, but I don't get them. It's a hundred degrees out. No breeze. Dressed in black? The summer air here sticks to you like flypaper soaked in shit. The Milwaukee Goths are teetering, close to heat stroke. They melt. But they'd die before they put on shorts.

I got a few words out of them. What brings them here?

"Vampires," the first Goth says. His name is Billy but he goes by Splint. Or Stint. Or Skint. I don't remember.

"Vampires?"

"Vampires. It's on the Internet."

Holy crap.

"You're here for the vampires?"

"We are vampires."

Holy crap. "Why are you out in the sun?"

"What's that supposed to mean?"

"Nothing. It's hot."

"Where are they?" This is Girl Goth. Her skin is white as paper, reddening by the minute. Her hair is black as ink. She

wears black eye shadow, black lipstick. She's skin and bones. She's really cute.

"Where are who?"

"The undead. It's all on the Internet."

"Here's the scoop. People are dying here. The head vampire's on a slab in the morgue. Dude's eighty years old. Doesn't look a day over twenty-one."

"We gotta see that."

"Dudes."

"What?"

"He's not like you."

"How so?"

"He's real. Don't go there after dark. Don't go out after dark at all." *I turned to Girl Goth.* "Where you staying?" *I can't believe the words actually came out of me.*

"Morrison Motel."

"I wouldn't stay there."

"Why not?"

"There was a murder there. Night before last."

"A blood-sucking?"

"No, the conventional, non-vampire kind. Death by ice pick."

"Not all that conventional."

"It is in these parts. What did you say your name was?"

"I didn't. It's Steele."

"No. Your real name."

"Steele."

"Cool."

I want her to stay. A lot. I think she likes me.

Anyway.

The Hooterville police chief's got a little task for me. Gotta go fight crime now.

The footlocker was right where Chief Sanborn said. Charley

wondered why the guy couldn't or wouldn't bring it back by himself. Just load it up and go. Maybe he hadn't parked nearby. Maybe Sanborn couldn't remove it because he wasn't supposed to be here. Aha. No warrant. Illegal search and seizure. This just kept getting better. The Chief *wanted* him to root through it and report back.

Charley had borrowed the Old Man's Chevy without asking. No worry. The Old Man was sick in bed again, hung over, puking up last night's supper. He wouldn't notice his baby, his car, missing for the ten minutes Charley needed it.

Charley hefted the locker and hauled it to the car and slid it into the trunk. He eased shut the lid, feeling conspicuous. What if this was a trick by Sanborn to get him on a charge of theft? He really didn't know Sanborn at all. Small-town cops, everybody knows they'll screw you. His mind raced with possibilities. Crime wasn't his calling.

He drove home with excessive care and lugged the locker to his bedroom. There was a low groan from the Old Man's room. Charley eased his door shut and locked it.

He thought for a thousandth of a second about calling Sanborn first, and then opened the locker. Inside were dozens of books about pirates, shipwrecks, and treasure. Clippings about Oak Island, off Nova Scotia. Something about Confederate Navy blockade runners. Something about the great lost fleet of galleons of 1715. Blackbeard's flagship, *Queen Anne's Revenge.*

And maps. Lots of maps. USGS quad sheets, coastal depth charts, copies of hundred-year-old surveys. Almost all the maps focused on the Big Bend area, all within a fifty-mile radius of Brigands Key. A guy could get lost in this.

A few of the books and maps Charley recognized. Roscoe sometimes thumbed through them in idle moments on the boat, when the fish weren't cooperating or it was lunchtime, skimming a page with the grimy index finger of his left hand while shoving a ham sandwich into his face with his right. At times, his eyes would light up with sudden inspiration and he'd drop both book and sandwich and grab a pencil and one of his little orange notebooks and start scribbling furiously. His orange books were his prizes. They were rugged things, hardbound and durable, not too big to fit into a shirt pocket. The kind survey crews use.

Roscoe wouldn't say a word until he'd gotten whatever little nugget was ricocheting around in his brain down on paper.

Charley looked through the pile of documents again. So where were the little orange notebooks? Roscoe must have filled a dozen of them, each with a capital letter handwritten on the cover in black marker, in alphabetical sequence beginning with *A*.

Charley picked up the books and looked at a few of them again. One caught his attention: *Lost Trails, Lost Cities.* The title jarred his memory, sent it reeling through time and space to the last day he'd seen Roscoe, their last day out on the water. To what Roscoe had said, with that peculiar look in his eyes.

When Old Roscoe kicks the bucket, you keep looking for them lost trails.

This book. Roscoe was sending him to this book. It made perfect sense. Charley knew the book well. It was the only one of Roscoe's pile that had captured Charley's imagination earlier in the year when they were idle on the water. What had interested him was the author's name. Colonel P.H. Fawcett. Another Fawcett, one that might actually be interesting. When Charley asked what it was about, Roscoe pursed his lips and looked at Charley. "Here, read it," he said, tossing Charley the book. "Ain't got time to explore Brazil anyway."

Charley finished the book that night. Colonel Percy Fawcett, a restless and reckless adventurer, had gone searching for lost cities in the Mato Grosso of Brazil in 1925 and was never seen or heard from again. His letters, notes, and maps were compiled by his son and published in 1953.

Charley had returned the book to Roscoe the next morning, and they spent the day arguing the theories about the doomed expedition and Fawcett's folly.

Charley picked up the old worn book and felt the rough canvas cover with satisfaction. He read the first page and riffled through the remaining pages.

A leaflet fell from the pages and floated to the floor.

Charley retrieved it and read it. It was a ruled-line page, five by eight inches, torn from a book. Heavy, durable paper.

A page torn from one of Roscoe's orange books.

On one side was a single, penciled note.

CF Sacré Bleu Remark 43.

What was that all about? Code words? With Roscoe, they almost had to be.

The note looked recent.

CF. Colonel Fawcett?

No. Charley Fawcett.

Sacré bleu? French, right? Seemed like he'd heard that in old cartoons, Warner Brothers, maybe Pepe Le Pew or Blaque Jaque Shellaque. Ah, the memories.

He typed the phrase into his computer and got an immediate search response. French, all right. "Sacred blue." A common curse way back that the French apparently no longer used. Had something to do with the corruption of dieu to bleu. Only Americans used it to mock the French.

It was an omen of bad things.

Charley settled back onto his bed, propped against the wall, and opened the book and began reading. Every couple of pages, he circled a sentence or paragraph with a pencil. He didn't eat, didn't get up to take a leak, until he'd read it straight through that night.

When at last he finished, he began at the first page again, skimming through and reading all the passages he'd highlighted. Nothing in the book had anything he could pin down about Colonel Fawcett finding some damned sacred remark.

He spent the next hour doing Internet searches. CF Sacré bleu remark. Colonel Fawcett remark. Colonel Fawcett sacred blue. Remark 43.

Nothing to connect the words.

The note had nothing to do with the lost explorer. The note was placed in that book because it was the one book of all of them that Charley had read. It was a note from Roscoe to Charley.

Cryptic as all get out.

There had to be more to this. If Roscoe had clued him in by mentioning "lost trails," maybe he'd hinted at something more. What else had he said that last day on the boat? Charley plumbed his memory, trying to recall the details of the conversation.

Read your Shakespeare.

Charley remembered thinking that was peculiar advice, and had shrugged it off as Roscoe being Roscoe. Roscoe was peculiar, just not very abstract. At least, that had been Charley's opinion at one time.

Read your Shakespeare.

Charley had never mentioned Shakespeare or any interest in it. His own house sure didn't have Shakespeare on the shelves.

It was a clue. And it wouldn't be here with this stuff. Roscoe was careful to spread things around, make paper trails harder. Lost trails. It was all part of his logic.

Charley pushed all the materials back into the locker, slipped a small lock on it, pushed it into a corner, and piled dirty clothes on it.

He grabbed his empty backpack, bounded out of the house

without a goodbye, and sped off on his bike. He pedaled past Roscoe's house twice, slowing, glancing this way and that, and whipped his bike into the driveway and behind the house. He dismounted and dragged the bike into a dying row of red oleanders.

Roscoe's backyard was hidden, due to lack of maintenance. Years of untrimmed growth had overwhelmed it. Charley had chalked it up to laziness, but now wondered if the overgrowth had been intentional, keeping prying eyes out. Whatever the case, Charley was invisible from the street. He climbed the three steps of the back stoop and tested the door. Locked, as expected.

A pile of bricks intended for a never-started pathway lay near the stoop. His heart began racing with the excitement of intrigue and lawlessness. He selected a brick, hefted it, returned to the door and smashed it against the doorknob. The doorknob snapped off. Charley tossed the brick aside, pushed the door open, and stepped inside.

He passed from room to room, stopping in Roscoe's office. Nothing caught his attention, and he headed back downstairs. A worn bookshelf lined one side of the front hallway. On it were a couple hundred books in no apparent order. Engine repair manuals, a row of John D. MacDonald novels, travel books. Treasure books like those in the footlocker were conspicuously absent.

Then he saw the volume he'd hoped he would find: *The Globe Illustrated Shakespeare*. He pulled the fat book off the shelf, stuffed it into his backpack, and left through the back door. He carefully propped the brick against the door to hold it shut and replaced the wounded doorknob back in it. At a casual glance, at least, the door wouldn't appear to have been broken into.

Back in his bedroom, Charley opened the Shakespeare to the first page. Boring introductions and whatnot. He flipped ahead to the first play, *The Two Gentlemen of Verona,* and started reading.

His heart sank. Five lines into the play, he saw what he was up against. Codes? Shakespeare damned near wrote in code. The language was gorgeous but dense. And the book was a good four inches thick, with over two thousand pages.

He stopped reading and flipped through the heavy tome. He turned it over and shook it, hoping a hidden leaflet would fall out, as it had with the Colonel Fawcett book. No such luck.

He turned back to the table of contents and read through the titles. A bunch of them he'd heard of, others he'd not.

One title caught his attention and he lingered over it for a moment: *Julius Caesar.* He'd never read it, never even seen it in a movie. Why did he stop on that title? He was a big believer in subconscious connections. He flipped ahead in the book, found *Julius Caesar.* And there, scribbled in the bottom margin on the first page of the play, was a line penciled in a shaky hand:

RTFIHS NWRPVJCRL YXAC UJMH

Whatever it meant, Charley knew he'd found Roscoe's clue.

He studied the cipher. Four words, apparently. But even that was unsure. The beginner's code book Roscoe had mailed to Charley made it clear that word spaces could be part of a code themselves.

The code book. Charley's mind raced, forming the link that had fixed his attention upon this, of all of Shakespeare's plays. He opened his code book and hurriedly found what he'd hoped for.

One of the most basic of codes was traced back to Julius Caesar himself. Surrounded by enemies, Caesar had invented his own code, now called "Caesar Shift."

It was a simple substitution code. Caesar shifted his Roman alphabet three characters over and encrypted his secret messages that way. In the modern English alphabet, *A* would be substituted by *D.*

Charley reread the handwritten cipher, mentally shifting the start of the alphabet to *D.* All he got was more gobbledy-gook.

He looked at the line again, and the solution jumped out at him. The first word, "RTFIHS," was written backwards. Reversed, it became "SHIFTR." Shifter? No; it was shift *R,* an instruction as to where the alphabet shift began. R-shift— Roscoe's Shift.

He took out a clean sheet of paper and wrote the alphabet out on one line. Immediately below it, he wrote the alphabet again, but with *A* lining up directly below *R.*

A B C D E F G H I J K L M N O P Q R S T U V W X Y Z
J K L M N O P Q R S T U V W X Y Z A B C D E F G H I

He then wrote out the last three words of the encryption and substituted the corresponding letter from the alphabet shift directly below:

NWRPVJCRL UJMH YXAC
ENIGMATIC LADY PORT

A thrill of excitement raced through him. He'd cracked the code. But the decryption was as mystifying as the encoded message. Enigmatic lady port? What in the world? "Enigmatic lady port," he said. He repeated it slowly, then again rapidly. It had a certain melodic ring to it. A familiar ring.

The answer fairly slapped him in the face and his estimation of Roscoe climbed again. Trickery this way, sleight of hand that way. "Roscoe, you old bastard," he said, laughing. "Can't ever play it straight, can you?"

CHAPTER FOURTEEN

By the time Jackie spotted Grant striding past her desk Wednesday morning it was too late. He was at Sanborn's office and pushing open the door. "Hey, you can't go in—" was all she managed before he shut the door behind him.

Sanborn looked up from a pile of paperwork, startled, angry. "Won't you please come in?"

"You and me, we both have a problem, and you're it," Grant said. "You're treating me like a suspect while your situation is spiraling out of control. Let's get this out of the way right here and now. You know damned well I've been telling the truth, so either charge me or get off my back. Do the first and you'll be wasting everyone's time when no one has time to spare. Do the second and we'll attack this little problem from the same side. What'll it be?"

Sanborn tossed his pencil carelessly on the desk and leaned back. "What makes you think I need or want your help?"

"Things fall apart. The center cannot hold."

"And what rough beast, its hour come round at last, slouches toward Bethlehem to be born?"

The door creaked open and Jackie appeared. "Tommy's here, Randy." A young officer stood next to her, trying hard to look pissed.

Sanborn kept his eyes firmly on Grant and motioned her away. "It's okay, Jackie."

Jackie withdrew and closed the door with a gentle click.

Grant took a seat and crossed his arms. He nodded slowly. "Think we're a bunch of morons, Grant?"

"I think we both recognize that something is seriously amiss. The rough beast's hour has come round and we better start working together. You don't have the staff to handle the crisis that's brewing."

"What can I do for you, Doctor?"

"Show me the truncheon I found. We need to start somewhere."

Sanborn studied him, then reached into his desk drawer and withdrew a key. "Follow me. And as long as I'm collecting brains, I want Dr. Nakamura's too."

Sanborn unlocked the door labeled "Evidence" and stepped aside. Grant peered in and snorted.

"Got a problem, Hoss?" Sanborn asked.

"None at all, Lieutenant Columbo. This looks suspiciously like a converted broom closet."

"Welcome to life in the slow lane."

The tiny room was crammed with the stuff of fishing village crime scenes. Street signs riddled with bullet holes. Half a case of Budweiser. A grimy tackle box or two.

Sanborn picked up a smashed crab trap. "This represents the most serious crime here in the last two months. Before the John Doe affair, that is. You don't screw with a fisherman's livelihood."

"How'd that one end up?" Kyoko asked.

"Broken trap, broken nose. We called it even and now the two are drinking buddies again." Sanborn slipped on a pair of white latex gloves and passed some to his companions. He selected a steel cabinet drawer, unlabeled but heavily padlocked, the only such one in the room, and opened it. "Our John Doe cabinet."

He carefully withdrew the truncheon. "Obviously beyond the capability of our forensics here, Dr. Nakamura. I could use Federal help with this."

Kyoko took the truncheon and studied it. "A sample, please?"

"Got it." Sanborn held up a small specimen jar, within which was a sliver of black wood.

They returned to Sanborn's office and Kyoko began dialing.

During her seventh phone call, she excused herself and went into the next room. There was a lot of shouting.

When she returned, she was glaring. "Success. After a fashion. We're overnighting it to the FBI lab in Quantico. Best in the world, but we've got a damned epidemic and they're sticking us in line."

"When will we get some answers?"

"With prodding, twenty-one days."

"I'll have you an answer in two, three days," Grant said.

They both looked at him skeptically.

He opened his phone, scrolled through a list of numbers, selected one, sent the call. "Rolando, Carson Grant here. Got you on speaker phone, by the way. Listen, I need a favor."

"Ah, Dr. Grant. It's been a while."

"I've got a hot item here. A wooden truncheon, manufacturer unknown. I need an analysis ASAP."

"I'd be happy to, but I'm on vacation in two days."

"You'll have it in your hands tomorrow. You can still go on vacation."

"You haven't changed. You think I will drop everything and deliver just like that? I have many loose ends to tie up before I go. You will have to wait."

"Remember that slow night in Bogota? When your wife was out of town?"

Silence.

"I guess you do," Grant continued.

"Very well. Send the sample. I will see what I can do."

"You're a gentleman and a scholar, Rolando. I owe you one."

"By my count, you owe me six."

"Who's counting? You'll have the sample tomorrow." Grant hung up.

Sanborn and Kyoko were smirking.

"Archaeologists have resources around the globe," Grant said. "Rolando Ruiz is the world's leading expert on identifying wood types."

"There are experts who do that?" Kyoko asked.

"They don't make the cover of *Newsweek,* but yeah. You'd be surprised how many grand Pooh-Bahs of arcane knowledge there are. Rolando will be hooked once he sees this bit of wood and won't relent until he's identified it. It's a point of honor to maintain his kingly stature. And he'll beat the FBI's best by three weeks."

Sanborn looked at his watch. "Come on. We've got a little meeting to attend."

Sanborn paused outside the door, listening. The meeting had started without him.

The mayor's bullish voice was rattling the windows, drowning out dissenting voices. A shame, that.

Without knocking, Sanborn pushed the door open and strode in. All talk ceased and all eyes turned to him. Grant and Kyoko followed him in.

"You're late, Randy," Mayor Johnson boomed. "The hell are they doing here?"

"Partaking of this great experiment we call democracy," Grant said. "Is that a problem?"

"Easy, Grant," Sanborn said.

"This here is a private meeting," Johnson said.

"No, it's not. State law says so."

147

"Afraid he's right, Ralph," said Clay Abbott. Johnson shot him a glance. Abbott looked away and pretended to study his note pad. "We don't have to meet, though," he quickly added, a note of hope in his voice.

"Damn it." Johnson turned to Hammond and Sanborn. "All right, then. Do we want to take a powder or continue?"

"We're not cutting out of this meeting," Hammond said.

"And I'm not letting them hear a word of it."

Sanborn shook his head and leaned close to Grant. "Listen," he whispered. "Important stuff is happening here and needs to happen, but it won't if you stick around. I already made my point to Johnson by bringing you here, so it's not a total waste. Do me a favor. Go back to your room. You too, Dr. Nakamura."

"I'm a popular topic of discussion. I want to be in on that discussion."

"Let's make a pact. If your name comes up, you'll hear it from me. That's better than nothing. Johnson won't air dirty laundry in public. Simple as that."

Grant held up a finger. "I expect a report in one hour."

"You got it."

Grant motioned to Kyoko and they stalked out of the room.

"Don't like that little mixer," Johnson said. "What'd you tell him?"

"The truth. He's wasting his time so he might as well waste it someplace else."

Johnson glanced at Hammond, a skeptical look on his face.

Hammond tensed. "Can we keep going? We've got nothing to hide. Do we, Mayor?"

A stiffness filled the room. "Course not."

"As I was saying," Abbott said, "Gulf Breeze's attorneys smell blood. That jackass, Pierce, has called me five times already today."

"And?"

"Last call, he's preparing legal action against Brigands Key, and against you specifically, Mayor."

"The hell ever for?"

"Susan's death, ostensibly."

"They blame me for that?" He grunted and rolled his eyes. "How much are they talking?"

Abbott cleared his throat. "Ten million bucks."

Johnson's face reddened, like a switch had been thrown. "That'll bankrupt us!"

"It's not a real lawsuit, just the threat of one. Call it insurance. Susan's murder is an excuse. Gulf Breeze sees an opening here, a highly likely vote of approval tonight. Pierce is sending a flunky to attend, just to make sure."

"Son of a bitch is too scared of getting sick to come himself."

"Bay View has been dragging for months while we dick around. The longer it drags, the more debt they carry. They want to see dirt moving. Susan told him your support was wavering. This lawsuit is intended to ensure you vote their way. Emma's death and Roscoe's absence make it two to none in favor, not counting you, Mayor."

"I can vote no and still watch it pass. But if Roscoe suddenly shows we got a two-to-one and everybody is looking at me. They force a tie vote and blackmail us with lawsuits. They've backed me into a corner, forcing me to vote."

"Isn't that part of the job, Mayor?" Sanborn asked.

"Don't get smart. You know I want the project approved."

"So approve it."

"And kiss my elected ass goodbye? I've been mayor for twenty years. I get re-elected one more term, I get my full retirement package. Then I can fish and drink beer. If I vote for approval, I'm as good as gone. Brigands Key voters are three-to-one against right now."

"Sounds like you're screwed."

"Randy, where the hell is Roscoe?"

"No one knows."

"Dead?"

"In my opinion."

"I don't like this one damn bit. Gulf Breeze had something to do with his disappearance. Susan's, too. Their own flack, murdered! Brilliant. Gulf Breeze is calling all the shots. Well, they grabbed the wrong bull by the balls. Roscoe ain't dead until a judge declares him dead, and I want to give him a chance to come back and vote. It ain't likely it'll be tonight. Clay, I want tonight's meeting canceled. Roscoe's unexpected absence is the excuse."

Abbott shook his head. "Can't do that. We still have a quorum. City charter dictates we meet."

"I want it canceled. Give me a reason."

Abbott's face knotted. "There's Hurricane Celeste. The charter allows us to cancel for emergencies and disasters."

"Do it."

"But Celeste is three hundred miles offshore and headed for Louisiana."

"Last I saw on CNN, the eye had jogged a couple degrees our way."

"Nobody's forecasting a sharp turn, though."

"Do it!"

Abbott's face took on a hurt look. He cast his eyes down, picked up a pen and notepad, and began writing.

"Sanborn," Johnson said, "find Roscoe before the next Council meeting, dead or alive. He's either voting or he's getting replaced because he's dead. We're not leaving this open-ended."

"Working on it."

"Not good enough. Get me some damn results." Johnson turned back to Abbott. "Well?"

"The threat of Hurricane Celeste has prompted Mayor Johnson to declare a state of emergency and begin evacuations. Tonight's City Council meeting is canceled. The safety of the citizens of Brigands Key takes priority over municipal business and the mayor is personally overseeing storm preparations."

"Heroic," Sanborn murmured.

Johnson ignored him. "You get to keep your job for another month, Clay."

"The Gulf Breeze sharks are going to blow a fuse."

"Let 'em. As mayor, I can appoint Roscoe's replacement until a special election can be arranged. Tell Pierce he'll be damned happy with the replacement I pick. The wait will be a pain in the ass, but it'll be well worth it to them. And tell that son of a bitch the next time he calls to talk to our attorney."

Sanborn left the meeting feeling slimy and disgusted. He wondered how much updating his resumé might need.

Kyoko Nakamura read through Hammond's notes, her stomach knotting as the picture became clearer. She glanced at him. "Is this headed where I think it is?"

"I sure hope not."

She set the notes aside and opened her laptop. "Your work is exemplary, Doctor. Few people are so detailed."

"Something peculiar was up from the start. I had to be thorough."

Kyoko scrolled through a menu of programs and selected one. "I'm plugging your data into a graphic plot. Every sickness, every death, excluding Susan Walsh's murder. We need to see an accurate progression of this thing. Give me an hour."

"Good. I've got to tend to my patients. I'll bring back an updated list for you."

When Hammond returned, an hour later to the minute, Kyoko was staring at the laptop. Fear lined her face.

"Bad?"

"Take a look." She turned the laptop toward him.

On the screen, a line graph glowed. Two white bars established time and incidence. Within the body of the graph, two lines, one red, one yellow, angled upward from the lower left start point.

"Yellow is reported illnesses," Kyoko said. "Red, confirmed deaths."

"The first instances are two days after John Doe was discovered."

"Yes."

"What about Nobles?"

"I'm not counting him. We can't be sure what's happened to him. But the confirmed incidences begin last Friday."

Both the yellow and red lines started at shallow angles, maybe five degrees, but increased over six plotted days to an almost vertical slope. "It's growing exponentially," Hammond said.

Kyoko felt a chill. "Within a couple of days, the entire island will be sick or dead. Mortality is holding to ten percent of the illnesses at each plotted point."

"It's not a single-event poisoning."

"Correct. We'd see an immediate spike and then a leveling and a drop. This is gaining momentum."

"Could be a contamination of food or water supply," Hammond said. "That would continue to increase as people continued to consume from the supply."

"True, the incidence would climb, but not the rate of increase."

"Then it still tracks like a highly contagious virus."

"Pray that it's not, Gerald. We're into a rampant killer we can't even identify."

He raised his eyebrows.

"If it's viral, it's a new strain. Good thing we're on an island, away from the mainland. And in a rural county. If this were a virus and had happened in Tampa or Miami or Orlando, there'd be no stopping it. It'd be all over the country by now. It may be anyway."

"What's your gut instinct, Kyoko?"

"I don't know what we're dealing with, but it's not a contagion."

"I agree. What if we're wrong?"

"Then America is in for a nightmare of epic proportions."

"What do we do?"

"I want you to call Mayor Johnson and Chief Sanborn. We need to make people stay indoors, stay home from work, stay out of the stores. Eat only canned foods, drink only bottled water. Anything to slow the spread of disease."

"And you?"

"I'm sending this report with extreme urgency to Atlanta."

CHAPTER FIFTEEN

ON the EDGE, with Charley Eff

I see Steele about an hour ago. She doesn't look so good, but I don't have a frame of reference for Midwestern street Goths. Don't they always look sick?

But she is sick all right. We talk about what to do in Brigands Key (nothing). And she turns ghost white and leans over and pukes. You okay, I ask. She shakes her head. Her pal, Billy the Splint, looks worried and a little sick himself.

"We got to get you to the doctor," I tell her.

Wouldn't you know it, Tyler Fulton comes strutting up the sidewalk right then. Him and his asshole friends. He points, laughing. "The Brigands Key vampire got the weird chick!" he says. Struts over and looms right over her. Asshole. Doesn't care that she's doubled over on her knees, heaving and puking. I stare at him. "You know we got people sick and dying on the island, don't you?"

"Spooky freaking vampires, don't you know."

Blood rushes into my face and my heart starts thumping. I shove him away from her. It's the first time I ever shoved anyone. Ever.

Tyler comes back and slugs me. Right in the mouth. I hit the pavement. The world spins. He laughs and gives me a kick for punctuation. "Charley Nutjob Fawcett."

In movies, the nerd always knocks the bully for a loop. What bullshit. In life, the bully is still twice your size and twice your

154

strength and still drops you like a sack of dog shit. I hurt. Man, did I hurt. Steolo puts her arm around me and helps me up. She's trembling. Me too. She smiles a kind of weak smile at me. "You were great," she rasps. "You can call me by my first name now. Callie."

I feel great.

Your Intrepid Correspondent, Charley Eff

Kyoko's phone beeped. She leaned away from her microscope, rubbed her eyes, flipped open the phone, put it on speaker, and peered again into her microscope. She already knew who it was. Only two hours had lapsed since she'd sent her findings.

"Dr. Nakamura, this is Dr. Greer. I read your report. It's a bit alarming."

Alarming? It was terrifying. "Yes, it is."

"You remember New Mexico?"

"Of course."

"I don't want a repeat."

"This is an entirely different situation, Paul. New Mexico was a hantavirus."

"And this—?"

"Not a hantavirus. I don't know what it is."

"You've had two days and you have no ideas yet?" The disappointment in his voice was patented, vintage Greer.

"It could be any number of things."

"All of them contagious."

"All of them deadly. I'm not convinced it's contagious."

Greer let out an exasperated sigh. "Then you're fighting the obvious. Nine deaths, that's starting to sound like Taos."

"Thirteen."

"Christ! Your report said nine."

"It was nine when I sent the report."

"Kyoko, you've got an epidemic!"

"Yes sir." Kyoko couldn't believe the words herself.

"I'm going to request the island be quarantined."

"I advise against that. Sir."

"Really? Why?"

"Turn on the Weather Channel."

"Hurricane Celeste? That's a non-factor. It's headed toward Mississippi."

"A couple of days ago it was Mexico. Then Texas. Yesterday it was Louisiana. Look, people need to get ready to leave."

"I was once vice-president at Midwestern Allied Insurance, in an earlier incarnation. Do you know how insurance works?"

"By playing it safe?"

"By playing the odds. Right now, the odds say Celeste hits Pascagoula. One in ten says it hits Florida's Big Bend region. That's what you put on one side of the ledger. On the other side, there's a one-hundred percent chance that Brigands Key is in the throes of a deadly contagion. I'm quarantining the island."

"Yes, sir."

"You need to back me on this. Play ball and I'll make a few phone calls into that DC transfer you wanted."

That'll be the day, she thought. "If you say so."

"And if you don't . . ." Greer was silent, letting the unspoken threat hang in the air.

"I have to go," Kyoko finally said.

"I want an update every three hours, day and night, Dr. Nakamura."

Kyoko snapped her cell phone shut and threw it across the room. She sank into her chair, shaking.

Charley sat on the dock, his long knobby legs dangling over the water, idly shooting peanut shells like marbles into the water, where curious sheepshead peeked at and investigated each one.

The sound of footsteps on the wood dock roused him. "Glad you could make it, Charley," Sanborn said.

"Did I have another choice?"

"Not really. I'm past following the rule book."

"That makes me feel so much better."

"Relax, kid. You're on the team now."

Charley kind of liked the sound of that, even if it was horseshit. "What'd you want me for?"

Sanborn pointed at *Electric Ladyland,* rocking gently against her moorings thirty feet away. "I want you to invite me on board."

Charley blinked suspiciously. "Roscoe's not here."

"That's why I want you to invite me on board."

Charley shifted.

"Come on, kid. You write all that crap about vampires. You know a vampire can't barge in uninvited. So invite me."

"Don't mock me, Sheriff."

"I'm not a sheriff. You going to let me on board or not?"

"Fine." Charley stood and strode over to the boat. He paused, thinking. He hadn't actually set foot on board since the last time he'd seen Roscoe. It was the obvious place to look for his boss, yet he'd avoided it.

Sanborn seemed to read his mind. "Don't worry, Charley," he said. "We won't find his body here. You'd smell it a hundred feet away."

Gross, but sensible. Charley shrugged and stepped aboard.

"Permission to board, Captain?"

"Why not?" He stepped aside and let Sanborn pass. "What you looking for?"

"Hell if I know."

The cop pulled on latex gloves, like he was some doctor or something, and tossed a pair to Charley. "Put these on but don't get the idea you can touch anything. When were you last on the boat?"

"Wednesday last week. Last time I saw Roscoe."

Sanborn went aft and studied the powerful twin engines, a pair of German behemoths. "Nice power plant here. How'd Roscoe afford motors like these?"

"He didn't have any girlfriends."

"Good point."

Sanborn expertly popped the hoods, checked the fuel lines. He knew his way around a boat, Charley decided.

"Spotless," Sanborn said. He moved along the starboard side, running his hands over the wood planking, all the way to the bow, down the port side, and back again to the engines. He moved into the small cabin and sat in the pilot's chair, looking about. He flipped a switch on and off. "Quite an array of electronics here."

"The best," Charley said.

"Why the best for such a shitty old boat?"

"Roscoe was like the city kid that drives a two-hundred-dollar car with ten thousand dollars' worth of gadgets in it."

"Male plumage?"

"Not Roscoe. He was always locking up, hiding his gear. He was sure everyone would rob him blind."

"Why the gear then?"

"He figured he needed the best to succeed."

"At what?"

"Treasure hunting."

"He got any gear on board for that kind of thing?"

Charley hesitated.

"Come on, kid."

Charley pointed. "There's a locker on the right side of the cabin."

Sanborn followed Charley's finger and found a padlocked latch. "Know where the key is?"

Charley shook his head.

Sanborn left the boat, went to his car, returned with a

crowbar, and snapped the padlock, latch and all, right out of the splintering wood.

"Breaking and entering," Charley said.

Sanborn shot him a glance and swung open the locker. Inside were several foul-smelling life preservers that may have once been orange. "Nothing," said Sanborn.

"Look under the life jackets."

He tossed the life jackets aside. A stained outdoor carpet lay over the bottom. He lifted the edge up and found another latch. "Clever," Sanborn murmured. Again, locked. Again, in splinters after Sanborn's assault with the crowbar.

Sanborn swung open the door. "Holy smokes," he said. Inside, surrounded by cables and winches, lay a gleaming tube with a nosecone on one end and four fins on the other. "He has a flippin' missile!"

"Side-scan sonar."

"Ah. Side-scan sonar. My next guess. What the hell is side-scan sonar?"

"Like the name says. It's sonar. You hang it over the side. It scans. You look for stuff on the bottom."

Sanborn pulled out a flatter object shaped like a manta ray. "And this?"

"Magnetometer. Looks for metal on the bottom. Ship hulls, cannons, anchors, whatnot."

"He ever use this stuff?"

"All the time. He was always looking for treasure. Fishing came first; had to get in a full day's work, but on the way in from a catch, Roscoe would throw one of these overboard and tow it all the way back to the island. He monitored it from the wheel and tracked the position with GPS."

"Ever find anything?"

"Lots. Nothing worth more than a nickel. The Gulf is littered with trash. Dumped barrels, scuttled boats."

"Did he use this stuff on your last couple of days with him?"

"No. Last time, maybe three weeks ago. Why?"

"This thing, the side-scan sonar. It's got fresh seaweed stuck in it. Still moist. This has been used in the last week."

Charley pedaled his bike two blocks and paused, waiting until Sanborn cleared the corner and was lost to sight. He hurried back to the boat and climbed aboard.

He faked busywork for any onlookers, straightening tackle, wiping down the windows. He worked his way toward the cabin and the compartment that Sanborn had just searched. He opened it, checked it briefly, and located yet another of Roscoe's hidden cubbyholes, this one devoid of hinges or bolts.

Charley opened his pocketknife and slid the blade under the edge of a small steel panel and pried it open. Inside, as hoped, was one of Roscoe's little orange surveyors' notebooks. Charley pocketed it, snapped the panel back into place, glanced about, and started cleaning again, working his way across the boat.

Finding the survey book was a piece of cake. Roscoe hadn't made much effort to keep that out of Charley's sight, once he'd begun to trust him. Now for the bigger secret.

Enigmatic Lady Port.

That was Roscoe's clue to Charley, meant to suggest his boat, *Electric Ladyland*. Something was hidden on the boat's port side.

Charley started at the port bow and cleaned, slowly. He examined every inch, running a finger along every seam, every joint, working his way aft, inch by painstaking inch.

Amidships, where the deck met the side, he found something. A faint line, as fine as a human hair, marked a low rectangle in the deck. In all his hours aboard the *Ladyland,* he'd never spotted it.

He opened his pocketknife and worked the blade into the

joint and pried it up. The wood came loose, revealing a small cavity. Inside was a length of white PVC pipe, an inch and a half in diameter by a foot long. The pipe was sealed on both ends with fitted caps, glued on with a solvent-weld compound. There was no pulling it off.

Charley stuffed the pipe into his backpack and climbed onto the dock. He hopped on his bike and sped home.

He bounded up the steps of the trailer, swinging the flimsy door wide against the wall with a loud slap. He rooted around in the tool closet and found a hacksaw and tucked it into his pants. It kind of hurt.

His mother came out of the bedroom, a worried look on her face. "Oh, Charley. Daddy's not doing well."

He never is, Charley thought. "Get him an aspirin, Ma. I'm kind of busy."

"Charley, I'm scared. Your father's in bad shape. He's caught the bug that's going around. I need you to go get Doc Hammond."

Charley leaned past her and peered into the bedroom. His father lay on his side, the covers pulled high. His chest rose and fell with long deep breaths. He snored softly.

An empty whiskey bottle lay on its side on top of the dresser. Sick. Yeah, right.

"Ma, quit pretending."

"This is different, Charley. He's sick, real sick."

"Ma! Not now!" Charley pushed his way past her and into his room. He slammed the door and locked it.

Outside, his mother started sobbing quietly. Ma, the perennial victim. If the Old Man wasn't doing it to her, she was doing it to herself. In twenty minutes, the Old Man would be old news and she'd be watching *The Beverly Hillbillies*.

He flopped onto his bed, pulled on his MP3 player, and drowned her out with Nirvana. He placed the orange notebook and the pipe on his bed.

Didn't they call this "withholding evidence" or "obstructing justice" or something? Sanborn seemed decent enough for Hooterville, but he'd confiscate the notebook and that'd be the end of it. If it wasn't plain as the nose on his face, all spelled out, Sanborn wouldn't get it. And Roscoe had intended this for Charley, not Sanborn.

He flipped through the book. It was some kind of log of the boat's activities. Strings of numbers filled the pages, Roscoe's own form of intentionally confusing shorthand.

In the upper margin of the first page was a number:

701220-12242

Below it were two columns of extremely long numbers. Each number in the first column was exactly sixteen digits. Each number in the second was exactly thirteen digits. The number of entries in each column was the same, nine in each.

Charley turned to the next page. The numbers were all different than those on the first page, but the ordering was the same. He flipped ahead. Each page was ordered in the same way.

A database.

The only time Roscoe ever wrote in this book was when he dragged out his magnetometer and side-scan radar for a bit of treasure hunting. This could only be the log of his search results. He had recorded more than two hundred searches over the last couple of years, hoping, always hoping. Each search was different, never on the same path. But the ocean is a vast place, and shipwrecks are not easy to find. If they were, we'd all be rich.

Now to crack the code. He returned to the first page and studied the top number, then looked ahead at the top page number of the next page.

702220-12452

He flipped ahead another dozen pages. The number always

began with "70." Then it abruptly began with "80" for the next twenty-three pages. Then "90" to the end of the book.

He returned to the first page.

The year, maybe? Did "70" mean 2007? The digits simply reversed? Charley turned to the last page and studied the top number.

906180-1953112

Charley mentally reversed the first six digits and added spaces to get 08 16 09. August 16, 2009. The last day anyone had seen Roscoe alive. But Roscoe hadn't dragged either piece of equipment that last day. Why was there an entry?

He must've gone out again. At night.

Charley went back to the first page. The date was February 21, 2007. That worked with what he knew; Roscoe had bought his equipment, secondhand, two years before. Charley grinned. This was classic Roscoe. The guy simply entered data in backward sequence. No brilliant encryptions, but as secure in Hooterville as if they were in a bank vault.

Satisfied he was on the right track, Charley studied the second part of the top number over a number of pages. If it were an entry of time, it almost made sense. On every page, the number (in reverse) always began and ended with either "1" or "2." It began about ninety percent of the time with "2." It ended in "1" or "2" roughly an equal number of times. From experience, Charley knew that Roscoe almost always alternated his use of each piece of equipment. He checked that knowledge against the number and found that it held up.

When Roscoe used the search gear, it was almost always at the end of the work day, not in the morning. So the beginning "2" likely meant P.M., "1" for A.M. And the ending "1" or "2" referred to the equipment used. The remaining three digits, read backwards, simply listed the time.

Charley studied the double columns of numbers. Read from

left to right, they made no sense. Read backwards from right to left, they jumped off the page at him. The columns were coordinates of latitude and longitude, calculated by global positioning, rendered as coordinates. The latitudes were all in the 29th degree, carried out to fourteen decimal places. Longitudinal readings were all west of the 83rd degree, carried to eleven decimal places. Accurate to within feet. If there was a hit, a note was scribbled in the margins. *J* for Junk. *SB* for Sunken Boat.

The last few entries were recorded the day of Charley's last trip out with Roscoe. Their coordinates covered a very small area, and there was a single notation, an X, next to the very last number.

X marks the spot.

Roscoe had found something. He had returned to the island. And he was never seen again.

One piece of the puzzle, solved. Charley knew where to look. The pipe would fill in the rest.

He tried once more to pull the glued cap ends off the pipe, without luck. He placed the pipe on the floor and drew the hacksaw blade carefully against it, scoring it all the way around. He began to saw, slowly and deliberately, careful not to cut deeper than the thickness of the pipe wall. He cut all the way around the pipe, lay the hacksaw aside, and twisted the cut halves apart.

Inside was a roll of laminated sheets of paper. He pulled them out and lay them on the bed. There were dozens of pages, each filled with line after line of typed, scrambled letters. Gobbledy-gook, like Roscoe's Caesar shift message.

Charley opened his notebook to a clean page and copied the first line into it. Then he wrote the complete alphabet on two lines, the second one with the alphabet shifted over to start below *R*. The R-shift code. This was going to be a snap. He started to decipher the code.

It didn't work. After a dozen letters, he still had nonsense. Okay. Roscoe wasn't going to be that easy. Charley started again, shifting to *N*. Maybe Roscoe had a shift code for his last name.

That didn't work either.

Charley swore quietly and went to work. After an hour, he'd tried a Caesar shift with every possible start position. None worked.

He tried writing the encrypted words backwards, like the orange book coordinates, and then applying alphabet shifts. Again, no luck.

He made a pot of coffee and settled down with his code book and started at the beginning, applying all sorts of codes to the encrypted pages, one after another.

As the sun rose the next morning, Charley sat back in despair. The pages had resisted every form of code that his little book could offer. Nothing worked.

The key to something huge was at his fingertips, tantalizingly close, but he was no closer to understanding it now than when he started. No discernible pattern peeked out from this scramble of letters.

This was a master code, something built by the very best to fool the very best.

Charley threw the codebook against the wall and picked up his phone and dialed Dr. Grant.

CHAPTER SIXTEEN

Mayor Johnson basked in the warm flickering glow of the Weather Channel, scarcely believing his luck. Celeste had jogged suddenly east and was gunning for Panama City. A Florida landfall was now a hundred percent chance, though the storm was still two hundred miles southwest of the Panhandle. Johnson had ordered an evacuation six hours ago and the governor's chief of staff, a toady by the name of Sara Simmons, had called him within a half-hour with a frantic "What the hell do you think you're doing?" No one else in the whole state, as far west as Pensacola, had done more than put out advisories. Johnson was manufacturing hysteria, she whined, and Governor Crawford was none too happy about it.

Too bad. Crawford hated getting beat to the punch. He figured it was his prerogative to order evacuations, not some small-town mayor's. And now every coastal town from Tampa to Pensacola was scrambling to issue evacuation orders. Johnson's people were mobilized and putting emergency plans into action while other mayors sat on their fat asses, hanging the citizenry out to flap in the gathering wind.

Mayor Ralph Johnson, Visionary. Man of the People. Man of Action. Had a damned good ring to it. Governor Johnson. Now that sounded even better.

CNN had called ten minutes ago and put him on live via telephone. How did Johnson know to act so early? "Just lookin' out for folks," Johnson said in his best down-home drawl.

That CNN spot was big. People knew him now. They had a camera crew on the way even now to put him on the air. They had to know all about the dark dangers threatening this small brave village by the sea. The epidemic, the hurricane. Life was good.

"Mayor, Simmons is on line two again," Faye called.

"Got it." Johnson let Simmons wait for a full minute before picking up. "Mayor Ralph Jack Johnson here," he said loudly.

"Mayor, this is Sara Simmons. We've got a problem."

"No, you've got a problem. I'm moving ahead with evacuation. Got a town to save."

"Put a sock in it, Johnson. Governor Crawford is ordering evacs all up and down the Panhandle coast. You made the right call but we both know it was dumb luck. We know you were up to something, pulling a stunt to get you out of a little political pickle down there in the sticks, but we don't really care. We also know there's little chance of Celeste making landfall as far east as Brigands Key."

Johnson hesitated. "I don't appreciate your assumptions and telling us how to protect our citizens."

"Shut up and listen. Ten minutes ago, the Centers for Disease Control ordered Brigands Key under a quarantine. No one leaves the island. You're to set up a road block immediately on the bridge. The National Guard will have units there to replace your guys within two hours."

Johnson got a sudden, cold stab of fear in his gut. "You can't do this."

"No, we can't. But the Feds can do whatever they want in the name of security. This goes all the way to the top. The White House bought into the CDC plan. No one gets on or off the island until we rein this contagion in. No one. That includes you."

★ ★ ★ ★ ★

Randy Sanborn tested the doors of the old high school gym. The ancient metal doors rattled and shook, but seemed solid enough. That was a delusion. If a storm wanted in here bad enough, it was coming in.

He'd swung by the Gulf to check things out on his way to Brigands Key High. The wind was picking up, whipping the sea into a frenzy, white-capping the waves and blowing the foam off like a head off beer. Any given day, you could count two-dozen boats on the water. Not today. Not a single boat.

When Sanborn got to the gym, Principal Chancy was fretting about uselessly, directing his custodial staff to straighten this or that, with little point to any of it. Sanborn stepped in and took control and Chancy looked visibly relieved. Readying emergency shelters was not Chancy's strength. He was new to the island, new to Florida. From Pennsylvania. A very safe state indeed.

Evacuation order or not, there would be holdouts and curmudgeons vowing to "ride the storm out." Morons. Most had never experienced a hurricane up close and personal. So a sturdy emergency shelter was vital. This gym had outlived most people on the island.

Sanborn kept an ear to the radio while hustling in cots, blankets, bottled water, and a truckload of life jackets, just in case, listening to the forecast while he directed the setup.

"Chief Sanborn," Chancy said, "I'm not an engineer, but I like to know my school."

"An excellent philosophy, Mr. Chancy."

"I was looking at the old school blueprints and surveys a few days ago. The school gym is the highest point on the island, outside of the lighthouse. It's thirteen feet above sea level."

"That's why it's the emergency shelter. The hundred-year storm event is twelve feet above sea level."

"So I hear, so I hear." Chancy still looked a little green.

"It'll be safe in here, Mr. Chancy. No storm in a hundred years here has topped that level."

"Yes, but the Gulf isn't the Gulf of yesteryear. It's hotter and more unstable than ever. Didn't Hurricane Katrina come ashore in Mississippi with an eighteen-foot surge level?"

More like twenty-five, Sanborn wanted to say. But what was the point? Chancy was right.

Sanborn's radio crackled, more static than usual. He unhooked it. "Sanborn."

He was surprised to hear Johnson's voice. As chummy as a little place like Brigands Key was, you just don't use the police band to make calls. Even the boondocks have protocol.

"You ain't gonna believe this, Randy," the mayor began.

Sanborn whipped his Jeep onto Bridge Street, gunned the engine, then slammed it into a skidding stop in the loose gravel at the island foot of the bridge, positioning the car so as to block both lanes. He slid out of the car seat and slammed the door shut.

A quarantine. Unbelievable.

He couldn't believe he'd acquiesced to Johnson. The fool had just ordered an evacuation, ahead of the curve for the first time in his life, but then caved in just like that.

The wind was picking up and the normally placid channel under the bridge was bristling. Several blocks south, fishermen at the marina scrambled over their boats, stowing, battening, tying, hanging extra bumpers over the sides, readying the fleet for the storm. Soon, some would be throwing their belongings on board and piloting their boats south toward Tampa and safe harbors. They'd better get in gear and get going now if they were going at all.

He toyed with the idea of calling Julie and giving her the scoop. He should. Her career was taking a new arc with this mess. She'd love the tip. But knowing her, she'd probably already got wind of it and was on her way over. Yeah, but he'd call her anyway. To be sure.

The Coast Guard already had boats en route to Brigands Key to enforce the quarantine.

What the hell was happening?

The sound of an approaching vehicle interrupted his thoughts. He turned and raised both hands, motioning it to stop.

This was going to be a lot harder than he'd imagined.

Ashley Gray, his childhood sweetheart, pulled up in her rusting Chevy Cavalier, her two little doe-eyed girls, Erin and Amanda, riding in the front seat with her. A silver compact disc dangled iridescently from the rearview mirror. Ashley stopped, cranked the window down as far as it would go, and leaned out. "Randy? What's going on? We're supposed to evacuate."

Sanborn swallowed hard, his throat suddenly very dry. "Change of plans, Ashley. The Feds have placed the island under strict quarantine. You'll have to turn around."

Ashley laughed. "Randy, cut it out. We got a long drive ahead. Going to Jacksonville to stay with the girls' grandma."

"It's for real, Ashley. No joke. No one can leave."

Her smile faded, driven away by sudden fear. "No one leaves? Have you not been watching the news?"

"Yeah. I wouldn't worry too much about it," he lied. "The Governor and the President are in a pissing contest. It'll be worked out in a couple hours. They're not going to leave anyone stuck here in a Cat-4 storm."

"Cat-4? It was just upgraded to Category 5, Randy, and it's turning again! People have to go now!"

Sanborn felt his stomach twist. He hoped to God it was the damn virus coming for him. "I'm sorry, Ashley. Two hours. Come back in two hours. It'll be worked out by then."

"I'm glad it didn't work out between us," Ashley shouted. She shoved the car into reverse and slung gravel backing up. The Cavalier roared off. The two little girls, Erin and Amanda, watched him through the rear window as they sped away.

He wondered if he'd just signed their death warrants.

Sanborn's cell phone chirped. He glanced at the caller's number. His cousin, Vince. Not one to dally, Vince had packed up and got going early in the morning, soon as the evac was ordered. Before the quarantine. Sanborn took the call.

"It's happening, Randy. Sons of bitches."

"You got your family off the island okay?"

"Yeah. We're on Route 19. Seven Humvees just passed us, heading your way."

"Vince, you've done all you can. Hurry on up to Ocala."

"Get out while you can, Randy. In twenty minutes you'll be stuck."

"Can't do that. I'll see you in a couple days, okay?"

"I sure hope so."

Sanborn climbed atop his Jeep and trained his binoculars on the mainland. In a few minutes, the Humvees appeared and spread out along the far end of the bridge. He climbed in behind the wheel and drove slowly across. The Humvees had fanned out across the road, blocking both lanes. Some thirty soldiers were setting up orange traffic barricades and blinking lights.

Sanborn coasted to a stop inches from the barricades and slid out of the vehicle. The soldiers hurriedly donned surgical masks. A young Guardsman hurried toward him, his palm upraised. His insignia identified him as a lieutenant. "Close enough, sir."

Sanborn kept coming. The lieutenant swung his M4 carbine about, directly at him. "I said that's close enough."

Sanborn stopped. The kid was nervous, a bank teller turned

weekend warrior. Best not to extend his nervousness to his trigger finger. "This is my jurisdiction, son," Sanborn lied. As police
chief, his jurisdiction ended at the Brigands Key end of the
bridge. These guys didn't need to know that. "The hell do you
think you're doing?"

Two more Guardsmen hurried to the young officer's side,
flanking him, guns ready. He looked relieved. He was younger
by a good ten years, and ill at ease with command. "Homeland
Security has ordered this sector under strict quarantine," he
said. "We're here to enforce it, sir."

"Who are you, Junior?"

"Lieutenant Louis Fisk, sir. Florida National Guard, 53rd
Infantry Brigade." Fisk puffed up with resolve. There was no
doubt why he became a Guardsman. A chance to do something
big that didn't involve getting blown up in a desert.

"You guys are a political football. You know that?"

Fisk didn't answer. Doubt flickered in his eyes.

"There's a bitch named Celeste on her way," Sanborn
continued. "And you're going to trap an island full of people."

"Sir, Hurricane Celeste is expected to make landfall near
Port St. Joe."

"The situation changes by the minute, Fisk. Celeste has
turned due east. Are you under orders to sit in your truck at
seven feet above sea level when she hits with hundred-and-fifty-
mile-an-hour winds and a twenty-foot storm surge? Are you
happy knowing you've trapped a thousand people on the island?"

"Sir, I'm assured that the storm will not strike here."

"Fine." Sanborn climbed back into his Jeep, switched on the
engine. "Self-sacrifice is a noble thing. Heroic. But take my
advice; get your men out of the area by tomorrow morning.
After that, it may be too late." He looked the other Guardsmen
in the eyes. "You may strongly want to consider desertion or

mutiny at that point. Junior here has no right to order the deaths of civilians and his own troops for a false cause." He gunned the engine and sped away.

As he reached the Brigands Key end of the bridge, a movement to the south caught his eye. He stopped to watch. A gleaming white boat, a seventy-five footer emblazoned with the bright red band of the Coast Guard, purred around the end of the island and into the channel. It cruised slowly up the length of the channel. Seven crewmen, all armed and wearing body armor, studied the small town. Their eyes met Sanborn's.

The boat continued north, passing under the bridge to the end of the island, and stopped. Two more boats appeared and growled slowly up the channel. One came about and took up a position fifty yards from the dock. The other set up at the southern tip of the island.

They were small craft, probably rushed up from the station at Yankeetown. Rumor had it that a seriously armed cutter was speeding up from St. Pete.

A rush of noise startled him. Overhead, an Army helicopter swooped past, a mere two hundred feet above. It sped over the island and began a long circle out over the Gulf. Two more choppers came in low and fast, settling into broad circling patterns over the north and south ends.

Brigands Key was cut off. No one could get in. No one could get out.

CHAPTER SEVENTEEN

Kyoko pushed open the door of the little restaurant and stepped inside. It was eight at night, but still hot and bright outside and her eyes took their sweet time adjusting.

The level of conversation dropped a few decibels.

Feeling a little uneasy, she scanned the room for the remotest and smallest of tables. She spotted it, a little square Formica thing with two chairs, and made a beeline, pretending to not see the sign that commanded all to please wait to be seated.

She was famished and a bit light-headed from hunger and heat. At least, she hoped that's all it was.

She took a seat at the table and pushed the other chair away with her foot. She quickly spread her notebooks and papers all over the table. Anyone not getting the message that she didn't want company was dense indeed.

And in walked Grant.

He came straight over and pulled the ejected chair back to the table. "Mind?" he said, sitting before she could answer.

Kyoko glared. "Apparently not."

The waitress, a young, pretty brunette, glanced at them. Grant nodded to her, smiling. She topped off another customer's coffee and swooped in on them.

"I've been here a couple weeks now," Grant said. "My advice; whatever the catch of the day is."

"That'd be flounder, mister," the waitress said uneasily.

"Flounder for the both of us," Grant said. "And a couple of

174

Cokes." The waitress jotted it down with a flourish and hurried off.

Kyoko gave him a sideward look. "Are you always so presumptuous?"

"Only when I'm right. Trust me on this one."

"I'm kind of busy here, Dr. Grant."

"Carson. I know you're busy. You've quarantined the whole damned island."

"That wasn't my doing. And if you hadn't noticed, I'm stuck here too."

"I noticed and that's why I've decided to help."

"I doubt you can help with forensics and epidemiology."

Grant gestured at the other diners. "Oh. Right. You've got such a good feel for the locals."

"My approach is calculated, Doctor. Well-meaning people tend to cloud issues and get in the way."

"You don't get out of the lab much, do you?"

"To the contrary. My job takes me all over the country."

"To New Mexico?"

She stiffened. "What do you know about that?"

"Not much. I remember the headlines. Charley Fawcett, now that kid's got a gift for mining the Internet."

"So I'm outed. Here's a little clue. Don't believe everything you read."

"I don't. With what Charley found, some of it internal to CDC, I'd say you were hung out to dry." He leaned in. "Know what? I've been there."

"That's very comforting."

"You don't have the full support of CDC, do you?"

"What makes you say that?"

"You're here by yourself. Hardly a big commitment."

"I like it that way."

"You have no choice but to like it."

175

"CDC field units are spread thin, what with the New Mexico containment. They're breaking a full unit loose for Brigands Key any minute now."

"Waiting for the cavalry, huh? Listen, here's your surrogate team in Brigands Key. Charley and me."

"Hmm. You know what they call unofficial problem solvers?"

"I can guess."

"Vigilantes. Thanks but no thanks. I'll work with the mayor, the chief of police, and the medical examiner."

"Work with them, by all means and by daylight. But you're already running into the logjam that is small-town politics. You need to work both with them and without them."

"Duly noted."

The waitress brought Cokes and set them on the table. Grant watched her go.

"Getting an eyeful, Doctor?" Kyoko asked. "What is she, seventeen?"

"He did a real number on you, didn't he?"

"Who?"

"Your husband. You've got a suspicious streak a mile wide." Grant reached into his hip pocket and withdrew a flask, jiggling it at her. "Vodka. Dinsmoor, of course. I was watching the lass to make sure she wasn't watching us." He poured two fingers of the clear liquor into his glass. "If she witnessed me sneaking a drink she'd be too timid or nice to say anything and she'd jeopardize her job. Now I'm having my drink, no two ways about it, and protecting her employment."

"You're a regular Sir Galahad."

"Lighten up, Kyoko. Have a drink."

She shook her head.

Grant reached out and poured vodka into her glass and pocketed the flask. "Drink, damn it. I don't know how much more of you straight and sober I can handle."

176

Her eyes flashed, but she picked up the glass and took a sip. A bigger sip than planned. The fire of the vodka burned her throat and the heat of the alcohol singed her nostrils. Her eyes watered.

It felt wonderful.

She finished it off and slid the glass toward Grant. "Another."

He obliged, and they got along fine.

"You're uneasy in a small town, aren't you?" Grant asked.

Kyoko leaned back. "Okay, Freud. Yeah. In big cities, too."

"Chip on your shoulder."

"No. I just don't like people."

"I know. That's the chip on your shoulder. Where did you come by it?"

"Naturally. My mother instilled it in me."

"And your father?"

"I didn't have a father." She looked at him challengingly.

He passed on the biological impossibility. Smart move. "Tell me about yourself, Kyoko."

"You already know my history, it seems."

"Yeah, I know written outlines. I don't know *you.*"

Kyoko looked at her drink, finished it, signaled Grant to pour another. "Okay, but not here. Let's go for a walk."

Grant motioned to the waitress and paid the bill. Kyoko gathered up her papers and they slipped out into the warm, salty night. The scent of the sea intoxicated Kyoko every time she inhaled it. Or maybe it was the vodka.

They walked to the dock in silence and took a seat. The breeze blew steadily, rippling the water, and the gold of the street lamps danced on the shivering water. Grant was at ease, comfortable with silence. She envied him for that. She had never been that way, but found that she liked it in him.

"I'm the child of a hibakusha," she finally said. "Know what that is?"

Grant shook his head.

"Hibakusha literally means 'explosion-affected people.' Survivors of the atomic bomb."

Grant whistled softly.

Kyoko touched her earring, jiggling it slightly. "See this? My mother made this earring for me. It's one of a kind. Mother found this pale green stone in the burning wreckage of Nagasaki. The stone is glass, fused from sand by the blast of the bomb.

"Mother was nine when the bomb fell. The city was obliterated. Seventy-five thousand people died. The unlucky survived. Mother was unlucky. Her entire family perished and she was charred, disfigured by the blast of heat. The flesh on her upper arm literally melted off. But she lived. She stumbled alone through the wreckage—there were no streets left—for a day, delirious, near death. Rescuers entered the smoldering city and saved her, removed her to a nearby town. She was clutching this stone in her hand when they found her.

"And she lived. She grew up in an orphanage. No one wished to adopt a hibakusha. The hibakusha were feared and an unpleasant reminder of a dark time.

"She grew to adulthood, surrounded but alone. In 1955, twenty-five young hibakusha girls, the Hiroshima Maidens, were taken to America. They received cosmetic surgery and were celebrated and both nations felt a little bit better. My mother was not among them. Hibakusha received support from the government, but Mother worked, cleaning floors, to survive.

"One night, the boss got drunk and came to her. She resisted so he raped her and threw her out. No one would take her in. She managed, somehow, to flee to America and I was born shortly thereafter. I was her only happiness in a world that defined her by her ugliness.

"She put everything into me and I was her life. But cancer

caught up to her like it does with all hibakusha and she died on my eighth birthday.

"I grew up in three foster homes. I went to college and med school. I married a brilliant, politically connected physician. He liked the idea of an obedient Oriental wife, but I didn't. And here I am, special operative for the CDC, on assignment in Brigands Key."

"Rumor has it that your ex is not unhappy that you're trapped in a hot zone."

"Word gets around in a small town, doesn't it?"

"It does when you've got a hacker sidekick like Charley."

"It's true; Ted could have gotten me out of quarantine. If he wanted. Greer could have too, for that matter."

"I know."

"How about you? Any significant others?"

"Yes. Everyone. They're all significant."

"You know what I mean."

"Why, Dr. Nakamura, I do believe you're flirting."

"Shut up," she whispered, slipping closer. He pulled her close and kissed her.

A watcher followed at a distance, sticking to the shadows, as Grant and Kyoko returned to Morrison Motel and entered his room. The lights blinked out. The watcher lingered for a moment, then headed down the street.

These two outside meddlers, for all their supposed brilliance, were pretty damned careless, the watcher thought.

Sex was careless, and carelessness made for easy prey.

Grant's cell phone chimed softly, playing "Smoke Gets in Your Eyes." He fumbled for it in the dark, recognized the number displayed on the LED, flipped it open. "Rolando," he said sleepily. "What you got for me?"

Kyoko stirred next to him, rolled over. Her fingers delicately traced lines down his back.

Grant listened intently, reached for a notepad, and started writing quickly, the phone cradled by his shoulder against his ear. He mumbled his thanks and turned to Kyoko. "Rise and shine, sweetheart. Got something to work with." He dialed Sanborn's number. "Meet us at your office in twenty minutes. Call Hammond. We have a lead for you."

Sanborn had coffee brewed and ready when they arrived. Hammond poured them each a cup. Kyoko took a sip, grimaced, and dumped a few spoonfuls of sugar into it.

"Randy's coffee is legendary," Hammond said. "He's been poisoning tourists with it for years."

"No Starbucks here, Kyoko," Grant said.

"I'll survive."

"Down to business. Rolando got back to me. The sample from the nightstick is an ash wood. Rolando knew that the second he laid eyes on it. Each type of wood has its own grain and coloring. This one was discolored from time underwater. Ash is a hardwood, ideal for clubs and baseball bats and such. That was the easy part. This wood is European ash, harvested from the Letea Forest in coastal Romania."

"You got to be kidding," said Sanborn. "How do you expect us to believe you pinpointed its origin?"

"Rolando spectro-analyzed it, scanned the cell structure. The guy's a genius. Then he ran everything he found against his global database of wood grains. His computer has a fingerprint on over ninety thousand wood samples from all over the world. He receives new samples from colleagues every day to expand his database. Identifying the species is easy; finding the home of the individual tree is trickier. The wood records what sort of environmental stress the tree has endured. He could identify a

180

board made from a live oak right here on Brigands Key."

"How?"

"The wood would exhibit traces of the salt content in the air and ground. It would pick up minerals from the soil. It would exhibit a grain typical of long growing seasons. It would show the stress of constant sea breezes.

"This truncheon was made from a Romanian ash tree, probably in 1940."

"He sees all that in the grain?"

"No. He's brilliant but not psychic. He emailed his results and photos to a dozen European military historians. This truncheon was manufactured for the Wehrmacht, the German Army. Romania joined the Axis Powers in 1940 in the hope of avoiding Hitler's wrath and army. The Romanian government supplied him with resources and raw materials for the war effort. Including wood. Including this piece of wood. This was shipped to a plant in Germany for fabrication into a truncheon. The hole down length of the club was for the insertion of an iron rod, to give it a lethal weight. The iron has completely rusted away. The plant at which this was constructed was also used in the manufacture of other weapons. It was bombed into oblivion in an Allied air raid in 1942. So this one was made between 1940 and 1942."

Sanborn whistled. "I need to get out more," he said.

"The wood is in such good condition," Hammond said. "Mint condition, almost. It can't have been in the water very long."

"False assumption," Grant said. "Wood can be preserved a lot longer under water than in the air. If fungi can't get at the wood and survive, the wood doesn't decay much. There are dugout canoes that have been found buried under silt in rivers, canoes thousands of years old."

"This wasn't buried under silt," Sanborn said. "It was laying on the sand bottom."

Grant thought for a moment. "Yet it wasn't just deposited. It's been there a long while." He held up the club. "The iron rod that filled this club is gone, rusted completely from contact with saltwater. That didn't happen overnight."

Julie Denton squinted, trying to focus on the mock-up she'd just finished for the morning paper. She rubbed her eyes and glanced at the clock. Oh what the hell, she thought. She was exhausted. If the paper didn't arrive at the doorstep, it wouldn't really matter. She was going to be on the air.

CNN wanted her live in twenty minutes.

So did ABC, CBS, NBC, Fox . . .

America wanted the story and she was the only person that could give it to them. She had to script it, deliver it, and shoot it, all by herself.

The National Guard was keeping the networks well away from the island. She was the only journalist in the whole world with access to the hottest story in the nation. Yesterday, she was nobody. Today she was the plucky voice of the damned.

The Bigs peppered her with anxious, breathless questions. Any leads on the killer? Will the standoff between the mayor and the governor and the President lead to violence? How many have died in the plague? Are the terrorists behind it?

What if Celeste hits?

Broadcast journalism. What a kick. She was out of her element with it but figured she could pull it off. She would write her piece, rehearse it once or twice, set up her web-cam in front of the frothing Gulf of Mexico or the damned Coast Guard boat and deliver it. The island didn't have a TV station, or even a radio station, but she could email her reports directly to CNN. They'd be airing it globally five minutes later, after making sure she didn't drop any F-bombs. Then she'd start working on an angle for the next report due an hour later.

The happy irony stung. She'd been dying to get off this sand-pile and move to a real paper. Now she was stuck on the sand-pile and was the hottest journalist on the planet. Christiane Amanpour would die for this gig.

Of course, Julie thought darkly, so might I.

The next story . . .

The mayor had his shot. He'd puffed up like a blowfish and came off like one. It was good look-at-the-small-town-politician stuff for the networks. Johnson thought he was working it. Julie knew better. She wouldn't let him make a mockery of himself again. Sure, he was a small-time windbag. But he was a small-time windbag with a penchant for screwing up colossally. She wasn't about to let him make Brigands Key look foolish, or worse, like it deserved this nightmare.

The next story . . .

CBS had dug up dirt. Carson Grant, it seems, had a checkered past. A rising star in the academic world at one point, he'd managed to get his closest friends and colleagues killed on his last expedition to Guatemala. No one believed his story. And here he was, neck-deep in death once again. Bad luck seemed to follow him.

Or maybe he brought it with him.

The next story . . .

Nakamura was a piece of work, too. Something didn't add up. Like Grant, bad luck seemed to follow her. Misdiagnosis in New Mexico. Seventeen people dead as a result.

The next story . . .

Celeste was plunging ever more eastward . . .

The single most critical moment in the history of Brigands Key was upon them and instead of the cavalry riding in to save the day, they got the Four Horsemen of the Apocalypse.

183

CHAPTER EIGHTEEN

There was no big chain supermarket on Brigands Key, and most of the island's residents drove thirty miles inland every week to shop for groceries. Charley's mother was no different. But Friday morning was different. No one could get off the island. She sent him hurrying over in the Chevy to the island's tiny general store to buy whatever he could to get ready for the hurricane.

The Island Mart was pretty much picked clean by the time he got there, the shelves nearly empty, like the sun-bleached bones of a rat. Mister Faraday was putting up plywood on the windows. "There's a box of Snickers bars behind the counter," he told Charley. "Take what you want. And you'll find a few batteries and a case of bottled water. Take it and get your folks over to the gym, son. This is going to get bad."

Charley nodded, mumbled his thanks, and collected the items into a box and headed for the door.

"Just a minute, Charley," Faraday said. He disappeared into his storeroom and returned with three bright orange life jackets and stuffed them into the box. "Don't know if these will help, but they sure can't hurt."

Charley drove back home. His mother burst from the house as he pulled up and ran to the car, her eyes glistening behind tears. "Charley, come quick. It's your father."

Charley jumped out of the car and bounded up to the house and to his parents' bedroom, his heart suddenly racing.

His father lay unmoving in a pool of vomit, his eyes open, glazed. Charley ran to his side. Trembling, he reached out and touched his father's face. He was warm. Charley felt his neck for a pulse. Finding none, he listened for breath.

He leaned back, tears welling in his eyes, and reached for the phone to call Doc Hammond.

His mother came in, cried out, and threw herself onto her husband, sobbing uncontrollably. "Why'd you let him die, Charley? Don't you care about nothing but yourself?"

Hammond hurried over to collect the body of Ben Fawcett. The door was open and he rapped once and let himself in. Charley was sitting at the dining room table with his mother, his arm around her. She was shaking. Charley nodded to him and waved him toward the back room without getting up.

Hammond felt for a pulse and a breath, but he knew at a touch that Ben Fawcett had been dead for a half-hour. Within two minutes, Hammond had assured himself that Fawcett was certainly another victim of the illness that was killing Brigands Key. He decided not to question Charley's mother about the illness. That was too much for her to handle.

He went back to the dining room and sat with Charley and Phoebe Fawcett for a few minutes, quietly consoling her. He tapped Charley on the shoulder, motioned him to follow, and went out onto the front lawn. "Be right back, Ma," Charley said, squeezing her shoulder gently.

The kid was red-eyed, taking it hard. "Charley, I'm really sorry. Are you going to be okay?"

Charley nodded slightly. "Yeah. I don't know."

"Charley, I need you to be strong right now. We've got a real problem here. The Brigands Key Plague killed your father. I'm supposed to take his body and autopsy him to be sure."

Charley's eyes narrowed. "That's bullshit."

185

"That's the law."

"I won't let you do it!"

"That's what I wanted to hear. I'm not doing it unless you direct me to."

Charley's anger melted. "I don't understand."

"Besides your dad, I've gotten two more victims within the last hour. I'm supposed to autopsy them, plus the six that died yesterday. Celeste will be here by tomorrow morning and we're all trapped on the island. There are a million things to be done and no way we can perform the autopsies and hold funerals before Celeste hits. And if she hits us head on, she may well swamp the island. Best I can do is have the bodies collected in the morgue, but the morgue may be destroyed and the bodies washed out to sea. That's unacceptable. So here's what you do. Take your dad to the cemetery and bury him yourself. You've got a family plot. Right now. We'll worry about paperwork if we live to worry about it. I've talked to Sanborn; he's going to turn a blind eye."

Charley glanced back at his house. His mother's sobs could still be heard. "Thanks, Doc."

"That's not all. All this is off the record, especially what I'm about to say." His voice dropped to a whisper. "I'm a doctor. I signed on to save lives, not preside over a parade of deaths. We're under strict quarantine here; a national emergency, they're calling it. But they're not the ones on the ground. I am. And I call it bullshit. Listen to me: whatever it is, it's not contagious. I don't care how you do it, if you love your mother, get her off this island."

He turned and left. He might be looking at a long jail sentence for what he just did. He didn't care. Right is right.

Fridays were supposed to be the good days, Governor Chase Crawford thought gloomily. Days you got the week's crap swept under the rug. This one, however, was turning into a crap-hole. He sat alone in his oak-paneled office, the lights dimmed, watching a flickering CNN newscast on the flat-screen TV on the wall, chewing a fingernail. He never chewed his fingernails. He shook his head, picked up the remote, and switched channels.

Same stuff. Brigands Key was all over the news.

That gal that produced the island mullet-wrapper was everywhere. She was good, too. Pretty and articulate, with a pinch of showmanship. He could use her on his own staff, yet there she was, destroying his career.

She was wrapping up a report on the National Guardsmen posted at the mainland side of the bridge. The unit had swelled to over a hundred soldiers, fanning out from the bridge to intercept any potential breaches by boat. Denton wondered aloud if the National Guard was there to account for any failures by the Coast Guard at intercepting boats.

She was there with a dozen locals, all looking angry and scared, confronting the Guardsmen, shaking fists, yelling. Children crying. The Guardsmen, looking worried, unsure of the mission. Denton even got one of them, some asshole lieutenant named Fisk, to admit he never signed up to imprison his countrymen. Great TV.

How had this happened?

He punched the intercom. "Sara, get in here."

Sara Simmons got in there in two seconds. She'd damn sure better. It was her damned advice that got him into this mess. "Are you seeing this?"

"Yes, sir. Very imbalanced reporting, if I may say so."

"Imbalanced? She's got a monopoly! They air this shit, then the talking heads all get together and tear me a new one. This is the first thing Democrats and Republicans have agreed on since World War II."

"It could be worse, sir."

187

"How could it possibly get any worse?"

"You could be the President."

Crawford stared at the ceiling in disbelief. This is the help you get for paying a public servant's salary. When all this blew over, he was cleaning house. "Sara, don't you get it? The President is who I want to be. I delivered Florida to him in the election. I took his side when he ordered the quarantine. This moron of a mayor, Johnson, suddenly looks like Teddy Roosevelt. I'm on the losing side here."

"I beg to differ. Your position has never been better. The President is taking a major beating. His approval rating has dropped twelve percent overnight. Everyone in the party is scattering from him. So this is how we frame it. Mayor Johnson acted rashly when Celeste was not a legitimate threat. But the plague is real. People are dying. President Rawlings acted cautiously, based on the welfare of the nation. He won't change course on this. The next time he changes his mind on anything will be the first. He's tightening his own noose. You, however, will not sit by and watch your people perish. The situation has changed. Prudence demands action and you will defy the President and stand up for all that is right and just. You are poised to seize the party's banner and hoist it." She picked up the remote and switched channels. The green and yellow swirl of the satellite radar image filled the screen. "Look at this, sir. Celeste has continued to shift. The chances of it hitting Brigands Key have been upped to one in three. It's picking up forward speed. It's strengthened to a Category Five."

"It'll hit in twelve hours. Christ, it'll be the worst disaster in Florida in eighty years."

"It's your chance to shine, sir. President Rawlings has usurped your power over the Florida National Guard and turned them against your own people."

"Yeah. I know. I approved it."

"Under extreme pressure. The President made it clear he was going ahead with or without you. Now you are going to reassert your control over the Florida National Guard. You're going to go down to Brigands Key and assume command. Within the hour. We've got a classic constitutional crisis on our hands, sir. States' rights and all that. You will not stand by and let Tom Rawlings trample the Constitution."

"I like it. But what if I go there and the Guardsmen refuse to submit?"

"Weren't you watching? Those guys are practically begging for a way out of this gig. They want no part of it. You'll give them the excuse they're looking for. It's a slam dunk."

"And if CDC is right? If we evacuate the island, we'll be dumping a shitload of misery on the whole country."

"If that's happening, it's already happened, but I'm hearing it's not a real threat. People were coming and going on daily business before the quarantine was set, yet no one is reporting illnesses breaking out in nearby towns. A hundred fled the island before the quarantine. Homeland Security is rounding them up. You win on all counts. And while the President spins down the toilet, you become Chase Crawford, patriot and savior."

Crawford drummed on his desk for a moment, watching the television. The hurricane swirled on the radar. It looked like the vortex swallowing his administration, his career.

He'd committed one misstep after another in this debacle. His options were few.

And then it hit him. His shot at the White House was not in seven years, as his grand plan had dictated. It was here and now.

He turned back to Simmons. "Get the convoy rolling and get some National Guard vehicles here. And get me some rain gear. Something in olive green, or camo. Army issue. And a side-arm. It's time to start looking like the future commander in chief."

Simmons beamed. "Everything is ready and waiting, sir."

CHAPTER NINETEEN

Julie Denton snugged her raincoat tight and stepped out into the street.

A squall line, precursor to the main event, lashed the island. Celeste's eye, a beautiful cobalt blue circle in the photos of monitoring satellites, was still a hundred miles west, whipping the coast with long strands of wind and rain. Low-flying clouds raced overhead, hurrying toward that eye, slinging rain as they went.

Brigands Key was battening down. The thudding of hammers and the sounds of saws came from everywhere. Ignoring the rain, men, women, and children were in storefronts and yards, working feverishly, hanging storm shutters and boarding windows with plywood. Those that had missed out on plywood were tearing apart scrap wood and metal and nailing it over windows.

Nearly everyone wore a mask. A surgical mask, a dust mask, or just a bandana tied over the nose and mouth. Few spoke.

Once in a great while, the petty squabbles of the island were forgotten. No one cared whose dog crapped on their yard, whose kids were caught smoking pot on the dock, how much City Council wasted on fireworks, what immoral books the library was stocking. Once in a great while, even the dying fishing industry was forgotten. Once in a great while, fear ran rampant through Brigands Key.

This was one of those times, only a hundred times worse.

This bordered on panic.

Brigands Key, forsaken.

The powers-that-be were going to pay dearly for what they were doing to this little town. Julie swore that she was going to live and carry out that promise.

Her excitement at being at the epicenter of the news universe had waned, replaced by frustration and growing anger.

Hemingway had unleashed his fury in print on an uncaring bureaucracy decades ago, after Matecumbe Key was devastated by a hurricane. That rage was in response to simple bungling and mismanagement. This time, an active war of egos and stupidity was consigning a whole town to death.

She stepped onto her porch, shook off the rain, and fumbled with the key in the door.

A hand gripped her shoulder.

She jumped and spun about, swinging a fist wildly.

Randy Sanborn dodged the blow. "Whoa, Julie," he said. "I called out but you didn't hear."

"Christ, Randy," she snapped. "I nearly pissed myself."

"Can I come in?"

Her eyes flashed. "Let me subdue my cardiac arrest first. Damn, man."

"Sorry," Sanborn repeated. "I just need to talk."

Julie stiffened, and relented. "Come on in." She shoved the door open and stormed in.

She looked in the refrigerator and pulled out two bottles of beer. "Drink up. Live for today. Tomorrow there won't be any power, maybe for weeks."

"Sorry, I'm still on duty," Sanborn said, taking the beer, twisting the cap off, and taking a long drink.

Julie laughed. "Don't worry. Your sudden dereliction of duty has missed the deadline for my next paper."

"Julie, things have spun out of control."

"Tell me about it."

"Anything you can do to help will be invaluable."

"What do you think I can do?"

"I need you to stop reporting the news."

Julie stared at him. "Randy, you're out of line. The news is what I do."

"I know. You're fantastic. But now you can do more. I don't need you to report the news. I need you to be the news."

"That's crossing a journalistic line."

"This is no time for professional ethics. You need to choose sides."

"Which one?"

"You know that already. You're worried about the food in your fridge going bad. That'll be the least of your problems. You won't have a fridge by this time tomorrow. You won't have a house. No one will. And we won't get the chance to hang someone for this unless we get off this damned island before the shit hits the fan."

Julie's head sank. "I know, Randy."

"Johnson's in over his head. You know as well as I do he's not smart enough to get elected dogcatcher outside this town, and yet he's got his eyes on the governor's mansion." Sanborn shook his head, incredulous. "And he's actually in the right for once. But he's losing us. Someone else needs to step in. That someone, Julie, is you."

She looked up at him, her eyes wide. "You've got to be kidding."

"I'm not. I've talked to Hammond and Grant about this. They agree. Your time in history has come. Your face is on every TV and computer monitor in America. Your stories are holding the nation spellbound. They want you. And the people here *need* you."

"They're getting all I've got."

"Wrong. You haven't even scratched the surface. You always were too big to be defined by this town."

"What do expect from me? A rebellion on live TV?"

"Pretty much."

She rolled her eyes. "Randy—"

"No, listen. So far, you've captured both hearts and minds. You've shined a light on the fear and the stupidity engulfing our predicament. You need to go a step farther. You need to force the issue. Confront the quarantine head on and dare them to enforce it."

"And what are the chances of my succeeding?"

Sanborn hesitated. "The National Guard is being pulled in multiple directions. They're under strict orders and regular army units are on their way to take control. Could get dicey."

"What are my chances, Randy?"

"Fifty-fifty at best."

Julie took a long drink from her beer. "I don't like it one bit. Why don't you go get shot up? You're the law."

"I'll be right there with you. Broadcasting you live to the nation."

Julie set her beer down and moved over to the battered upright piano. She took a seat, stretched her fingers. "I need to think it over, Randy." She placed her fingers lightly on the keys and began playing. "Für Elise" never failed to crystallize her emotions and thoughts into one.

"Julie, there's no time."

"A half-hour. Please."

"Fine. I'll—"

He stopped in mid-sentence. Julie glanced at him. He stared past her, at the top of the piano. Dozens of family members—a few living, most dead—watched over her when she played, from photos framed in polished mahogany, displayed across the top of the old upright.

She stopped playing. "What is it?"

Sanborn stepped closer, picked up one of the old photos, peering at it closely. He held it for her to see. "Who is this in the photo?"

"These pictures are all of my family. Why?"

Sanborn switched on his radio and raised Jackie at headquarters. "Get Hammond. We're coming to see him in ten minutes."

Sanborn banged on the door, shaking it in its frame. He kept banging until it opened.

Hammond peered out. "Chief of Police Randy Sanborn," he said. "Shocker."

"Don't mind if I do," Sanborn said, pushing past him. Julie Denton followed. She pulled a small picture frame out from under her raincoat, wiped it against her denim work shirt, and tucked it under her arm.

Kyoko Nakamura stood and stretched, her face pale. Sanborn knew that neither Hammond nor Nakamura had left the lab in hours.

"Jerry, we got something," Sanborn said. "Fetch John Doe."

Hammond glanced at Julie. "We have a bit of an urgent situation here, Randy. If this is just so Lady Sound Byte can crank out another media gem, you can forget it."

Julie's eyes flashed. "Bring him out, Hammond. I can identify him."

"She's never seen the corpse," Sanborn said. "It's high time she did."

Hammond sagged, as though someone had opened a valve and let air escape. "Sorry, Julie. I'm a bit on edge."

"Just get the body."

"Follow me." Hammond led them into the next room.

The chill struck Sanborn and he shivered. Eighteen bodies, zippered in bags, lay wherever a space had been cleared. Never in his career had he seen more than two bodies in here at the same time.

Hammond motioned toward the bodies. "Randy, you know what'll happen to this lab, right? And to these bodies?"

"We can't worry about the dead anymore. Except this one. If we're ever going to identify this guy, it's now. He likely won't be around tomorrow and if he is there won't be any power to keep this room cold."

Hammond went to a corner isolated by a hospital curtain. He yanked the curtain aside. Like the others, the body was zipped up tight in a bag. "An autopsy is not a pleasant thing, Julie. I'll open his bag to the neck only."

"That's all I need."

Hammond pulled the zipper. John Doe lay there, as fresh as the moment he arrived.

Julie gasped. She looked from the man on the slab to the picture frame she carried, and again to the man.

Sanborn leaned closer. "Can you—?"

Julie nodded. "It's Andy Denton."

Sanborn studied the man's face and then Julie's. The resemblance was striking. Her brother? But she was an only child. Or was she? Every family had a skeleton in the closet. Maybe she had a brother no one on the island knew about.

Hammond looked from the corpse to Julie and again to the corpse. "I'm very sorry. Was he a cousin? A nephew?"

"He was my grandfather."

"But he's . . . he's almost a boy," Kyoko said.

Hammond sat heavily on the lab stool, staring at the body. "Incredible. But it makes sense. I knew deep down something was out of whack—way out of whack—with this whole case. Now I feel like a damned genius."

"Grandpa Denton," Julie said. "He was only twenty-one when he died. Or disappeared, I should say. His death was never confirmed. Until now."

"You're sure this is him?" Sanborn asked. "This could be a relative you haven't met."

Julie shook her head. "It's him. I have albums full of old family photos. I have one of him holding my dad when Dad was a baby. It was taken two months before Andy disappeared."

"When was that?"

"May 1945."

"Maybe you better start at the top."

Julie drew a deep breath. "Andy grew up in Chiefland. His folks moved here in 1931. His father, Daniel, thought commercial fishing might be a steady income during the Depression, and if it wasn't, he could at least catch fish for the family to eat. He found something better than fishing, though. Rumrunning. He was a bootlegger during the Prohibition and did all right. Daniel had introduced Andy to all aspects of the family business at an early age. In 1933, Prohibition was repealed and everyone was happy. Except the bootleggers. The family sank into poverty when that source of income dried up. Fighting between my grandfather and great-grandfather escalated. The war came and Selective Service called Andy up in 1944 when he turned twenty, but he bombed out. 4-F. Diabetes and flat feet. A double-whammy. They worried he could drop dead at any moment, and if he didn't drop dead he wouldn't be able to run twelve miles on those paddles he had for feet. Andy wondered what the big deal was; he wanted to go to war to kill or be killed anyway, and diabetes and flat feet had never stopped him from working twenty hours at a stretch. The Army disagreed. That wasn't easy on a young man at that time. Health issues or not, if you weren't in uniform, people looked at you funny. Andy met my grandmother and they married. Dad was born four months later."

"Didn't waste time, did they?"

"Nope. And then one day my grandfather and great-grandfather were out on a fishing trip and just never came back."

"Were they caught in a storm?"

"No. Perfect weather. And they were old salts by then and had worked in gale-force winds without a hitch. But neither they nor the boat were ever seen again."

"Well, your grandfather was murdered," Hammond said.

Sanborn scratched the stubble on his chin. "Any theories circulated back then?"

"Of course. Lots. It's a small town. Nothing official was ever decided, other than fishing mishap, but no one bought it. There was talk that Andy hated his new role as husband and father and people figured he would just up and leave one day. He threatened to. Andy never got on too well with his father after he washed out of the Army. Daniel was real old school and figured something was wrong with the kid. Really wrong, and he let him know it. The rift grew. The rumor went around that Andy went a little crazy and killed his own father and then took off in the boat. To Cuba, maybe."

Sanborn faced Julie, forcing himself to speak softly. "Is there a chance Daniel killed Andy?"

Julie's eyes burned him with the sudden guarded heat of family secrets. "No. I don't know. Families murder the ones they love first, don't they?"

The lull that followed the first squall line was short and temperamental and soon vanished. As dusk gathered, a second squall raced in, a train of charcoal clouds slicking the streets. Gusts buffeted Sanborn's Jeep as he drove Julie back to her house. She was quiet on the way. When they arrived, he swung out of the vehicle and hurried to her side and put his arm around her, shielding her against the rain. She didn't resist and leaned into him. His body felt warm and strong. A port in a storm.

"What we talked about earlier," he said. "Will you do it?"

She hesitated. "Lead an insurrection? Get shot to pieces?" She turned to look him in the eyes. In the failing light, they were points of gold, full of passion. She suddenly knew. "My family has a history here," she said in a small, calm voice. "I'm the good Denton, the good girl from the questionable family, the good girl that keeps her nose clean, does her job, stays out of trouble. I think it's about damned time all that changed."

CHAPTER TWENTY

Darkness fell hard and early Friday in the shadow of the approaching hurricane. Lieutenant Louis Fisk leaned against the Humvee, sheltering against the breeze and a light rainfall, trying to light a cigarette. At last, the tip glowed red and he puffed it into life.

His initial unit of seven Humvees was up to ten, with ten more fanned out along the mainland coast, watching for any movement off the island. At the bridge, crossbucks now barred the roadway, with half a dozen klieg lights lighting the area like day, powered by a pair of roaring generators. Two more floodlights swept the channel in both directions. The troops were in full combat gear, body armor and all.

And gas masks. His men all had gas masks dangling from their necks. They hadn't even used the masks when he was in Iraq.

What a screwed-up mess this was.

He'd lived his whole life in Florida and had seen some bone-rattling weather, but this monster had him worried like no other. You got out of the way when a hurricane came, even a run-of-the-mill one. You don't sit there in the path of a Big Nasty, hoping for the best, hoping it turns aside.

Sergeant Jennifer Stokes climbed down out of the cab and came to join him. "Not good news, Lieutenant," Stokes said. "Brigands Key looks more and more like the bull's-eye for Celeste."

"Damn it. Okay, get Captain Garcia on the radio. I want directions."

"But we heard from him only two hours ago."

"Just do it, Stokes! Two hours is forever in this situation."

Stokes trundled off unhappily.

Fisk took another drag off his cigarette.

That hick cop was a jack-off, but he was right. Fisk was standing guard over doomsday.

He and his men had turned away folks ever since they took on this rotten post. Three-dozen families at least. The first were meek and compliant. They turned with little argument and slunk back home. Since then, they'd been more and more frequent, more and more belligerent. Anger and desperation were stewing.

His stint in Iraq had shown him that kind of mix. Frustration had a knack for festering. After Iraq, he'd had enough of the Guard. Finish out his stint, no more re-ups. Yet here he was, with an M4 and a gas mask.

A pickup approached over the bridge, its headlights arcing up and lowering as it topped the crest of the bridge. At a hundred yards, it slowed to a crawl. Fisk tossed his cigarette and crushed it beneath his heel. "Stokes, you get hold of Garcia yet?"

"Yes, sir, his secretary is patching us now."

"Give me the radio. I want you down here. Swing the search beam onto that pickup. In their eyes."

Stokes brought him the radio and angled a searchlight toward the pickup. Its beam pierced the darkness, the slanting rain glowing bright within it like meteors. The pickup was one of the big, super-cab ones. A monster Chevy. A real dick-compensator. Great. All they needed right now.

The beam bathed the interior of the truck in white. Inside, squinting and shielding their eyes, were a young man, a pretty young woman, and a little boy standing in the seat between them.

Fisk kept his eyes on the pickup and squeezed the transmit switch on the radio. "Captain Garcia, this is Lieutenant Fisk. Request a status update, sir."

Static crackled on the radio. "Lieutenant, the status has not changed. Stay with your post."

"Sir, people are getting real antsy out here."

"No doubt. But no one gets by you. Understood?"

"Yes, sir. Seems a little extreme, is all. The Guard usually helps people when hurricanes come."

"Extreme? Fisk, listen to me. There is some serious shit going on. This is not Governor Crawford's doing. This is national. The Florida National Guard has been federalized by President Rawlings."

"Holy crap."

"It's a national emergency, Fisk. That bug gets off the island and we got the apocalypse loose among us. No one, do you hear, no one is to get off the island. No matter what the weather does."

Easy for you to say, Fisk thought.

The pickup crept forward slowly, cautiously. At twenty yards, Sergeant Stokes signaled it to stop.

The driver complied.

"Excuse me, Captain," Fisk said, "we've got another family to turn back. I'll stay on the line." Fisk waved at his troops. "Masks on, people. Stokes, keep the lamp on them. Ferguson, come with me." He pulled his own mask back over his face and breathed in the stale air.

They approached the pickup carefully, Fisk with his hand raised high. He motioned the driver to lower his window. The man complied, scowling.

"Sir, you're going to have to turn the vehicle around and

return to the island."

"Like hell," the young man said.

"Sir, this is not a request. Turn the vehicle around."

The man shook his head angrily. "Look, I got a little boy and a pregnant wife here. You got to let us off the island. You got to."

Fisk hesitated. A pregnant wife. Wouldn't you just know it? He became aware of the quickening of his own breathing, ominous in the gas mask. He glanced at Ferguson. The soldier's eyes were watching him intently, judging his leadership. Why was nothing ever easy? He steeled his nerve, drew himself up. "I'm sorry, sir. Orders are orders, and these are from the highest level. Turn your vehicle around."

"No, you don't understand—"

"Turn the damned truck, sir! Now!"

The young guy muttered something under his breath, his eyes burning into Fisk's. He put the pickup in reverse and backed at an angle and turned the truck around. The truck moved slowly back up the bridge to Brigands Key and disappeared over the crest.

Fisk pulled his mask off and blew a sigh of relief. The seal of the mask was moist; he'd been sweating heavily. He nodded to Ferguson and they plodded glumly back to the roadblock. Fisk picked up the radio. Garcia was still there. "Captain, this is frankly an unworkable situation."

"Maybe so. But that's not for you to worry about, now is it? You'll carry out your orders to the best of your ability or I'll have you court-martialed. Got it?"

"Yes, sir. I'm just expressing my concern for my men."

"We've got regular Army moving down from Pensacola, Lieutenant. A whole battalion. I don't want them shoving us aside because we can't handle a job. I—"

Garcia's lecture was drowned out by the roar of a gunned

engine. Fisk spun about, looked out at the bridge.

The pickup, its headlights switched off, had turned and was speeding over the bridge straight for them.

Stokes swung the searchlight back onto the pickup. In the cab the young driver squinted into the light, his face clenched with fury. His wife and son stared ahead with wide, terror-stricken eyes.

"Crap," Fisk shouted. "Ferguson, fire a warning shot!"

Ferguson fired a short burst into the air. The truck raced ahead, ignoring the gunfire. Fisk pounded on the lead Humvee. "Everyone out! Positions!"

Three Guardsmen poured out of the Humvee and deployed to the side.

The pickup accelerated. Its headlights flashed suddenly on, high beams. Fisk squinted against the sudden bright glare.

The pickup couldn't possibly squeeze between the Humvees, couldn't blast them out of the way without destroying itself. Fisk glanced at the ends of the bridge. There was only one way past, a narrow gap between the lead Humvee and the guardrail on the south lane of the bridge. The driver planned on crashing through the guardrail at that point and banging off the front of the Humvee onto the shoulder of the road. A massive truck with four-wheel drive might just be able to pull it off. There was no time to shift the Humvees and close the gap.

"Ferguson, disable the vehicle. Shoot out the tires."

Ferguson shook his head, lowered his weapon.

The Chevy bore down, gaining speed. There was no time to spare. Fisk raised his M4 and fired.

Bullets struck the pavement below the Chevy. Sparks flew off the concrete. He drew careful aim, fired again.

The pickup's front tire exploded, rubber flailing out and away from the vehicle. The truck swerved crazily, first one way, then another. It slammed into the concrete guardrail, shattering it, throwing chunks of concrete spinning into the air. The truck broke through the guardrail and plunged over the side.

And then it was gone.

The sound of a great splash reached them. Fisk ran to the shattered rail and peered over.

The tailgate of the pickup was all that was visible. With a hiss of bubbles, it slipped under the water. Red taillights glowed and sank.

Oh God oh God oh God . . .

"Ferguson, Stokes, get down here!" The Guardsmen stripped off their masks, jackets, and shirts, cast aside their weapons, and plunged into the water, headed for the truck.

Fisk swam to the foaming bubbles that marked the point of the truck's descent. In the dark water the lights still glowed.

He drew a deep breath, steeled his nerves, looked under . . .

Below, through the rear window of the cab, the little boy stared upward, screaming in silence, his eyes wide with terror. Eyes that sank like knives into Fisk's soul.

His stomach lurched and he vomited.

Kyoko stabbed the buttons on her phone and waited impatiently through the ringing of the phone at the other end. She glanced at the clock. It was late, but with a national crisis on their hands, Greer had damned sure better be at work.

His secretary answered. "I'm sorry, Dr. Greer is in a very important meeting at the moment."

"Interrupt it. I don't care who he's with."

"Dr. Greer flew to Washington and got there an hour ago. He's meeting with the Secretary and the President as we speak. It's of the utmost importance."

"Don't you think I know that? I'm caught in the middle of the thing and I've got the inside view they need. Get him on the line, Roberta. Now."

Roberta hesitated. "Let me see what I can do."

Kyoko tapped her foot anxiously. She heard a door open and turned to see Grant and Hammond enter. She motioned them to take a seat.

Roberta spoke again. "Go ahead, Dr. Nakamura."

Greer's voice came on the line. "How are you, Kyoko?"

"I want to know what the plan is."

Greer snorted. "Very well. The quarantine will go forward."

"You can't do this to us!"

"Calm down, Kyoko. I might add that I'm with the President and you're on speaker phone."

"Good. He should hear this. You're making a huge mistake. This town is exploding. Three more have died, fifteen minutes ago."

"We understand. That's why we're containing the problem. The virus cannot be allowed to reach the mainland. Our computer models . . ."

"These three were a young family. A fisherman, his pregnant wife, and their little boy. They died when their truck went off the bridge. When the National Guard shot at them."

"Oh Jesus." It was the President's voice. "Are you sure?"

"You'll see it on CNN any minute now. Julie Denton is leading a march across the bridge, with cameras rolling, as we speak."

"Oh Jesus. Okay. Ron, get to work on that. Pre-emptive press release. Regrettable loss of life, difficult job, accidents under stress, that sort of thing."

"Already on it, sir," Ron said.

"Dr. Nakamura," the President said, "thanks for the heads-up. These things have a way of biting you in the ass. Well done."

They don't get it at all, Kyoko thought. "When are you going get us out of here, Mr. President?"

There was a pause, a murmur of voices. Greer spoke. "Dr.

205

Nakamura, you know the situation. The threat to the nation is real. No one leaves the island."

"We're all going to drown!"

"Doctor . . . Kyoko, listen to us. We might be dealing with a Biosafety Level 4 virus. The worst of the worst, and as yet unidentified. Our computer model shows a viral plague this infective, once it crashes into the human population, could leave twenty million Americans dead within a month. If the mortality rate is only 10%. So far, we have no real idea what the rate is. Suppose it's 50%? Then we could be looking at 150 million dead in the U.S. alone, and a total collapse of society. And there's no way of knowing if it'll run its course or just keep spreading and killing. Weigh that against a thousand dead on Brigands Key. Do you want the deaths of 150-million on your head?"

"Paul! Listen to me! It's not viral. It's environmental."

"And you base that conclusion on what?"

Kyoko hesitated. She didn't have a good answer, but she knew she had the right one. "Instinct, sir. This isn't behaving like a virus."

"Nor like a poisoning, which is what you want to believe."

"Doctor," the President said, "you can appreciate the gravity of the situation. My experts tell me the chance of Celeste hitting you is less than fifty-fifty. She'll make landfall about forty miles north. You'll get some nasty weather but nothing you can't get through. I've directed FEMA to move units into place on the mainland. Bio-containment is our first priority. CDC and USAMRIID are mobilizing field hospitals and labs, and a Navy hospital ship is being deployed from Key West. As soon as the storm passes they'll be moving in to assist."

"There won't be anyone left to assist."

"The decision's been made, Doctor."

"The decision is wrong. Governor Crawford is on his way

here to say so himself."

"Ron, what the hell is she talking about?"

"I—I don't know, sir . . ."

"Guess Crawford didn't let you know," Kyoko said. "He's going to re-commandeer the Florida National Guard and abandon the quarantine. He's going on CNN to tell the nation that you've usurped states' rights."

"Like hell he will," bellowed the President. "He can't de-federalize the Guard. That's executive privilege. Ron, get that son of a bitch on the phone."

"Right away, sir."

"Damn, Tom," Kyoko said. "You've got a full-blown constitutional crisis on your hands. Bet you didn't count on that. Paul, are you sure you want to be tied to this sinking ship?"

"Careful, Doctor," Greer said.

"Have it your way, Paul. Mr. President, I sensed something was wrong down here and I had to sneak in to be allowed to investigate. Now that we know something is wrong, Greer is overreaching. He bungled Taos and I took the blame. He's bungling this and I'm taking the blame. He's a panicked little man and he is refusing to take less than draconian measures. We're being sacrificed to his stubbornness."

"Young lady," Rawlings said, "I didn't get where I am by second-guessing. You are an officer of the United States government. You have a job to do and you'll do it to the best of your abilities. Do I make myself clear?"

Something in her, a dark ambitious thing she had always pretended didn't exist, surfaced, urging her to succumb, to submit. To say yes. She wavered, faced her fear, her ambition, and seized the thing and ripped it to pieces. Her voice lowered, laced with rage. "Crystal clear! Now you listen to me. Effective immediately, I am no longer an officer of your government. And when I get out of this, I'm going to do everything in my power to bring you down, you contemptible sack of shit."

She slammed the phone down. She was trembling.

"Wow," Hammond said.

"Shut up. Rawlings never changes course. He's certain of the rightness in everything he does. I may have just made the situation worse. A lot worse. The course of the nation is about to be played out at the foot of the Brigands Key bridge."

On Edge

I never understood history before today. How passions rule and how events change lives and the future.

Now I know.

Shock and rage are sweeping through Brigands Key as I write this. I won't call my town joke names anymore. This is Brigands Key. This is my town. This is home.

You're on the outside watching us and hearing about us. You probably know more of what's going on than we do, but we have a perspective no one else has. I understand what makes history.

Three more died a half-hour ago. Not by plague, not by the hurricane that's about to take the rest of us, but by the hand of our own.

I knew them.

They lived a hundred feet from me in our trailer park. Steve and Dottie Walters and their son, Pete. Pete turned six last week. I went to his birthday party. Mrs. Walters was pregnant. If you haven't seen the news, here you go. The Walters tried to get off the island. The Guard wouldn't let 'em. Now they're at the bottom of the channel.

How did it come to this? Who's calling the shots? Not us. We have no say in our survival. But we're not going down that easy.

If you're reading this, get off your ass and help us. Call your congressman. Storm the White House. Riot in the streets.

Get us off this island.

I've got work to do. The weather's getting worse; I may not get another blog out. I may not be alive in another day. But like I said, we're not going down that easy.

Yours, Charley Fawcett

The fluorescent lights flickered and hummed overhead, bathing Kyoko in an unsteady white. She glanced at her watch, stretched, rubbed her eyes. Bad lighting and long hours had left them bloodshot. Her mind still raced from her little chat with the President of the United States. That was forty minutes ago. She'd had to immerse herself in her work to regain control of her anger.

Ten more minutes, she told herself. Then she'd hurry over to the bridge. She was part of Brigands Key now and would be there when the shit hit the fan. They needed her; maybe the Guardsmen would listen to a federal official. They didn't need to know that she'd just told their commander in chief to go to hell. Or maybe they did. Maybe they'd listen when they found that out. Besides, how much good would she be here? She'd gone over her work again and again, picking it apart, rerunning data. It was wrong. Something was missing, but refused to reveal itself.

Her stomach twitched, again, and nausea passed through her like a wave. She leaned back, closed her eyes, hoping it would pass. She reached for the aspirin bottle on her desk and took two pills, swallowed them, chased them down with a drink from her water bottle. This was no time to get sick. Too much was riding on her figuring this thing out. Yet the illness was almost inevitable. Everyone was feeling it.

She'd begun taking her own vital signs every twenty minutes since she first felt the nausea two hours ago. She needed the most detailed record of every slight change.

She expected a fever. Yet there was none.

She studied the glowing screen of her laptop, toggling the mouse pointer back and forth between tables of raw data and the time graph of incidences. Something was there, begging to be found. But what? What was she missing?

Geography.

She'd not given a thought to the geographical distribution of the incidence of disease and death. Brigands Key was so tiny it didn't seem to matter. A viral plague in such a small, confined area wouldn't reveal its origins through a plot. That only worked at a regional scale. Didn't it? By the time anyone contracted an illness on Brigands Key, they'd have traversed the island two dozen times before the next victim showed signs. And she already knew that a bacterial contamination was not to blame. But a point-source of poison just might show up in a spatial analysis.

She opened the aerial photo, with superimposed street names, on her screen. She highlighted the list of address and dragged them into the aerial and hit enter. The addresses blinked out, replaced by glowing red dots scattered across the aerial, across the island, but clustered ever tighter in one small place.

She stared, dumbstruck. How could she have been so stupid? There it was, the obvious.

She counted off the symptoms she and Hammond had observed. They all pointed to a virus of unknown type and origin but in her heart, she knew it wasn't a virus. The symptoms hinted at another possibility, one of mind-boggling remoteness. But only partly; her new theory couldn't be right if the symptoms didn't all line up like they should. She shook her head, angry, frustrated.

Unless . . .

She reached for the phone and dialed Hammond's number.

"I wouldn't," a low voice behind her said. She spun around and an instant of recognition flashed in her mind before a gloved fist slammed into the side of her face. Her head snapped sideways from the blow and she crashed against the lab table, scattering microscope, racks of slides, and papers everywhere.

Sparks filled her vision and the world tilted crazily. She caught herself and tried to pull herself up.

Her assailant rushed her and knocked her to the floor and was upon her. She lashed out, striking the assailant in the mouth.

"Bitch," her assailant hissed. She was struck twice more and a hand grabbed a fistful of her hair and yanked her head back. The other arm encircled her neck. Pain shot through her neck and throat and her head was forced ever backward. The pressure at the base of her neck ratcheted higher.

My neck is breaking.

She kicked and fought, desperation giving her renewed strength.

The arm tightened around her neck, squeezing her trachea shut, cutting off her breathing. Panic, the panic of airlessness, of suffocation, exploded in her mind.

She heard a distant sharp click. Something glinted in the light. She caught a glimpse of a shiny knife blade near her face. She wanted to scream but couldn't. The knife inched closer and dipped toward her throat. It delicately pressed into her neck. She felt a drop of blood trickle down.

"Don't fight it," a voice whispered. "I could miss."

The knife blade withdrew from her throat and traced a line over her chin and across her cheek. It came to rest behind her ear and lingered there for an impossibly long moment. Then it bit in. Pain overwhelmed her and she struggled, helpless, feeling the razor-sharp blade sink in, feeling it sawing downward through her ear, hearing it, feeling it crunch through cartilage, the sickening sound reverberating in her skull. Warm wetness splashed onto her shoulder and ran onto her breast.

The world became only screaming pain and terror. Darkening, receding, shrinking, dissolving, an old movie fading to black.

Chapter Twenty-One

Grant couldn't believe his eyes. A mob was gathering at the foot of the bridge on the island side, fury building by the minute. Julie Denton and Chief Sanborn were at the forefront.

Denton shouted above the raised voices. "We've collided with judgment hour. Brigands Key perches at the edge of its own death."

Grant spotted Charley with a young girl. The girl was shouting into a cell phone, gesturing futilely.

Grant went to them. Charley looked at him fearfully. "We're in some shit, Doc."

"Tell me about it. Trouble follows me." Grant nodded to the girl. "Who's this?"

"Callie. I met her a couple days ago. She's from Milwaukee, came here to hunt vampires. Now she's trapped and she's telling her folks she loves them, in spite of everything." Charley looked into Grant's eyes. Gut-kick pain haunted the kid's face. "I've fallen for her," he whispered. "And she came here because of nonsense I spewed on the Internet. The kid she came here with died an hour ago. Because of me. Now she's going to die here because of me. I already buried my Dad. I'll probably bury my Mom. I finally found someone to love and I'll be burying her too." His eyes glistened and he wiped them with the back of his hand.

"It'll work out," Grant said, not believing it. "Look at Denton and Sanborn; they're a pair, working the crowd. They're

213

working an angle that'll get us out."

"I won't let her die on my account. I'm taking her out of here."

"Charley, listen. We're in lockdown here. The National Guard and the Coast Guard have both been ordered to use whatever force it takes to enforce the quarantine. They won't let you off the island. The government has panicked and now we've got a governor and a president in a pissing contest. We're stuck."

"I won't let her die, Doc."

Grant's phone chirped. He glanced at the LED screen, saw that he was receiving a text message. Kyoko's name. He pressed a button to accept the message.

Go 2 lab. Urgent. K.

Grant snapped the phone shut. "Charley, I've got to run. Sit tight until I get back. Don't do anything stupid, okay?"

Charley gave a weak nod. " 'Til you get back."

Grant looked at Callie. Beneath the black paint and silver studs, she was a frightened child. He put his hand on her shoulder. She looked up at him, her eyes glistening through the tears. "It'll be okay, Callie," he said. "Charley's strong and more importantly, he's in love with you." She glanced at Charley and nodded, forcing a weak, hopeful smile.

Charley blushed.

Warm yellow light shone through the frosted glass in the door of the lab. Grant rapped on the door. "Got your message," he called, giving her a moment.

No answer.

He pushed the door open and entered.

Papers were scattered on the desk and floor. A waste can lay on its side, its contents spilled across the floor. A desk chair was toppled.

He scanned the room, his heart thudding. "Kyoko!" The

room was empty. The floor was streaked and etched with footprints in red wetness. A bloody handprint smeared the desktop.

He turned and his blood froze.

Stuck into the oak paneling of the rear wall was a human ear, impaled on an ice pick. A tiny drop of blood gathered and suspended on the earlobe, fell, and splashed onto the floor.

Dangling from the ear was an earring of pale green glass.

Kyoko . . .

Grant rushed out into the hallway, looking in all directions, and out of the building. "Kyoko!"

He raced around the building, a complete circuit. It was no use. There was no one in sight.

He ran back into the room. Crime scene purity be damned. He pulled the ice pick out of the wall and cradled the ear, and set it gently upon the desk. He turned on the tap, rinsed the ear off. He tore a handful of paper towels from a dispenser and wrapped the ear and placed it in the specimen refrigerator.

His cell phone rang. He answered.

"Scary, isn't it?" a voice whispered.

"Who is this? Where's Kyoko?"

"Listen and don't speak. You know what I want. You know where to find it. Get it and leave it on the dock. You have until one in the morning. Four hours. That gives you time, but not time to screw with me and get cute. Four hours. Not a minute before, not a minute later. Then drive away. Signal with a boat flare into the sky from the high school and go inside the gym. Succeed and you get your girl, mostly in one piece. Fail and you'll receive another little something to remember her by. Maybe her other ear, maybe her nose. Haven't decided yet. And more pieces for each half-hour you're late until there are no more pieces. Tell Sanborn and she dies."

"I don't know what it is you want!"

215

"You're a smart guy, Doc. You just need a little motivation."

The phone clicked, followed by a dial tone.

Grant felt as if his guts had been torn from his body. He slowly closed his cell phone with trembling fingers. He had no idea what to do, what to think.

And he had just four hours.

The crowd stood at two hundred. And growing. Each passing minute brought more from their homes to see what was brewing. No one wore surgical masks any longer.

Sanborn watched Julie with admiration that approached awe. She'd always had a gift for words but he'd thought it was limited to the written word. She wasn't a particularly gabby person, preferring, like the best journalists, to listen and take notes.

Not this time.

Her thin voice rose angrily above the din and commanded attention. "We're hostages, all of us," she cried. "Hostages to politics, hostages to stupidity, hostages to overblown egos. Well, Brigands Key is well named. We are the blood of ne'er-do-wells, of fishermen, of pirates. We are not of the blood of people that would be hostages. Our parents, our grandparents, wouldn't accept it then and by God we're not going to accept it now!"

Shouts of approval and anger rose from the crowd.

Mayor Johnson ambled up, sweating, his face red. He paused, catching his breath, worked up a broad grin and reached for the microphone.

Julie shoved his hand away.

A murmur ran through the crowd. Power had shifted in Brigands Key.

"Step aside, Ralph," someone cried. "You got us into this mess." Sanborn turned to the voice. It was Frank Walters. Steve Walters's father, the father of the young man killed by the

216

National Guard. His eyes were red and drawn, his face lined in grief.

Johnson raised his palms in a conciliatory, understanding gesture. "Now calm down, Frank. You've suffered mightily today, but you know I'm doing everything I can. My staff has been working long hours toward resolution. We're not giving in."

"Don't bullshit me. I lost a son, a daughter-in-law, and a grandson today. My guts have been kicked in and I got no family left on this planet. Nothing's going to change under your watch. Nothing has ever changed, long as you been mayor, and nothing ever will. As for the morons you call a staff, the hell are they now that we need them? Answer me that. Where's that worthless Clay Abbott? Hiding under his bed?" He paused, and a sob shook his body. He wiped his eyes and looked at Sanborn.

Johnson glanced about, confused. "Clay will be here. You can count on it." He grinned sheepishly, trying to look like he was in charge, failing miserably. Johnson leaned closer to Sanborn. "Get Clay on the damn phone," he whispered.

Walters said, "Yeah, Sanborn, get Clay on the phone. You ain't gonna do anything else here. Only one here with a backbone is Julie."

"Frank," Sanborn said, "I won't pretend to understand the depth of your pain but we've got to go carefully here. We're not holding any cards. Why don't you head home for now. If anything good happens here, we'll come get you."

"I ain't going nowhere and you ain't taking me nowhere."

Sanborn shook his head, flipped open his phone, and dialed Abbott's cell phone. After a half-dozen rings, he got a message that the customer was unavailable. "Not answering," he said.

Johnson swore under his breath.

Principal Chancy arrived, pushing his way to the front of the crowd, with a couple of students in tow, lugging a pair of floodlights and a video camera. A third kid, Tyler Fulton, lugged a gas-powered generator. "Right there," Chancy said, pointing.

Fulton nodded and went to work. The kid's face was slick with sweat, clearly pale even in the dim light. He positioned the generator and turned the ignition key. The generator roared to life and the lights were plugged in, the area bathed in yellow-white.

Fulton slumped heavily to the grass and hung his head, disinterested in the commotion swirling all around.

Sanborn went and knelt beside him. "You okay, Tyler?"

The kid nodded slightly. "Just a little tired from dragging all this junk around."

"I've got the CNN uplink, Julie," Chancy said. "They're ready when you are."

Grant raced across town, cutting across lawns, leaping fences, toward the mob assembled at the bridge. He arrived, gasping for breath.

Things were ratcheting up quickly. Julie Denton was the focus of riveted attention, shouting an angry broadside into the camera and mike held by Chancy. Johnson stood impotently by, opening and closing his mouth silently, as if hoping to get his two cents in.

Denton had the crowd in her hand. Probably had the whole nation in her hand.

Brigands Key was exploding and Grant didn't give a damn. All he could think about was Kyoko Nakamura. Sanborn was with Denton, preoccupied with her and the stirring crowd. He cast about, spotted Hammond nearby, collared him. "Doc, I need your help. Now. Don't ask questions. Where's Charley?" Hammond had a quizzical look, but nodded and pointed. Grant followed Hammond's finger and spotted the kid talking animatedly with his mother and the girl, Callie.

"Follow me," Grant said.

He hurried over to Charley, grabbed him by the arm, and pulled him a few feet away. "Kyoko's in trouble. She's been kidnapped." He quickly explained what had happened, what he'd found. Charley turned pale.

"Good God," Hammond said. "We just saw her less than an hour ago."

"I need your help, Charley," Grant said, peeking at his watch. "In three hours and fifty-two minutes, some goon will start slicing her up and express-mailing her to me in pieces."

"What can I do? I don't have any idea . . ."

"Roscoe found it, whatever it is. Some Goddamn treasure. We know he didn't hide it in his house or on his boat. Maybe it's on the island, but I don't think it is. The killer doesn't think so either."

"Why do you say that?" Hammond asked.

"Because he—or she—has been watching us. All of us. If the killer thought we could get to it that easily, he wouldn't give me four hours. He'd give me a half-hour. He's convinced it's off-island."

Charley's eyes widened. "The coordinates . . ."

"Exactly. You and Roscoe scoped out my spring out in the Gulf. I know the coordinates down to the foot. Roscoe's return trip was close, really close, but not exactly the same spot. I need the exact fix."

Hammond shook his head. "What's the point? You can't get off the island. We're in lockdown by both land and sea. The Coast Guard will intercept you or gun you down before you get a hundred yards. And you can't seriously be thinking of going onto the water in the teeth of a hurricane."

"That's why I need your help, Jerry."

"I'm not liking the direction this is going."

"You're going to like it a lot less once you hear me out."

Charley glanced at his mother and Callie. "I'm not leaving them, Dr. Grant."

Grant saw the pain in Charley's face. He turned toward Hammond. "We can't infect the mainland. That would be criminal. How sure are you this thing is not a contagion?"

"It's not contagious."

"How sure?"

"A hundred percent. We're a political football. The island has been poisoned. It's not contagious."

"Good enough." Grant turned back to Charley. "You love them, Charley. I know that. And this is how we fix it." And Grant told them his plan.

Grant crept from the shadows toward the dock. The Coast Guard patrol boat had moved closer from its earlier mooring and had anchored in the channel a mere fifty yards out. Five seamen milled about on the boat, watching the commotion on the bridge, some two hundred yards to the north. Some had binoculars. Another seaman leaned against the stern railing, keeping an eye southward. His silhouette was black, but a tiny red glow marked the cigarette he was working on.

Grant swore silently. The dock lay in the pool of white light from a trio of overhead lamps. He wouldn't be able to set foot on it with the patrol boat so close.

The crowd was buzzing at the foot of the bridge. As if on cue, Julie strode out onto the bridge. A cheer arose and the entire crowd fell in behind her.

The march had begun.

The Guardsman on the stern flicked his cigarette into the water and said something to his mates, pointing to the bridge. The anchor line was hauled in and the engine rumbled. The boat moved slowly farther out into the channel and turned toward the bridge.

Grant slipped out of the shadows, crouching along a tattered hedge, and ran out onto the dock. His boat, *Lost Expedition,* was moored in slip twenty-eight, near the end of the dock in the least protected spot, one of a handful of slips rented to visitors at an inflated rate. A single lamp lit that end of the dock with a weak light. He reached the boat and slipped quietly aboard. He took a baseball bat out from under the console and knocked out the light bulb with a pop and a show of sparks. He ducked low and watched the patrol boat for a second. No reaction. They hadn't noticed the blown bulb.

He stood and waved. Four figures emerged from the shadows at the foot of the dock and hurried toward him.

One of the figures stopped at slip seven and clambered aboard the giant cabin cruiser moored there. The *Ellie June,* Mayor Johnson's pride and joy. Only it wasn't Johnson that climbed into the captain's chair. It was Hammond. One of only three people on the island that knew that Johnson kept a spare ignition key hidden on *Ellie June,* taped to the underside of the console.

The remaining three reached *Lost Expedition.* Charley helped his mother and Callie aboard. "Ma," he said, "this is Dr. Grant. Dr. Grant, this is my mom."

"Call me Phoebe," Charley's mother said. Her eyes were red and misty.

"Phoebe, Callie, welcome aboard." He handed them each a life jacket. "Put these on. Are you good swimmers?"

Phoebe nodded. "I'm an island girl."

Callie shook her head. Her eyes were wide. "I can't swim."

"We'll do our damnedest to stay afloat. If we go in, don't panic. You can't sink with your jacket on. Just kick toward shore."

The rain began falling again.

A guttural purr sounded. *Ellie June* eased out from her slip. Her running lights were dark. A whiff of oil and gas drifted across the dock.

"Everyone down," Grant whispered.

Hammond guided the cruiser slowly away from the dock and into the channel and headed south. Away from the bridge.

Grant peered over the gunwale, watching closely. The first Coast Guard boat was still moving toward the bridge. So far, so good. *Ellie June* had not been spotted, and drew slowly toward the patrol boat guarding the south tip of the island.

Grant tossed the lines and slipped *Lost Expedition* free of its moorings. The wind was a good ten knots, blowing from the northwest, the backflow from one of Celeste's feeder bands. Grant pushed the boat clear of the slip, hopped back onto the dock, and dragged the bowline southward, orienting his boat. He jumped back on board and let the wind push the boat out.

The engines of *Ellie June* throttled up to a full roar. She rose up on a heavy, white wake and accelerated southward.

Grant's companions eased up beside him, unable to resist the show.

Ellie June rushed headlong toward the patrol boat. A spotlight flashed on and lit the water, illuminating rain like fireflies, and swept in the direction of the oncoming cabin cruiser. The patrol boat's engines sounded to life.

The searchlight found *Ellie June* and she glowed a brilliant white. A distant amplified voice barked out a warning. Still, *Ellie June* rushed ahead, straight at the Coast Guard boat.

The patrol boat swung broadside toward *Ellie June*. Grant focused binoculars on the boat. It was eighty feet long, armed with two mounted deck guns. He counted seven crewmen on deck, each unslinging weapons and assuming firing positions along the gunwale. Two more appeared and stepped behind the deck guns and swiveled them toward *Ellie June*.

Ellie June had one advantage: the bigger patrol boats would lack her maneuverability and would be pinched by the narrow channel.

Another warning echoed across the water. Then, a gunshot and a spray of white, ten yards ahead of Hammond.

To the north, the first Coast Guard boat had swung about. Two seamen were pointing southward, shouting. The boat seemed unsure.

Forty yards from the patrol boat, *Ellie June* swerved hard left, kicking up a high foaming wake, and raced northward.

The southern boat throttled up and gave chase.

"It's working!" Charley said.

Grant nodded. "Keep your fingers crossed." He slid into the pilot's seat and fingered the ignition. *Ellie June* was fast approaching and would pass by fifty yards out, with the Coast Guard in hot pursuit, leaving its assigned post.

The first boat swung about and moved to intercept.

Hammond showed no sign of slowing.

Just a few more seconds . . .

A beam of light suddenly played across *Lost Expedition*.

"Charley Fawcett," a voice called from behind.

Grant wheeled. A burly young man stood ten yards away on the dock, pointing a flashlight. He took a step closer, staggered a bit.

In his other trembling hand he carried a revolver.

CHAPTER TWENTY-TWO

Randy Sanborn hurried to the edge of the bridge and peered over. The crowd turned in the direction of the roar of engines and jammed against the guardrail, straining to see.

At the far end of the bridge, a searchlight swept out over the water from the cordon of National Guardsmen.

A large cabin cruiser zigzagged toward the bridge. Sanborn recognized it immediately.

Mayor Johnson trundled up beside him. His jaw dropped. "Who the hell is stealing my boat?" he bellowed. Not his best moment as mayor.

The patrol boat nearest the bridge revved its engine and swung wide to intercept *Ellie June* but she swerved hard to starboard, drawing the Coast Guard boat with it, and cut sharply back to port, blowing past the accelerating patrol boat. The cruiser raced underneath the bridge, a glowing white wake trailing behind, directly underneath the onlookers. A man leaned out from under the canopy, into the pursuing spotlights, and waved at the crowd with a grin.

"Thanks for letting me borrow your boat, Ralph," the man yelled. "Handles like a dream!"

"Damn you, Hammond!" Johnson roared. "You're fired!"

Hammond flipped him off and *Ellie June* raced northward, the two Coast Guard boats in hot pursuit. At the far north end of the island, the third Coast Guard boat moved into position.

★ ★ ★ ★ ★

Charley looked from the revolver to Tyler Fulton's face, and back to the revolver.

"Kid," Grant said, "what the hell are you doing?"

Tyler shined his light in Grant's eyes. The beam of light quivered. "You think you're getting out?"

"Yeah, Fulton," Charley said. "We're getting out. You're not stopping us."

Tyler swung the beam back onto Charley. Charley's foot felt for the oar lashed against the interior of the gunwale. It would make a decent weapon, with a lot of reach. He might be able to strike Fulton with it if the bastard was distracted. He ran through a mental count of how quickly he could seize the oar and bring it into play. A couple seconds at least. Not promising. Even a moron like Fulton could squeeze off six shots before getting whacked. And Fulton was a very quick moron.

"Kid, you don't want to shoot us," Grant said. "Put the gun away."

Good. Grant was keeping his attention. Charley steeled his nerves. Years-long rage at Fulton and his asshole buddies, at the bullying, the jokes, bubbled to the surface. On three, he told himself, drop and grab the oar and swing it with all your might.

"Think . . . think you can do it?" Fulton asked.

One . . .

"With a lot of luck."

Two . . .

Tyler turned the revolver handle first and extended it to Charley. "Fawcett, man, let me come with you. I'm real sick."

Charley was stunned.

"Charley," Tyler said, "please, man. My aunt died today. I got no other family. And I don't want to die on this shit-pile alone." He sank to his knees and keeled over, clutching his gut, and vomited.

225

Charley felt his rage evaporating. He glanced toward Grant. Grant nodded gently. "Let it go, Charley. It's time to be a man."

Charley looked at his mother and at Callie. He turned to Tyler and swallowed. He climbed onto the dock and took the revolver and handed it to Grant. "We got to hurry, Tyler," he said. "Each second wasted is a second we might get caught. Or killed." He hesitated, and put his arms around Tyler, still hunched over and heaving. "Come on, man. I've got you."

Tyler nodded weakly.

Charley hooked an arm around him and helped him aboard. Turning to Grant, he said, "Let's get out of here."

Grant shoved the boat away from the dock and switched the engine on. The engine rumbled and *Lost Expedition* swung into the channel.

"Keep down," Grant said. "The boats are gone but we don't want to attract attention."

Running dark, with no lights, Grant kept near the edge of the island, skirting the channel. When he was sure he was out of sight of the bridge, he throttled up and raced southward. *Lost Expedition* cleared the lee of the island and storm-driven waves smacked the boat. Everyone aboard stumbled and grabbed onto anything they could find to steady themselves.

"Rough sledding, people," Grant said. A big wave struck broadside, threatening to swamp them. "This is why they issue small-craft warnings." He angled the boat sharply into the oncoming waves and rushed out to sea.

Lost Expedition flew southwest as fast as Grant dared take her, bouncing hard off the waves, jarring everyone with each bounce. After ten minutes, he veered left, southeast, and headed toward the mainland. With the waves at their backs it was like surfing, riding along with long, high waves.

Another ten minutes and the blackness that was the shore loomed ahead of them. Grant slowed, checked his GPS. They were seven miles south of the island.

A pair of headlights blinked on and off twice, a hundred yards ahead. He glanced at his watch. Right on time. Grant plowed ahead toward the lights. "Take the wheel," he said to Charley. "Try not to kill us."

The coast was more marsh, mangrove thickets, and flats than solid land. Grant slowed to a crawl thirty yards from the swamped edge and swung the boat hard about, bow into the waves, and throttled the power to keep them in place. Waves crashed into the mangroves, threatening to throw the boat into the tangle. He motioned to Charley.

Charley nodded and took the wheel with a death-grip. Grant stumbled in the pitching boat to a stowage locker under the cabin and retrieved the rubber raft he kept there. He unrolled the material and yanked the cord. A CO2 cartridge hissed and the raft ballooned into shape.

Grant handed Phoebe a pair of short paddles. "Keep low, keep balanced, and paddle like hell," Grant shouted, lowering the raft onto the churning water. "You'll be there in thirty seconds. My friend Terry is there and will haul you in and take you to Tampa. He'll get you rooms and keep you under wraps until its okay to come out."

Phoebe Fawcett and Callie climbed into the raft. Tyler Fulton hesitated.

"Go ahead, son," Grant said.

"Just a minute," Tyler said. He stumbled over to Charley. Charley tensed.

Tyler held out his hand. "Charley . . . thanks. I'm sorry. I don't deserve this."

Charley nodded. "Better get going, Tyler."

"I owe you."

"Just keep my mom and my girl safe."

Callie and Phoebe looked at Charley, a realization dawning

upon them. "Charley," Callie said, "what are you doing? Get in the raft."

"Can't. Kyoko's in big trouble. I came this far without saying anything because I knew you'd fight me on this."

"Charley . . ."

"It's okay. We have to find Kyoko. I'll see you in a couple of days."

"Charley, you won't be alive in two days!" Phoebe cried.

"I'll come for you, Ma. I promise."

"We're not leaving you!"

"Row for shore, Ma. I love you. Tyler, I need that favor now. Get them to shore."

Tyler nodded, a look of resolve in his eyes. He shoved the raft clear and leaned into his paddle, pulling hard.

Lost Expedition pulled away.

Callie's cries were lost in the rush of wind and water.

Lieutenant Dave Perault leaned close to the cockpit window of the Apache helicopter, wondering if his eyes and the weather were playing tricks on him. A flash of white had been il-luminated by lightning for an instant. Then all was blackness on the sea below once more. Hurricane lightning was rare enough in itself. That it may have found something, out here, in this mess, was almost unthinkable.

"I need video, Adams," he said. "Fifteen degrees south of west."

"You see something?"

"Yeah. Maybe."

The screen flickered and the eerie whites and blacks of night vision danced on the screen. Endless whitecaps of waves rolled across the screen like interference on a crappy old TV.

"There it is, sir. Small craft." The screen image zoomed closer.

"Got it. Criminy."

A small sport boat was heading out to sea, straight into the teeth of the approaching storm.

"They're breaking quarantine, sir," Adams said.

"No shit. What's our range?"

"Two miles distant. They have no idea we're here."

"Take us down to a hundred feet, and two hundred in front of the boat."

"Down?" Adams clearly hated the idea. "We're at five hundred feet already."

"Yeah, down. Take us to a hundred."

"Sir, we can take 'em out from here with the guns."

Perault shook his head. You could always count on a snot-nose to recommend the guns. Snot-noses loved the sheer destruction a 30-mm cannon could wreak. "Take us down. Now."

As if to suggest that it wasn't a good idea, a gust of wind rocked the helicopter. "Shit," Adams said, struggling to correct.

The chopper dipped and banked southwest. "Close enough," Perault said. The little boat plowed through the unceasing parade of waves below them, heading out into the open sea. Waves were coming in ragged, rearing to ten feet, blasting white against the boat's bow, and whitecapping as the wind blew the crests apart.

"I've seen stupid before," Adams said. "This beats all."

The boat lumbered onward. Two men were aboard, and glanced up at the aircraft but made no change in their direction.

"Flash 'em," Perault said.

Adams nodded and flipped the searchlight on and off.

The boat continued on its path, undeterred.

"What should we do, sir?"

"Squeeze off a burst in front of her. That'll get their attention."

Adams swung the gunship around. The ghostly image in the night-vision screen filled with flashes of light as the cannon rattled and spat. The sea before the boat exploded.

The image settled. The boat plowed onward.

"No change, sir. Shall I hit 'em for real?"

Perault watched the screen.

"Sir? The target's not responding to threats. Recommend we take 'em out."

"Adams, when we get back to base I'm going to beat the shit out of you."

"Sir?"

"What made you so damned bloodthirsty? We ain't taking out our own."

"Sir, national security is at stake!"

"Bullshit. I fired across their bow to get 'em to turn back so they wouldn't die. They ain't turning back so they got good reasons, I reckon. They're heading into a hurricane. They're heading into death, and any damned fool could see that. Let 'em go."

"Sir . . ."

"Turn the bird around, Adams. Our mission's done. We're going home."

CHAPTER TWENTY-THREE

Sanborn dashed from one side of the bridge to the other. The *Ellie June* blasted through, kicking up a high wake. Hammond had the engines opened full throttle.

The two trailing patrol boats roared along in pursuit. "No Wake Zones" be damned. Maybe they could be ticketed for that.

The boat to the north arced across the channel to cut Hammond off, but it was hopeless. Short of slamming into *Ellie June* or opening fire, there was little the boat could do to stop her. There was little chance of either happening. Wasn't there?

To Sanborn's horror, the boat opened fire, spitting flames in staccato bursts. Screams erupted around him.

Bullets struck the water in a line of geysers that raced toward *Ellie June*. Hammond swerved east, bullets smacking the water where he would have been a split-second later. He crouched low. *Ellie June* raced toward the mainland, and the northern patrol boat accelerated after it. She was faster than the bigger vessel and separated from it, swinging northwest once more and straightening course.

Heading straight for the patrol boat.

"Oh God," Mayor Johnson murmured next to Sanborn. He was chewing his fingernail. "I'm going to skin Hammond alive and fly his hide from a flagpole."

A hand clamped onto Sanborn's shoulder and turned him. Frank Walters. "They're shooting us again. You gonna do something this time?"

"Frank, calm down. What do you think anyone can do right now?"

Walters turned and stalked away.

Sanborn hurried over to Tommy Greenwood. "Keep an eye on Frank Walters. He's losing it."

Greenwood nodded and edged his way through the crowd toward Walters.

The deck gun of the Coast Guard boat rattled, yellow fire spitting from it. Again, a line of geysers exploded around *Ellie June*. Pieces of the boat flew apart, splintering with the smack of bullets. Still the boat raced onward.

The deck gun spat again and the windows of *Ellie June* exploded. The bow rail leapt upward, fell, and dragged alongside the boat, skimming the water.

"Turn, Jerry," the mayor groaned. "They'll kill you!"

Ellie June closed swiftly, coming apart as it charged into the hail of fire. Still no change in course. Closer, closer . . .

The Coast Guard boat swerved at the last second. The gunner stumbled from the deck gun, but his harness kept him attached and flailing wildly. The gun discharged into the night sky. Tracers flew into the blackness and fell in the distance.

Ellie June blew past the lighthouse and thundered into the rough seas off the north end of the island. The three Coast Guard boats chased her. The gunner on the lead boat recovered and regained control of his gun. He swung it about and took long aim. Fire leaped from the deck gun and the bursts of sound echoed across the water.

More pieces of *Ellie June* flew off, some of them skipping along the water's surface, keeping pace with her.

A flash of light, an explosion, a shock wave. *Ellie June* blew apart, its tanks pierced by white-hot bullets. A deafening roar. Chunks of the boat flew high and fell burning like meteors and crashed into the sea.

Burning flotsam littered the sea, the flames streaking the black water with gold.

Carson Grant leaned into the wheel of *Lost Expedition,* bracing himself against the impact of waves. Rain and ocean sprayed horizontally, splashing his face, dimming his vision, as the boat climbed and fell across tossing waves. He glanced at Charley. In the dark, he couldn't make out the kid's features, but he could read posture. The kid had a death grip on the gunwale and dash.

"You alright?" Grant shouted.

"Time of my life," Charley shouted back.

The bow raised high on a wave, teetered on the crest for a moment, and slammed down into the trough. The impact jarred Grant, running up and down his spine.

He tried to project a devil-may-care spirit but felt far from it. For the hundredth time he cursed himself for such lunacy.

What had he been thinking? Ramming a twenty-four footer straight into the mouth of a monster hurricane? And putting Charley's life in mortal danger bordered on criminal.

Just thirty minutes ago, he'd considered one last time the wisdom of it all just before turning the boat out from the south leeward edge of Brigands Key. Celeste was still miles out at sea, churning for the island, packing hundred-and-fifty-mile-an-hour winds. The leading edge wouldn't hit for another four hours, plenty of time to find whatever the hell it was they were supposed to find. It could be done. *Lost Expedition* had ridden plenty of storms in its day.

Madness. Those storms were thunderstorms, mean sons of bitches to be sure, but kittens against the hurling waves fueled by the coming hurricane.

The boat lifted and slammed down again, laboring forward.

He had the powerful engines open full, but they were making half-speed at best.

But turning back was out of the question. Always had been. Kyoko had just one chance, and that lay with Grant succeeding. She wasn't going to die if he had a breath left to fight for her.

He pushed aside thoughts of what lay ahead in the furious open sea.

He peered at his watch, though reluctant to take his eyes off the pounding waves for even a second. "Give me a reading," he shouted.

Charley wiped the glowing screen of the GPS with his sleeve. "Getting close. Half a mile." He pointed. "Got to correct, ten degrees starboard."

Grant made the correction and felt the impact immediately and nervously. He'd been holding as best he could to a line slightly off straight into the waves, letting the boat pierce them and ride over them. Moving even slightly farther to starboard allowed the waves to crash into the port side. *Lost Expedition* rolled and shuddered.

"Hell of a boat, huh, Charley?"

Charley didn't answer.

"Take the wheel, Charley."

"You crazy? I can't handle this storm."

"Time is of the essence. We're passing my spring right about now, and we're a couple hundred yards from the target coordinates. I want to be ready to go soon as we get there. Take the wheel."

Charley shook his head vigorously.

Grant released the wheel and stepped back. The boat lurched and rolled.

Charley grabbed the wheel and shoved it back, nose into the waves. "Don't do that!"

"You're a natural-born sea captain, kid. You've got to navigate and steer at the same time now. But I got faith."

Charley shrugged angrily away but leaned into the wheel and glanced at the GPS. "Getting close," he grumbled.

Grant peeled off his wet clothes and pulled on a swimsuit. He went to the locker underneath the cabin, dialed up the combination, and removed scuba tank, regulator, BC vest, weight belt, mask, fins, lamps. He moved quickly, trusting in his maintenance of the gear. The tank, the only one he'd kept juiced, had a couple thousand psi, maybe a half-hour's air, if he didn't go too deep. That should do; if he wasn't back in a half-hour, he was most likely already dead.

He shouldered vest and tank on, fitted his belt, pulled on the fins, and took a good spit into the face mask and rinsed it clean. "Ready here, Charley,"

"And . . ." Charley said, squinting at the GPS, "ready here. Right smack dab over the target." He reached for the ignition key.

"Uh-uh," said Grant. "Leave the engine running, throttled way down. The wind and waves will shove you hundreds of yards in minutes without power, and in this storm you'll need to correct constantly to stay nose up into the waves. Plus, boats are finicky; you kill the engine, it may not start up again."

"Comforting."

"Charley, I've got a half-hour's air. Check your watch. After thirty-five minutes, get the hell out of here and go find your girlfriend."

Charley nodded. "What you think is down there?"

"You know what it's all about. Treasure. Gold, silver, jewels. That was Roscoe's passion. This area wasn't on the Spanish Main but pirates plied these waters. Could be a pirate's wreck. Could be a Confederate blockade runner, full of goods bound for England or full of gold back from England. Could be a cargo-hauler. Almost all wrecks have monetary value if you know what to look for. But this can't be just any old wreck, to inspire kidnapping and murder. Roscoe finally found the strike he'd been after, but someone got the drop on him."

"Be careful, okay?"

"My middle name." Grant pulled the mask down onto his face and took the mouthpiece in. He hooked the lamp on his vest and switched it on. He stepped over the transom, seated himself on the dive platform, gave a thumbs-up, and pushed himself off and into the sea.

A wave tumbled him end over end, disorienting him. The tank shifted on his back, throwing his balance further. The regulator hose twisted around his neck. He shoved the tank back, just as another wave rolled him. He had to get below the storm right away or this mission was still-born. He righted himself and kicked hard down into the ink of the night sea.

Below the surface the waters pushed and surged but were child's play compared to the tempest on the surface.

He became aware of his heart thudding in his chest.

Calm down, damn it.

Grant gripped the lamp and pointed downward. All he could see was blackness, a peculiar clear blackness, with flecks of white drifting and surging through.

The primeval gut-fear of the unknown ran through him. Blackness, water with no bottom.

Down he went, sweeping all directions with the beam of his lamp.

He knew the depth before getting off the boat. Eighty-three feet. A good fifty feet deeper than Grant's Eye. Whatever it was, it rested at the foot of a slope.

The slope came into view. To his right, the craggy limestone plunged into the depths at forty-five degrees. Sea fans clung to it, waving in the currents, and sponges and urchins gave it an otherworldly beauty, brilliantly colored, starkly shadowed, in the glow of the lamp.

He followed it downward.

Forty, fifty, sixty feet. Equalizing the pressure in his head. Seventy . . .

And then he saw it.

He stared in disbelief, forgetting to breathe.

CHAPTER TWENTY-FOUR

The wreck lay on its side, split wide in the belly, its profile as recognizable as if it were a page in a book. The long slender hulk, rusting, covered with growth, torn and gaping amidships, the jutting prow, the tower, the shattered deck gun . . .

A German U-boat.

Grant was a student of ships and the sea. He knew the maritime history of the Gulf of Mexico as well as anyone. This ship shouldn't—couldn't—be here.

He shook himself. This was nothing he'd imagined but this wasn't the time to wonder how it got here.

He kicked down to the U-boat's bow, touched the bent railing that lined its deck. A cloud of white drifted from it. The steel was rotting and coated with the slippery growth of the sea.

He gripped the rail and pulled himself slowly along. Instinct urged him to hurry the hell up, but reason kept his brakes applied. It would do no good to rush through and miss something vital. He paused and surveyed the sea bottom nearby, looking for anything that may have spilled free of the wreck. Finding nothing, he continued.

The deck gun lay half-buried in silt, intact, undamaged save for the corrosion.

He moved on, stunned by the immensity of the vessel. He had thought that World War II-era U-boats were not that big, but this craft stretched into the blackness.

Amidships, the conning tower jutted from the deck. Cor-

238

roded spears of steel—the periscope and antennae—projected sideward from it. Aft of the tower was more weaponry, a two-barreled anti-aircraft gun.

He swam through the spires atop the tower, found the hatch. He tugged at the door. It refused to budge, fused by years and rust to the tower itself. He gave up and moved down the tower to the deck.

There, just aft of the tower, yawned the submarine's death wound.

He shone the lamp into the hole and looked down the length of the hull toward the prop. There were a few small holes but no other breaks in the hull big enough for passage. And only a few pieces lay strewn along the bottom. Not much point continuing to the stern. This was it.

He again shone the lamp into the black gash. The gash was perhaps six feet wide. Inside, shadows danced in light.

Now or never. He pulled himself inside, careful not to snag his gear on the jagged metal.

The interior was a tangle of twisted metal. He peered fore and aft. Submarines were notoriously cramped even in the best of times. When they've been shipwrecked at the bottom of the sea for six decades, they're impassable.

As he wriggled his entire body within, a brown wisp swirled and drifted up around him. Just what he needed and feared most. The wall of the sub below him had silted up. He reached down, fanned it, and put his hand into the silt. His hand sank into the mud to his elbow.

It was a diver's nightmare. Many times, he'd explored submerged limestone caves under Florida, and many times he'd pulled the bodies of drowned divers free. Most had become disoriented in the twisting labyrinths of caves, their disorientation heightened by the clouds of silt they'd inadvertently kicked up, reducing visibility to zero. Lost and blind, underwater, underground. The very definition of terror.

This drowned sub mimicked those conditions, amplified by a hundred, with jagged edges ready to slice him up.

Despair crept into his thoughts. Success was an impossibility. Everything looked the same inside the sub and he still had no idea what he was looking for.

Was Kyoko's kidnapper simply mistaken, simply expecting a treasure-laden merchant ship?

Did U-boats carry valuables? Maybe in movies, carrying the hoarded gold of escaping officials of the Third Reich. But that was Hollywood. Real warships carried weapons of war, provisions, sometimes cargo, sometimes spies. They weren't operated for profit; they were operated for mayhem.

He glanced at his pressure gauge. Sixteen hundred psi left.

He had little idea of the layout of a U-boat, other than generally. The torpedo tubes would be forward, although some U-boats could also fire torpedoes from the stern. Engine rooms would logically be close to the stern and the propeller. Command and control would be amidships, under the conning tower. Right where he was.

He began to pick out details around him that verified the control center. Dials, gauges, and switch-panels, obscured by growth, lined the wall. Grant wiped one gauge clear, exposing the intact glass and needle within. A few words written in German showed through.

He moved along, studying the instruments. He pulled his way around a collapsed section and squeezed through an open hatch.

Jumbled along the bottom were the bones of five human skeletons. Their skulls gleamed a sepia color in the beam of his light. He instinctively recoiled from the bones and brushed against a tangle of pipes. A skeleton, held together by a tatter of rags, fell apart from the pipes and clattered into him. The skull fell against his face mask, loosening it, and sank to the bottom.

Steady now . . .

He shook the bones free, adjusted his mask, closed his eyes for a moment. Claustrophobia, his old inner demon, threatened to take him.

He desperately wanted to remove himself, calm himself, steady his pulse. But the situation forbade it. Put it behind you. Think of Kyoko . . .

He moved on.

His light flickered and went out.

He shook it. It blinked once and went dead again.

He was immersed in total darkness, in a tomb of human skeletons at the bottom of the sea, at night in a hurricane.

Chapter Twenty-Five

Charley fought the boat with all his strength. He'd piloted boats bigger and smaller than this before in bad weather, but this was a whole new level of fury.

The sea morphed and grew with each passing minute as Celeste thundered ever closer. The wind was whipping, not consistent with the waves, pushing him one way while the sea tried to push him another. Plowing ahead from the island to get here was bad enough, but the momentum of the boat had given it stability. Trying to keep *Lost Expedition* hovering over one point in a pitching sea was another thing altogether. He could only run the engine at a low throttle to keep it from moving, while the elements lashed at it.

A sudden strong gust swept the boat's stern wildly, pushing the beam nearly broadside to the waves. He strained against the wheel, forcing it back, just as a ten-footer reared and slammed into the boat. Spray flew into his face and eyes, the salt stinging. He spat, dragged his forearm across his eyes.

The boat heeled over crazily. This is it, we're going over, he thought. He spread his stance wide, gripped the windshield, and shoved the throttle lever forward. He needed momentum or the boat would be capsized with the next wave.

The engine roared and *Lost Expedition* lunged. He regained control of the boat and turned into the next wave just before it struck.

In ten seconds, he moved fifty yards. He had to get back on

point, back over whatever the hell Grant was diving on. He cupped his hand over the LED screen of the GPS to guide him back.

The GPS screen was dark.

Cold fear kicked him in the pit of his stomach. He was navigating blind. He glanced at his watch. Grant would not be back for another fifteen minutes.

Immersed in impenetrable darkness, Grant glanced back in the direction he'd come. Pointless. Light was absent, except for the ghosts of light that played in his eyes and mind.

He was out of reach of the gash in the hull, it being back one compartment. He might be able to feel his way back to it, but that would be exceedingly risky. It had been hard enough picking his way through the tangle of metal with the light.

And even if he could, he would have failed in his mission if he succeeded in finding his way out.

He cursed himself for not having a ready backup light on the damned boat. He slapped the flashlight once. The bulb flickered, died again. He shook it. The light came on.

He exhaled a burst of bubbles, realizing he'd been holding his breath.

He resumed his search. The way grew more treacherous as he neared the aft of the boat. He entered a room of narrow shelves, some littered with bones. The shelves were what once passed for sleeping bunks on the cramped submarine. Men had died in them. The skeletons seemed almost restful, at peace with fate, unlike the twisted jumble of bones in the fore rooms. Those seamen had died in a mad scramble of terror.

Small lockers lined the walls. He pried open one after another. The decayed remains of sailors' personal effects spilled out. From one drifted a framed photo. Miraculously, the photo of a little dark-haired girl, smiling, cherubic, was still intact. The locker and picture frame had combined to protect her sweet image from the corrosion of salt and the invasion of sea growth.

Beyond the bunkroom, he squeezed into another room. His eyes fell upon the sepia collection littering the bottom.

More skeletons.

The port wall above was crowded with heavy steel racks angling inward. Piled below him, below the skeletons, were massive tubes, thick as tree trunks, partially covered in silt. He studied them. Pipes? Cases? He didn't know what they were, but they might be what he was looking for. He scooped aside the bones and gently whisked the silt away. It muddied his vision, but there was no alternative.

He uncovered a tapering end of the top tube. A long, thin blade of metal projected from it. A fin.

It was a torpedo. A pile of unexploded torpedoes.

Just gets better and better, he thought. He eased away.

He shone his light aft. Sure enough, there was a portal for rear-facing torpedo launches.

He was in the stern of the U-boat. No treasure, just death and the machines of death.

He pulled himself forward. Moving through the bunks and control room, he found more small compartments. One was jammed with boxes. That looked promising. He gripped one and pulled it apart. It gave easily. Inside were jars and cans. The foodstuffs of the ship.

He checked his pressure gauge. Eight hundred psi.

Throwing caution aside, he seized box after box, tearing them apart, spilling the contents. Nothing but the remains of what had once been food.

Moving farther, he found a group of heavier containers. He pried one open. Ammunition. By the look of it, shells for the deck gun. Another container yielded smaller ammo, probably for the anti-aircraft gun on the conning tower.

Three hundred sixty psi. Five minutes.

He had to make some educated guesses now. The first was that these boxes would only give up more ammo. He abandoned them and hurried forward.

Another torpedo room, the main one, bigger than the aft torpedo room. More bones. More spilled torpedoes.

No storage crates, no lockers. Nothing.

He returned to the control room. Two-sixteen psi. Three minutes. Not enough time . . .

Think, damn it. You're not going to find a treasure. What's the next best thing?

Information.

He remembered the photo of the little girl, still smiling after six decades under the sea. If that survived, other information could survive.

He scanned the control room. The gauges and instruments were corroded and covered. He found a locker that he'd pried open earlier. Various effects were inside, mostly dissolved. He found a cup, glinting in the beam of light. A tin cup.

Tin doesn't rust.

He took the cup, turned it over. There, stamped on the bottom, clear as the day it was struck, was a phrase. *Unterseeboot-498.*

The name of the vessel.

Suddenly, he felt a straining in his lungs. He glanced at his pressure gauge. Out of air.

He sucked hard on the mouthpiece, drawing another breath, and pulled himself toward the gash in the port wall.

His tank clanged against a steel panel. He heard the groan of metal, and the panel tore loose from its rotted fixtures and crashed into him. A rusted conduit an inch thick speared his thigh, piercing him all the way through, driving him down, pinning him to the floor.

Pain shot through his leg. A cloud of red billowed from the wound, enveloping him.

The lamp flickered and went out.

Charley stared at his watch. Thirty-five minutes. Time up. Grant had ordered him to not wait beyond that.

Worse, he was blind. No GPS. He had a compass, but that meant little, other than that he could find a general direction back to the island. He had lost his bearings. He didn't know where the hell he stood relative to Grant's position. The best he had done was keep the engine churning, the boat nose into wind and waves, guessing and praying that he was applying just the right amount of power to keep her running in place.

The storm was worse now than when they'd gotten here. Celeste was bearing down on them.

A wave reared and crashed over the boat, spraying him, staggering him. He shook it off. The boat pitched as the wave lifted it over the crest and dropped it into the trough. He veered a couple degrees to port, turned back into the wind. Had he drifted in that few seconds? He couldn't know. In this mess, if he wasn't right on point when Grant surfaced, he could miss Grant entirely. A couple more minutes. He'd give it a couple more minutes.

The boat might not last much more than that.

Grant didn't bother with the light. There was no time. He drew the last straining bit of air from the tank.

His leg screamed in pain, and sudden nausea washed through him like a wave. His stomach knotted. Light or no light, the image of his impaled leg was seared into his mind.

He vaguely recalled a medical admonition that impaling objects should not be removed until a doctor is ready to seal the wound. If a major artery is pierced, the object might be the only

246

thing standing between you and bleeding to death.

Moot damned point. He was pinned to the sub wall by a spear of rusty steel, a bug pinned down in a display case. Bleeding to death weighed less on the threat scale than drowning while impaled on the sea floor.

His air gone, he unfastened his weight belt and let it fall to the floor. He tried to lift his leg. Impossibly, the shooting pain grew even worse, and the leg didn't budge.

No time for pussy-footing. He drew his free leg up under him, braced it against the floor, and gripped the heavy panel attached to the conduit. He gritted his teeth and yanked the panel upward with all his might.

He could feel the corroded conduit drag through his thigh, the roughness of it tearing at his flesh, scraping against bone like an inch-thick steel file. His mind fogged, threatening to shut down, to end the debilitating pain. Sparks flashed in his mind. He fought his rising unconsciousness.

His leg came suddenly free. His head struck the wall above.

His lungs craved air. And he was still inside a shipwreck, fourteen fathoms deep.

The rupture in the port side of the U-boat was a few yards ahead. He dragged himself toward it, feeling carefully, fighting back panic. He pulled quickly through the wreckage, not worried about the silt that could blind him. How much blinder can a guy get than one hundred percent blind?

His lungs ached. How close was he?

His right hand ran along the port wall, the skin of his knuckles getting stripped. Suddenly, his hand fell through into emptiness. He'd found the opening. With a kick, he propelled himself through and clear of the wreck of *U-498*. He angled up. His lungs screamed for air. He had none, yet the air in his BC vest would carry him upward.

He pushed toward the surface. Every impulse in his body

drove him to rush upward, to get to sweet air as quickly as possible. With all his will, he fought the urge. If he succumbed to temptation and rocketed for the surface, he'd guarantee himself a mortal case of nitrogen narcosis. The bends. His blood, what little there might be left of it, would literally boil with nitrogen and he would die a slow, wretched death.

Pick your poison, he thought grimly.

And storm or no storm, he was trailing a river of blood that every shark within a mile would soon scent.

Starved for oxygen, his mind began to fog. He couldn't go faster than rising bubbles. How fast did a bubble go, anyway? And he couldn't see a goddamn bubble. He could count . . .

One-Mississippi, two-Mississippi, three-Mississippi . . . four . . .

The numbers were slipping, sliding over a cliff . . . what number was next . . .

Seconds stretched to forever . . .

And then he broke the surface.

He gasped long and hard, drawing air into his body. Cool, delicious air. Life. For an eternity, he gulped air, uncaring about anything but air.

Slowly, awareness returned. He was rising and falling across huge tossing waves. He looked around. *Lost Expedition* was gone.

He was alone on the open, thrashing sea.

CHAPTER TWENTY-SIX

Her mother, disfigured, radiant, stood amid black ruin, a turbulent red sky framing her.

She tried to call out but sound would not pass her lips. She tried to go to her mother but could not move her feet.

Mother raised her arms. Kyoko, my light, my joy. You must find strength. You must. For yourself. For your friends. For everyone . . .

I cannot, Mother . . .

You must come up from the emptiness, my child. You must do it now.

Yes, Mother, I will . . .

Her mother faded into the red and the red became black.

All was blackness . . .

And Kyoko realized she was awake. And as in the dream, though her eyes were open, all was blackness.

With wakefulness came a dull ache in her skull.

She lay still, hoping to let the ache pass. It became a hammering instead.

She tried to sit up and found herself unable to. Her arms and legs were confined. Cords bound her wrists painfully together behind her. Between her teeth, forcing her jaw open, was a heavy cloth, tied behind her head.

She struggled against the bonds, but only managed to spike the pain. Her heart was racing now, sapping energy. She willed herself to relax. She had to think, to assess the situation.

She lay on her side, arms behind her. She became aware that her blouse was open in the front. Her bra was gone, her breasts exposed. She had not been that way before, even right before she was overwhelmed in the attack. Of that she was certain. She realized that her belt was also loose and open. She could feel his filthy hands on her. Anger welled up within her.

The ache in her head worsened, became a sharp localized pain, emanating from the right side of her head. She turned her head and touched it gingerly against the floor in an effort to judge the extent of the wound. She winced with sudden sharp pain, but felt a soft thickness. A pad of some sort was taped over the wound. A bandage, slightly moist. She had no doubt that the wetness was her own blood.

A sudden remembrance chilled her and she felt the bandage again. It was much too flat against her skull. She remembered the terrible pain, the crunch of steel working through cartilage. She stifled a cry. Her ear! The bastard had cut off her ear! Her anger boiled into rage.

Someone would die for this.

Shaking, she forced her rage aside, bottled it. Anger would simmer but letting it consume her would not help. She had to think, coolly and distantly from emotion. She was a scientist. All she could do was gather data about her world and make deductions.

She was on a hard, rough surface. A floor. She moved, trying to understand that little bit of information. Hard, rough. Concrete. No, maybe not. Like concrete. She could feel joints in it. Masonry joints. A masonry floor? That wasn't a common thing. Was it?

The masonry was hard and painful against her body. Hard. Not clean. It felt moldy. It reeked of mold. Mold suggested little or no maintenance of this place.

She had deduced this much; she was being held in a seldom-used place built of masonry.

She listened.

Nothing. Not a sound. Unusual in itself. Must be a solid place, to have no sounds at all. Just the ringing in her own ears. Almost any place you went, you heard something. The hum of appliances, footsteps, car doors, the whisper of air condition-ing . . .

No air conditioning here. The place was hot and muggy, the air stale and dank. A happy home for mold, indeed.

Mortar and masonry floors. Quiet as a tomb. Seldom used. She was getting an idea of her prison. But she needed to test it.

With great effort she rocked backward, onto her back, and brought her legs over, their momentum carrying her over onto her stomach. Bits of litter ground into her flesh. She shifted her weight and rolled onto her side.

With two more complete rolls, she smacked face-first into a wall. The collision stunned her and she relaxed, letting the pain ebb.

She drew close to the wall and faced it. She reached out with her bound feet and touched the wall, and felt it as far in every direction as she could. It too was of masonry. She bent her knees and scooted a few more inches.

She felt the gentle concave curve of the masonry in both directions. And suddenly, she knew where she was.

She was a prisoner inside the old lighthouse. Hammond Lighthouse.

A distant, muffled sound came to her, the first she'd heard. She placed her ear against the floor and listened intently. There it was again, a distant, sharp sound. Something hard against something hard.

A key turning a lock?

A heavier sound. And then a soft, regular padding. Footsteps, coming nearer.

She heaved back away from the wall, and rolled over and over, back to where she guessed she had been deposited.

A rattling, metallic sound, a key turning in a lock. There was a loud click, and the rasp of a heavy bolt being slid.

She ratcheted down her rapid breathing by sheer will. Her eyes narrowed to slits. She pretended to sleep. Her captor didn't need to know she'd learned a thing or two.

A door opened and yellow light poured in. A dark silhouette stood, framed in the light of the doorway. A man. Who, she couldn't tell. All she could see was his silhouette.

He fastened his light on her and stood, silently watching. He took a step closer, stopped. The light flicked around the room briefly, along the walls, across the floor, and returned to settle on her again. Looking at her. Studying her.

Go away . . .

She made a decision; she would feign unconsciousness only up to a point. If he put one filthy hand on her one more time, he was going to pay. She would swing her bound legs together, bringing the force of her knees straight for him. With a little luck, she might even connect with him right in the temple. A well-placed knee to the temple could kill.

She tensed the muscles of her leg and back, readying herself for her one desperate attack.

Grant rose and fell with the growing waves. All about was darkness and wind-lashed water. He shouted, his voice lost in the rush of wind and water.

He shook the lamp, tried the switch on and off. A wave crested and blew over him. He submerged and bobbed to the surface again.

He blew more air into his BC vest. The vest lifted him slightly higher in the water.

The pain in his leg grew. He reached down and touched the wound, and could feel the warmth of his blood escaping into the water.

Charley had gone, just as Grant had ordered him to. Ninety-nine percent chance of that. But that left one percent contrary. That was something. And the lamp was his only hope if Charley was still out there looking for him.

He tried the lamp once more. It failed. He gripped the rubber casing that held the lens plate intact, and twisted. It resisted then began to slip. He carefully unscrewed the casing and withdrew it. He tucked it into his swimsuit and gently tapped the exposed bulb. No response. He twisted it looser, then tighter. The bulb flickered, went out, and came to brilliant life.

"Ha!" Grant shouted.

He held the glowing lamp aloft just as a wave washed over him. He kicked hard with his fins, driving himself higher in the water. Couldn't let this baby short out. The wave rolled past, and Grant quickly replaced the lens casing and screwed it tightly into place.

A wave suddenly struck and tossed him, tearing the lamp from his grip. It sank beneath the surface.

Grant plunged under after it, caught it, and returned to the surface, his heart pounding.

He swept the beam of light all around him, a full circle. He waved it up and down. He zigzagged it across the waves. He shined it up into the rain and clouds, the beam glowing against them. Anything that might attract attention.

He listened intently for an engine.

A sudden movement to his left caught his attention. He spun and aimed the beam in that direction. No boat. An angular black shape cut the surface and disappeared some twenty yards away.

His leaking blood had rung the dinner bell.

He reached down to his lower leg, unsheathed the dive knife he kept there. Puny, worthless thing, but it was all he had.

He studied the nearby water, all the while waving the lamp.

Below the rush of the wind, he heard a low throaty rumble. An outboard engine.

He looked in every direction, sweeping the light.

Two hundred yards away, a black button lifted above the waves. Two tiny lights, one red, one white, blinked above the waves. The running lights.

The boat plowed toward him, rising and falling.

"Yeah, Charley, over here," he cried, waving the lamp.

Something bumped his foot. Something big.

He drew his legs up under him and slashed down with the knife, striking nothing.

The boat drew nearer. A hundred yards now. Ninety.

The bump came again, against his calf. He felt the shark's rough skin, sandpaper, scrape against his skin. He kicked it, his heel making contact. It darted away.

It was a big one, powerfully built. He had a good idea that it was a bull shark, the nastiest, deadliest creature in the Gulf of Mexico.

The boat was fifty yards away.

At forty yards, Grant could see Charley, grinning and jumping up and down.

"Hurry the hell up," Grant shouted.

Lost Expedition rumbled up and Charley turned its beam toward Grant. "Thought I'd lost you, Doc," he shouted.

Grant tossed his light onto the boat and swam toward the dive platform on the transom. Charley killed the engine as Grant neared the propeller, and rushed aft and swung the aluminum ladder out into the water with a splash. Grant reached out, caught the ladder, and pulled himself up.

The shark hit his fin, bit down, and thrashed its head side to side, yanking Grant back down, shaking him like a toy. He was pulled free of the ladder and into the water. The shark headed downward, pulling him under. He stabbed downward with the knife and felt the blade sink into the animal. The shark flinched and released him and darted away.

Grant wasn't going to wait for the fish to change its mind. He lunged upward, caught hold of the platform, and hauled himself out of the sea. "Son of a bitch! Another ten seconds and I'd have been fish bait."

Charley hooked Grant under the arms and pulled him over the transom. He helped him into one of the twin seats behind the dash.

"Easy, boy," Grant said. "I'm a bit torn up."

Charley felt about, found the light, and shined it on Grant, stopping at the blood welling from his thigh. "Jesus," he mumbled.

Grant pointed. "Hand me the first-aid kit. It's right under the console. And so's a bottle of Dinsmoor. I'll need that, too."

Charley fished out the kit and the vodka. Grant took the bottle first, unscrewed the cap, took a hard pull off it, and poured some over both sides of his wound. "Christ, that hurts."

"Find anything, Doc?"

"Son, you're not gonna believe it."

Kyoko held her breath, tensed, waiting, waiting for the bastard to make his move. One shot. That's all she would get. She listened intently, judging his movements.

After an eternity, the man stepped back out the door and shut it. She heard the scrape and click of deadbolt and lock and she was alone in the dark once again. She gasped with relief.

She listened for a minute. Satisfied, she rolled across the floor again. If she had to die here, it wasn't going to be for lack of trying.

Kyoko dragged herself around the perimeter of the dark room, learning all she could, feeling with bound feet, feeling the floor beneath her, searching for weakness. After twenty minutes, exhausted, she sagged and rolled onto her back, panting heavily. Sweat slicked her body and ran into her eyes, stinging.

The room was quite small. It couldn't have been much more than a storeroom when it was in use. She tried to recall what Hammond had told her of the old lighthouse. It hadn't been in active service in years. More recently, it had been kept up as a historic site, but lack of funds had let it sink into a murk of disrepair and neglect.

In the best of times, there was little chance of anyone finding her here. With a hurricane at the doorstep and the island in turmoil, there was no chance. She was on her own.

Something skittered across the floor and brushed against her leg. She recoiled from the rat, kicking in its direction and making contact with the creature. It squealed and darted away.

Her heart raced. She took a deep breath, gritted her teeth, rolled onto her stomach again, and resumed her search, pushing herself inch by inch.

She suddenly felt a sting in her breast, pricked by something sharp. She shifted her weight, easing off whatever it was. She felt a warm trickle of blood on her breast.

She scooted up, bringing her bound hands even with where she thought the object lay, and rolled her back toward it. She settled down and felt about with her hands. After a moment, she found it. She gingerly gripped it between two fingers, dropped it, picked it up again, felt it. It was a shard of glass, no more than an inch long. A glimmer of hope stirred in her.

Her arms straining, she worked the glass upward between her clasped hands, bit by excruciating bit. It sliced the palm of her left hand. The pain was minimal to her numb hands and the wound bled only a little. At last she felt it come into resistance against the thick rope that bound her wrists.

Slowly, a fraction of an inch at a time, the glass lacerating her fingertips, she rubbed the razor-edged shard against the ropes.

Randy Sanborn put his hands on Julie's shoulders and looked her in the eyes. "Sure you're ready to do this?"

She nodded. "Now or never, Randy. Take a look around. The weather is getting worse. Celeste will be here before dawn."

He looked out at the burning wreckage of the *Ellie June*. "Things are out of control. We've got heavily armed troops doing a job they weren't trained for, following orders they don't believe in. They're on edge."

"Let's go," Julie said. She pushed past him and marched toward the mainland.

Sanborn caught up to her and kept pace. "Anyone wants off the island, follow us," he shouted. "We probably won't make it, but it's better than waiting for a Cat-5 to drown us all."

Artie Blount stepped forward. "I'm with you, Randy. Folks, if we want out of this mess, we've got to force the issue."

Sanborn nodded his thanks to Blount.

A murmur ran through the crowd.

"Mayor?" Sanborn said.

Johnson nodded dully and fell in behind him.

"Thanks, Mayor. Don't worry about it. A boat is just a material possession. If you couldn't escape on it, it wasn't going to last another day anyway."

Johnson scowled. "Save the homespun philosophy for your girlfriend."

"You bet. We'll get the taxpayers to buy you a new boat."

One by one, the crowd fell in behind them.

"Think this'll work?" Julie whispered to Sanborn.

"Not a chance. Will you go to a movie with me tomorrow?"

She laughed. "You really should work on your timing, Randy."

"That wasn't a flat-out no. Works for me."

They neared the barricade at the opposite end of the bridge. The National Guardsmen fanned out along the foot of it, gas masks on, weapons ready. Three search beams swung out onto the crowd. Sanborn raised his hand—slowly—to shield his eyes.

When they'd come within forty yards of the barricade, a Guardsman held up a hand. "Close enough, folks." His voice was muffled through the gas mask. "You know you can't come past us."

The crowd behind them hesitated. Julie didn't. She continued straight toward the soldiers. Sanborn stayed right with her. She glanced questioningly at Chancy and his makeshift camera crew. Chancy nodded and hurried forward.

The soldiers shifted nervously. The one that had spoken turned to his comrades and spoke softly. They raised their weapons, pointed them at her and at Chancy.

She stopped ten yards from them. Chancy caught up to her, motioning his cameraman into position.

"You in charge?" she asked, looking at the soldier that had spoken.

"Yes, ma'am. Lieutenant Fisk. You have to turn back now."

"Smile, Fisk. The whole nation is watching you."

Fisk glanced nervously at the camera. "Don't make this difficult, ma'am."

Julie took two steps closer. "Going to shoot me, too?"

"Turn it around, ma'am."

Sanborn stepped forward. "Easy, Lieutenant. We're unarmed. My men and I have left our weapons at the other end of the bridge."

"How do I know that?"

"You can search us."

"Search you? I don't even want to breathe the same air."

"Let us off this island," Julie said. She took another step.

Fisk straightened, held up a hand. "Close enough, ma'am."

A gunshot exploded nearby, from behind and to Sanborn's left. He wheeled. Two more shots came and Fisk staggered and fell, clutching his shoulder.

Frank Walters, his eyes wild, waved a .38 pistol at the Guardsmen. He fired once more. People scattered.

"Frank, no!" Sanborn cried.

Too late. Bursts of automatic weapons fire roared. Walters was spun and thrown backward by the impact of dozens of bullets. His body hit the pavement.

Screams.

Sanborn grabbed Julie and yanked her backward. The crowd panicked and ran. The Guardsmen dropped to their knees, in firing positions.

Fisk writhed on the pavement. A sergeant, a young woman, rushed to his side. Fisk shoved her aside, struggled to a sitting position, his hand clamped onto his shoulder. "Hold your fire," he barked.

Julie pulled free of Sanborn's grasp. "We can't lose our foothold," she said. "If we retreat to the island, we've lost our last chance."

Sanborn nodded. "Chancy, Johnson," he called. The men were crouching nearby. "Over the railing. Bring the camera." Johnson shook his head, backing away. Chancy grabbed him by the collar and shoved him toward the rail. Johnson reluctantly dragged his bulk over the railing, followed by Chancy.

Sanborn and Julie scrambled over the opposite bridge railing and crouched in the darkness under the bridge. His feet sank into the mud. "Stay down," he whispered. "They saw us slip down under here."

Sanborn leaned out from under the bridge, paused, and gripped the steel beam above and pulled himself up. The citizens of Brigands Key were fleeing toward the island. A pair of

Guardsmen stooped over the body of Frank Walters.

A low rumble of vehicles came from the east. "Hold on," Sanborn said. He eased out farther and craned his neck to see.

The lights of vehicles appeared in the distance, approaching. The Guardsmen turned. "Who the hell is that?" Fisk said. "Ferguson, get Captain Garcia on and ask why we weren't alerted to reinforcements."

A dozen military vehicles pulled into position behind the National Guard units and arrayed themselves, blocking the entire roadway and shoulders. The headlights bathed the confused Guardsmen in blinding light.

The doors of the center vehicle opened. A dozen soldiers spilled out and took positions. From another Humvee a handful of civilians climbed out.

A news van, WCMT in Tampa, rolled up. A camera crew leapt out and began panning the scene.

"News media? How'd they get in? They're not allowed past Checkpoint A, a mile back."

Governor Chase Crawford, dressed in camo fatigues and body armor, stepped out of the central vehicle, bullhorn in hand. He glanced at the news crew. He raised the bullhorn to his mouth. "This is Chase Crawford. You men are Florida National Guardsmen. Now listen carefully. This ends here and now. As you can see, I've brought more Guardsmen with me. The U.S. government illegally federalized you. I am hereby removing you men from the command of the President of United States."

Fisk's troops glanced at him. He struggled to his feet, wincing in pain.

Crawford raised his bullhorn again. "I repeat; I am moving you to State command."

"The hell you are," shouted Fisk. He waved to his men. They trained their weapons on Crawford.

The troops that had arrived with Crawford drew aim upon the Guardsmen on the bridge.

Even in the glare of the lights and the gloom of the storm, Sanborn could see Crawford's face turn ashen.

Under the bridge, Mayor Johnson hustled through the mud to Sanborn's side, panting heavily. "What's happening up there?"

"Just a civil war."

CHAPTER TWENTY-SEVEN

Grant lifted his bandaged thigh and studied it in the beam of his dive lamp. The heavy bleeding had stopped, though a trickle seeped out through the red-soaked bandage. Charley, piloting through the churning Gulf, let the boat slam down coming off the crest of a wave. The impact jarred Grant and pain shot through his leg. He winced and grunted and glared at Charley.

Charley looked down at him. "Sorry. Almost there. Coming up on the south end of the island. Smoother water ahead."

"Is the Coast Guard still there?"

"Don't see them. They must be at the bridge or still chasing Doc Hammond."

Not much chance of Hammond still eluding them, Grant thought sourly. Unless they want to be outrun, it isn't happening.

They rounded the tip of the island.

Two of the three patrol boats were nowhere in sight. The third prowled the middle ground between the bridge and the dock, its searchlights swinging across the bridge. One probed the shadows beneath the bridge structure on the mainland side. There was a shout. One search beam swung about and lit the *Lost Expedition*. The patrol boat's engines revved and kicked up a wake and looped toward them.

"Charley, forget the dock. Beach us in the mangroves. Do it now."

"Aye, Cap'n." Charley rounded the tip of the island and

entered the calmer waters. "Hang on." He shoved the throttle forward. The engine roared and the boat shot forward. He turned the wheel and the boat rammed into the tangle of mangroves that lined the south end of the island, snapping the thin trunks and limbs before coming to rest ten yards in.

The Coast Guard boat rumbled in the channel behind them. The searchlights set the mangrove thicket ablaze with light. There was no chance they weren't spotted. Charley flipped a middle finger in the boat's direction.

"We're being chased by angry men with cannons," Grant said. "Was that really necessary?"

Charley killed the engine and helped Grant to his feet. "Can you make it?"

"Got no choice. Let's get going."

Grant sat on the gunwale and swung his legs over the side. Charley hooked his hands under Grant's armpits and lowered him into the muck of the mangrove swamp. Grant tried to catch his weight on the arching roots of the mangrove, but slipped and sank into the mud, knee deep. The pain in his leg surged. He sucked in his breath and dragged himself from the mud and higher into the roots and moved ahead.

Charley followed. In a few minutes of fighting the jungle, they emerged onto the cleared upland that was to become Bay View.

The patrol boat idled just behind. A shouted discussion was taking place aboard it. The boat swept away in the direction of the bridge.

"Something's going on," Charley said. "They've lost interest in us."

"A break at last." Grant looked at his watch. "Let's go."

Grant took two steps and stumbled, grimacing in pain.

Charley hooked one of Grant's arms around his neck and helped him up. "I've got you."

Two minutes' walk netted fifty yards. "This rate," Grant said, "it'll take us all night."

A car approached from the north. "Should we run?" Charley asked.

"I can barely walk. Let's just hope it's on our side."

The car drew near and pulled alongside. The driver's window hummed open and Gerald Hammond leaned out. "Need a lift?"

He parked the Benz, got out, and hurried over to Grant. He swung open the back door and eased Grant toward it. "I saw your boat enter the channel. Cripes, what got into you?"

"Rusty steel pipe. German U-boat."

Surprise lit Hammond's face. "Sounds like a hell of a story. You can tell me about it in my office." He tossed the car keys to Charley. "You drive."

Charley climbed in behind the wheel, keyed the ignition. The engine purred. Charley put it in gear. The car lurched.

"Easy there, leadfoot."

"Sorry." He leaned forward stiffly and the car rolled out onto the street.

"You eluded the Coast Guard," Grant said. "Pretty slippery for a sawbones; I gave you a one in ten chance."

"I'm fine, thanks for asking. You'll find Johnson's boat in the dictionary under the heading 'flotsam.' Nothing bigger than a breadbox left of it." He described the boat chase and the gunfire. "I bailed off the north end of the island just before the explosion and swam underwater a hundred feet before surfacing. Made my way back to the island. I don't think I'll be collecting my Christmas bonus this year."

"What's going on out on the bridge?"

"Not sure. I'm dying to find out but everyone thinks I'm dead. Figured that was some small bit of advantage, so I hid and kept an eye out for you. People were running back to the island."

They pulled up near Hammond's office. "Kill your lights and park on the next block," Hammond said. "I want to stay dead a while."

Charley nodded and passed Hammond's clinic. He parked in a dark lane behind an overgrown hedge.

"We'll use the back entrance," Hammond said. He helped Grant out of the car and they crouched and hurried across the empty parking lot in the shadows.

Hammond passed Grant off to Charley, fished his pocket for his keys, and opened a narrow back door and shut it behind them. He switched on a single light in the rear hall.

"Someone'll see the light," Charley said.

"Nope. Got my hurricane shutters up today. Not a single photon will escape this building." He led Grant into an exam room.

"No," Grant said, shaking off Hammond's arm. "We're running out of time. Patch me later."

"You may not know it but that's a nasty wound you've got there. And you've lost a lot of blood."

"Grab your medicine bag and fix me up somewhere else. We need a computer."

Hammond grunted. "You make a lousy patient. Very well. My office. Second door on the right, Charley. Make him comfortable. I'll be right there."

Charley helped Grant into the room and settled him into Hammond's overstuffed leather chair. He brought up a stool and placed Grant's wounded leg onto it. Grant gritted his teeth against the rising pain. "Boot up the computer, kid. Hurricane's coming and we'll lose the opportunity soon."

Charley nodded and switched on Hammond's desktop computer.

Hammond returned, loaded with medicines and bandages. He eased the fabric of Grant's blood-soaked swimsuit above the wound. "Yow," he said softly. "I'm going to get some industrial painkillers and antibiotics into you." He soaked a cloth with alcohol and gently wiped the leg clean, front and back. He got out a syringe, selected a bottle of anesthetic, filled the syringe, and squeezed out a thin stream of the medicine. "This is going to hurt you a lot more than it hurts me," he said. He pressed the needle into Grant's thigh.

Grant winced. "You weren't kidding," he grunted.

"Computer's up and ready, Prof," Charley said.

Grant reached into his hip pocket and withdrew the tin cup and slammed it on the table. "Souvenir of *U-498*. Google it."

Grant and Hammond crowded Charley, peering over his shoulder at the computer, making him nervous. He hated when people looked at his screen.

Charley had found a website for submarine history buffs. A list of German U-boats filled the screen, bright red against a charcoal background, with sounds of wind and waves accompanying.

"Wow, there were hundreds of them," he said. "Over fifteen-hundred."

The ships were listed numerically. He scrolled quickly down the list. "Here we are. *U-498*." He clicked open the tab and was rewarded with a page full of details.

"Constructed in a Hamburg shipyard, commissioned in 1941. Type IX-C. A long-range Atlantic boat, designed for extended stays at sea, 13,000-mile range. Over two hundred and fifty feet long. Armed to the teeth with fore and aft torpedo tubes, two deck guns, a 105-millimeter and a 37-millimeter; and a 20-millimeter anti-aircraft gun on the conning tower."

Charley clicked on a graphic link. Several photos of *U-498*, in happy times, crew smiling, waving. One taken in rough seas. A painting of a typical Type IX-C boat was included.

"That's what I saw down there, all right," Grant said.

"Damaged in 1942," Charley continued. "Rehabbed, sent back out again. Took part in Operation Drumbeat, the first U-boat assault on shipping along the U.S. Atlantic coast. Says here, *U-498* was credited with sinking thirty-seven ships. Quite a lethal boat."

"Look at this," Hammond said, putting a finger to the screen. "It was attacked and sank off Cape Hatteras, North Carolina, May 1945. That's not your boat, Carson."

Grant waved the tin cup. "I've got evidence to the contrary."

"Maybe that cup was just a supply picked up from another boat."

"I don't think so."

"But the record of the sinking . . ."

"Charley, open this link, about U-boat activity in the Gulf of Mexico."

Charley opened it. "Very active German sub presence in the Gulf in 1942. Lots of commercial ships torpedoed. Says here only one U-boat was sunk in the Gulf, the *U-166.*"

"Open the *U-166* link."

Charley clicked on *U-166.* "It was sunk in 1942 south of Louisiana. The wreck was found in 2001 in five thousand feet of water."

"So history got it all wrong. More than one U-boat was sunk in the Gulf."

"Maybe *U-498* was crippled in the Atlantic and presumed lost, but made its way into the Gulf before dying."

"Charley, what else you got?"

"*U-498* carried a crew of forty-eight on its last voyage. No survivors. The captain's name was Kommandant Friedrich Remarque. Here's his photo." A young officer, with tousled yellow hair and piercing eyes, grinned broadly in the black and white photograph. Charley sat back for a second, puzzled. Something about that name . . .

"What is it, Charley? No time to hold back."

"Remarque. I found a little note in Roscoe's stuff. Simple substitution code. It said, 'CF sacré bleu remark 43.' It was in that book about Colonel Fawcett's disappearance in the Amazon, but Roscoe was being his usual cryptic self. 'CF' was addressed to me, not to Colonel Fawcett. I pulled my hair out trying to figure out what 'sacré bleu remark 43' was. Roscoe was pointing to this guy, Remarque. And 43-something."

"Except Remarque went down with his ship. Any ideas about the '43'?"

Charley shrugged. "None."

"And sacré bleu?"

"Sacred blue. A curse, a bad omen, something like that."

"Remarque didn't go down with his ship," Hammond said softly.

They turned to him.

He tapped the photo on the screen. "Friedrich Remarque. Fred. Crazy Fred."

"What are you talking about?"

"This guy used to live here, on Brigands Key. Died when I was a little kid in the sixties, but I remember him. He was a lot older than the young officer in the picture. Crazy Fred Remarque. Quiet sort, kept to himself. Rumored to be keeping a huge secret."

"Now we're getting somewhere," Grant said. He looked at his watch, shook his head. One hour to go. "What time is Celeste supposed to make landfall?"

"One and a half hours," Hammond said.

"Some son of a bitch planned this to the minute, didn't he? He's letting the hurricane cover his tracks. Did you know Remarque was German?"

"Sure. He couldn't hide that, nor did he try. Said he came to

America to get away from a wrecked continent and start a new life."

"A Nazi?" Charley asked.

Hammond shrugged. "A German. Said he'd been in the army, the Wehrmacht. Obviously, a little lie there. He was navy, the Kriegsmarine."

"Looks like he had a little unfinished business," Grant said. "He came back to salvage the treasure."

"Where did he live?"

"235 Lee Street."

Charley's eyes widened. "That's Roscoe's house!"

Hammond nodded. "Pieces are beginning to fit."

"Did Roscoe know Remarque well?"

"Nobody knew Remarque well. He was a recluse, the kind of guy kids throw rocks at. Hence the name 'Crazy Fred.' "

"But Roscoe bought the place from Remarque?"

"No. After Remarque died, the place sat empty for years, getting more and more run down. It was vacant when Roscoe bought it."

"Well, Roscoe had to buy it from someone."

Hammond glanced at the ceiling, thinking. "The Property Appraiser's website lists all current owners and who they purchased from."

"Charley?"

Charley started typing at the keyboard. "I'm on the case." A moment later he said, "Got the website." A county map of towns and roads appeared on the screen. Charley windowed and zoomed in on Brigands Key, selecting the lot at the south end of Lee Street, the last house before the cleared field that was soon to be Bay View.

Charley clicked again and a table of data appeared. "The previous ownership was corporate. Brigands Key Land Holdings. Rather innocuous."

"Heard of it, Jerry?"

Hammond thought for a moment. "Sounds familiar. Where've I heard that name? I thought I knew everything about this island, certainly every business. This one is low-key."

"We need names, Charley."

"Right." His fingers typed rapidly. "Here we go. Brigands Key Land Holdings, Incorporated. Uh-oh."

"What?"

"It's owned by Mayor Ralph Johnson."

"Wow," Hammond said.

"We need to have a little chat with the mayor," Grant said.

There was flash of light and a crack of thunder, so close it made them jump. The computer screen flickered and blinked off. The lights failed. The world went black.

CHAPTER TWENTY-EIGHT

Julie squeezed Sanborn's forearm. "See that?"

"See what?"

"The island has lost power."

Sanborn gripped the structure of the old steel bridge and hoisted himself up level with the bridge deck and peered through the railing back toward Brigands Key. Sure enough, the entire island was dark. "Celeste has got us in her grip." He turned back to the confrontation taking place just yards away.

Crawford was a wreck, paralyzed, stuck between two armed forces. His hands were raised above his head, trembling. He was babbling.

Sanborn hopped back down. "Now or never, Julie. We've got to get everyone out of here."

Julie nodded. She took a deep breath and trudged out from beneath the bridge.

Half a dozen soldiers aimed at her. She stopped and raised her hands. "Lieutenant Fisk," she called.

The Guardsman, still in his gas mask, turned to her. His arm was blood-soaked and a medic had peeled back his sleeve and was bandaging the arm. "Yeah?"

"It's time to end this."

"Can't do that, ma'am. We're under orders."

"You're under multiple orders, conflicting orders. How do you know which ones are right?"

"I don't. So I'm sticking with the President's orders."

"President Rawlings is not here, now is he? He's safe in the Oval Office."

"Don't matter. He's Commander in Chief."

"Not for long. Sure you want to have your wagon hitched to that horse?"

No answer.

"He's not even your commander. The states have dibs on National Guard units, with the governors each commanding their own. Rawlings has usurped that right. Ever heard of a constitutional crisis? This one's going down in the history books, and your picture's going to be plastered all over the losing side."

"No one gets off the island, ma'am. We ain't letting the plague hit the mainland."

"There is no plague, Lieutenant. This is a poisoning. An intentional poisoning. Murder."

"How do I know that? I'm no doctor."

"Neither am I. That's what the only two doctors who've seen it up close agree on, though."

"That's not the report I got."

"Fisk, listen to me. You've killed four people already today. More are dying because of poisoning. All of us will die if we don't get off this island in the next half-hour. You're the only person on the planet that can prevent a thousand more deaths."

No answer.

"It's time to be a man, Fisk. Governor Crawford is right there in front of you, ordering you to stand down. He wins this in court, you get court-martialed."

Crawford nodded vigorously.

"Why does CDC think it's contagious?" Fisk asked.

"Because they won't listen to their expert on the ground. Because egos have piled on top of egos. Because the President has never been wrong in his life and he's not about to start now. Pick one."

Fisk looked about, confused.

"Heard the latest weather forecast?" Julie continued. "Celeste is packing a hundred and fifty with a hundred percent chance of making landfall on Brigands Key. It's going to shove a storm surge twenty feet high in front of it. With ten-foot waves on top of that. Where you're standing is seven feet above sea level. Do you think you're going to float?"

After a pause, Fisk said, "I'm listening."

"I'm coming over, Lieutenant," Julie said. "Gun me down if you must. I can get you out of this mess." She strode forward. Sanborn followed, both hands raised and empty.

The soldiers tensed, weapons on her.

Julie and Sanborn approached Governor Crawford and faced him. His eyes were panicky.

Julie waved Fisk over. He peeled off his mask and tossed it aside. He had a boyish, serious face.

"Leap of faith, Lieutenant?"

Fisk straightened with obvious, unconvincing effort. "Gonna die anyway."

"Not if I can help it. Fisk, you're cut off from your command post."

"No. We've got contact."

"You don't understand. You're cut off. The storm has caused you to lose contact. You tried your best to get through, but just couldn't. Damned leftover communications gear they expect you to use."

"Ah. Now that you mention it."

"That leaves you to make the call for your side."

Fisk nodded. "Guess it does."

"Yet you have sworn to uphold the quarantine. Governor Crawford, you have a half-hour to evacuate an island. You face the unthinkable, watching your people drown. You have the Florida State Penitentiary in Raiford, two hours away. Maximum security, solid as a rock. Hell, if these folks are sick, the only people that can catch it there are inmates. No political risk. Safe from the storm of the century. Like King Solomon, you solve the quandary. You and Lieutenant Fisk negotiate a deal. You escort the entire population of Brigands Key under armed guard to Raiford. The population is safe; the population is quarantined. You are the man of the hour. The nation will hang on your every word after this."

Crawford's eyes slowly brightened. "It could work. Yeah. Fisk? You on board?"

Fisk studied the Governor for a moment. "Deal."

"It's your show now, Governor."

Crawford seemed to swell in size. He swung to his men. "Lower your weapons. We're evacuating the island."

Fisk slung his rifle over his shoulder and strode toward his own men. "Saddle up!" he shouted. "We got a town to save. Ferguson, I understand the radio ain't working."

Hammond's car slid through a dark turn. Grant, in the passenger's seat, peered through the rain-spattered windshield and spotted the line of vehicles rolling off the bridge onto the island. The convoy loomed suddenly and unexpectedly before them. Hammond slammed on the brakes and the car skidded to a stop a few feet from one of the Humvees.

"Looks like Julie worked a miracle," Hammond said.

"Fall in behind them," Grant said.

A sudden gust caught the car and threatened to push it off the road. "Getting bad out," Hammond said.

They tailed the convoy to the high school. The vehicles circled the campus and pulled up in front of the gymnasium.

Hammond parked near the entrance and Grant swung open the door and ran toward the lead Humvees. Soldiers spilled out of them, along with Principal Chancy, Sanborn, Julie, and Crawford.

A squall line blew in, driving rain sideways.

Mayor Ralph J. Johnson lowered his great bulk from a Humvee and lumbered toward the gym.

Hammond placed a hand on Grant's arm and restrained him. "Easy now."

Grant tore free of his grip and hurried toward Johnson, his nausea and punctured leg fighting him every step. He grabbed the mayor by the jacket and shoved him against the vehicle. "Where is she?" he shouted.

Johnson's eyes widened. "What—"

Grant shoved him again. Sanborn rushed in and clapped both hands onto Grant's shoulders and jerked him backward. "Back off, Grant!"

One of the soldiers positioned himself between Grant and Johnson and raised his rifle.

Grant stabbed a finger at Johnson. "He's kidnapped Dr. Nakamura. I don't have time to play nice."

"Simmer down or the cuffs come out."

"I don't know what you're talking about," Johnson yelled.

"Neither do I," Sanborn said. "Grant, we have an island to clear out. Make it quick." He turned to Chase Crawford, who had eased closer. "Governor, this is a local matter. Go inside the gym and roust everybody out into the trucks. If they've got cars here, they can use them. If not, they've got ten minutes to get home and get their cars to the foot of the bridge. No one leaves the island until we're all set. In eleven minutes we start across the bridge."

Crawford nodded eagerly, turned and hurried to the open gym door. His star was on the rise.

"Julie, Mr. Chancy, get inside and make sure he doesn't screw this up, too."

Julie and Chancy ran to the gym, splashing through the water piling up on the street. Sanborn turned back to Grant. Hammond and Charley had joined him. "What's this about a kidnapping?"

"This son of a bitch has been working us good," Grant said.

Hammond shook his head. "I'll handle it from here, Grant." He described Kyoko's disappearance, the call from the kidnapper. Hammond's commandeering and destruction of *Ellie June*, the wreck of the *U-498*. Crazy Fred. He ended with the revelation that Remarque and Roscoe had two things in common: the house, and real estate transactions with a corporate go-between owned by Mayor Ralph J. Johnson.

"He showed up late to the rally tonight," Grant said. "Right after Kyoko disappeared. Pretty odd timing for the town's most important official."

Sanborn turned to Johnson. "Well?"

"I was readying things at my place. And yeah, it's true. I owned that property. I came into it legitimately. But I don't know about a damned treasure. And I don't have no idea where Roscoe or Nakamura went."

"It's a whopping big coincidence, Mayor."

"Careful, Randy. I'm still your boss."

"Well, Boss, you're an eyelash from arrest. You've got ten seconds."

"I tell you I got nothing to do with their disappearances. And I didn't know anything about Crazy Fred. That was just an investment property to me."

"Got an alibi for the night Susan Walsh died?"

"You know I don't. I'm a homebody, and there's nobody there with me to verify that since Billie died."

"No alibi the night Roscoe disappeared either, I'll bet."

"No."

"Seems everyone with an interest in Roscoe's property ends

up missing or dead. Everyone but you. Roscoe led a double life, Ralph. A friend of his, from his other life down in Tampa, said you were pressuring him on the Bay View vote."

Johnson snorted. "You think you're the only person in town that knows about Roscoe's secret life? You're not. I knew that stuff years before you caught a whiff of it. Yeah, he had boyfriends in Tampa. Well, here's something you didn't know. You didn't know who Roscoe's lover here on the island was."

"He didn't have one here," Sanborn said. "He kept that life out of town and out of sight."

"Ha! He was discreet all right, but I didn't get to be mayor by being blind. Roscoe was on City Council. Has been for quite a long time. I make it my business to know all about the councilmembers. Especially when they're involved with my business partner. Then private lives affect my well-being."

"What business partner? You're the sole proprietor of Brigands Key Land Holdings."

"I had a partner. I bought him out."

"Who?"

"Artie Blount."

"Blount was involved with Roscoe?"

"You bet. Me and Blount, we used to quietly buy rundown places and flip 'em. We bought the old Remarque place and slapped a little paint on it and put it back on the market. Artie had his real estate license by then and did the brokering for us. He showed it to Roscoe. I guess you could say they hit it off real well. Blount divorced Maureen over it. She never told nobody, and moved away. Blount spent many a night at Roscoe's. Would walk there after dark and leave before daybreak. But I knew.

"Roscoe started renovating the old pile of sticks not long after moving in. He worked on it real slow. Artie let on how Roscoe started renovating one of the upstairs bedrooms, knocking out a wall or two. That's when their little romance cooled. Roscoe never allowed Artie around his house again."

"Blount," Sanborn said. "So Roscoe found some tantalizing clues hidden by Crazy Fred. He knew he'd found something big. My guess, Blount got real nosy and found out the same stuff. Roscoe figured Blount was trying to horn in on his big find and threw him out."

Charley had been listening quietly. He stepped forward. "Roscoe lived there for years. Then all of a sudden, he got on this kick about treasure hunting. And codes, and code-breaking. Got the bug real bad, right after he started remodeling the place. He was after a big treasure but he never knew what he was looking for."

Sanborn motioned to Greenwood and started for the gym. "Okay, Tommy. Let's go collect Artie Blount."

"He ain't here, Boss. There's a handful of folks missing and we're going to their houses to check on them. It's easier to spot who ain't here than who is. Artie ain't here."

Sanborn turned to Governor Crawford. "I need a favor."

"Name it."

"Place three of your troops under Officer Greenwood's command for the next ten minutes."

"Can't do that. I just stuck my neck on a Constitutional chopping block to claim they're under my command."

"Under Greenwood's direction, then."

"Done. Lieutenant Fisk! Get over here."

"Tommy, take these Guardsmen to Blount's house. Arrest him and cuff him and meet us at the bridge. Use extreme caution and extreme prejudice." Sanborn faced Grant. "You satisfied that the mayor's clear?"

"Not really. Keep him under guard."

"Damn you," Johnson snapped.

Hammond said, "Does 'Remark 43' mean anything to you?"

Johnson looked puzzled. His eyes widened. "Hell yeah. Crazy Fred's safe deposit box, number 43. The longest-held safe deposit box on the island. It's a legend down at the First Bank. Fred left an open account that has kept the box active since his death, paid for years in advance. The bank's honored it, figuring a relative would claim it some day."

"What's it take to open a safe deposit box?" Grant asked.

"Probable cause and a court order," Sanborn said.

"We've got probable cause and I'm not waiting for a circuit court to hold session. Johnson, issue the order."

Johnson hesitated.

"Got something to hide, Mayor?"

"I'll get you keys to the bank and assume responsibility for the order to open the box."

A gust of wind hammered them, spraying them with rain as they huddled at the door of the bank. Sanborn handed Charley a flashlight and carefully followed bank president Sally Jansen's reluctant instructions for robbing her bank.

He keyed open the multiple locks on the main entrance and they entered the dim, quiet bank. Half the security systems, including the front door alarm and motion sensors, had failed when the power on the island had blinked out. Sanborn made a mental note to get after Jansen about such an unreliable system if . . . when they got out of this.

A set of LED lights, powered by battery, ghosted the interior in pale green light.

"This way," Sanborn said, sweeping the lobby with his flashlight. He moved across the room, unlocked a door to the tellers' stations, and another behind that into the rear of the building. Beyond that lay the vault and a barred room. Sanborn examined the combination lock and withdrew the slip of paper Jansen had scribbled on. He read the paper, shielding it from his companions. He glanced at them. "You mind?"

They turned away. Sanborn dialed the combination and was rewarded with a loud click. He turned another key and pushed the barred door open. "Here you go. The safe deposit boxes."

The room was little more than a hallway, lined with rows of safe deposit boxes. They scanned the numbers and found Box 43. Its door was a large one, two feet to a side. "Crazy Fred had one of the bigger boxes," Sanborn said.

"I've got the key," Grant said. He raised a crowbar and wedged its point into the hairline crack of the drawer slot. He raised a sledgehammer and struck the end of the crowbar. The steel clanged sharply, throwing off sparks. He struck five more times and the frame around the drawer bent inward. He struck twice more and leaned into the crowbar. There was a snap and the door bulged forward an inch and sprang open.

Inside were two items; an envelope and a wooden box.

Grant handed the envelope to Sanborn, pulled the box out, and set it on the central table. It had a hinged lid. Grant slipped the hasp and raised the lid, revealing a black machine.

"Some kind of typewriter," Hammond said.

The machine had a set of typewriter keys, arranged in standard QWERTY layout. Above the keys were three rows of small round windows, each window the size of a dime, each containing a single letter, also arranged in QWERTY layout.

Above the windows were three vertical slots. Each slot had a metal wheel set down inside the machine. The rim of each wheel projected just above the slot. A wood panel opened on the front of the box, revealing rows of small, cabled plugs fitted into sockets. A small metal plaque was attached to the front of the machine, inscribed with a single word.

Enigma.

"Incredible," Charley said. "It's an encryption machine. The German Enigma, used in World War II." He pulled out his code book and the stack of laminated sheets from Roscoe's boat. "Enigmatic Lady Port! Roscoe was telling me to find and use the Enigma. That's why this was unsolvable."

Sanborn tore open the envelope, withdrew a slip of paper. "Just three digits here," he said. "Seven-four-nine."

"It's code stuff, man," Charley said. "I read about the Enigma machine. It was freakin' ingenious. A message is encrypted by an Enigma technician, typed in. The machine's wiring scrambles the message and each transposed letter is lit in sequence on the machine, copied down, and sent via Morse code to the receiving Enigma technician, who types the encrypted message into his machine and writes down the corresponding light. The encryption contains some fifty-billion-billion possible combinations. That's impossible enough to crack, but the real beauty of it was that the code was changed every day. It was thought for years by both sides to be absolutely unbreakable. Capturing and possessing a machine wouldn't solve the code. Only knowing the daily settings would solve it, and the Allies eventually figured out how to anticipate the daily sets. U-boats carried an Enigma machine to receive their orders. Chief, let me see that paper."

Sanborn handed Charley the sheet.

"We've got it! These numbers are the day-setting, telling us what presets to program the machine to." Charley read aloud the numbers and turned the three wheels to match them.

Grant pressed one of the keys. Nothing happened.

"It's battery operated," Charley said. "The battery's dead after this many years."

Grant and Sanborn hurried out into the outer office, rummaged through a supply cabinet, and returned with a 9-volt battery. Charley had already opened the cabinet of the Enigma and removed the wires from the ancient German battery. He placed the fresh battery beside the machine and twisted the wires onto its terminals. He pressed a key and the light above it blinked on. "We're up and running!"

"Who's a good typist?" Grant asked.

"Sixty words a minute," Hammond said. He pulled up a chair in front of the machine.

"Type like there's no tomorrow." Grant sat next to him and opened a notebook and readied a pencil. "Read us the code sheets, Charley Eff."

Charley began calling out the scrambled letters, Hammond typing each as he went, Grant scribbling down the reordered letters.

In seconds, they knew they had cracked the code.

CHAPTER TWENTY-NINE

Captain Remarque's Journal
October 1962
Committing this to paper is not necessarily smart but after much deliberation it is my decision. Recent events (and a too-close familiarity with the baser instincts of our species) have prompted this history. It is all I have left to offer. I pray that the chance of good outweighs the chance of evil this story might bring.

I am old and cannot live forever, but the events I record will not die with me. Furthermore, I set these thoughts in code for English decipherment. I have acquired a working Enigma from a collector in Belgium, and with it I secure this story from the casual thief.

I am known on this strange, friendly island as Fred Re-marque. Crazy Fred. The odd old bird with the funny accent.

My name is (or was) Captain Friedrich Remarque. I am German. I grew up in Pirmasens, near the French border. My happy childhood ended abruptly when the guns of August 1914 came to bear. At seventeen, I entered the German Navy.

The Great War ended badly for Deutschland.

I returned to Pirmasens and became a shopkeeper, a seller of linens. I failed at it. And my country failed and rage and misery led us into nightmare once again. In 1936, I was again conscripted into the Navy, now called Kriegsmarine. I became commander of Unterseeboot-498.

Our boat was a Type IX-C, sturdy, built for long-range missions. A top speed of over eighteen knots. Seventy-six meters long, with a draft of under five meters. She packed twenty-two torpedoes, a 105-millimeter deck cannon, and two anti-aircraft guns. My crew of forty-eight was the best in the fleet.

We prowled the Eastern Seaboard of America, killing ships and Americans. Upon occasion, we let ships slip away, to avoid detection. Intelligence was often more valuable to the Reich than the tonnage of sunken ships. We deposited spies on American soil and we collected spies from American soil. Never did we ask what they knew. They were an elite class of warriors. Untouchables, Americans might say.

In 1942, U-498 steamed into the Gulf of Mexico. In a week, we had sunk three freighters. Airplanes swarmed, searching for us. We slipped quietly back into the Atlantic and crossed the ocean to celebrate our success, and returned and did it again.

So it went. The wolfpacks ruled the Gulf for a year, sending fifty-six ships to the bottom. But the Americans grew stronger and committed men, planes, and ships to the Gulf. In summer of 1942, the U-166 was attacked and went down. It was, history tells us, the only German submarine lost in the Gulf of Mexico.

That is a lie.

By 1943, the wolfpacks were in retreat across the Atlantic. The enemy had decrypted the Enigma code, and he designed ships and planes to kill us. Three out of every four German submariners lost their lives.

By spring of 1945, the war was a nightmare for the Fatherland. The Soviets were destroying Berlin, the Americans and British had retaken Italy and France and were crossing the Rhine. The war was all but lost. The Kriegsmarine was a shell of its former self. In 1940, we lost twenty-four U-boats. In 1944, two hundred and fifty. Yet we fought on.

The U-498 cruised the Mid-Atlantic, still on the hunt. Forty

284

kilometers northeast of Savannah, we targeted a rusting cargo ship making a dash for the city. Three kilometers separated us. Another seven northwest prowled a destroyer, keeping a protective eye on the merchant ship and another vessel, ten kilometers farther. If we could slip in quietly and claim our prize, the destroyer would be tasked with collecting survivors, unable to give chase. Good. The Führer had ordered all U-boats to kill any survivors, to take no prisoners. The captains universally hated the barbaric order. The threat and presence of the destroyer would excuse me from carrying it out.

We shadowed the freighter, watching, alert for trouble. When the destroyer drifted farther out of range, we closed swiftly. The torpedoes were armed, slicked with Vaseline, ready for firing. I took the periscope and drew upon my target. It would be an easy kill.

I hesitated. To this day, I'm not sure why.

I could feel the eyes of my crew upon me. They were waiting, wondering.

First Watch Officer Becker burst into the room, frantically waving a piece of paper. "Captain, do not fire! We have received a radiogram."

I took the paper and read it. "You are certain of the decryption?"

"As certain as ever, Captain."

I turned to the crew. "There will be no attack. We have been redirected. Mueller, take us to ten fathoms, course southeast."

"Where are we headed, Captain?"

"Into the Gulf of Mexico."

The crew exchanged glances. The Gulf had been abandoned by the U-boats for two years. A sudden, hurried course change to the Gulf meant only one thing. A spy mission.

The men hated spies. There were only two tasks a sub could perform on spy missions. Insertion and removal.

Both were dangerous. Both required shallow water maneuvers, creeping close to shore, damn near beaching oneself.

A sub was as good as dead if a patrol plane spotted it in such a place.

Farther abroad, safely removed from Savannah, we surfaced under cover of darkness and switched from batteries to diesel engines. Conditions were favorable and we moved swiftly. We passed Jacksonville far out at sea and turned due south. In fifty-four hours, we rounded the Florida Straits and entered the bathtub that is the Gulf of Mexico. In another twenty-four, we passed Tampa.

Since '42, Gulf patrols by plane and destroyer had become untenable to submarines. Now we had returned to challenge them on a dubious mission in the waning weeks of a war we had no chance of winning.

Our mission had already extended far beyond our planned stay at sea. Morale was low and water and food supplies even lower. I cut rations of both, further eroding morale.

On the night of April twelfth, our drinking water ran out, but we had reached our destination. We crept to within three kilometers of shore and eased into position in gentle seas. I stood atop the conning tower, scanning the darkness ahead. A low ceiling of clouds blotted out a quarter moon. Rendezvous with spies are always performed under new moon, the darkest of nights, yet we were under less than darkest conditions. The men swore about poor planning, but they knew better. For us to be sent here, now, optimum conditions had been willfully ignored.

Someone had deemed the mission vital.

I had memorized my charts of the area. The water was a mere seven fathoms at high tide. We hoped. The charts were not the best, as this was an area of little shipping. I had crewmen fore and aft taking soundings, and found that the depth was less than six fathoms. We were close to running aground. There was no need to be here. This coast was rural, sparsely peopled. Tal-lahassee lay one hundred and twenty kilometers northeast, Panama City seventy kilometers northwest. Strung along the coast like a necklace were tiny fishing hamlets.

Ahead, small barrier islands girdled the bay of the Apalachi-cola River. We dared not enter the shallow bay, but I could smell the land and forest and the fresh, muddy water. I breathed deeply. Though we could see nothing of the land ahead and dared not lay a foot upon it, the nearness of solid earth, however foreign and hostile, never failed to stir the imagination and yearning of submariners too long at sea.

"It is time, Captain," said Becker, at my right.

"The signal, then."

The signalman flashed his light twice rapidly, paused, and flashed once more.

We waited.

There was no signal in reply.

"The pick-up has not made rendezvous, Captain. We have performed our task. Perhaps we should leave."

"Patience, Becker." I was as anxious as he to be out of that dangerous place. We waited in silence, watching, listening for two hours. I glanced at my watch. "Signal once more."

He did so and we waited.

"Mein Kapitan, the tide is ebbing. We were already shallow when we came in at high tide. In another ten minutes, we will be aground."

The sky was already graying in the east. In an hour, the sun would be up. I felt relieved, absolved. "We have fulfilled our mission to the best of our ability. We shall be on our way."

"Captain!" Mueller cried, pointing.

A hundred meters ahead, a dark shape, barely visible, crept over the gentle waves. A small boat approached, its small engine rattling.

"Arms at the ready, men."

Mueller and Becker unshouldered their carbines and aimed at the small craft. I unholstered my Luger and clicked the safety off and raised it to eye level.

The black figure throttled the boat's engine to an idle and the dinghy coasted. The figure raised its arms toward us. Becker sucked in his breath and leaned into his carbine.

"Steady, Becker," I said.

A light flashed on the boat, five short times, followed by a single long one. The correct response signal.

"Proceed, sir," I called softly.

The figure maneuvered his tiny craft and pulled alongside the sub. Crewmen scrambled to haul the man aboard. He was dressed head to toe in black, his face painted black. A canvas bag was slung over his shoulder, clearly containing something of considerable bulk. He struggled under the weight of it. I offered to help him with it. He waved me back, with a piercing angry light in his eyes. *"Captain Friedrich Remarque,"* I said, saluting. *"At your service, sir."*

"I am Shreck," he replied in a raspy, tired voice. *"Max Shreck."* A good name for a spy who wishes to remain anonymous. Max Fear, after the gaunt actor that played F.W. Mirnau's ghastly vampire, Nosferatu.

Becker chuckled. Shreck shot him an angry glance. Becker shut up. Shreck looked over my men with that look we usually receive from our dry-land compatriots. They see a smelly, dirty, bearded lot of submariners. Undisciplined. Unpatriotic. It gives them a smug feeling of superiority. They do not want to know that a U-boat crew dispenses with shaving and bathing out of the critical need to save scarce water.

"Captain Remarque," Shreck said, *"Let us make way."*

"With eagerness, sir. Our destination?"

"The Fatherland. Posthaste."

U-498's *diesel engine hummed and the boat withdrew, backing out from the shallows. I watched nervously from the conning tower, scanning the dark shore with binoculars. Several sets of headlights, each set a twin pair of glowing pinpoints, appeared near where we had been. The headlights froze. I imagined men scurrying about, searching the shore, scanning the sea. And radioing an urgent call for help.*

I prayed for reliable engines and deep water.

Four kilometers from shore, as the sun peeked above the horizon and painted the eastern sky a dazzling red, my prayer was answered; the water deepened to ten fathoms. I gave the order and the crew happily sealed the boat. U-498 *slipped under the water, to periscope depth. The old rhyme played in my thoughts: Red sky at morning, sailor take warning.*

By the dim light inside our old warhorse, our guest was not much more to look upon than he had been in the dark. He was a young man, rather slight of build. Unremarkable in every aspect, certainly not one of the Aryan supermen Americans imagined us to be. Shreck's hair was brown, his eyes brown, his face plain. Average all around. Which is good for someone undercover.

Average, yet sick. His pallor was ghastly and his hands trembled. He avoided talk. He kept his heavy bag with him at all times, an arm clamped around it.

We gave him dry clothing and fed him. Like all our remaining food, the food we gave him was moldy. He ate ravenously nonetheless. His eyelids drooped with exhaustion; I offered him my bunk. He declined at first, then relented and was asleep within seconds, his prize still tight in his grip.

He roused after seven hours and returned to the control room. I nodded to him.

American jazz music, quite popular among submariners, played softly. Shreck seemed annoyed by it.

He looked at me coolly. "What is our position, Captain?"

"Eighty kilometers south of our rendezvous point."

Shreck stared at me. "That's all? What is our speed?"

"You have an urgency?"

"Our speed, Captain, if you please."

"Seven knots."

"And that is as fast as we can go?"

"Underwater. On the surface, we are considerably faster, a top speed over eighteen knots. We are just below the surface, running under diesel power with our snorkel raised. The diesel cannot run at a greater depth as the engine requires air intake. Deeper, we switch to electric batteries, but we cannot stay down forever on battery power."

"Then return to the surface at once. Speed is of the essence."

"My orders, sir, are to fetch you back to Germany. I shall do so. But I am also sworn to protect my ship and crew to the best of my ability. That prescribes a degree of caution."

"To the surface, Captain. Now."

"You'll have to do better than that, Shreck."

Shreck leaned back, rubbing the stubble on his chin, studying me. "Is there a private place we can talk?"

"On a submarine? Not many. But follow me. The officers' wardroom will do."

I showed him to the tiny, wood-paneled wardroom. We took seats and stared at each other for a moment.

"Captain, you haven't much use for spies, have you?"

"They have a place, I suppose."

"I am a judge of men. I doubt I can bully you, so I'll reason with you. Listen to me: the war is not over."

"For all practical purposes, it is. Germany is doomed. But you know that. Moving among the Americans, you have better news than a submariner weeks at sea. Germany's fortunes cannot be reversed. The Reich is collapsing. Nothing you say will

persuade me to further jeopardize my men for a lost cause."

"That borders upon treason, Captain."

"It is the truth."

Shreck regarded me for a long moment, nervously tapping his fingertips together. "I'm going to tell you why we must be swift."

"It's a long trip home. I have time."

"My stay in the United States has been largely pointless. Until now. For three years, I have reported troop and ship movements. I have reported political infighting. I have monitored aircraft plant output. And none of it mattered one iota in the prosecution of this war. Yet recently I received an assignment that, at long last, would matter.

"In early April, I received new orders from Wolfe. That's all the name you need. Wolfe is an intelligence-gatherer like no other in the world, but has little or no stomach for the more distasteful assignments. So I left Chicago and took a train south. I disembarked in Atlanta and purchased work clothes and boots. I found a general store that had a few old hunting rifles for sale, and as luck would have it, I purchased a weathered M1917, a .30-caliber American Army-surplus weapon, a fine rifle designed to kill men.

" 'Going on a little springtime shoot?' the clerk asked.

" 'Hogs are tearing up my land,' I said. 'I'll need two boxes of ammo.' Language fluency is a necessity for a spy, and my English is flawless . . . but not for that part of the country.

"The clerk had to pry. 'Where ye from, Mister?'

" 'Chicago,' I said in all honesty.

" 'Why ain't ye in the Army?'

" 'Shot in the foot on Guadalcanal,' I replied. The clerk glanced at my foot and slid the ammo toward me.

"I worked my way south through the countryside, through small towns. I hate them. They are bad for spies; it's easier to blend in a big city. When I drew within twenty kilometers of my

destination, I moved at night until I arrived in Warm Springs.

"I prowled woods and farms in darkness until I found a suitable place of little security, a towering grove of pines. The house was in the distance, patrolled lackadaisically by guards. A shallow ditch transected an open field, within a hundred meters of the house. It would do. I loaded the rifle and crept onward. Stop, watch, wait, proceed. At the edge of the woods, all appeared well. I cradled the rifle across my forearms and belly-crawled across the darkened field and into the stagnant water in the ditch.

"I found a suitable vantage point. Soldiers patrolled the grounds, disinterested in venturing afield. A fatal laziness.

"The target appeared.

"Franklin Delano Roosevelt, slumping, rolled onto the porch, his wheelchair pushed gently by a nurse.

"I raised my rifle and peered through the scope.

"Things were worse for Roosevelt than the public had been led to believe. His face was drawn and pallid, his hands trembling. Gone was the confident, reassuring smile. Sickness and pain gripped his frail body. All knew that polio had tortured him and that his trips to Warm Springs revived his spirit and strength. This was no longer the case. This was no longer the same man. Death was creeping upon him.

"Yet orders were orders. And the mission was to shock, to stun . . . and to distract America from the details of war. Only assassination could accomplish that.

"Or so Wolfe had claimed. I snugged closer into the rifle, pulling it firmly against my shoulder. The shot would be a long one, but within my range. I paused, waiting patiently for a lull in the breeze that drifted across the field. It came, and I held my breath, steadying myself for the shot.

"I slowly squeezed the trigger . . ."

CHAPTER THIRTY

The cords binding Kyoko's wrists began to yield as she sawed with the shard of glass. Though her hands were numb, the pressure lessened and suddenly the bonds loosened and gave way and she pulled free.

She put the piece of glass in her pocket and rubbed her wrists. Feeling and blood slowly returned to her hands and with it the sharp pain of her lacerated fingertips. The cuts were open and had been dry but now the blood began to drip from them.

She wiped her fingers on her blouse. No time to worry about minor cuts now. She felt the bandage over the wound where her ear used to be, the ear that was no longer there. The wound throbbed with pain.

She tried the door. It was a massive, heavy door, hung on great iron hinges. Locked, as she knew it would be. She pressed her ear to it and listened. No sound of movement or life came from beyond. She shook it. Ancient though it was, it wasn't about to yield.

She gave up and felt about in the dark and began to search the masonry wall. She felt as high as she could but could find no openings. The room was almost certainly once a storehouse, harkening back to days when perhaps the only resident on the whole island was the lighthouse keeper. The keeper would have benefited from a storeroom that was virtually impregnable to rats and raccoons. Such a room makes an excellent prison.

She completed her circuit of the room, finding no openings,

no windows, not even a promising crack. The door was the only way in or out.

She scoured the floor for anything of value. Finding nothing, she withdrew the shard of glass from her pocket. That was her sole weapon. She experimented with her grip on it, settling on a tight pinch, almost a pencil grip. She practiced a slashing motion, finding that a backhand slash gave her the most power in her swing.

She tore a bit of cloth from her blouse, wrapped it around one edge of the glass, and gripped it tightly. That might save her fingers.

She backed against the wall adjacent to the door and flattened herself against it. Her heart was thudding as she pictured how this could unfold. She tried to visualize each possible combination of moves and the chances of success for each. The outcomes didn't look promising.

Outside her prison, the wind whistled, growing in intensity. Celeste was closing in. A crack of thunder split the air nearby. Below the sound of the rising storm came another sound. Footsteps. Approaching.

There was a soft clink of metal against metal and the heavy sound of a bolt being slid in an outer door somewhere. She drew a deep breath, gritted her teeth, and raised the shard of glass even with her shoulder. She would get one chance. She had to make it count.

Captain Remarque's Journal

Shreck paused importantly, letting me imagine him about to put a bullet through the face of Franklin Roosevelt. "A voice hissed at me from behind, in German," *he said at last.* " 'Agent, abort the mission immediately!'

"I twisted about, ready to kill. It was Wolfe. The last person I expected. As I said, he was not the field type.

" 'This mission is ended,' he continued. 'We are withdrawing.'

"I was of no mind to continue the discussion within shooting range of armed guards. We backed out of the wet ditch and slipped through the pine woods, silent as the night, until we had removed ourselves a kilometer from the kill point.

"At last, Wolfe spoke. 'You have a new mission.'

" 'How did you find me?' I asked.

" 'Child's play. I found the only point at which you could succeed.'

"My estimation of Wolfe rose. 'I was mere seconds from completing the assignment,' I added.

" 'The new mission is vastly more important.'

" 'More important than assassinating the President?' I was incredulous.

" 'That would amount to mere noisemaking. Now you have an opportunity to alter the war, perhaps even win it.'

"And then I received my new orders.

"Wolfe took me back to Atlanta. My cover changed once more. I bathed and shaved and was furnished with a business suit and briefcase. I was provided a car. Wolfe vanished and I was on my way once again.

"I drove north from Atlanta, crossing mountains, into Tennessee. From Chattanooga, I turned northeast and in a few hours I entered a small valley.

"I consulted my map. I was to find Robertsville, a tiny hamlet. There it was, on the map . . . but it was not there. In its place was a sprawling installation.

"I was baffled. I knew the names and locations of all major military installations in America. Or so I thought. But here was something very big, and very secret.

"I left my car by night in a wood and covered it in brush, kilometers from the installation, and began my examination, skulking once again through the night forest, crawling upon my belly through ditches.

"Over the next two days, the enormity of it all sank in. The complex sprawled across tens of thousands of acres, across small valleys, each separated from the next by high ridges. Security and isolation were endemic to each. No one moved between the isolated areas; no one working in one area would be aware of what happened in the next.

"Barbed-wire and guarded gates everywhere. Armed patrols everywhere. All of it new. A new city, with no name, on no map.

"Entering was impossible and pointless. If I somehow gained entry, I had no earthly idea what to do or look for.

"Someone else would do it for me. Wolfe had given me a name. Dr. Lawrence Roth. PhD. Physics.

"Roth was not a traitor, but he had two critical things: access and weakness. Why governments guarding secrets allow such weaknesses is a mystery. But they do and duty compelled me to take advantage of that weakness, distasteful as I may find it.

"The homes were new but ugly, the ugliness varying with the status of the worker. Roth's house was among the more attractive ugly houses.

"Security, so impenetrable around the vast factories and labs, was weak in the housing districts. When Dr. Roth returned to his sparkling ugly home late one night, he had an unwelcome guest. I sat in his living room, smoking a cigarette. I hate the things, but they lend an ominous air when smoked in the dark of one's home by an intruder.

" 'Welcome home, Dr. Roth,' I said. 'Do not run. I would kill you before you reached the door.'

"Roth froze. 'Get out of my house,' he said. His face paled as he glanced about the small house. 'Where—?'

" 'Doctor, please sit. Your wife and daughter are safe. Do as I say and you will soon be with them.'

" 'Where are they?'

" 'Safe and sound. Now. You have a choice before you.'

" 'How much do you want? I'll pay anything.'

" 'You can't be that stupid.' The good doctor was laboring under the misconception that he had any control over the moment. I decided to disabuse him of that notion. I stood and punched him in the stomach, doubling him over. 'Now. You have access to something precious. You know what it is.'

" 'Information,' he said resignedly. 'Very well. I will tell you what I can.'

" 'Information,' I repeated. 'We have all the information we need. Why else do you think I'm here? No. I want the prize itself.' I spoke my lines well, though I had no idea what I was actually after. I just had a phrase. 'Deliver Manhattan to me.'

"Roth's eyes widened with fear. 'Manhattan? Who are you?'

"I punched him again in the stomach, where no mark would show. I needed him looking well if this was to have any chance of success. 'Why, I'm a Nazi spy, of course.' There was no point in lying; any moron would have deduced as much by now.

" 'Are you insane? You think I can steal the core and pass it off to you?'

"I had no idea what the core was, but it was clearly of paramount importance. 'Precisely. Bring me the core.'

" 'I won't do it!'

" 'Doctor, what do we know about the war?'

" 'Your side is all but beaten,' he said.

" 'Yes. Therefore, the core won't make any difference, will it? The war will be over before I return to Germany. So you can't really affect the outcome. Yet you can save your family. Bring me the core and you have your family back. Fail, and I will begin with your wife. While your little girl watches. When I'm done with Judith, I will move to your little girl. Sally is a precious thing; how old is she, ten? After I am finished, you will receive the both of them, or what's left of them. And Germany *will still lose the war. So therein dwell the difficult choices. Your loved ones in exchange for a piece of hardware that in the greater scheme of things won't matter. You have three seconds to decide.'*

"Roth trembled and tears welled in his eyes.

" 'Time's up,' I said.

" 'I'll . . . I'll steal it,' he said in a breaking voice.

" 'Tonight,' I said. 'Now.' In my work, I find it unwise to give desperate men time to mull over options."

A sliver of light appeared beneath the door. Kyoko tensed, swallowed her breath. The lock rattled and the door creaked slowly inward. Light flooded into the blackness. A hand appeared against the door . . . and stopped. Time to act. Kyoko slashed downward with the glass shard, slicing the intruder's palm open, and sprang into the doorway and drove her knee hard into the intruder's stomach. She slashed at his face, creasing it with a line of red across the cheek.

The man staggered and swung a fist, striking a glancing blow to the side of her head. Sparks flashed in her mind and she stumbled sideward. She recovered and slashed again. The shard snagged in the man's shirt and was nearly wrenched from her grip, cutting deeply into her fingers, but she maintained her hold on it. She struck wildly, knocking the flashlight free. It clattered to the floor, throwing light and shadow into a frenzy. She caught a glimpse of her enemy.

Blount.

One of only a handful she had trusted on this island.

She clawed his face and lunged again. Blount stumbled and she was past him. She kicked the flashlight through the door, snatched it up, and bolted out of the room and raced for the outer open door and slammed it behind her. She felt for, found, and shot the bolt home, locking the door.

The door thundered and shuddered. Blount had thrown himself against it. "I'm coming for you, bitch!" he screamed. He slammed against the door again and again. She backed away, unable to see but mesmerized by Blount's fury. She shook herself, collected her thoughts. She'd done it! Hope surged through her. She allowed herself a moment's joyous relief, and faced the reality again. She was still trapped in a black tower with a murderous lunatic.

Blount's assault on the door suddenly ceased and all was quiet. He was going to find another way in.

She groped frantically about for the flashlight, banging her shin painfully against something hard and unyielding. She reached down and felt a horizontal steel plate and found another recessed above it, and another above that. A staircase. The spiraling interior stairwell of the great lighthouse.

She found the flashlight and twisted the lens casing. The light blinked on. She shined it all about and up the stairwell.

Nowhere to go but up. She began to climb.

A soft low sound, a moan, came from above. She shined the light in the direction of the sound, searching the rusting steel wedges of the steps. The way looked clear . . . except for a black shapeless mass on the stairs fifty feet above her.

She fixed the light on the mass . . . and the mass moved.

CHAPTER THIRTY-ONE

Captain Remarque's Journal

"I confess I had no confidence Roth could pull off the heist," the spy continued. "Security at the installation was paramount, and whatever undertaking this place had set itself to was guarded with extreme prejudice.

"Yet two hours after I'd sent him in, he returned, lumbering under the weight of the prize, his eyes filled with terror and guilt.

"He had blood on his clothes yet he was unhurt. He set the bag gently at my feet. I opened it and peered in. 'Manhattan,' he said.

" 'Dr. Roth, you have a natural aptitude for espionage,' I said.

" 'Damn you to hell. Give me back my family.'

" 'In time. At the moment, they are my insurance. Tomorrow at five P.M. they will be released. We will examine the prize. If you've tried to be cute, they die.'

" 'It's the real thing,' he snapped. 'You can count on one hand the number of persons in the world that have access to it, including me.'

" 'Go home,' I said. 'Get some rest. You've done well.'

" 'Damn you.'

"I made short work of him, slipping my needle deftly between his ribs and into his heart, killing him before he knew what was happening. This was distasteful but I could not run the risk of

*him revealing our collaboration. Don't look so disgusted,
Captain Remarque. He was a casualty of war and his family
was spared.*

*"The Appalachian foothills afford the darkest countryside
one could hope for. The remoteness of the region suits well the
aims of a secret city, but also makes for perfect cover for
getaways. I hurried by foot out of the valley, heading north,
then east and finally south. I ignored my hidden car and
searched instead for an abandoned barn described by Wolfe. As
promised, I found, hidden among baled hay and covered with
canvas, a dusty Ford pickup, its ignition keys taped to the
underside of the chassis. I hid my prize in hay bales stacked in
the pickup's bed, discarded my suit and tie, and donned the
dirty overalls and work shirt tucked under the seat. I switched
on the engine and pulled out of the barn and headed south on a
dirt road.*

*"Before daybreak, I entered Georgia and passed west of
Atlanta on a paved highway.*

*"As the sky turned gray with first light, I detoured onto
another dirt road through woodland. Not a moment too soon.
With binoculars, I glimpsed the paved road upon which I had
been traveling. The police were hastily assembling a roadblock
and cars were queuing up to it.*

*"The word had been put out to stop and interrogate everyone.
Without doubt, military blocks would soon be added to the ring.*

*"Following instructions, I hid the truck among cut brush and
constructed a separate hiding place of brush several hundred
paces away and buried myself in it. I lay motionless for the
remainder of the day, pistol in one hand and prize in the other.
When night fell, I retrieved my truck and resumed my journey,
zigzagging south. In Albany, I bought more petrol and overheard
talk of a frenzied search for an armed and dangerous prison
escapee. Fitting my description, or at least my former descrip-*

tion. The escapee was believed to be in the south of Georgia, heading for Savannah. An accomplice had been gunned down in that city.

"My estimation of Wolfe rose once more. He had diverted the chase and sacrificed himself to the cause.

"I hurried west and reached the narrow, swift Chattahoochee River. There I found a small motor launch, laden with fishing tackle and extra cans of petrol, just as Wolfe had promised. I abandoned the truck and set off downriver for the Gulf of Mexico.

"The swift stream helped my speed and gasoline and in five hours I entered Florida.

"The Chattahoochee joined other small rivers and emptied into the Apalachicola, a much easier stretch to negotiate. The river was remote and wild and cut through sand banks and limestone bluffs alike, overhung with rampant growth and towering trees. The escape by river seemed a stroke of genius. I was a country fisherman on an outing. But illness had beset me. I vomited frequently and became dehydrated.

"As I neared the coast, the danger grew. I saw military aircraft in greater numbers prowling the coastline. Perhaps the Americans believed I was headed for Savannah but they were taking no chances. I lay up the last day, the day of our appointed rendezvous. With nightfall I plied the last stretch, passing the mouth of the river, the village of Apalachicola to my right. The narrow course opened into a broad bay, traversed by a long, low highway bridge. I had to pass directly beneath the bridge. As I did so, slowing to avoid collisions with the bridge pilings, I heard shouts from above. The beams of flashlights swept across the water as I emerged from the opposite side of the bridge. One beam found me. More shouts, a warning to stop. I throttled the motor full out and shot ahead. A gunshot echoed and the water on my starboard splashed white. I took an evasive

course, swerving left and right. Two more shots, one striking the gunwale and spraying splinters of wood.

"The gunfire ceased as I drew out of range but the lights followed me as I turned east across the bay. Once I was out of sight I veered southwest for the narrow pass separating St. George Island and St. Vincent Island. I raced ahead, aware that I was beyond the window of our rendezvous. I cleared the pass and entered the turbulent Gulf. My tiny skiff threatened to capsize in the waves.

"And so I found the U-498." Shreck was silent for a moment. "Now you know why we must make all possible speed. I have brought something aboard of unrivaled importance to the Americans and to the Reich. Make no mistake; they will hold nothing back in the effort to recover it and will be ruthless in the trying."

The spy's words bore into me. I no longer believed I would live to see home.

Kyoko steadied herself, watching the dark shape on the staircase above slowly shift.

Blount had given up trying to batter down the door behind her. All that could be heard behind her was the worsening storm.

Who—or *what*—lay before her? An unknown, shapeless black mass, writhing, blocking her path. She could turn back and take her chances with Blount. That appealed on a gut level, taking her from the dark unknown to a known terror.

She steadied herself. All Charley's nonsense about vampires had seeped into her psyche, amplifying anything that went bump in the night.

The thing moaned, a deep pained noise, all too human. She took a step closer.

"Help . . . me . . ." the man said. His words were garbled and wet, croaked more than spoken, as if forced through a wreckage of a throat. "Please . . ."

Kyoko took a breath and approached cautiously, her fear overcome by sudden wrenching pity.

A stench of rotting, living flesh enveloped the man. She'd known that smell once before, on a woman dying from a gangrene-riddled leg in Darfur.

She placed a hand on him and turned him gently toward her. He flinched and a moan of pain escaped. She could not turn him all the way; something restricted him.

"Cut . . . me . . . loose," the man rasped.

She reached for his arms and felt the ropes binding his wrists to the railing. His hands were soft and sticky, and she realized with a shudder that his flesh was open and oozing. His feet were similarly bound, the flesh there also split open.

"It's all right," she whispered. "I'll get you out of this." She began to saw his bonds with her shard of glass. "Was it Blount?" she asked. In a moment his hands and feet were free.

The man coughed. "Yeah," he rasped.

"What's your name?"

Kyoko glimpsed the man's face and recoiled reflexively. His entire face was swollen, balloon-like. Red, hanging flesh draped his cheeks. His lower lip was grotesquely swollen, five times normal, like an egg. His upper lip was a rope of pulpy flesh hanging from the left side of his mouth. His right eye was swollen nearly shut, a faint glimmer of the eye seeming to peek out from the slit. The other eye was sunken, seemingly not there at all, a streak of wet matter staining his cheekbone beneath it. Thin tufts of hair clung to his scalp.

Kyoko knew in an instant what it all meant, what the mysterious plague of Brigands Key was. The nagging, wildly improbable idea that she'd been considering was confirmed.

"My . . . name?" the man croaked.

His sticky, oozing hand closed on her wrist and tightened in a grip like steel and his other hand grabbed a fistful of her blouse. She struggled but he pulled her closer to his destroyed face. His cracked voice drifted on foul breath to her. "Nobles. I'm . . . Nobles . . ."

Captain Remarque's Journal

Shreck leaned forward, a peculiar light in his eyes. "Well, Captain? You now know the nature of my mission. Of our mission. Take us to the surface and resume full speed."

I did not know what to make of it. His tale was fantastic, yet I had no reason to doubt a word of it. We had been summoned as a matter of the utmost urgency; men in high places obviously felt that Shreck's mission was critical.

"That would not be prudent," I said. "We are within striking distance of patrol planes."

"We are at war! There is always risk involved."

"The Gulf of Mexico hasn't been safe for the Unterseebooten *since '42. America's military has grown exponentially since. They have aircraft with nothing to do but search for subs."*

"Captain, I know more about submarine tactics than you assume. American anti-sub patrols follow the coast from Texas to Florida, seldom venturing more than a hundred kilometers from land. We're well outside their patrol range. There are not more than five hours of daylight left. At the surface we will be thirty kilometers farther along by nightfall. I insist we surface."

I turned numbers over in my mind. We were ninety kilometers from land. Shreck was a fool if he thought American planes wouldn't patrol beyond a hundred, and by his own admission they were hell-bent on finding us.

I could feel by the rocking of the vessel that the weather had worsened. The morning sky had hinted that bad weather lay in store. And we sorely needed rainwater for drinking. "Very well," I said. I reluctantly ordered the crew to take us to the surface. The diesels would continue to recharge the batteries, and we would sail under diesel power through the night. Shreck didn't need to know I intended to submerge again, deeper and under battery power, at dawn.

And so I made the greatest mistake of my life.

As we neared the surface, I raised periscope and surveyed the sea a full three hundred and sixty degrees. There was no sign of ships. A squall had blown in, filling the view with gray in all directions. I glanced at Becker inquiringly. "Anything on the hydrophones?"

Becker tapped Grothe on the shoulder. Grothe huddled over his equipment, headphones cupped tightly against his ears. He twirled the dial delicately, listening in first one direction and then another. He shook his head. "No ships near, Captain."

I took a deep breath. "Breach the surface, Becker."

U-498 rose to the surface. The motion of the boat changed as it began to roll with the waves. "Becker, accompany me to the tower."

We climbed the ladder to the conning tower hatch, Becker first, myself following. He twisted the latch open and shoved the heavy door upward. Seawater splashed in, wetting us both, and we climbed through.

The squall showed no sign of being short-lived. Good. Visibility was limited by the rain and low-ceiled clouds, and with it, the risk of our being spotted. I clapped my hands happily and let out a shout. "Becker, we have drinking water! Fetch barrels for collection." Rain pattered down on us. I breathed deeply of the damp cooling air.

But the bad thing about a squall is that it deafens one's hearing. On a clear, calm day, you can hear an airplane for many kilometers. With rain beating down, you hear little other than the rain.

We didn't hear the airplane until it was diving on us, its guns rattling and spitting.

CHAPTER THIRTY-TWO

Kyoko tore free of Roscoe's grasp and backed away.

The man looked at her, opened his mouth, sank back against the stairs as if air had been let out of him. "Won't . . . ," he gasped. "I won't . . . hurt you . . ."

Kyoko, breathing hard, watched him fearfully. "You're the missing fisherman," she said. "Have you been imprisoned here all this time?"

Nobles shook his head weakly. "People . . . could find me here. No . . . bound . . . gagged in closet . . . Blount's house."

"Why did he bring you here?"

"Hurricane," he wheezed. "Will . . . swamp the island. This is only safe . . . place. Blount needs me . . . alive."

"Why?"

"Wants . . . the treasure." He shuddered and coughed violently, a wet, rheumy cough.

"The treasure did this to you, didn't it?"

Nobles nodded. "Ain't . . . no treasure . . . in this world."

Captain Remarque's Journal

The airplane swept down, its guns blazing. Bullets slammed into the hull and struck the water, sending spires of water high. A bullet whistled close to my neck, plucking at my collar.

Our attacker was an American PBY Catalina, the most hated of aircraft, designed to kill subs.

I shoved Becker back into the hatch. "Alarm! Down below!

307

Commence dive!"

The plane roared low overhead. I fired twice with my Luger, a futile gesture. I could see the airplane's waist gunner swiveling in his glass blister, peppering us as he flew past. The plane climbed and banked, preparing for another run at us.

I plunged into the hatch after Becker and jammed the lock shut. "Bow, down thirty, stern up five. Get us down quickly!"

The submarine was a beehive, instantly on order and on task. Air hissed as it was expelled from the ballast tanks even before I landed from the bottom rung of the ladder. U-498 was slipping under the waves.

"We surprised them as much as they surprised us," I said. "If they'd had time to prepare, they would have bombed us into oblivion and we would not be discussing it. If luck is with us, the cannons have done minimal damage."

I could feel the shift in the boat as we went under. I did a mental calculation, guessing at the recovery time of the Catalina before it could come about and resume the attack. I did not like the results of my calculation, though we would be beyond the grasp of machine gun and bomb.

"Brace yourselves for depth charges," I shouted.

The crew fell silent, listening.

Sure enough, two distant, faint sounds reached the sub.

"Grothe?" I asked.

"Two charges, one off starboard beam, one starboard aft."

"Hard to port," I said.

The boat veered, heeling over as it went.

We continued to dive. An explosion shook the boat, followed by another seconds later. The hull groaned in protest.

A jet of water splashed across my face. The lights flickered but held.

"Maintain dive," I ordered. "Descend to fifty fathoms. The Cat is hunting a moving mouse. We want to be invisible and

dead to them." I took off my jacket and cap and handed them to Becker. "Take this, collect whatever expendables you can find and shove them into the aft torpedo tubes. Only items that float. Load another tube with a barrel of diesel. Eject all as quickly as possible. We'll give them a debris field and an oil slick and tonight they will toast their heroism and make unskilled love to the ugly local girls in celebration."

At fifty fathoms I turned to Becker. "We're now too deep for them to find us with a magnetometer. Due east, Becker, seven knots. We must get quietly away; the Catalina has undoubtedly summoned a destroyer to finish us off." I glanced at my watch. "The Cat itself may land on the water to listen for us. No shipboard talking unless absolutely necessary for two hours."

The boat made a long slow turn toward the east. We put distance behind us at an agonizingly slow pace.

Something felt wrong in the movement of the ship. I sent Becker aft. He returned with Brandt, the engineer, in tow.

"Becker, your report?"

"The boat is manageable . . . for now," he replied. "Brandt?"

"The starboard screw is damaged and inoperable," Brandt said. "We have sustained multiple hull leaks. We're welding the splits and we've driven leakage plugs into the damaged pipes and neutralized a battery-acid leak with lime."

"Continue sealing the leaks as quietly as possible. What speed can you give me?"

"Three knots, sir."

"And at the surface?"

"Nine knots. With a following sea."

Becker's face was pale and haggard. Sweat glistened on his forehead. Not unusual in a submariner, but unusual in the hearty Becker. "Are you well, Becker?"

He looked at me, nodded. "A bit seasick today, I think."

It was a lie. Becker hadn't been seasick in four years. "Inspect the boat for further damage, from end to end," I said. "After that, get some rest."

The boat limped east, the batteries slowly running down.

When my watch told me that twilight was gathering above I returned to the control room. "Bow up five," I said to Becker. "Periscope depth." Carbon dioxide was building up in our air and we could not stay down much longer. U-498 angled upward and leveled off just below the surface. We raised periscope and I scanned the darkening horizon.

All was clear, yet I waited for total darkness. I refused to make the same mistake twice. When the night satisfied me, we surfaced and switched to diesel. The vessel picked up speed.

Our guest became impatient. "Why are we heading east?" he demanded.

"Because the enemy will be looking for us where they bombed us or where they expect us to flee, south or west. Not east, not toward the Florida peninsula. We shall turn south in due time, thirty kilometers from land. Until we leave American waters, we travel submerged by day and at the surface only under cover of darkness. It is the only sane option."

Shreck paced back and forth for a moment, and suddenly rushed me. "Again you waste time," he shouted. "You will turn this boat south!"

I spun on him, collared him with both fists, and shoved him against the hull. "Against my judgment, I acceded to your demand that we surface in hostile waters," I shouted. "And you nearly sent us to our graves. No more! I am captain of this vessel!"

His hand shot under his coat and withdrew an ice pick. He handled it with a sureness that informed me that it was a practiced weapon of choice.

Three of my men drew Lugers and leveled them at Shreck. "Careful, Shreck," I said, struggling to contain my rage. "It's *unwise to discharge guns inside a submarine; my men must really want to use them."*

The spy settled back, fire in his eyes, regarding me. He replaced the ice pick, gathered himself, rose, and stalked past me. He stopped, his eyes widening with fright, glancing about.

"Over here," I said, nodding toward Shreck's precious bundle. In the violence, Shreck had lost his grip on it for the first time since he'd joined us. It had fallen open and I glimpsed two gray boxes inside. He cinched it quickly closed, hefted it, and struggled past us, casting suspicious looks, and settled into a corner of the control room, scowling and mumbling. I directed him to bunk with the crew. He declined and huddled with his treasure. That was perfectly fine with me.

Becker arose from his bunk. His pallor had not improved. I placed him in charge and retired to my cabin to catch a few hours' sleep.

As directed, Becker woke me two hours before sunrise. I noted his condition but he shrugged it off. "A full third of the men are seasick, Captain," he said.

"Seasickness is not contagious," I said. Shreck lay bundled where I had left him, softly snoring. I approached and kicked his boot. He stirred.

"Shreck," I said, "you are quite ill."

He mumbled something and sat up. "A cold," he said sleepily. "It's passing."

"My men have it now."

"Bless their poor hearts."

"You've been with us one day. I'm not a doctor, but I know that flu and other viruses take days before symptoms show. So let me ask you: in God's name, what poison did you bring aboard my ship?"

Shreck clutched his bag tighter. "A common cold, Remarque. And though the gravity of my mission is dawning on you, you

*are forbidden to inquire further into the matter. Now then; I
believe it is time that we steer southward."*

I was tempted to cast the son-of-a-bitch overboard. "We shall
see. Kohler, our position?"

"Thirty-two kilometers from the coast, Captain."

"Depth to bottom?"

"Twenty fathoms."

"Hofmann is still on watch topside? Good. Let's join him." I
climbed the tower and emerged onto the bridge to find Hofmann
peering out into the darkness. No stars were visible. Far to the
north, silent lightning illuminated towering black thunderheads.
The fresh, cool air felt good on my face.

"What news, Hofmann?" I asked.

"None, Captain. The sky will be graying in an hour."

I peered through binoculars at the horizon. "Not a single
light," I said. "Not even the lighthouse the charts say is to the
east. It would be just visible if lit; we're at its maximum range.
Wartime blackout. That's good; there won't be any local vessels
abroad tonight. Becker, new heading, due south. Brandt, all the
speed you can muster. In forty-five minutes, we dive and will be
once more reduced to a crawl."

The sub wheeled southward, heeling as it turned.

Kohler drew a sharp, sudden breath. "Captain!" He pointed
twelve degrees off our starboard bow.

A pinpoint of red light glowed there, a hundred meters away.

Someone smoking a cigarette.

Lightning flashed and boomed nearby, illuminating the sea,
illuminating the U-498.

The pinpoint of light suddenly went out, dropping into the
sea. We heard a man shout. The boat's engine popped and
rumbled to life.

"We've been spotted. Light it, Kohler. To the cannon, Hofmann. Quick!"

Kohler flipped on the searchlight and swung it onto the fishing boat. Aboard it, two men scrambled, one hauling up an anchor line, the other shouting and looking into our light. The boat began to pull away.

We could not afford to have our position reported.

"Fire, Hofmann!"

The cannon blasted, spitting fire that lit the sea. Far beyond the fishing boat, a spray of water erupted.

"Steady, Hofmann," I said. "Make it count."

Hofmann took careful aim. The cannon roared again and the boat exploded, a fireball tearing it asunder. Flaming debris flew into the air and rained down onto the water.

I called below. "Twelve degrees starboard, two knots. Kohler, sweep the surface for survivors."

We eased into the burning flotsam. The seas were still rough and not even a strong swimmer would last long here.

"There, Captain," Kohler said. His beam fixed upon a single man treading water.

As we drew near, he swam farther away. "Get the hell away, you sons of bitches," he yelled.

I addressed him in English. "Sir, unless you feel up to the challenge of swimming thirty kilometers, I suggest you surrender and exact your revenge upon us another day."

After a moment, the man turned toward the U-498.

Roscoe Nobles worked his fingers weakly. Where the bonds had bitten into his wrists, the flesh settled, open and hanging. White bone shone through the red and black flesh.

"Thank . . . you," he whispered.

Kyoko's mind raced, a feeling of panic creeping into her. For the first time in her life, she had no idea what to do next. The man needed urgent medical care . . . but would probably die anyway. And the storm was worsening. She had but one direction to go in the lighthouse. Up. But he did not appear capable of climbing the tower and she couldn't carry him to safety with her. And she couldn't leave him here.

Nobles seemed to guess her mind. "Leave me," he rasped. "Blount . . . is coming . . . thinks I'm trapped . . . still." He coughed, his flooded lungs rattling. "I'll . . . stop him."

"You can't stop him and I can't leave you."

"What . . . choice . . . ? None . . ."

"But—"

"Go!"

Kyoko heard the rattling of the door lock below her. She stood and looked into Roscoe's destroyed face. "I'll come back for you. We'll both get out of this."

Roscoe slowly shook his head.

She turned and clambered up the creaking spiral stairs.

Nearing the top, she heard the door clatter open far below. She switched off her light and leaned over the railing, peering down into the darkness. A beam of light flickered at the bottom. Blount had returned with another flashlight.

The beam began to follow the curve of the staircase, and its light got stronger. Soft footsteps came to her, and her hand on the railing felt the faint vibrations. Blount was climbing.

He paused where Nobles would be, and swore angrily.

What was happening?

The beam suddenly swept up toward her and for an instant she was caught in its light. She pulled away.

A gunshot rang, deafening in the hard close space inside the tower. The bullet pinged off the wall next to her and grains of concrete stung her cheek. She scrambled up the staircase and her head struck a ceiling. She reached up, felt it. Steel, set in a rectangular frame. Hinges. A trapdoor. Her fingers traced the outline of the frame and she determined that it opened upward. She shoved against it. Rust flaked off and fell into her eyes, but the door failed to budge. She heaved her shoulder painfully into it, once, twice. Still it failed to yield.

The footsteps below grew louder, quicker, ringing against steel, pounding upward and closer.

Chapter Thirty-Three

Captain Remarque's Journal

The fisherman said his name was Andy Denton. He was bruised but in otherwise good condition. He was fed and clothed and cuffed to a ladder. I gave him a cup of whiskey to ease his pain.

His fishing mate had been torn in half by the blast.

Denton was a strapping young man of conscription age. "Why are you not in the armed forces?" I asked.

"Not that it's any of your Goddamn business, but I washed out on account of flat feet and diabetes."

That was not good. He had no medicines for diabetes and we had but a tiny stock. Not enough to cross the Atlantic on. All I said was, "Lucky man."

"Not in my book. Why'd you shoot us?"

"We could not afford witnesses. Why are you abroad at night?"

"We're fishermen. Half the fishing fleet has gone to war. Somebody's got to feed everybody. We spend a lot of nights on the water."

I nodded. "I trust you will enjoy your voyage. You shall be treated well."

"Can I get a drink of water?"

I shook my head. "We're out of fresh water. If we're lucky enough to catch some, you'll get a sip."

"You got no drinking water? How you expect to get back to

Kraut Land?"

"We will collect rainwater and distill a little from seawater."

"You'll spend all your time collecting drops. I got a better offer for you."

"And what might that be?"

"An unlimited supply of fresh water, a hundred yards from here. We anchored over it."

"I have no time for nonsense." I turned to go.

"No, hear me out! There's a hole in the ocean here. A dang freshwater spring in the Gulf of Mexico. There's a few of 'em up and down both coasts of Florida. Rainfall collects on land and seeps underground and goes where it goes. There's springs all over the place and a few of 'em happen to be offshore."

"This is true?"

"You bet. Me and my father, that you murdered, we found this spring three years ago. Pure dumb luck. We free-dive to it. Found us a couple arrowheads and stuff. Damnedest thing."

"Your father?"

Denton nodded.

"You are taking his death remarkably well."

Denton glared. "Don't you go worry yourself about that."

I decided to drop that issue. "You are sure the water will not be salty?"

"Sweetest water you ever tasted."

"So you'll show us this spring. I assume you want your freedom in return."

"What you got to lose, Adolf?"

"You'll report us as soon as you land."

"Of course I will and I hope we bomb you into little pieces. So you fix that by dropping me off on Cuba. By the time I find an American to talk to, you'll be a thousand miles gone."

Denton was shrewd and something in his eyes told me that he could read people. He had no way of knowing I wouldn't simply put a bullet through his head after he showed us to the spring. Yet he seemed to sense that I was not the barbaric sort.

"We will deposit you in Cuba. Show us the spring."

"Can't. Not yet anyhow. It's nighttime and I ain't a damn bat with night vision. Come first light, you'll have your water."

I thought for a moment. "We will wait until first light. That is nearly an hour of precious time we could make at top speed before having to submerge. When the sky lightens, this boat will become a target. But we need water and I will give you fifteen minutes to find and deliver the water. I will not accept failure. Do you understand?"

"You bet, Adolf. The spring's barely reachable by free-dive. To bottle some water, I'll need to stay down a few minutes. You got a dive helmet and suit? I'm going to need some gear and something to ship water with."

I shook my head and turned to Becker. "Outfit him with a Dräger." Becker left and returned with the Dräger. Resembling a baggy life vest, it was a forerunner of modern scuba and dispensed oxygen through a valve. "This is a Dräger rebreather," I said. "Designed for escape from a sunken submarine. It will give you a few minutes of air."

I ordered Denton to strip nude. He growled about that but relented. I showed him how to wear the Dräger. He strapped it snugly on and took the mouthpiece in and tested it. "Good enough, I guess," he said.

We escorted him to the deck. The seas had slackened and the eastern sky grayed as dawn approached. When the sky and sea resolved into distinct planes, Denton asked for binoculars. I handed him mine and he searched the eastern horizon. "There's the Hammond Lighthouse," he said, pointing. "Brigands Key. Where I live. The lighthouse is dark these days, but you can just see the tip of it over the curve of the Earth." He looked southeast. "And Bishop Bay Lighthouse, way over yonder." He held up his hand to arm's length and counted six palm-widths between the lighthouses. "We ain't drifted far since you blasted me off the water. Go north about a quarter-mile."

I took the binoculars from him and looked all around. All clear. I ordered the new course and the U-498 headed north.

After a minute or so, Denton pointed and said, "There she is." I followed his direction and spotted a small object apparently adrift forty meters ahead. We closed on it, and I could see that it was merely a glass jar bobbing in the water, nearly invisible.

"If Daddy and me had a marked our little secret with a buoy, some bastard would have found it. We marked it with trash, a hundred yards east of the actual spot."

"Clever," I said.

Five empty barrels were brought onto the deck for water collection. Each was filled with seawater to allow them to sink. The idea was that the full barrels would be dropped by ropes above the spring and guided by Denton into its mouth. The barrels would be opened and tipped and the denser seawater would settle out and the less-dense freshwater would replace it.

Over the side man and barrels went.

Two minutes later, a tug came on one rope. We hauled the first barrel onto deck. I opened the valve and water trickled into my cupped palms. I tasted it. The water was fresh and cold.

As the second barrel was hauled aboard, the deck shuddered beneath my feet. Startled glances passed among my men. I motioned to Becker. "Accompany me to the engine room." As I scrambled down the ladder of the tower into the control room, the vessel shuddered again, accompanied by an ominous groan of metal.

I had heard that sound before. It was a ship's death-knell.

Kyoko desperately threw her shoulder against the unyielding trapdoor above her. The door creaked but held fast.

A second gunshot reverberated through the lighthouse. The

bullet plucked at Kyoko's blouse and ricocheted off the wall, striking the steel handrail beside her with a clang. The handrail shook, bent outward by the bullet.

Kyoko grabbed the bent rail and pulled it inward. It yielded slowly; the bullet had torn through the rotted metal.

The footsteps were close now.

She strained against the broken rail. With a snap it broke free, sending her falling backward and into the rail opposite her. She teetered, losing her grip, and nearly tumbled over the rail. She regained her balance, gripped the rail, and jammed its sharp, broken end between the steel door and its frame.

She lifted herself bodily off the platform, using all her weight. The steel shaft crow-barred the door upward a hair. She pulled down hard on the rail.

The footsteps stopped, just below. She could hear the panting of the man.

With a pop, the door jerked upward, fell, and slammed back into its frame. Kyoko fell to the deck, scrambled to her feet, pushed open the door, and bounded up the stairs. She slammed the door shut behind her.

The door jumped open a few inches as Blount shoved it. Kyoko threw herself onto the door, forcing it shut again.

Blount swore and pushed again.

Kyoko whipped the flashlight about, taking in her surroundings. Glass walls encircled the small round room. In the center stood a gigantic glittering glass, the Fresnel lens, standing taller than her. Light played through the great lens, splitting and dancing among the dozens of angular glass ribs that encircled its surface.

She returned her attention to the trapdoor. Two small metal rings attached the frame on either side of it, apparently a security measure. She slid the metal railing through the rings and stepped back.

The door shook and yielded a fraction of an inch, but held.

Blount was barred on the other side, cursing and pounding on the door.

The windows rattled in a powerful gust of wind. She clicked off the flashlight, wiped the glass, pressed her face to it and peered out.

After the inky blackness of the lighthouse interior, the world outside resolved itself in the charcoal twilight of the predawn. She caught her breath. She had read of the fury of a hurricane and had seen the film of flying debris and falling trees. The reality of a Category 5 was far worse. She doubted anyone possessed film of that type of event.

Outside, a ferocious rain flew horizontally in the roar of wind. Across the island debris was flying. A roof peeled off a house two hundred yards away and somersaulted down the street.

The Gulf of Mexico raged. Towering waves crashed into the west of Brigands Key.

A plateau of water on the Gulf, topped by raging, white-capped waves, rolled toward the island.

The storm surge would swamp the island.

Chapter Thirty-Four

Captain Remarque's Journal

I pushed into the engine room. Oily black smoke billowed out. Brandt stumbled into me, coughing, his face streaked and filthy.

I caught him and steadied him. "Brandt, what has happened?"

"The engine has blown its seals. I put out the fire. But that's not the worst of it."

"What then? Speak, man!"

"Captain, we cannot continue. The depth charges ruptured the pressure hull. The boat is shifting in its own skin."

I looked at him with surprise. "But our damage was minimal!"

"Initially, yes; but insidious and inevitable. Multiple leaks starboard and aft. Diesel is leaking, too."

"The diesel will leave a trail on the surface a blind man could follow. The engine is shot, Brandt?"

"Soon."

"What can you coax from it?"

"A hundred nautical miles. At best."

"And then?"

"And then we sink."

I knew what had to be done. "Follow me." I headed back to the control room.

All eyes turned to me. Shreck gave me a narrow, sidelong

look. I believe he suspected my next orders. "Men," I said, "we have lost. Our mission is ended. The U-498 is crippled and cannot make the Fatherland." I turned to Becker. "We retrieve the American. Then, full ahead. Due east."

Shreck bounded to his feet, his face contorting. "Due east?" he shouted.

"We are sinking and my men need medical attention. We cannot survive another hundred kilometers, so we shall raise a white flag and run aground on the coast of Florida."

"This is treason!"

"I'll not sacrifice my crew to your fantasy that Germany might yet win this war."

Wildness blazed in Shreck's eyes. His hands clenched into white-knuckled fists. I readied myself to parry the blow and return it many times over, but the blow never came. Brandt and Becker took a step toward him. Shreck shook with rage.

"You have a choice, Shreck," I said. "Control yourself and you may move about. Do not, and you shall be bound and gagged and shoved into a dark hole where you can bother no one."

Shreck turned away in disgust. He found a hard corner and slumped down, clutching his prize. "I look eagerly forward to your court-martial, Remarque. And your hanging. I shall raise a toast to justice when that fine day comes."

"Don't be an idiot. The Reich will have ceased to exist before we return, even if we could return."

"Coward," Shreck muttered.

The blood of anger rushed into my face. I would have throttled him on the spot, had not my diminishing sense of loyalty to duty and Fatherland stayed my hands. I glanced at my silent, staring crew, and turned again to the spy. "The thought of surrender tears at me. I would sooner go down with this bucket of rust than surrender. It is instilled in me. Yet such a course is folly and these men will not die for my folly, even though they gladly would if I asked. They have wives and children to get home to, or to obtain for the first time. And that's what they shall do. That is my order."

Shreck glared.

"You accept my course of action?" I asked.

He nodded sullenly. "Thus has war ended for me."

"You shall end the war alive, Spy. Rejoice." I turned and climbed the tower.

On deck, I approached Hofmann. "Summon Herr Denton to the surface. Forget the barrels. There is no need to fill them. The ship is dying and we cannot get home. Our only course is surrender."

Hofmann grimaced and cut the third barrel loose even as it broke the surface.

I heard someone climbing the tower behind me and turned to see Shreck emerge from the hatch, still clutching his bag. I tensed, readying myself for another of his outbursts.

"Permission to bridge, Captain?"

His sullen anger, his hate, seemed gone, his expression one of resignation. I was wary but considered the situation. I had not expressly forbidden him from coming topside. Within hours our war would be over; we would make the best of it, I reasoned.

"Permission granted," I said. I returned my attention to Hofmann's work.

What happened in the next moments happened as if in a dream; time slowed for it. Hofmann gave several quick tugs on Denton's line, trying to signal the American. A sudden swift movement from Shreck caught my eye. I turned to see him now wearing a Dräger. He heaved his heavy bundle over the side. It struck with a great splash and disappeared under. The spy leapt in after it, clutching a rolled bundle under one arm. His free hand gripped a nightstick and his wicked ice pick.

324

The deck suddenly heaved beneath me. I staggered, fell to one knee, caught the railing. A deafening roar filled the world. Black smoke surged from the open hatch.

Hofmann, off-balance, pitched forward into the rail, his head striking it with a sharp crack, and somersaulted over the side and disappeared into the sea.

The pressure hull groaned. I felt metal bending, shifting underfoot. Amidships at the waterline, oil and smoke billowed from a great gash. Orange flickered underwater and another explosion shook the boat. The diesel tanks had exploded.

Shreck had bombed the U-498 from within.

The deck lurched and tilted at a crazy angle and hurled me over the side. I slammed into the hull, gashing my scalp, and caromed into the water.

The bow of the U-498 reared above the water and slapped back, throwing up a great wave that shoved me away. The bow settled under and the sub's aft lifted above the water and angled downward.

The sea around me rushed in to fill the void created by the sinking sub, sucking me under. I kicked furiously and managed to escape the water's grasp.

U-498 disappeared with a hiss. I ducked my head under and watched it drift west as it sank. It settled on the edge of an undersea escarpment, rolled slowly over, and disappeared over the edge.

Nary a soul escaped the boat.

I returned to the surface, searching for Hofmann. There was no sign of him. Fury burned in me. I spun about, searching under the water for Shreck.

I spotted him below, emerging from the mouth of the spring, his ice pick clutched in his hand. A cloud of red drifted past him from the spring. Another line of red streamed from his mouth.

Denton was no doubt dead but had inflicted damage before dying.

Shreck glanced at the rush of bubbles and slime that marked the disappearance of the sub. He looked about and located his prize on the sea floor, eight meters from the spring vent. He swam to it, gripped it, and planted his feet against the bottom. He heaved into it and began dragging it toward the vent. It was clearly of great weight and he would exhaust his limited Dräger air quickly. He managed to reach the vent and disappear inside. A moment later he emerged, no longer burdened with his precious bundle.

He had hidden it in the spring and eliminated all witnesses.

Except one.

The second bundle he'd carried overboard floated on the surface, an inflatable life raft, thirty meters away. He was making his way toward it, his back toward me.

I shook off my boots and shirt, as they threatened to drag me under, and swam after him. He reached the surface and stripped off his Dräger, gasping, and let it sink. He caught hold of the raft, still holding the ice pick. He must have realized the folly of bringing a sharp weapon aboard a flimsy inflatable at sea, and cast the ice pick aside. He scanned the surface, searching for survivors. I was a mere dozen meters from him. I anticipated his move and ducked underwater. As I closed in, he swung one leg onto the raft and began hauling himself up.

With one last powerful kick, I shot toward him and grabbed his trailing leg. I burst to the surface, gulped air, and went back under, rolling his leg under me as I went.

His grip on the raft was wrenched free and he was dragged under, with me above him. He'd been surprised and had not drawn much air, so sudden was his immersion. Bubbles streamed from his mouth. He flailed wildly at me. I raised my face above water once more and drove down into him again. Life was a

*contest of breath-holding now and I had drawn the last breath
between us.*

*Terror took him and he fought and clawed desperately. I
drove him deeper, one fathom, two fathoms, not releasing my
grip on his legs. He tore at my face. I shut my eyes to protect
them.*

*My lungs burned for air. I wanted nothing more than to
return to the surface, yet I held my grip, absorbing his blows.*

*His struggles at last weakened. He shivered, and his blows
stopped. He became still. I opened my eyes and studied him. His
eyes stared blankly; his mouth was agape. No breath issued
from him. I shoved him away. His body hung in the water, a
puppet. I hurried to the surface and gasped in the air.*

*Exhausted, I drifted in the raft for hours until a fishing boat
picked me up a few kilometers from land. I was a sorry sight,
without strength or will.*

*The Americans held me for two days in a prisoner of war
camp in the town of Orlando then whisked me away to a
destination I still do not know. I was interrogated for days and
nights without end. The Americans wanted badly to know of my
submarine.*

*I told them everything but the truth about our guest and the
location of the U-498. Shreck, I reasoned, had stolen something
of terrible significance, of top secrecy. The Americans had stopped
at nothing to retrieve it. If I had knowledge of this secret, my
knowledge might best die with me. If I had no knowledge of it,
if I were merely an unlucky submariner, they might let me live.*

*So I lied. I had slipped into the Gulf of Mexico to disrupt
shipping, one last hurrah for the Kriegsmarine. I had no
knowledge of any spies. I had not come within sight of the coast.
Yes, we were attacked by a Catalina and we sank, nearly two
hundred kilometers to the west. I was the only survivor.*

I doubt they believed me. I learned later that a great number of vessels and airplanes had scoured the coast for hundreds of kilometers in both directions and far out to sea. But the sea is a vast place, and they were searching for a needle in a haystack.

I spent the remainder of the war, and then some, sequestered. When finally they released me, I was escorted back to Germany.

Two bombs, super-weapons of terrible power, had forced the surrender of Japan, only months after Germany had collapsed.

I knew then the nature of Shreck's prize.

I studied and pieced together the story. Shreck had stolen Uranium-235, the fuel for the weapons, from the vast secret city thrown together in the remote Tennessee countryside.

The theft has never been acknowledged. Even the destruction of the U-498 in the Gulf of Mexico was erased. Wiped clean. I was promised extreme recrimination if I ever claimed such an event. To this day, the only sub lost in the Gulf is the U-166. My boat apparently sank in the Atlantic, off North Carolina.

I lived with silence and fear for twelve years and I was forgotten. I wished to live out my years on solid, dry land, a gentleman vintner of the Rhineland. But restless memory squirmed in my brain.

As the world left war behind, alliances and hatreds shifted and world powers again struggled for dominance, armed with unspeakably powerful weapons. History seems fated to repeat itself yet again. I cannot stop the madness. But I knew where the heart of one such weapon lay.

A forgotten man, I emigrated to America without incident in 1957. I settled in the little town of Brigands Key. I fell in love with the island and its peculiar inhabitants, of which I am now the most peculiar.

I had one mission left. I could not begin to locate the sunken sub and the lethal thing that lay nearby, nor did I want to. No, my mission was to make sure that no one else found them. I would keep the murderous thing out of the hands of men for the remainder of my life.

And so ends my story. You know the secret of U-498.

Denton's spring and the weapon will someday be discovered. There is no doubt of that. I am taking the risk that the industrious, intelligent person that decrypts this message will be wise enough to guide that rediscovery toward a sane conclusion. To that end, I wish you courage and peace.

Captain Friedrich Remarque

October 1962

CHAPTER THIRTY-FIVE

The wind howled and thrummed against the walls as Grant finished. He stared at the last line and set the page aside and looked at his companions.

Hammond paced, deep in thought, his face clouded. "Damn me straight to hell," he said. "How could I miss the signs? How could I be so stupid? The plague of Brigands Key is acute radiation poisoning."

"The mystery of ageless John Doe is solved," Grant said. "Shreck's treasure is what preserved Andy Denton. He was bathed in radiation since he was murdered in the spring."

Hammond nodded. "Radiation killed all the bacteria in his body; bacteriological decomposition was put on hold while enzymic decomposition was unaffected. A man dead sixty years looks like he died this week. Like using radiation as a food preservative. Incredible."

"And we've got a killer running around the island trying to get his hands on the guts of an atomic bomb," Sanborn said.

Charley held his head in his hands, staring at the floor.

Grant put his hand on the young man's shoulder. "Charley? You got something on your mind? This is no time for shyness."

Charley looked up at him, his eyes glistening. "Roscoe . . . he found his treasure but he had no idea what he was after. He was obsessed with gold. Probably thought Remarque had a cache of gold bullion stolen from Fort Knox." He shook his head.

"Radiation poisoning is not going to stop," Hammond said.

"The best thing that could have happened to us was this hurricane forcing everyone off the island."

"I wish it was that simple, Doc," Charley said. "If I ever got off this island and got to college, do you know what I was going to study? Physics."

"I'm getting a sinking feeling, Charley," Grant said, glancing at his watch. "Spill it. Time's wasting."

"Physics is my bag. I read everything I can about it. Max Shreck didn't just steal nuclear fuel. He stole enriched Uranium-235 from Oak Ridge. It took years to produce enough for one bomb. Officially, the U.S. built three bombs from two different designs in World War II. Two of the bombs were implosion-type devices. In an implosion device, a plutonium core reaches critical mass and a chain reaction kicks in when an outer shell of conventional explosives goes off and implodes violently on the core. The implosion bombs used plutonium produced in Washington state. The first of them was used in the Trinity test in New Mexico. The other was Fat Man and was dropped on Nagasaki.

"The third bomb was called a gun weapon. It used U-235 produced at Oak Ridge. The material was produced there and made into a weapon at Los Alamos. The gun-type trigger fires a mass of U-235 into another mass of U-235, slamming them to critical mass and unleashing a chain reaction. That bomb was Little Boy and it obliterated Hiroshima. If Remarque's story is true, guess what? A second mass of U-235 was produced in Oak Ridge and actually fabricated into a bomb core there. But there's no public record of that. Because of the theft, its existence has been kept secret.

"Gun-type uranium bombs were of a much simpler design but they were virtually abandoned soon after that. Here's the problem. The weapon is a shit-storm of unreliability; too much can go wrong and start a chain reaction before you're ready.

But the simplicity of the design makes it a huge threat today. Any dirtbag country with enough U-235 can build a Hiroshima-type bomb, but the damned thing might go off if there's a mistake in construction.

"What we're facing is a ready-made A-bomb core that could be fashioned into a horrific weapon by anyone with a physics degree and a good machine shop. We've got two masses of U-235, each one subcritical. If they're forced together and critical mass is reached, even by accident, even a partial detonation, even a fizzle, we could get a chain reaction that would blow Brigands Key off the map."

"Wait a minute," Sanborn said. "How do you know there are two chunks of it?"

"U-235 in small amounts isn't dangerous at all. But put together enough, roughly a hundred and fourteen pounds, it goes critical. The Little Boy core weighed a hundred and forty pounds. Remarque peeked at Shreck's treasure. He saw two boxes jostling in the bundle. Two masses, physically separated, yet close enough together that gamma radiation was being sparked. The fact that Shreck was deathly ill and Remarque's crew got sick proves it. And the fact that Brigands Key is now sick backs it up. Kept apart, you only get alpha and beta radiation, not enough to make you sick. We've been getting dosed with gamma, which penetrates the whole body. If the two masses had been kept apart there wouldn't be a problem."

"Christ," Sanborn muttered. "I hope everyone got off the island."

A bang shook the bank; something had slammed into the roof. "Celeste is here," Hammond said. He went to the front door. It was unlocked, but he was unable to push it open; the wind had barred it shut. "Must be blowing a hundred miles an hour."

"We haven't seen the worst of it yet," Grant said. "The eyewall's packing a buck-fifty."

"We can ride it out here," Hammond said hopefully. "This bank is built solid. One of the strongest buildings on the island."

Grant shook his head. "No good. This is a one-story building. The storm surge is going to sweep in here, twenty feet or more. We'll drown here, and if we wait ten more minutes, we may be in the strongest winds and unable to leave at all. We have to get out now."

"The high school gym?"

"You can go there. Not me. I just figured this thing out. Blount's onto the score of a lifetime. To hell with gold; he can sell weapons-grade uranium for a billion dollars to any one of a dozen banana republics. He can't slip out without risking losing it. His best chance is to let Celeste chase everyone off and kill anyone else stupid enough to stick around, and then slip out of here unnoticed after she leaves, in the dark, before search-and-rescue squads can enter. But we've got a playing card now; he doesn't have the uranium and he thinks I might. He's desperate." Grant looked at his watch again. "I have exactly fourteen minutes to meet his deadline. Now that I know what he's after, I'm going to fake my way through it."

"We don't have any idea where to start," Hammond said.

"Yes we do. I'm going where Blount is hiding out, and where he's got Kyoko. He's sitting pretty right now in the securest place on the island, a place he magnanimously maintains for the City, and that only he has keys and access to. The only place on the island strong and high enough to escape the storm surge. Hammond Lighthouse."

Blount's furious pounding on the door suddenly stopped. Kyoko waited, shaking with tension. She had no weapon, except for the tiny shard of glass. The broken metal railing she'd wedged the door shut with would make a worthy, even lethal, weapon.

Yet she dared not pull it from the door.

What was Blount up to?

She stared out at the raging storm, transfixed. Amid the thrashing and whipping of trees and the flying rain, something caught her eye, something unnatural in that fury of nature. Something far below her.

She leaned against the shaking glass and peered down, hoping to catch a glimpse. A lone figure, black and hunched, leaned into the wind, stumbled to its knees, and crawled onward.

Roscoe.

Somehow, he'd slipped by Blount, hidden in the dark. No, he couldn't have sneaked past in such a confined space. Roscoe had played dead. That was the only explanation. He was near death anyway and it wouldn't have been difficult to fake the rest of the way. Blount had found him motionless, probably kicked him in the gut and left him for dead, thinking Kyoko, a low-paid government physician, wouldn't have just abandoned the poor soul to his own fate.

Guilt stung her. Abandoned him? That was exactly what she had done. She had to, she forced herself to think. There was no other way.

Roscoe crawled into the brush at the edge of the yard and disappeared. Kyoko swallowed hard. Out of the frying pan, into the teeth of the storm of the century. Roscoe would surely drown when the sea swept in.

The lantern room was walled with heavy glass panes framed in riveted, rusting steel from floor to ceiling. Storm panes, Hammond had called them. In the center of the room the gorgeous Fresnel lens towered over her, fixed upon a vertical axle. Her light played on the lens and the lantern room glittered and sparkled, rainbows of color dancing all around, the lens's hundred prisms scattering it in a dazzling display.

Outside the storm panes was a sagging steel deck, a catwalk

encircling the lantern room, topped with a handrail.

There had to be an access way to the catwalk. She glanced about at the storm panes and realized that one set had a slightly heavier frame. A glass door.

She found and tried the door handle. The mechanism refused to budge, likely fused into a solid, unmoving mass by years of salt air. She threw her weight into it, with no results.

Abandoning the glass door, she felt about quickly. She needed something, a weapon, a plan, a hope, anything. A dark heap at the base of the Fresnel lens caught her attention. She hurried to it and found it to be a canvas tarp covering a mass of bulging objects. She threw the tarp aside and examined the items. There were empty paint cans, brushes, a small broken chair, a coil of steel cable.

She hefted the chair. It was a wooden chair, a small rocker, missing one leg, its cane seat rotted through. Decades old, no doubt sat in by a lonely lightkeeper whiling away the hours. Kyoko pulled off a leg. It splintered, rotten in places. The chair felt puny and irrelevant against a gun-wielding enemy. It would have to do. She set it behind the lens.

A crash at the trapdoor startled her. Blount had returned with something heavy and was bashing his way inside.

Again he struck the door. It bulged upward and she threw herself onto it. She prayed he couldn't shoot her through the steel and doubted he would risk being killed by his own ricocheting bullet. She could hold him out indefinitely.

He struck the door again. No, not the door. The frame that secured it. The door was not the weak point; the aging mortar holding the frame in place was.

He struck again and again. She reached down and felt the mortar. It was cracking and crumbling with each blow.

She abandoned the door. Attempting to hold him out was futile. When the mortar and frame gave way, she would tumble down with it. She returned to the pile of debris, running her hands over each item. Nothing of value, nothing.

She felt the cable.

It was a long coil of twined steel, the thickness of a pencil. Metal threads bristled along its length like tiny quills, painful to the touch.

A thought, an insane, impossible one born of desperation, sprang into her mind.

Grant hesitated, gripping the handle of the bank door. "Ready?"

"There's not a damn thing will get me ready for this," Sanborn said. "Let's do it."

"Once more unto the breach," Hammond said.

Grant shoved the door open. The angle of the wind had shifted enough so that it no longer pinned the door shut. The door was leeward, sheltered by the building itself, in relative calm. Just a few feet beyond, the wind roared. Spray flew in sheets, a whipping wall, and foliage and debris sailed past.

Dawn was breaking somewhere, washing the scene in shades of gray and black. Across the street, the giant live oak that had stood guard over City Hall, that had outlived two hundred hurricane seasons, lay on its side. With a metallic shriek, a huge sheet of steel roofing peeled off the Island Mart and flew spinning away, becoming a blade that could slice a man in half.

The street was under a foot of racing water, the rain falling too fast, too hard, to drain anywhere.

"Surreal," Sanborn muttered.

"Flat against the wall," Grant shouted. "Wind's blasting southwest to northeast, so if we stay on the north and east faces of buildings we'll avoid the worst of it. Keep to the back of the bank and try and make the next building. That's forty feet unprotected. We take it that way, building by building, all the way to the lighthouse."

He stepped out, glued himself to the wall and edged his way along the building, his companions following close behind. He reached the end of the bank, looked across to the drugstore. He steeled himself and sprang out into the open.

The wind caught him like a great hand and threw him sprawling to the ground with a splash. Rain stung him like needles. His face slid over pavement and he felt the skin on his cheek strip open.

The pain of his punctured thigh welled up, a great searing wash of agony, overwhelming the painkillers Hammond had pumped into him. He squeezed his eyes shut, forced back the pain.

He struggled to his feet and ran with the howling wind, being shoved ahead. He reached the lee wall of the pharmacy and escaped the wind, gasping for breath.

His companions, stumbling, pushed along by the wind, staggered up after him.

"How the hell did we do that?" It was Hammond.

"Clean living," Grant shouted.

Charley grabbed Grant by the arm. "Doc!" He pointed west across town.

Grant's blood froze. Two hundred yards away, driven by the tempest, a wall of water raced through the streets, engulfing houses, crashing into them with great sprays of white. Trees uprooted and were swept along with the flood. An old Victorian was lifted off its foundation and swept along, disintegrating as it came, slamming into other buildings.

The surge would be upon them in seconds.

Grant shoved Charley along. "Run! If we don't make the lighthouse before the flood they'll never find our corpses."

CHAPTER THIRTY-SIX

Blount lashed out at the door frame again and again. It bulged upward and tore free from the mortar and clanged onto the floor. Kyoko considered abandoning her wild scheme for an instant. This is it, your last chance, she thought. Charge headlong into the son of a bitch and win some tiny advantage before he's all the way in. But hesitation robbed her of the fleeting opportunity and Blount surged through the shattered doorway, pistol in hand, ready for any attack she may have planned.

She backed against the storm panes, positioning herself so that the Fresnel lens stood between her and Blount.

"End of the line, bitch," Blount said.

She willed herself to be calm, or to at least sound calm. "I thought you needed me alive."

Blount's voice was tinged with something from the dark boundary of morality. "I gave your boyfriend instructions; find the prize and deliver it or the Chinese bitch comes back bit by bit. Time's up. It was worth a shot, leveraging you with your boyfriend, to see if he knew something about the treasure. But he failed and has either fled or will be dead soon, so you've got no value left. Blame him for your death." He leveled his pistol at her.

Kyoko stared at the gun, transfixed. Panic welled in her, and she forced it down. No time for that. Be cool, be smart. Buy some time. She wanted to run, but where? She willed herself to be still. "I know what this is all about, Blount," she said, struggling to keep her terror from her voice.

Blount sneered. "I doubt it."

"It's about a huge payday. An unimaginable payday."

"You have no idea." He took aim.

"What's bomb-grade nuclear material sell for on the black market these days? The answer is, sky's the limit."

Blount's eyes widened and his gun hand sagged for a split second. So she was onto something. The realization sent a shiver of fear through her. He really was after a nuclear weapon. *But he hasn't got it yet.*

"I don't know what you're talking about."

That lie was a good sign, Kyoko thought. Blount was suddenly struggling with the thought that she might be worth keeping alive a little longer. She had to keep him on the hook.

"We wring our hands about nuclear proliferation but can't find enough spare change to buy up old Soviet stocks. Yet there are monsters in the world with exceedingly deep pockets who'll find the money. You're auctioning off a warhead! The flaw in this marvelous plan is that you don't even have it. Otherwise, there'd be no point to all the kidnapping and murder."

"You're a smart bitch, I'll give you that, but things have to add up. The bomb core is on the island and I'll be the only person alive that knows it. Nobles hid it and managed to keep his secret. Soon as I tried to pry it out of him, the quarantine was dumped on us. But this hurricane's a Godsend. Once Celeste passes, I'll sweep this sand pile with a Geiger counter, house by house if I have to. Brigands Key isn't so big I can't find it in a single night. It's as good as mine."

Kyoko's mind raced. Blount's scheme could only succeed if she, Grant, Charley, Hammond, and Sanborn were all dead. He would kill them all. "You won't pull it off without drawing attention. I have a better idea."

"And what's that?"

"I can take you to it."

"Bullshit. You don't know where it is."

"Roscoe told me. Right after I released him and right before he died."

"Why would he tell you?"

"I was his last hope. I'm confused, though," she said. "I take you to the bomb core, you kill me, you eliminate one witness. But Grant, Sanborn, and Hammond also know what you're after. You're rolling the dice, betting the hurricane kills them all. If even one survives, you're screwed. He'll bring hell down on you. How do you think you'll get out of here?"

Resolve crept back into Blount's eyes. "I don't survive officially. There'll be a lot of missing persons to sort through."

"Ah. A casualty of Celeste. Good plan."

"Say goodbye, bitch."

"I can guarantee your escape."

He hesitated.

"Sanborn's missing a walkie-talkie. You had free run in City Hall and the Police Department. You stole the radio to eavesdrop, keep track of their movements and guesswork. Pretty thorough, you are."

"I'm still listening."

"Call him on it. Tell him to steal the mayor's Hummer and rush it over here. It's the only vehicle on the island that can make it in a storm like this. I lead you to the atomic core and you make your getaway."

"No good. They don't know who I am and I plan to keep it that way."

"And you will."

"How?"

"They stay in the lighthouse. It's the only way I can save them. You get away and I save my friends."

"No good. You know my identity."

"But I'm your insurance policy. You'll take me hostage. That's your only chance. You cross the bridge as soon as the eyewall passes. In two hours you'll be in Tampa. You ditch the Hummer and lay low. You can kill me then." She edged a few inches closer to the coil of steel cable on the floor.

Blount watched her through narrowed, wary eyes. Cold, calculating, sorting through the idea, weighing it. He shook his head almost imperceptibly. "And then I'm tracked down. I learned a long time ago, you don't act impulsively. Things add up, then you act. This doesn't add up. Tough luck, huh, lady?" He leveled his pistol at her face, an eager fire in his eyes. His knuckles flexed as his finger tightened on the trigger.

Kyoko grabbed the broken chair and hurled it at him and dropped to the floor in one swift motion. Blount jerked reflexively aside, trying to dodge. The chair smacked a glancing blow across his face. The gun roared and the bullet hissed past her face. The glass behind her exploded and wind gushed into the tiny interior.

Blount wiped a sudden line of blood from his eyes. "You whore!"

Kyoko darted behind the Fresnel lens. He whipped his pistol toward her and fired. The bullet nicked the lens and glass sprayed from a shattered prism. The light of the gun blast refracted through the great lens, flashing bands of colored light in all directions.

Kyoko scrambled across the floor, hooked the coils of steel cable into the crook of her arm, and darted through the shattered window. Broken glass raked her shoulder, slicing her blouse and skin. She gained the catwalk, in the leeward side of the lighthouse, away from the blasting wind.

Blount fired again. Another storm pane exploded.

Kyoko crawled quickly, staying low.

Above the rush and roar of the hurricane, she heard a metallic groan, a giving of rotted steel. The catwalk shook under her and dropped a few inches. Another couple of seconds . . .

The catwalk broke under her weight. She grabbed a slat of steel and clung to it, its ragged edges digging into her fingers. The cable slipped off her arm and tangled in the decking. Her legs swung crazily out from the wall of the tower. The deck lurched and twisted, catching Kyoko's hair and pinning her head against the wall. She could not move.

Blount staggered forward. He raised his gun, took aim.

She was suspended, immobile, a mere six feet from the gun. This time, there was no way he could miss.

With all her might, she lunged toward the coiled steel. Her outstretched hand caught it, and with her other hand, she released her grip on the catwalk. The gun roared again. She felt her hair tearing out by the roots and an instant later she was plummeting into wind and rain and space.

CHAPTER THIRTY-SEVEN

Charley was slammed to the ground by a powerful gust. He staggered to his feet, pushed ahead, and shot a glance behind him. The flood rushed through the street, seventy yards behind, closing in fast. If it caught them . . .

He stumbled forward. The lighthouse loomed ahead, towering above them in the dim gray world.

A street sign whistled through the air inches from his face. He dodged, trying not to think about the carnage it would have done to his good looks.

They closed in on the lighthouse. They were going to make it! They passed into the wind shadow of a stand of leaning, thrashing cedars and raced up the driveway.

He skidded to a stop, colliding with Hammond.

The gate was locked.

They glanced about. The chain link fence was ten feet high, topped with three strands of barbed wire, the result of a lame attempt by the City Council to thwart vandalism. The Council had overlooked situations like this.

A roar rose behind them. The flood was within thirty yards. There wasn't time enough for all of them to climb the fence.

"There!" Hammond shouted, pointing. To their left, a giant magnolia had fallen, and lay in a heap across a tangle of crushed fencing between them and the on-rushing water.

They raced to the breach in the fence, climbed onto the trunk of the magnolia, and scrambled through the tangle of branches and dropped onto the other side.

Water poured over the driveway and enveloped the base of the lighthouse, striking it with a great splash and spray of white.

The lighthouse was cut off.

Hammond waved to them and ran ahead to the lighthouse keeper's home.

The building was a sturdy old concrete and brick house. It was the second one built, the first having been destroyed in a hurricane in 1901. It stood on an ancient Mississippian mound seven feet higher than the island; the house's first floor was another four feet above that. It had withstood hurricanes but none like this. It would have to do.

They bounded up the brick steps as the flood rushed in. Five feet of water slammed into Charley and knocked him off his feet and off the steps. Panic grabbed him as he felt himself irresistibly swept along. He struck the heavy brick pilaster at the corner of the steps and clawed for a finger hold, slowing himself for an instant.

Grant, clinging to the wooden handrail, reached out and hooked his arm under Charley's, and pulled him free of the surging water, dragging him onto the porch.

Hammond tried the door, found it locked, and threw his shoulder against it. It didn't budge. Sanborn stepped back, steadied himself against the howling wind, and leapt and crashed through the window to the right and into the interior. Broken glass became airborne and sailed off into the gloom.

There came a tortured shriek of twisting metal. Overhead, the tin roof peeled upward and tore loose and flew away.

They scrambled through the shattered window as water poured onto the porch.

Kyoko hurtled downward, the flooding ground below rushing up to her. The cable, wound three loops around Kyoko's right arm and once around her left, yanked with a ferocious jerk, nearly wrenching her shoulder out of its socket. Her legs swung wildly below her. The steel fibers of the cable bit into her flesh.

The base of the lighthouse below was swiftly engulfed by the flood. She swung out of the leeward side into the winds of Celeste and was instantly whipped out and away from the lighthouse. Raindrops, flying laterally at one hundred fifty miles per hour, stung like bees. Again her shoulder was yanked sharply as the cable reached its length. Pain shot through her and radiated down her arm.

The wind flung her far out from the lighthouse and shoved her back into the narrow wind shadow of the structure. She slammed into the lighthouse with a bone-jarring impact, caromed off the wall, flew out, and again struck the wall. The breath was knocked from her and she gasped, desperately trying to suck in air.

Water splashed in her face. Not from the rain, she realized; she was in the shadow protected from the driving, stinging bullets of rain. She looked down. To her horror, she realized how high the sea had climbed. Twenty feet below, water rushed by, encircling the lighthouse, submerging the main door at its base. The storm surge was at least ten feet and climbing. Above the surge, waves ten feet high peaked and fell, racing past, their tops blown off by the thundering winds in sprays of white foam. A wave crashed into the lighthouse and exploded upward, dashing her with water.

The surge climbed inexorably. A rectangle of blue floated past her, rolled, and revealed a windshield. A car, tumbling along in the storm. It struck the lighthouse with a crunch, rolled again, and disappeared under the water.

What was it they had predicted about Celeste? A storm surge of twenty feet, with waves ten feet high over that?

The water rose, sweeping lethal debris along with it. Within minutes it would engulf her and pluck her off the lighthouse like an insect. She would be at its mercy.

Something pinged against the wall next to her. She looked up. Far above, Blount leaned out over the edge of the lighthouse. The gun flashed and barked. A bullet whistled past, grazing her hip, nicking her flesh with a stab of intense pain.

Water swirled around the keeper's house, rising with each second. Grant cast about inside, searching. The house was empty, devoid of furniture. "Nothing here. We've got to fortify the door and hope the water doesn't reach the windows."

"The lighthouse and the keeper's house were already on an Indian mound and then built up a century ago," Hammond said. "New buildings are mostly on stilts, to get above the flood level, but I'll bet eighty percent of the buildings are just a few feet above sea level. We're on the highest point on Brigands Key right now. The whole island is under water. If anybody didn't get off the island . . ."

Water was now a foot deep inside. "How strong is this building?" Grant asked.

"Damned strong. Strongest building on the island. Poured concrete walls a foot thick, reinforced with steel, faced with brick. Built to survive. When the town was in its infancy, this house was the storm shelter for the whole populace."

"Yet it already lost the roof."

Hammond raised his hands in a so-what gesture. "Roofs come and go."

Grant looked out the window, awestruck at the unleashed fury. An ancient oak, forty feet from the house, leaned and toppled into the water. "Another tree down," he shouted. "We've got a problem."

"There are going to be a lot of them blown over," Sanborn said.

"This one wasn't blown over. It was undercut. It was on the edge of the mound we're on." He turned to face them. "The house may be strong as granite, but the mound is washing away. No house can stand on dirt that's not there."

His companions hurried to the window. A great slab of mud calved and slid down the side of the mound.

"Son of a bitch," Hammond growled.

Sanborn twisted his head, listening. "Did you hear something?"

Hammond shook his head. "No. What . . . ?"

"A gunshot. There's another one."

Charley pointed. "Look!"

Grant felt the blood drain from his face. Across the flood, dangling just above the crashing waves and rushing water, whipped by wind, was Kyoko. And high above her, Artie Blount took careful aim at her and fired.

"Take him out, Sanborn," Grant shouted.

Sanborn nodded, drew his pistol. He set up in the window, his elbows propped on the sill, his left hand cradling his gun hand, steadying it. He sighted carefully. "I'll never hit him at this distance in a storm with a pistol, you know."

"Take him out!"

Sanborn held his breath, aimed high, taking a wild guess at an adjustment for gravity and hurricane winds. He squeezed the trigger.

The gun roared, deafening in the small space of the room.

A puff of white sprayed off the wall of the lighthouse, a few feet below Blount and to his side. He jumped, startled, and glanced about. Sanborn adjusted his aim, fired again.

The second bullet struck inches from Blount, shattering one of the long rectangular panes of glass that enclosed the light. He backed away from the destroyed window and his silhouette reappeared on the opposite side of the lantern room.

"Kyoko will be dead in minutes from the storm or from Blount," Grant said. "I'm going after her. How many rounds you got?"

"This a Glock .40 caliber. Fourteen left in the magazine, two more magazines of fifteen each in pouches. Forty-four rounds."

"Don't save them for a rainy day. Keep Blount pinned down." He began to climb through the window.

"Wait!" Hammond said. "You won't be any good to her dead. You won't get thirty feet before you're tumbled underwater." As if to punctuate his sentence, a sudden swell rolled over the porch and water poured through the open window.

"I'm a hell of a strong swimmer," Grant said. "And I don't have a choice. I can make it."

"You'll never make it. I can give you a chance. Everybody upstairs, quick. We're losing the first floor anyway."

Grant hesitated.

"Trust me, Grant. I know you need to help her. But just trust me. Come upstairs."

Grant nodded reluctantly and slipped off the window sill. A gunshot sounded and a bullet struck the window frame, splintering wood.

"Blount's got a fix on us now," Sanborn said.

They bounded upstairs, the old steps threatening to cave in with each step. "This is the keeper's bedroom," Hammond said, trying the first door they came to. Locked. He stepped aside, motioning to Sanborn. "You're the law. Nobody will arrest you for breaking and entering. More importantly, you're the biggest guy here." Sanborn nodded and kicked the door in.

There was no ceiling, it having been ripped away with the roof, and the wind howled overhead. The room was cluttered with odds and ends. Old furniture, wood crates, boxes of nails, stacks of lumber. "This room became the storage closet of the various agencies that maintained the lighthouse since it was shut down," Hammond said.

Hammond hurried to a crate along the far wall and pried open the lid. "Still here," he said. He pulled out a pair of old, faded life preservers. "Take these," he said, tossing them to Grant. "They're old but serviceable. We bought 'em for the last lighthouse keeper. I think you'll drown anyway, but at least you'll have a fighting chance." He handed more lifejackets to Charley and Sanborn. "You too. I have a feeling we'll be fighting to keep our heads above water in another ten minutes."

Grant pulled one on and snapped the straps into place across his chest. "Thanks." He went to the upstairs window and looked out. Blount still held guard in his tower, searching for them. He apparently considered them his only threat at this point; Kyoko was as good as dead.

"Not while I'm alive," Grant muttered. He turned to Sanborn. "Cover me. I need ten seconds."

"You got it." Sanborn took up a position at the north window, looked up, took aim, and fired.

CHAPTER THIRTY-EIGHT

Roscoe Nobles staggered across the loft of an ancient, ramshackle warehouse on the waterfront, his right foot dragging lifelessly.

The building leaned and groaned as if alive, slowly giving way to the bludgeoning power of nature.

Burning, blinding pain coursed through his body. He had never imagined how much an entire body, how every cell, from his skin right down through his muscles and organs, could burn like fire. Searing pain was all he could feel, a universe of pain. His thoughts were muddled and confused, but he had a purpose and when confusion threatened to overwhelm him, he concentrated on his purpose. That was all he had left. Everything else, his life, his home, his unquenchable, incurably romantic dream . . . all gone. Swept away by furious, uncaring nature and an evil human being.

Mother Nature you forgive. You just do.

Not so with a human being that has destroyed your life.

All he had left was his purpose.

Revenge.

He hoped like hell he had enough life left in him to exact it. He coughed up a sticky mass of blood and phlegm and stared at it numbly. He had his doubts.

Snap to, he thought. Stick to your purpose.

He had somehow stumbled, dazed, across the island, ducking into the lee of buildings, crawling, to reach the wharf seconds before the flood. To get here, the best place on the island to hide something from that pig, Blount.

In one of Blount's own properties.

Blount, the realtor, the land speculator, was the biggest property owner on Brigands Key, outside of that carpet-bagging outfit from Tampa. And Blount was in cahoots with them, too. Son of a bitch was never satisfied. Never.

Blount owned over two-dozen properties but not for the hell of owning them. He'd always put on a big show of opposing big development, and all the while he was buying up derelict properties from bankrupt fishermen. That was part of his scheme. Fight the developer, be the friend of the little man, and buy 'em out. Once Bay View got up and running, land values would skyrocket.

So Blount had all these properties and never spent a plugged nickel on them and never set foot in them. Just sat on them, waiting for his big score.

Until he stumbled onto a chance for an even bigger score.

Claim-jumpers got strung up in the old days. And a claim-jumper was exactly what Blount was. Except he'd also graduated to kidnapper and murderer.

Blount was looking all over the island for Roscoe's treasure. He'd looked everywhere except in his own rundown warehouse.

The warehouse stood a hundred feet from Roscoe's boat slip on the dock. Roscoe had hid it there, high in the loft, the night he'd found it and brought it to the island.

Revenge . . .

Except for three people, the island had been abandoned. He was sure of that. No sign of another human being anywhere on the island. Even the high school gym, the storm shelter, was abandoned. Good thing. It wouldn't be standing in another hour.

Just as he reached the warehouse, the flood had swept in,

engulfing everything. He'd managed to pull himself up the ladder to the loft. From there, he'd peered out to witness the
destruction of his town. Houses collapsed and rushed past in
the apocalypse.

Three people left. Himself, Blount, and that woman that had
cut him free. He'd never seen her before. All he knew was that
she was an outsider and an angel. She was now a victim too.
Blount had surely killed her.

With swollen, pulpy hands, he pried up a loose board in the
deck of the loft. Beneath it were two bags. He withdrew the
bags and opened them, studied the contents. Not the great
hoard of gold he'd once envisioned. But far more valuable. And
lethal. He knew what it was from what it had done to him.

He strained to lift the heavy bags from the cubbyhole. He
raised them an inch or two, struggling mightily. It was like lift-
ing a grown man. He gasped and set them down again, panting.
Too heavy! His strength was a shadow of what it had been.
Failure . . .

He saw in his mind Blount's smug face and remembered the
years of lies. His anger swelled. The son of a bitch would not
get away with it. He gritted his teeth, tightened his grip on the
bags, and heaved. He swung them free. He gasped, his breath
rattling wet in his lungs. Groaning, every fiber of his body
screaming in agony, he managed to drop them to the flooded
floor of the warehouse, making sure he kept them apart. Water
poured into the building through the sagging door, and the two
bags struck with a splash. He descended from the loft and
waded through the water and retrieved them. He dragged the
bundles to the leeward side of the warehouse, facing the dock.

The marina had been devastated. Boats were capsized and
shattered and submerged, others were broken free and being
driven, rolling, across the channel toward the mainland by the
shrieking wind and towering seas. Only one boat remained

moored in place: *Electric Ladyland.*

Roscoe had been held captive since before he knew a hurricane was headed this way. He wouldn't have known at that time to moor it to swing with the wind and waves on a long chain, long enough to ride above an impossibly high storm surge. Someone had rigged it for him.

Charley. His friend.

Roscoe found the cobwebbed aluminum skiff Blount kept in a corner and turned it over. It appeared okay . . . for a calm day on a pond. It would not last a minute in this storm.

But all he needed was a half-minute. He emptied the water from the skiff and it floated free. A small two-horse motor was fixed to its transom. On a shelf above the boat was a gasoline can. He lifted it, shook it. It had maybe an inch of gas inside. Or maybe it was water. It would have to do.

A splintering sound cracked nearby. The building shifted and a seam opened in the west wall from floor to ceiling. The building was about to go.

He opened the tank on the motor, poured in the gas, fumbled the cap, replaced it. He had no confidence Blount had ever done any maintenance on the motor and that there was any chance of it starting.

He gripped the starter cord and pulled. The tiny motor coughed and sputtered to life.

Summoning his strength, he hoisted the bags into the boat. God, they were heavy. He dragged himself over the gunwale and into the little boat and pushed open the side door of the warehouse. The flood rushed in, raising the skiff. The tempest raged just inches away.

One shot. He aimed the skiff at *Electric Ladyland* and chugged out into the tossing storm.

All doubt washed out of his seared body. Doubt was for men who still had lives. He had nothing but revenge and spiteful sea gods aligning events to guide him to success.

Sheets of rain whipped around the lighthouse, lashing Kyoko. She turned her face from the stinging water and pushed with her legs away from the wind, edging more into the wind shadow. Water reached upward and lapped at her feet.

Blood squeezed from between her fingers and ran down her arms, the cable biting deep, making slippery her hold on it.

Miraculously, Blount had stopped firing at her. Maybe he'd run out of ammo, but she found that unlikely. Something had distracted him.

As if to punctuate the thought, a sharp sound echoed, masked by the dense noise of the storm. It sounded like a gunshot, but with a different pitch than the shots fired by Blount.

Another gunshot, from somewhere off to her left on the opposite side of the lighthouse. She was sure it was a gunshot. Hope surged through her. Someone was engaging the bastard in a gunfight!

Her strength was fading fast and she had a choice to make. She could hang on and hope that someone succeeded in killing or wounding Blount. Yet it was an almost impossible shot for someone to hit him at that height, in that wind.

Or she could release herself and plunge into the water and hope that she could swim, blown by the storm, to one of the trees that still clung to weakening ground, and ride the storm out. There was no chance of swimming around the lighthouse into the teeth of the storm to reach whoever was firing on Blount. That was a physical impossibility.

She felt a sudden vibration, a tug, in the cable that suspended her. She felt it again, stronger. The decision was being made for her. Blount was unfastening the cable to let her plunge into the flood.

The cable plucked again and she dropped a few inches. She

had only seconds before she would plummet into Celeste's furious waters.

"Blount's backed away from the glass," Sanborn said, maintaining his aim upward. "Now's your chance."

Grant didn't bother to respond. He threw himself through the window. The force of the rushing water grabbed and tumbled him head over heels, forcing him under. The lifejacket righted him and pulled him back to the surface. The second lifejacket he carried was nearly torn from his grasp by the water. He reeled it in and clutched it under his arm.

The wind and waves drove him toward the lighthouse, but he could see that the angle would blow him past it, missing by ten feet. No good. He had to make contact with the structure. He would only get one chance.

He kicked furiously against the current. His angle improved but he saw with dismay that it would not be enough. He would be swept past the tower and out into the channel.

He slammed into something hidden just under the surface. The old concrete monument that detailed the history of the lighthouse. The blow drove into his ribs and he heard and felt a snap and a sudden shooting pain, the snap of a rib breaking. He arched his torso sideways to ease pressure on the wound.

He was caught up on the submerged monument, pressed against it by the surging water. He worked his way around, braced his legs against the monument, and pushed from it with all his might.

The maneuver gave him the few extra feet he needed.

The water whisked him within inches of the lighthouse. He lunged and caught hold of the frame of the door and pulled himself against the concrete wall. Pain and nausea coursed through his body. He winced, gritted his teeth, willing the pain to ease. It refused and paid him back in spades for his effort.

He released his grip on the door frame and flattened himself against the wall, letting the current drag him along against it. He was carried around the wall.

As he entered the lee of the tower, he looked up. Twenty feet ahead, just above the reaching waves, Kyoko clung to a thin line. She was looking up.

She dropped a few inches. She was about to fall to a drowning death. He shouted at the top of his lungs, barely hearing himself over the din of the hurricane. She certainly had not heard him. He shouted again.

She dropped another two feet, suspended a moment, and plummeted into the sea, the steel cable falling down after her, whipping the water.

She disappeared under the water.

Grant shoved ahead, reaching the spot where she disappeared. Suspended by his lifejacket, he was unable to plunge under after her. He reached frantically downward, feeling nothing but the surging current. "No!" he screamed.

He was pushed away from the tower by the relentless water and wind.

CHAPTER THIRTY-NINE

Kyoko had gulped one last breath before plunging under the water and she felt her air waning rapidly. The cable had fallen in after her and coiled about her like a snake in a great, sinking tangle. She unwound the cable from her arms, but the steel line bunched and dragged her deeper. She was shocked at the weight of the tangle.

She pulled frantically at the cable, tugging, bending, trying to wriggle free.

Something bumped into her shoulder.

She grasped at it, hoping to pull herself free. Her hand closed on the object. Recognition stunned her. It was the leg of someone struggling in the water.

For just a moment, she clung to the booted foot, and then the weight of the cable and the inexorable power of the water tore her free and pulled her to the bottom.

Her lungs ached, screaming for precious air. Clouds gathered in her mind.

She settled onto the bottom and gathered her legs under her. She felt the coils relax as they settled, held open in their own tangle by the bottom. She ripped at them and felt first one, then two coils slide down her body, scraping her skin off as they went.

She lunged upward and away and pulled free of the cable. She broke the surface and gasped for air. A wave rolled over her and she went under again.

An arm hooked under hers and pulled her to the surface. She turned, coughing, and looked into her rescuer's face.

"Grant!" she cried. She broke into sobs and buried her face against his shoulder.

Grant held her tight against him. "Hang on! I've got you." He helped her into the second lifejacket and cinched it tight. "You couldn't go under now if you tried, but don't let the waves catch you off guard."

The driving current pushed them clear of the lighthouse.

The bulk of a large fishing boat appeared from a tangle of trees, churning up what used to be the driveway. The boat rolled and yawed on the storm, and would surely have been quickly capsized if it were on open water. Kyoko caught a glimpse of the boat's name. *Electric Ladyland.* At its helm clung a wreck of a human being, leaning into the wheel.

The boat plowed through the heaving water, driving straight ahead and crashing into the lighthouse, splintering what little of the door remained unsubmerged. Its bow wedged into the doorway and the relentless rush of water and wind pushed the stern about. Pieces of the door frame splintered and swept out with the current. Nobles, carrying two bundles, slid into the water and disappeared into the doorway.

The boat pulled free from the doorway and was blown into the limbs of a fallen oak and held fast.

Kyoko and Grant were swept from the lighthouse, through the grasping branches of the last few trees and out into the channel, toward the mainland.

Charley couldn't imagine being more scared than he already was, but this got him there. Hammond, Sanborn, and Charley had just witnessed the sudden appearance of *Electric Ladyland,* white and ghostly in the storm, and the broken man escape from it, struggling under the weight of his burden.

"Unbelievable," Hammond said. "Roscoe! The guy is still alive. Barely."

"We have to get out of here," Charley said. "Now."

"Our options are in short supply," Sanborn said. "We're best off hoping this house remains standing through the storm."

"Don't you know what we just saw? Roscoe has the bomb core with him." His voice cracked. "Roscoe's going after Blount. We can't stay here."

"God almighty," Sanborn whispered.

There was a sharp crack of splintering wood. Through the window, they saw the front porch of the house sag, split apart, and tear away. Charley felt the floor underneath his feet shift.

"That ends the debate," Hammond said. "The foundation is caving in."

"Get ready. We're going for Roscoe's boat. Swim like hell; once we're in the water there's nothing we can do for each other. You'll be on your own."

The house tilted crazily. Charley lost his footing and fell into the wall. The wall ruptured in the corner, opening at the floor and separating.

"Get out now!" Sanborn cried. "We can't be caught inside when it collapses." He pulled himself through the window and disappeared. Hammond, his face ashen, followed.

Charley cinched his lifejacket tighter, counted to three, drew a deep breath, and climbed onto the window sill.

Another splintering of wood. The wall came apart under him and a timber tore loose and pinned his leg against the sill. He winced in pain and tried to pull free.

A hand seized him by the wrist. Sanborn had him and pulled mightily. Charley thought his shoulder would separate, but he was suddenly free and in the tossing water. He tumbled and went under but was quickly righted by the lifejacket.

They fought the short, unbearable hundred feet toward *Elec-*

tric Ladyland. Wave after wave washed over Charley's head, filling him with terror, but he remained afloat.

After the longest minute of his life, Charley was in the tangled branches of the oak, which itself was uprooting and beginning to drift. He scrambled through and clutched the transom and pulled himself aboard. Hammond huddled on the floor of the boat, coughing up water.

Sanborn came rolling over the gunwale in a waterlogged heap. He motioned to Charley. "It's your boat now. Get us out of here."

Blount leaned out over the rail, drawing aim at the swimmers, and squeezed off two shots. The bullets fell short, spiking twin sprays of white off the surface, sprays that were instantly flattened and torn apart by shrieking hurricane winds. He screamed at them and fired again. It was no use. They were swiftly moving out of range. Sanborn, that rube of a cop, had distracted him with his potshots just long enough that he'd missed seeing Grant reach his Jap girlfriend.

They'd gotten hold of lifejackets. That was bad. They had an even chance of living, and the storm was hurling them eastward. If the bitch lived . . .

Rage filled him, causing him to waste two more shots. He willed himself to lower his weapon.

If the bitch lived, he was sunk. He couldn't stay on the island. He'd be caught in a heartbeat, thrown in jail, probably executed. But if he fled, he'd miss out on the score of a lifetime, and he sure as hell couldn't escape and return to Hicksville.

Or could he?

If he went missing in a monster storm, he'd be presumed dead. In fact, without witnesses, he'd be a dead hero, just like Sanborn and his asshole friends. With witnesses, he'd be a dead villain. Either way, he'd be presumed dead.

That was the answer. He would ride out the storm in the tower. Sanborn and friends couldn't stick much longer in the keepers' house. It was already disintegrating. The roof had been thrown aside as if God had swatted it away. The porch had collapsed. The first floor was underwater and the waves were slashing at the upper windows. It couldn't last. If they had lucked into more lifejackets they would soon have to throw themselves into the tempest and hope for the best. The storm would carry them close by the lighthouse.

He would be there, pistol ready, when it did. He would wedge himself into the door frame and would pick them off, one at a time, fish in a barrel, assholes in a hurricane. Then he'd slip off the island as soon as the worst passed.

He readied himself for a good kill shot.

Charley stumbled into the captain's seat in the pilothouse, checked the ignition. All was ready. He threw the switch. The starboard engine coughed and rumbled to life. The port engine remained silent. Charley swore and shoved the remaining prop into reverse. Wood groaned, and branches yielded and snapped, and the boat withdrew from the tree and listed to starboard. The boat rode deep and Charley looked at Sanborn. Sanborn nodded and darted to the forward cabin and threw open the hatch. The small room was flooded. Water gushed into the room through a series of inch-wide ruptures in the hull.

"We're sinking," Charley cried. He tried the switch for the bilge pumps. He heard one click into service, while the other two remained silent.

"Can we make the mainland?"

"Half an engine, half-speed, sinking vessel. In a hurricane. I don't see why not." He coaxed the dying boat free of the oak tree and gunned the remaining engine. It yawed and pulled sluggishly away.

Free of the branches, the wind and water grabbed the boat and threatened to capsize it. Charley felt himself slipping. The boat rolled back upright. Charley snapped it into alignment with the ferocious wind and moved it away from the lighthouse.

"Full up for the mainland, Charley," Sanborn shouted.

The boat labored into the open water doing twelve knots. A hundred yards ahead, black shapes rose and fell with the waves. Charley veered toward them, hoping against hope, his heart surging.

They pulled alongside Grant and Kyoko and hauled them aboard. Slowed in the water, the boat rolled and yawed, riding even lower than before. *Electric Ladyland* was breathing her last. Charley swung her about and urged it toward the mainland. Every second, he knew, was distance. And distance meant survival.

But could *Ladyland* give them a mile before going under?

Something caught Blount's eye, far below. Something white.

A boat.

No, he told himself. No boat on the island could survive this howler.

The boat churned away, close to sinking yet under power, shifting its aft to the following, crashing waves. For an instant, he caught a glimpse of the name on the transom.

He froze.

Electric Ladyland.

It couldn't be. Of all the boats on Brigands Key, what were the odds?

Yet there it was, pulling away. Roscoe had escaped. No . . . there were at least three people on board. Those other bastards had gotten away.

Sudden doubt and fear raced through him. He had to get moving. He turned to head for the spiral ladder downward.

Standing over the trapdoor, ten feet away, was Roscoe Nobles. In the howl of the storm, Blount had not heard him enter. He was a nightmare of rags and swollen, hanging flesh, dripping wet. What remained of his face twisted into a hideous grin. In his hands he held a dull silver cylinder about four inches in diameter and seven inches long. At his feet stood a stack of metal rings, also of dull silver, seven inches high.

"Going somewhere?" Nobles rasped.

Blount stopped. "You ought to be dead."

"Unfinished . . . business."

Blount glanced at the metal objects. "Is that it?"

Nobles nodded. "My . . . treasure."

"What do you want for it?"

Nobles laughed, a sound that came out wet and broken. "Nothing. First you try to steal my treasure. Now you want to buy it?" Nobles coughed. "You . . . you ain't got to hunt no more. I'm givin' it to you."

Blount hesitated. "What are you up to?"

Nobles cackled. "Weapons-grade. Come and get it."

Blount shook his head, aimed his pistol. This didn't add up. "Asshole," he growled. "I don't negotiate and I don't fall for tricks." He squeezed the trigger.

Nothing.

Blount glanced at his gun. Out of ammo! He had lost count of his shots.

Roscoe Nobles cackled, a wet laugh that rattled deep in his chest. "Things add up."

He lowered the cylinder slowly to the stack of rings. The two were meant to be fitted, joined, mated. Consummated. "I am become . . . Death," he rasped. "The Destroyer of worlds." He inserted the cylinder into the rings and rammed it down.

In the last split second of his life, Artie Blount experienced two things. He saw blinding blue light, filling the world, dazzling, clear, pure, the blue of the clearest deepest sky multiplied a thousand times over, impossibly clear blue. In the same instant, he felt searing pain pass through his entire body, a wave, a hurricane, through every cell, destroying, burning, killing . . .

Blue light.

Sacred blue.

Grant glanced back. The island and the lighthouse, now a mile behind, were invisible, obscured by the driving rain. A brilliant light flashed, lighting the sky, flaring brighter and brighter.

"Detonation!" Charley cried. "Grab something and hang on."

An instant later the shock wave struck, grabbing the boat and shaking it, threatening to lift and toss it. The stern spun wildly. Grant was hurled into the console and Charley was thrown over the wheel. Grant seized the wheel and swung the heeling boat back into the wind.

"Roscoe took his revenge," Kyoko said.

A vast ball of light and fire rose from the gray of the storm and was instantly torn apart and shot northward, blasted by the shrieking wind.

A deafening roar, deafening even above the freight-train roar of the hurricane, pealed across the tossing sea.

A wall of water, twice the height of a house, raced toward them. More on instinct than thought, Grant spun the wheel and turned the struggling boat into the wave.

Electric Ladyland climbed the wave as it raced beneath, broke through the churning whitecap, teetered and slammed down, and slid down the following trough. Grant nosed into the wind once more and angled back to trail the tsunami. The fishing boat was swept along.

The swamped mainland loomed suddenly before them. Grant

aimed for a gap between the limbs of the inundated trees and drove the boat with a crash into the snapping tangle of branches. *Electric Ladyland* listed dangerously and came to rest, pinned into the trees, and its stern sank beneath the water.

A foot-thick branch, broken and pointed, pierced the wooden hull, impaling the boat, holding it fast. A miracle in disguise. *Ladyland*'s passengers huddled in a corner of the pilothouse, clutching each other tightly, eyes clinched shut, as Hurricane Celeste howled and raged, ripping and tearing at them, trying to kill them.

CHAPTER FORTY

Two days later, Grant sat in a camp chair on the shattered waterfront of what was left of Brigands Key, sipping putrid coffee that Sanborn had inflicted on them before sneaking away. The morning was muggy and clear, and sweat rolled off his brow. The steaming coffee exacerbated the heat and he thought about dumping it. But the need for caffeine ruled all in the morning.

He was a wreck. His punctured thigh was heavily bandaged and he was chock full of antibiotics and painkillers. Not enough painkillers; his entire torso ached with every breath, each a shooting reminder of his cracked rib. He'd been trampled by stampeding buffalo. Atomic buffalo.

Kyoko sat next to him. Her head was bandaged tightly. Miraculously, her severed ear, retrieved from the remains of Hammond's wrecked clinic, had been reattached, Hammond doing the work himself. She'd insisted, saying she trusted no doctor more than him.

Charley sat on the ruins of the dock, the planking tilted steeply, more than half of it missing entirely. His bare feet dangled in the water, something impossible before Celeste turned the once-straight dock like a tangle.

None of them spoke. They were content to watch the buzz of activity taking place off the north end of the island.

Helicopters buzzed round and round overhead. Most were military. Some were network news, and were kept at arms' length from the island by the Army choppers. Cameramen leaned out of the news choppers, desperate for footage. Two dozen Coast Guard vessels were anchored in and around the channel. A canvas enclosure encircled the area of the lighthouse. The lighthouse that no longer existed. A tent city had sprung up this side of the enclosure. A couple dozen vehicles—mobile labs and trucks—were lined up outside the tent city. Some were CDC. Most were Army. Some were mysterious and unnamed.

The north end of the island was gone.

Men and women in hazmat suits prowled, sweeping every square inch with weird instruments, like spacemen in a bad movie. A floating lab anchored in the channel and divers came and went from it in waves. Officially, it was a "search for survivors."

Except for the military and government types, Brigands Key remained deserted. Angry residents fumed on the mainland, sequestered in the state pen at Raiford, talking to any camera they could find, clamoring to be allowed to return to their homes, anxious to see what little was left.

No. That was the succinct government answer to those residents. Not until the rescue operations are satisfied and the island made safe. And, oh yeah, to prevent looting.

Grant, Kyoko, Charley, Hammond, and Sanborn were the only ones allowed back in, and that was because the government was in a pickle with them. Those five alone knew the truth. So a bargain had been struck; keep mum until we give the word. Then blab all you want. They had the run of the island and everything they wanted . . . so long as the truth was tabled for a while. No one was getting on or off Brigands Key soon.

"Mind if I join you?"

Grant turned to see Sanborn, not waiting for an answer, pulling up a chair. He'd been out walking up one debris-choked street and down another, a good cop working his beat.

"How's it look, Randy?" Kyoko asked.

Sanborn shook his head. "My town is gone. Wiped away. Seventy percent of the buildings have been completely destroyed, the rest all beat to hell. On the northern third, not a single building or tree is standing. That's blast damage. Most of the rest is Celeste's doing. We got the double-whammy of all time. The bank we were in . . . gone. City Hall . . . gone. All public records gone with it. The high school gym, gone. The fishing fleet . . . gone. How the hell Jerry's place survived, who knows, but Kyoko is suitably grateful, I expect. We all are. Good news is, I haven't found any bodies. They'll start to stink today if there are any, but I believe—fingers crossed—everybody got out okay. They're ninety-nine percent still at the prison. In lockdown. The mayor's royally pissed. He's tearing the governor and President both a new one. Fisk says public anger at the President is off the charts right now and there's talk of impeachment."

"Sounds like Blount worked the miracle of actually uniting both sides of the aisle with a common purpose," Kyoko said.

"Kyoko," Grant said, "CDC is going to want you back now."

"They just might get me if there's an appropriate string of firings in management."

Sanborn leaned closer to Charley and placed a hand on his shoulder. "Your mom and your girlfriend are safe in Tampa. They're telling your story, talking you up. Even Tyler is talking you up. You're becoming a folk hero. And just wait 'til the whole story gets out; you'll be a legend."

Charley's eyes misted. "Thanks, Sheriff."

"Stop it. You know I'm not a sheriff."

"Charley," Grant said, "your home washed away. Listen; you want to go to college. I'm going to score a full scholarship for you. Physics will get a new hero."

"You can do that?"

"I guarantee it."

Sanborn nodded toward the divers and boats. "Think they'll come clean on what happened, Professor?"

"You know I'm not a professor. They have to eventually. Officially, Celeste blew away the north end of the island. Hurricanes have done that to barrier islands before. But there are people already figuring it out. Strange images in satellite photos, impossibly hot readings in thermal imagery, talk of a brilliant light seen from thirty miles away . . . people are putting it together and will demand an explanation. The Feds will spill eventually, but not until they sweep the island for remnants and radioactivity."

"Celeste did us a favor. The wind blew the entire burst out to sea. So far, the island is coming up clean. No fallout."

"We lucked out," Charley said. "The blast was a fraction of what it could have been. The timing of a gun-type detonation is very specific. A perfectly timed critical mass would have been worse. A lot worse."

Sanborn shook his head. "One thing I don't understand; how did Roscoe find the bomb core? Grant and I both searched the spring before he did. We should've found it."

"You're a cop, the Professor is a professor. Roscoe was a treasure hunter. The core was covered in sand and silt. Roscoe was looking for gold, silver. He swept the bottom with his metal detector and found it right away."

"Guess that makes sense."

Hammond nudged Sanborn. "What you going to do now, Randy?"

Sanborn averted his eyes. "Julie's a national hero," he said. "All the networks want her. I might see if she needs some help. I guess."

"Ah," Hammond said. "I guess."

Sanborn blushed and changed the subject. "It's not all good, Grant. There's a lot of finger-pointing. Seems trouble follows you around."

"I'm almost learning to enjoy it." Grant turned to Hammond. "What are your plans, Jerry?"

Hammond sat in stony silence for a moment, gazing at the wreckage of his hometown. "My practice is gone," he said, almost in a whisper. "My livelihood is gone, my town is gone." He turned to face them, his eyes glistening. "Brigands Key was aptly named. The town was built by scoundrels and prospered on the misfortune of others. If you believe in karma, you'll think Brigands Key got repaid in spades for its sins. My great-grandfather founded this town. He fell into ruin but came back. Julie's grandfather was the town ne'er-do-well, the loser everyone mocked. Yet he may very well have stopped Hitler from acquiring a nuclear weapon. Roscoe Nobles was our latest public laughing-stock loser, yet managed to keep one of the town's leading citizens from selling an atom bomb to the highest bidder. I'm going nowhere. I'm rebuilding Brigands Key. This is home."

"Doc," Grant said, "I'm unemployed and unappreciated once again. Brigands Key sounds like my kind of place. Might as well hang around a while."

"Me too," Kyoko said. "I think I'll take back my CDC job and leverage my clout into pulling in some huge FEMA money. We'll put Brigands Key back on the map and build it back indestructible this time."

A Coast Guard boat chugged past, its crew eyeing them suspiciously. Grant waved.

A pair of dolphins swam languidly alongside the vessel, in long, slow rolls. Small silver fish, disturbed by the boat, scattered and leapt. The dolphins darted after them, corralling them, catching them.

"Smart animals," Kyoko said.

Grant nodded. "Smarter than us." He took her hand, stood, and stretched, the motion causing him to wince. "Man, that hurts," he grumbled. "And I'm famished. You can see if Fisk's cooking is worse than Randy's coffee. As for me, I'm going to have the National Guard scare up some Dinsmoor and orange juice and make me the meanest screwdriver yet devised by humankind."

ABOUT THE AUTHOR

Ken Pelham grew up in the off-the-radar South Florida farm town of Immokalee, sandwiched between coasts and snuggled against wild, wooly Big Cypress Swamp. He holds a degree in landscape architecture from the University of Florida, and has applied his training to the thorny problems assailing land and water across the state, designing parks and working on land development issues. Before turning his attention to novels, he wrote numerous short stories and articles. He lives in Maitland, Florida, with his lovely wife, Laura.